PRAISE FOR BENTLEY LITTLE
The Revelation
Winner of the Bram Stoker Award

"Grabs the reader and yanks him along through an ever-worsening landscape of horrors. . . . It's a terrifying ride with a shattering conclusion."
—Gary Brandner

"*The Revelation* isn't just a thriller, it's a shocker . . . packed with frights and good, gory fun. . . . A must for those who like horror with a bite."
—Richard Laymon

"I guarantee, once you start reading this book, you'll be up until dawn with your eyes glued to the pages. A nail-biting, throat-squeezing, nonstop plunge into darkness and evil."
—Rick Hautala

The Ignored

"This is Bentley Little's best book yet. Frightening, thought-provoking and impossible to put down."
—Stephen King

"With his artfully plain prose and Quixote-like narrative, Little dissects the deep and disturbing fear of anonymity all Americans feel. . . . What Little has created is nothing less than a nightmarishly brilliant tour de force of modern life in America."
—*Publishers Weekly* (starred review)

Turn the page for more praise . . .

The Store

"If there's a better horror novelist than Bentley Little working today, I don't know who it is. *The Store* is . . . frightening. The perfect summer read."
—*Los Angeles Times*

"Must reading for Koontz fans. Bentley Little draws the reader into a ride filled with fear, danger, and horror." —Harriet Klausner, *Painted Rock*

The Mailman

"A thinking person's horror novel. *The Mailman* delivers." —*Los Angeles Times*

University

"Bentley Little keeps the high-tension jolts coming. By the time I finished, my nerves were pretty well fried, and I have a pretty high shock level. *University* is unlike anything else in popular fiction."
—Stephen King

Also by Bentley Little

THE
TOWN

Bentley Little

A SIGNET BOOK

SIGNET
Published by New American Library, a division of
Penguin Putnam Inc., 375 Hudson Street,
New York, New York 10014, U.S.A.
Penguin Books Ltd, 27 Wrights Lane,
London W8 5TZ, England
Penguin Books Australia Ltd, Ringwood,
Victoria, Australia
Penguin Books Canada Ltd, 10 Alcorn Avenue,
Toronto, Ontario, Canada M4V 3B2
Penguin Books (N.Z.) Ltd, 182–190 Wairau Road,
Auckland 10, New Zealand

Penguin Books Ltd, Registered Offices:
Harmondsworth, Middlesex, England

First published by Signet, an imprint of New American Library,
a division of Penguin Putnam Inc.

First Printing, May 2000
10 9 8 7 6 5 4 3 2 1

 REGISTERED TRADEMARK—MARCA REGISTRADA

Printed in the United States of America

PUBLISHER'S NOTE
This is a work of fiction. Names, characters, places, and incidents either
are the product of the author's imagination or are used fictitiously,
and any resemblance to actual persons, living or dead, business
establishments, events or locales is entirely coincidental.

For the Dobrinins, the Tolmasoffs,
and all of my Molokan relatives

Prologue

Loretta Nelson hated working at night.

The real estate office stayed open after dark only during the weeks preceding the Copper Days celebration each August. The rest of the time, the doors closed at five, like a normal business, and that was the way Loretta preferred it. Still, she recognized the importance of the celebration, and that was why she never put up a fuss. Copper Days was the town's big claim to fame, and it was the closest thing to a tourist attraction that McGuane had. Each year it brought in people from all over the state—hell, all over the Southwest—and a lot of local shops, restaurants, and hotels were able to survive only because of the business they did that weekend. Last year an estimated ten thousand people had descended on their sleepy little town during Copper Days, and the huge and sudden influx of cash had helped offset an otherwise dismal season.

Their office had sold more homes that Friday, Saturday, and Sunday than in the combined months of June and July.

This year they had a jump on things, though. Gregory Tomasov had bought the Megan place, which had been on the market for years now and which they thought they'd never be able to unload.

She hadn't seen Gregory since junior high school, but he hadn't changed at all. He was the same arrogant know-it-all he'd always been, and he still acted as though his shit didn't stink. He was rich now. He'd won several million dollars in the California lottery, and he'd apparently come back to town to lord it over everyone else.

He *said* he just wanted to raise his kids in a good, whole-some small-town environment, and he *pretended* to be nice to her when he found out who she was, but she knew better. She sensed the real reason for his return to Arizona, and she could feel the smug disdain behind his casual conversation.

His wife looked like she was a Molokan, too—which was not a surprise because those people always stuck together—and she seemed as stuck-up as he did.

As petty as it was, Loretta was glad Call had conned them into buying the Megan place, and she couldn't wait to tell her friends that the sucker they'd finally hooked was old Gregory Tomasov.

Although she would be grateful if Gregory were here right now. Or if anyone were here.

She did not like being alone.

Not at night.

Loretta stood, walked over to the front window, looked out at the highway.

Nothing.

Only darkness.

In the decade and a half she'd been Call Cartright's secretary, she could count on one hand the number of people who'd called or stopped by after dark.

She shivered. It was the mine behind the building that spooked her. She knew it was a childish fear. She'd lived in McGuane her entire life, and there was nothing in the pit at night that wasn't there in the daytime. It was empty, abandoned. But after nightfall, having that black hole behind her gave her the heebie-jeebies. It *was* abandoned, and that absence of human activity was one of the reasons she felt unnerved here at the edge of the pit.

It had been abandoned since before she was born.

That made it even scarier.

She shook her head. She'd been watching too many monster movies lately.

Lymon was supposed to have shown up to keep her company, but he was even more unreliable than he was slow, and it didn't surprise her that he hadn't arrived. She continued to scan the highway, searching for the lights of his four-by-four, but there was no one on the road at all tonight. She glanced up at the clock. Nine-forty. Twenty minutes to go.

She walked around the edge of the office, looking out the windows, ending up back behind her desk, straightening the brochures she'd had printed this morning and peering out at the inky blackness of the mine. The moon was new, a pale sliver in the sky, and its faint illumination made the pit seem even darker. It was as though the mine was a light vacuum, sucking the slightest hint of radiance out of the land and sky.

She was about to turn away, about to call Lymon and give him a lecture on laziness and thoughtlessness, when she saw something out of the corner of her eye. Something white against the blackness of night.

Movement.

Loretta sidled next to the window and peered out. It was a light. A light down in the bottom of the pit.

But there hadn't been a light down there for nearly half a century.

A cold chill passed through her. She was afraid to look into the mine, but she was afraid to look away, and so she remained in place, staring, as the light, a vague, shapeless glow of indeterminate size, first floated upward, then began darting around, moving not with any visible motion but winking on and off, appearing at different points around the massive pit in rapid succession.

It was accompanied by a sound that reminded her of rats screaming.

Loretta looked away, concentrated on the warm, friendly, illuminated interior of the office, trying to tune out everything else. She checked to make sure the windows were all closed, then hurried over and closed and locked the front door.

She looked down at the desk, at the brochures, tried to tell herself that it was nothing, just her imagination, that there was nothing unusual happening outside. But she could still see the light in her peripheral vision, buzzing around the deep interior of the mine.

Then it winked off.

Appeared instantly next to her car.

Loretta's heart leaped in her chest. There was no way she could continue to pretend that there was nothing going on. She quickly reached for the phone, intending to call Lymon. She picked up the receiver, but there was no dial tone. The line was dead.

She looked back out the window, saw nothing but blackness.

There was a knock at the door.

She let out a small yelp. Her pulse was racing, her heart thumping, and she was more scared than she had ever been in her life. She swallowed, tried to sound brave. "Hello?"

There was another knock, louder this time.

"Go away!" she yelled.

All of the lights went out.

She screamed, an instinctive reaction but not a practical one. The office was too far from downtown for anyone to hear her. She could scream all she wanted and no one would ever know.

Another knock.

Crying, terrified, she slumped against the wall.

And in the darkness, something grabbed hold of her hand.

One

1

Lawn grass, freshly cut.

It was the smell of suburban summer, and Adam had always loved that rich, unique scent, but it depressed him now, and as he walked down the sidewalk past the Josefsons' yard on his way to Roberto's, he thought about how unfair life was. Especially if you were a teenager. Or almost a teenager. It was an adult world, adults made the rules and made the decisions, and they always got their way. Forget black, white, brown. Adolescents were the true minority. They were the ones really being oppressed. They had the thoughts and emotions of adults but none of the rights. He might be only twelve, but he considered himself mature for his age, and he knew better than anyone else what was good for him. He should at least be consulted regarding decisions that would affect his life and his future.

But his parents had decided to move to Arizona without even discussing it with him.

They'd just told him.

Ordered him.

Adam sighed. Life sucked.

His friend was already waiting for him, sitting on the trunk of his dad's old Chevy parked in the driveway.

"Hey, Ad Man," Roberto called.

"Dick," Adam said. No one had ever made fun of his name except Roberto, although he'd always been embarrassed by it and considered it supremely goofy. Babunya, his grandmother, had picked out the name, and it sounded okay when she said it: *Uh-dahm,* with the accent on the second syllable. It sounded exotic that way, not quite so stupid. But when it was pronounced the normal way, the American way, he hated it.

He was glad Babunya was going to be living with them, he had to admit. He liked the idea of having her around all the time instead of just going to visit her on weekends. But he was not happy to be moving.

Not happy?

He was miserable.

He'd postponed telling Roberto that they were moving, not sure how to break the news to his friend.

Sasha, if possible, was even more upset than he was. Teo was only nine and didn't seem to be all that concerned, but Sasha was furious. She'd had a big fight with their parents last night, refusing to move, threatening to leave, threatening to run away, and she and their parents were still arguing when he finally fell asleep.

For the first time in his life, he'd been rooting for his sister to win an argument.

But of course that could not happen. She might be a senior in high school, but she was only a teenager and they were adults, and hierarchy always overrode logic.

They were going to be forced to move to Arizona, and there wasn't a damn thing they could do about it.

Roberto walked quickly over to him, glanced back at his house. "Let's hit the pavement," he said. "My mom's on the warpath again, and I know she's gonna try and make me wash windows or pull weeds or do something stupid. She was all over my old man last night about how I don't do anything around the house, and she's been looking around all morning trying to think of something."

"Roberto!" his mother called from inside the house.

"Haul ass!" Roberto took off, and Adam followed. They sped down the block, turned the corner, and didn't stop until they were out of hearing range. They were both laughing and breathing heavily, but Adam's laughter was tinged with sadness as he realized that in a few more weeks he would not be able to hang out with Roberto anymore, would not be able to rescue him from the hell of household chores, and his amusement faded much faster than his friend's.

"Let's check out the AM/PM," Roberto said. "The new Marvel cards should be in."

Adam nodded his agreement. "All right."

They walked through the neighborhood, cut through an alley, and headed down busy Paramount Boulevard to the gas station mini-mart. Roberto found a plastic spider on the ground next to a sewer grating, and Adam found a quarter in the coin return slot of a pay phone, and they both agreed that this was turning out to be a fine day.

At the AM/PM, they walked straight to the trading cards rack. The new Marvel cards had indeed arrived, and the two of them pooled their money and bought five packs. Adam was the Spiderman fan, so all Spidey cards automatically went to him. There were four this time, so Roberto got four choices from the remaining cards, and they divided up the rest on a one-for-you-and-one-for-me basis.

They were walking slowly past the pumps, back out to Paramount, sorting through their cards, when Adam told him.

"We're moving."

"What?" Roberto stopped walking and looked dumbly over at him as though his ears and brain had somehow mistranslated what had been said.

"My parents bought a house in some small town in Arizona. That's where my dad's from. Ever since he won the lottery and quit his job he's been lost. He doesn't have anything to do. He doesn't know what he wants to do. So he decided to try to recapture his childhood or something and he dragged my mom out to Arizona and they bought a house out there and now they're going to force us to uproot our lives and take off and live in the middle of the desert." The words spilled out in a torrent, with barely a pause between sentences, and Adam realized that he had a lump in his throat and was very close to crying.

Roberto was silent.

They looked around at the building, at the cars, at the pumps, at the street, at everything but each other, both of them too embarrassed to acknowledge what they were feeling.

"Shit," Roberto said finally.

Adam cleared his throat, starting to say something, then thought better of it.

"I never said anything against your old man, you know. Even after everything you told me, I always thought he was pretty cool. But, Ad Man, your dad's an asshole."

Adam nodded miserably.

"Fuck."

There was a horn honk behind them. Adam jumped, turning around to see a mustached man in a beat-up Chevy waving them away from the gas pumps. "You're blocking my way!" he yelled.

Adam followed Roberto out to the sidewalk. "You can come out and visit," he said. "You could stay for, like, a week or two. Have your mom and dad pick you up. If it's all right with them," he added.

"Or you could come back here. Stay with us."

Adam smiled. "Even better."

Roberto shook his head. "Arizona, huh?"

"Arizona."

"It's gonna be tough, man. You'll have to go to an all-new school, have to meet new people, make friends. Probably everyone there's known each other since birth, so you'll be an outsider. Big ol' hillbilly kids'll kick your ass for no reason."

Adam hadn't thought of that.

"There'll be nothing to do but watch TV and stare out at the cactus."

"I'll tell 'em I'm a major surfer from California. They've probably never even seen an ocean. What do they know? I'll lie my way to the top of the school."

Roberto smiled. "There are some possibilities there."

They were both silent as they started to walk back toward the neighborhood. It was going to be as tough for Roberto, Adam knew, as it would be for him. He was Roberto's best friend, and Roberto would have to find someone new to hang with, too.

They were both depressed as they headed down the alley.

Adam looked over at his friend. "You gotta write to me, man. You gotta keep me up on current events, tell me what's going on in the real world so I don't turn into some inbred Jed."

"I will," Roberto promised. "I'll write to you, like, once a week. And I'll put in a new Spidey card every time."

Adam tried to smile. "Yeah. That's cool."

"They probably don't have 'em out there."

"Probably not."

But Roberto wasn't much of a writer, he knew. His friend might send a letter or two the first couple weeks, but that would taper off as he found some new best friend, and probably by the time school started there wouldn't be any letters at all.

Once his family moved, he might never see Roberto again.

He tried to imagine what his friend would be like in ten years, what kind of job he'd have, whether or not he'd go to college. Would Roberto's life turn out differently because he wasn't there with him? Would *his* life turn out differently? They were good influences on each other, Roberto's mom had always said. Maybe their new friends wouldn't have as much influence, wouldn't be as good.

Roberto cleared his throat, looked away. "You'll still be my best friend," he said embarrassedly.

"Yeah," Adam said.

He wiped his eyes, and tried to tell himself that they were only watering because of the smog.

2

In her dream, Gregory was a little boy again. He was standing on the steps of the old church in Arizona, staring down at what looked like the dead body of a deformed child. Wind was blowing, a strong wind, kicking up dust, and there were shapes in the dust, vague, dark outlines that resembled the small, twisted body on the steps.

She herself was a viewer of this scene but not a participant in it, and though she wanted to call out to her son, wanted to yell for Gregory to get away from the body and run into the church, she could only stand there and watch as he bent down and tentatively touched the figure's face.

The wind instantly grew stronger, and the deformed child lurched to its feet. She saw unnaturally short legs and unnaturally long arms, a tilted head that was far too large for the supporting neck and was of a disturbingly peculiar shape. Gregory backed up, backed away, but he was already changing, his head enlarging, his arms lengthening, his legs shriveling, and in a few brief seconds, he became the identical twin of the malformed child before him. He screamed, a piercing cry that carried over the howling wind, and then the blowing dust obscured them both, fading them into the vague shapes that were hovering behind the curtain of sand.

She awoke drenched with sweat.

She sat up, breathing heavily, a muffled pain in her chest. She did not know what this dream meant, but it did not bode well and it frightened her. Closing her eyes again, she folded her hands, bent her head.

Prayed.

TWO

1

They followed the moving van, making quick stops only for gas and pee breaks. Gregory didn't trust movers on general principle, and he wasn't about to let these jokers out of his sight. They looked like men even a carnival wouldn't hire. The kids had been moaning and complaining since Phoenix, begging to stop at McDonald's or Taco Bell or some other fast-food place for lunch, but he told them to eat the pretzels and chips they'd brought along.

They sped through Tucson, headed east toward Wilcox.

The night before last, they'd had a going-away party with all of their friends and family, a big blowout at Debbie and John's that had spilled back to their own house, the revelers sitting on packed boxes and the floor, drinking out of paper cups placed on the empty kitchen counter. Julia had ended up crying most of the evening, hugging people and promising to keep in touch, accepting invitations to stay at various homes on the promised frequent Southern California vacations, issuing invitations to all and sundry to visit them in Arizona, but he himself had not teared up at all. He'd been more excited than sad, looking more toward the future than the past, and that forward-looking optimism still held. He felt good driving across the desert, and despite the kids' complaints and Julia's sagging spirits, he felt happy. They were getting a new start, their future was bright and wide open, and they had the freedom to do whatever the hell they wanted.

God bless the lottery.

They'd bought a new vehicle for the trip, a Dodge van, and it was nice to experience a smooth ride, air-conditioning that actually worked, and a state-of-the-art radio/cassette/CD player. He'd grown used to the tepid air-conditioning and rough-and-ragged suspension of the old Ford, and the striking contrast between the two vehicles made the van's pleasures that much more enjoyable.

He glanced in the rearview mirror, saw Sasha reading a Dean Koontz book, Adam and Teo playing Old Maid. Behind them, in the backseat of the van, his mother stared straight ahead. Her eyes met his in the mirror, and she favored him with a slight smile.

He smiled back.

His mother was with them on a trial basis. She'd brought her clothes and Bible and a few other necessities, but she had not even tried to sell her house, her furniture was still safely in place inside the home, and she reserved the right to return at any time. As he'd expected, as he'd known, she was not really enthused about leaving her friends and her church and the rest of her family, but she did seem to recognize that she was not as young as she once had been, and since he was her only son, she'd agreed to come. On some level, she seemed to realize that she was more dependent on him than she was ordinarily willing to admit, and he was encouraged by the fact that her love for her family appeared to be stronger than her ties to the Molokan community.

This was the first time in his life he'd ever gotten *that* impression.

Like most of the other Molokan women her age, his mother lived for church, and her entire life revolved around the religion and its attendant social functions. She was getting on in years, though, and lately she'd been spending even more time at church than usual, going to funerals. He didn't like her driving into East L.A. by herself. There was a lot of gang activity in the neighborhood adjacent to the church, but she continued to see the area as it had been years ago, her mind not recognizing the changes that the years had wrought. He expected to hear one day that his mother or one of her

friends had been gunned down in a drive-by or mugged
on their way to their cars, but so far the Chicano gang
members and the strangely garbed Russian churchgoers
had managed to peacefully coexist.

He himself had not gone to church for years, not since
they'd moved to California. As a child, his parents had
taken him to church each Sunday. The service lasted all
day, and though he liked eating the food when they
broke for lunch—the cucumbers and tomatoes, the
freshly baked bread and the freshly cooked *lopsha*—he
had been frightened of the service itself, of the old men
and women and the way they acted when the Holy Spirit
entered them. These were his relatives and his parents'
friends, people he knew and saw on a daily basis, but
they seemed somehow different in church, like strangers,
and he held tightly to his parents' hands as, one after
the other, the churchgoers were possessed by the Holy
Spirit and began leaping up from their benches, lurching
spasmodically across the open room, stomping loudly on
the hardwood floor, and crying out in Russian. It was
disturbing to see, this sudden abandonment of ordinary
behavior and individual personality, terrifying even to a
little boy who had been raised in the religion. There was
one old, old man who had to be in his eighties, a man
he didn't know and saw only at church, who scared him
even more than the others, who jumped up in the air
with his eyes closed, screaming and lashing out with his
hands. Once, he'd even had a vivid nightmare about the
old man, a dream he'd never forgotten, and in which the
possessed man, eyes closed, screaming, had attacked
him, leaping on him, hitting him, taking him down.

Gregory himself had never felt the intrusion of the
Holy Spirit into his body, and as a child that had worried
him. He felt guilty, unworthy, because God did not see
fit to possess him. Even his parents were periodically
invaded by the Holy Spirit, his father weaving back and
forth in place, his mother crying and humming psalms
as she danced, and though no one ever said anything to
him, Gregory always assumed that the other Molokans
viewed him as not being sufficiently good or righteous,
not deserving enough to be touched by God.

It was one of the many reasons that, try as he might,

he attended church as an outsider, as an observer, rather than a participant.

The Molokan religion was indeed a strange one, but although he had not felt a part of it, he'd always felt protective of it. In McGuane, they'd been the object of ridicule, the town joke, harassed by hard-drinking cowboys and teetotaling Mormons alike. Molokans were foreign, they spoke with Russian accents, they were clannish, and in small-town America that made them suspect.

He remembered one Sunday morning in particular, when some cowboy-hatted rednecks outside the bar on the way to the church made fun of their clothes, derisively referring to his father as a "milk drinker." That was exactly what the word "Molokan" meant, but it sounded mocking and disdainful coming from their mouths. He and his parents had ignored the men, who'd hooted and hollered as they passed by, and Gregory had felt ashamed of both his father and his religion. It was at that moment that he'd decided he would not go to church when he grew up.

He also decided that he would come back and kick those rednecks' asses.

Those same feelings had once again emerged within him in the mid-eighties, during the witch-hunting McMartin days in Los Angeles, when the public seemed to see child-molesting satanists behind every tree. Someone had reported spotting a group of devil worshipers in a cemetery, and the LAPD had ended up disrupting a Molokan burial service. It was understandable. The anonymous tipster had reported a group of robed figures, all dressed in white, walking through a graveyard at night, chanting, and the police had been obliged to investigate. But the Molokans, also understandably, were not only deeply offended but angry.

Despite America's guarantee of religious freedom, they had never had an easy time of it, and what the Constitution promised and how citizens actually acted were two different things. The Molokans had left Russia, fleeing religious persecution from the czar and the Russian Orthodox Church. They were pacifists, living strictly by the laws of the Bible, and the fact that they recog-

nized both Christian holidays and Jewish celebrations
such as Passover led to as much misunderstanding in the
United States as it had in Russia. Even more offensive
to Americans was the fact that Molokans were conscien-
tious objectors, opposed on religious grounds to partici-
pation in the military. That had led to discrimination
against them in the United States as well, particularly
during World War II, and far too often that prejudice
had been validated and reinforced by civic authority.

The police had not been the problem here, however.
It was the media. The cops had merely investigated,
apologized, and moved on, but the local news stations,
in their insane quest for ratings, had milked the "satan-
ist" angle for all it was worth. Million-dollar anchors had
joked about smog and marine layers with their comical
weathermen, then expertly shifted their smiles into expressions of grim seriousness and solemnly reported that
perpetrators of the satanic rituals described by molested
preschool children had been spotted desecrating a cemetery in East L.A.

Even though it was not true.

Even though the police had already rejected and dis-
counted any connection between the Molokan burial service, satanism, and child molestation.

He'd been embarrassed by the Molokans when they'd
made the news for those two days, but he'd also been
angry at their accusers and had fired off a series of letters to the local television stations and the *Los Angeles
Times,* taking them to task for their inaccurate and in-
flammatory reporting.

Embarrassment and defensiveness.

It was the constant duality of his life.

Teo and Adam finally tired of their Old Maid game,
and Teo asked him for the hundredth time to describe
their new home to her. Adam and Sasha both groaned
loudly, but Gregory launched into a by-now-pat spiel,
recounting how he and their mother had found the
house and instantly fallen in love with it, painting a picture of the huge lot on which the house sat and the hill
that abutted the back of the property, and describing the
location of each of their bedrooms and how they were
going to fix them up.

He caught his mother's gaze in the rearview mirror once again.

He'd saved the best news for last, and it was time to reveal it.

"There's also a *banya*," he said.

His mother's eyes widened. There was a tinge of excitement in her voice. *"Banya?"*

He smiled. "Remember the Shubins? They used to live right next to our new house—"

"The Megan place?"

"Yes!" he laughed. "The Megan place. It's our place now. And the Shubins' burned down quite a while ago, so the people who bought the Megan place bought their property as well, and now it's all ours. Both lots. There's nothing left of the Shubins' house at all, but the *banya*'s still there."

"Completely untouched," Julia said.

"What's a *banya*?" Teo asked.

"It's a bathhouse," Julia explained. "In the old days, houses didn't have water or indoor bathrooms. You had to get water from a well, and you had to go to the bathroom in an outhouse. And instead of taking a bath or a shower, people used *banyas*."

"Not all people," Gregory amended.

"Russians," Julia said. "Americans filled up tubs with water or took sponge baths, but Russians used the *banya*. The women and girls would all go in at once, and the men and boys would all go in later."

"They were all naked?" Teo giggled.

Julia smiled. "Yes. They sat around on benches and heated rocks in a fire and put them in the middle of the floor and poured water over them to make steam. The steam cleaned the skin, and they used eucalyptus branches to lightly slap their back and chest and legs."

"Why?"

"Because it smelled good. And they thought it helped open the pores and get them even cleaner. Afterward, they'd go down to a stream or a river and rinse off with cold water."

"So it's just like a steam bath," Sasha said.

"Yes," Julia agreed. "Like a steam bath."

"And we have one?" Adam grinned. "That's cool."

"Dork," Sasha said, hitting him with her elbow.

"I used to do it myself," Gregory said.

Sasha grimaced. "That's gross. I don't even want to think about it."

Gregory and Julia laughed, and they followed the moving truck off the interstate and onto the highway that led to McGuane.

It was an hour or so later when his mother suddenly let out a Russian oath. There was a hint of panic or fear in her voice, and Gregory quickly turned around to make sure she was okay, that nothing was wrong.

A stricken look had come over her face. "Jedushka Di Muvedushka," she said.

Oh, no, he thought.

He fixed her with a glare and shook his head, indicating the kids, before turning back around to face the road.

She paid no attention to his hints. "You don't ask him to come, do you?"

He sighed, not knowing whether to argue with her or humor her. "I forgot," he said.

"Jedooshka Dee—what?" Adam asked.

"Muvedushka. Moo-VEH-doosh-ka."

"What's that?"

"He's the Owner of the House." His mother's voice sounded pinched and strained.

"It's a Russian"—*Superstition,* he'd been about to say—"tradition," he said instead. He'd never been able to make his mother understand that he and Julia did not hold the same beliefs she did, that they had purposely kept their children from many of them, and he shot Julia a glance of apology.

She nodded, understanding.

"Is my fault," his mother said in the back. "I should have told you. Should have remind you."

"It's okay," Gregory said.

"It's okay," Julia repeated.

"I should have known. I should have ask him to come myself."

"Why?" Adam said.

"He's the Owner of the House. He protect you. He

make sure everyone in the house is safe and healthy, that nothing happen to you. You ask him to come with you so he protect you in new house."

"You mean he's been living with us all the time?"

She nodded. "That is why nothing bad ever happen."

"What's he look like?"

"A little man with the beard."

"Where does he live? In the attic? Or under the house?"

"He live where you cannot see him."

"I'm scared!" Teo announced.

"If he came with us, would he ride in the van or would he ride on the roof? Is he invisible?"

"I'm sacred!"

"Mother," Gregory said sternly.

She put an arm around Teo. "No. Not scary. Good. He there to protect you, keep you safe." She smiled. "My father saw him one time. We live in Mexico, on the farm, and Father went to feed the horses. At night. Little man was standing there giving hay to the horses. And Father watch and he came and told Mother, 'Jedushka Di Muvedushka feeding the horses.' He don't get scared, nothing. In the morning we go look, the horses' hair all braided. So beautiful! All their hair braided." She shot Gregory a defiant look. "So there is such a thing."

"You weren't scared?" Teo asked.

"No. Not scary. But the braids, you cannot even undo them. Jedushka Di Muvedushka help Father by feeding the horses and just want to show us that he . . . that he's watching us, taking care of us. But Jedushka Di Muvedushka not scary. He's the Owner of the House. He don't do nothing bad."

Gregory remained silent, waiting for the subject to go away. Teo was already frightened, and being in a new house after hearing this story, she was bound to have nightmares. Adam wasn't entirely immune either. Moving was tough enough without having to put up with scary folktales, and he hoped his mother knew how upset he was, how angry he was with her. They were going to have a long talk later, and he was going to have to set down some rules of the house, rules she would have to follow if she lived with them.

He glared at her, but she looked neither embarrassed nor apologetic. Her face was set and grim, and when he met her gaze in the rearview mirror, it held his own, reproachfully.

"I should have invite him myself."

2

Julia stared out the window as they drove. The scenery was amazing, like something out of a movie. Endless vistas, blue sky, clouds that appeared to be the size of continents. They could see hundreds of miles worth of weather patterns: a rainstorm far off to their right, gathering thunderheads to their left, clear skies straight ahead. A series of dark mesas and jagged blue mountains on the horizon before them seemed to remain perpetually the same size, serving only to reinforce the vastness of this land and the awe it inspired.

She looked out at the late-summer wildflowers that lined both sides of the highway. Blooming ocotillo, deep-green saguaros and lighter-green paloverde trees filled in the landscape and belied the common conception of the desert as a dead, arid place devoid of life. Indeed, she'd been surprised herself by the beauty and lushness of the land when they'd first driven out here to look for a house. She'd been hesitant at first about Gregory's sudden brainstorm, his plan to just pull up stakes and move. As she'd told him, she had always lived in Southern California, and despite her chronic complaints, she had never really been able to imagine herself living anywhere else.

But traveling through the open country, Liz Story on the stereo, she'd actually been able to see herself living in a small town, a town where everybody knew everybody else, where neighbors helped each other and cared about each other and were willing to work together for the good of the community. It was a comforting thought, a welcome thought, and her belief and conviction in

Gregory's plan had grown stronger the further they traveled from California.

Even the kids were quiet as the road dipped through dry washes, wound around low hills, and finally began snaking through the canyons of a rugged desert mountain range. McGuane was in these mountains, and once again Julia found herself captivated by the rough beauty of this wild countryside. To their right, cliffs with the same multicolored striations as the Grand Canyon towered above them. Huge cottonwoods grew on the canyon floor, the trees providing umbrellas of shade to barely visible corrals and occasional ranch houses.

"Almost there," Gregory said. He pointed ahead. The road passed through a tunnel carved through the rock, the zigzagging remnants of an old dirt trail still visible on the cliff above. "McGuane's just on the other side."

"Cool!" Teo said.

And then they were there.

According to Gregory, the town was almost exactly the way it had been when he'd left. There were no chain stores, no corporate gas stations, not even one of the name-brand fast-food joints that had taken over most of small-town America. There was no Wal-Mart or The Store, no Texaco or Shell, no McDonald's, Burger King, or Jack-in-the-Box. McGuane had retained its local individual character rather than succumbing to the increased homogenization that was sweeping through the land, and from the first that had impressed her. Emerging from the tunnel was like coming out of a time machine, and she felt as though she'd been transported back thirty years and had entered the world of Gregory's childhood.

They passed a small diner, saw a pickup truck and several bicycles parked in front of it, five or six teenagers clustered around a picnic table to the side. They looked up, waved as the van drove by. In Southern California, she thought, they would have yelled something or flipped off the vehicle. Across the road, two boys jumped down from a tree house into the dirt, laughing.

It was a refreshing change, and she understood what Gregory had meant when he'd said that McGuane would be a good place to raise kids. It was a Huck Finn world, a children's paradise, a place where boys and girls could climb rocks, explore canyons, build forts and clubhouses instead of simply sitting inside the house and watching TV or playing Nintendo.

The highway came into town from the west, ending at the tan-brick courthouse, where it split into two narrow streets that wound through the diverging halves of the community.

The geography of the town was determined by the geology of the land. At McGuane's south end was the mine, an ugly open pit long since closed down and fenced off from the highway by rusted chain-link. The old mining office was now the realty, where they'd bought their new home, and it sat dwarfed at the edge of the massive hole, a matchbox next to a drained swimming pool. The rest of the town snaked northward from the mine up two branching canyons to a sagebrush plateau. At its peak, according to Gregory, McGuane had had a population of thirty thousand, but that had been down to ten thousand when he'd lived there, and he was not sure what it was now.

"Are we almost there?" Adam whined.

Gregory looked over at Julia and smiled.

"Almost," Julia said.

There was not enough room to back in, so the moving truck parked on the street rather than in the drive, its wide bulk blocking both lanes of the narrow road. Gregory pulled the van into the dirt driveway and stopped just in front of the carport next to the house. The movers had not even gotten out of the cab, much less opened the rear door of the truck and started unloading, so he sorted through his keys in order to open up the house before hurrying back to oversee their work.

"Hurry up," Sasha said. "I have to go to the bathroom."

"Wait!"

He'd unlocked and opened the front door and was about to walk inside, when his mother stretched a bony arm across the doorway. She looked up at him. "We have to bless the house."

Gregory nodded, motioning the kids back and shooting Julia a look of apology as his mother recited a prayer in Russian. She told them to remain outside, then walked in, going through each room, ordering out all evil spirits and repeating the same Russian prayer.

Adam's eyes widened. "Are there really evil spirits in there?"

Great, Julia thought. Now Teo would never get to sleep.

"No," Gregory said.

"Then why's Babunya—"

"It's a tradition."

She emerged from the front door a few minutes later, nodded that it was safe to go in, and Sasha hurried past her, heading for the bathroom.

Julia hoped the utilities company had not forgotten to turn on the water.

"Are there evil sprits in our house?" Teo asked.

Gregory looked at his mother. She smiled, patted her granddaughter's head. "If any there, they gone now."

Teo and Adam ran inside, yelling and laughing, rushing excitely from room to room.

"Adam!" Julia yelled, stepping over the threshold into the entryway. "Teo! You stop running right now!"

From behind them, up the drive, came the sound of the truck's cab doors slamming shut. Gregory looked over at his mother.

"You should have invite him," she said. "Jedushka Di Muvedushka."

"I know," he told her. "I'm sorry."

She patted his back, sighed, and followed the rest of the family inside.

Three

1

Copper Days.

Gregory remembered the celebration from his childhood, but it had since grown into something entirely unrecognizable. Downtown McGuane was festooned with flags and banners and balloons, and a traffic jam worthy of Los Angeles at its worst clogged the narrow streets. They'd walked into town instead of driving, in an effort to avoid the rush, and the cars they'd passed even a block back had still not caught up with them. He glanced into the driver's window of the unmoving Saturn next to him and saw an irate bald man swearing at the wife seated beside him.

Julia saw where he was looking, smiled. "Charming."

Adam and Teo were both very excited, but Sasha had wanted to stay home with Babunya, and having been made to come, she registered her protest by walking several steps behind, sullenly accompanying them, not speaking.

From somewhere up ahead came the sound of gunfire from the Wild West Stunt Show.

"Hurry up, Dad!" Adam begged.

"It'll be on again at noon," he told his son. "We'll catch it then."

On the open lawn in front of the courthouse, booths had been set up by local organizations. There was a fair in the parking lot and the park next to it, complete with Ferris wheel and carnival rides.

"Can we go in the mirror house?" Teo asked.

"Yeah!" Adam chimed in.

"Later."

Gregory led them up to the highway, and they picked out a spot next to the announcer's booth and settled in to watch the parade, which was already in progress.

Back in the old days, the parade had been a real community affair, the floats little more than flatbed trucks decorated with crepe paper, but now there were Shriners from Tucson, one of Arizona's senators in a chauffeured 1940s Cadillac, assorted floats sponsored by some of the state's major stores, businesses, and corporations. It was more professional and, he had to admit, probably more entertaining to the kids, but it had lost something in the translation, and he missed those innocent raggedly amateur days in which little Sunday school children walked the parade route dressed in prospector garb, pulling their pets in wagons made up to look like mine cars.

The announcer was a deejay from some big country station in Tucson, and his patter, too, seemed far slicker than it should.

After the parade, they followed most of the rest of the crowd and wandered over to the fair. The local tribe had set up a booth out front and were making fry bread, and Gregory bought the whole family Indian tacos. That brought back memories. Fry bread was one of the few types of ethnic food not available in Southern California, and the kids had never had it before. Though the deep-fried dough was perhaps one of the most unhealthy meals in the world, it tasted wonderful, and even sullen Sasha remarked on how much she liked it.

Adam finished his taco, wiped his dirty hands on his pants, looked around. Gregory saw his son's eyes light up as he spotted something down the makeshift midway.

"A haunted house!" Adam said. He turned toward his father. "Can we go, Dad?"

Gregory followed the boy's gaze. It was one of those shoddy prefab carnival attractions, all gaudy oversized front with an almost nonexistent ride behind it, but Adam was ecstatic and next to him Teo was frightened, and he could tell this was a big deal to them. He remembered how excited he'd been himself when as a child at the county fair he'd seen a booth advertising the frozen body of the Abominable Snowman. Even his parents had known it was fake, but he *had* to see it, and although it turned out to be merely a hairy plaster mannequin in a glass box, he would have regretted it for the rest of his life if he hadn't been able to view the attraction, and he had no intention of denying his own children access to the haunted house.

"I don't know," Julia said.

"It'll be all right," he told her.

"Are you guys coming too?" Adam looked hopefully up at his parents.

"No," Gregory said.

"Sasha?"

"Yeah, right."

Adam turned toward Teo. "What about you? Are you coming? Or are you too *scared*?"

"I'm not scared!" Teo said defiantly.

"Then you're coming with me?"

"M-maybe," Teo said hesitantly.

"You *are* scared!"

"Am not!"

Gregory smiled. Adam was only goading his sister because *he* was afraid to go into the haunted house alone. Gregory finished his Indian taco, tossed his napkin and paper plate in a nearby trash barrel, and took out his wallet. "Teo," he said. "Will you go if Sasha takes you?"

Teo nodded happily.

"All right" Adam said.

Sasha threw away her paper plate. "Gee, thanks, Dad."

He smiled. "You get to go, too."

"What a thrill." She took the money he gave her, and after listening to her mother's warning not to scare her brother or her little sister, led Adam and Teo across the grass toward the haunted house.

"She'll adjust," Julia said, putting a hand on his arm.

Gregory watched Sasha's retreat. "We'll see."

The two of them started walking slowly toward the midway, stopping at various stalls along the way. Julia looked at the local historical society's display of photographs and documents from the town's past and picked up some pamphlets from an Arizona chapter of the Sierra Club. The crowd had swollen, the entire parade audience having now left the highway and merged with the existing throngs of people exploring the booths and exhibits spread across the park and parking lot.

Julia had heard someone mention a Molokan Heritage Club booth, and they were looking for it—Gregory saying that if his mother had known the Molokans were participating she would have come no matter how badly her arthritis was acting up—when a man in front of them said tentatively, "Excuse me."

Gregory looked up and saw a heavyset middle-aged guy with thick hair and a thin goatee. The man squinted at him. "Gregory?"

The face of the man was familiar, and Gregory ran through the catalog of mug shots in his brain, trying to determine which of his past friends could have grown into the man before him.

"Paul?" he said.

The other man grinned, offering a calloused hand to shake. "Jesus! I thought that was you. How you doing, man?"

"Not bad," Gregory said, smiling. "Not bad." He put an arm around Julia, gave her a small squeeze. "This is my wife, Julia. Julia, this is Paul Mathews, my best friend from elementary school."

"Elementary school? Try elementary, junior high, and high school."

"My best friend from McGuane," Gregory said. "How's that?"

"Better."

Julia nodded. "Hello."

"Nice to meet you," Paul said, smiling. He reached forward, shook Julia's hand.

"We just moved back here," Paul said.

"No shit?"

Julia touched Gregory's cheek, motioned toward the row of booths in front of them, and he nodded. She started walking, smiling a good-bye to Paul.

"I'll catch up," Gregory told her.

There was a moment of awkward silence.

"So you're married, huh?"

"With three kids."

"Girls? Boys?"

"Two girls, one boy. Sasha's seventeen. Adam's almost thirteen. Teodosia's nine."

Paul shook his head. "Man. Time flies, doesn't it?"

"Yeah," Gregory said, "it sure does." He looked at the man in front of him, saw within that man the boy he had once known.

It was nice to see an old friend, he admitted, but there was also something disconcerting about it. They were both grown men, middle-aged, so the years had obviously passed, but the fact that they were both here, in McGuane, gave him the unnerving feeling that they had both been spinning their wheels, that they'd accomplished nothing in all those years, that their lives were pointless and useless and they were just killing time until they eventually died.

It was completely illogical, an idiotic thing to think, but he thought it nonetheless, and he realized that he'd been feeling adrift ever since he'd won the lottery, ever since he'd quit his job. He'd never considered himself one of those people who were defined by their work, who needed the imposed structure of a job to bring meaning and order to their lives, but perhaps he wasn't as free and independent as he'd always thought.

"Are you married?" he asked.

Paul nodded.

"Anyone I know?"

"Deanna."

Gregory was shocked. "Deanna Exley?"

"She lost a lot of weight her last two years of high school," Paul said defensively.

Gregory laughed. "I'm sorry," he said. "I'm sorry."

"That's okay." Paul grinned wryly. "What's my life for if not to serve as the butt of jokes for my buddies?"

"Just like old times." Gregory looked around. "So where is she?"

"Visiting her mom in Phoenix. Me and the old broad don't exactly get along, so I drop Deanna off, she stays a week or so, then I go back and pick her up. Everyone's happy."

"I can't believe it." Gregory shook his head. "Deanna."

"So what brings you back here?"

"I don't know."

"Getting back to your roots, huh?"

He smiled. "Yeah. I guess."

"There aren't a lot of jobs around," Paul warned. "It's gonna be tough finding work."

"I'm okay."

The other man's eyebrows shot up. "Don't tell me you're independently wealthy?"

"I won the California lottery."

"No shit?"

Gregory laughed. "It's not quite as exciting as it sounds. There were three winners, and it's paid off over twenty years, so I only get, like, eighty thousand a year."

"Eighty thousand a year? I've never cleared that in my life."

Gregory felt suddenly embarrassed. "Well, it's not that much in California. The standard of living's quite a bit higher there, and . . ." He trailed off, not sure what to say.

"Well, it's quite a bit back here. You're going to be one of our most important and respectable citizens."

"I'd rather not broadcast it," Gregory said.

"Wise decision." Paul whistled. "The lottery. Eighty thousand a year."

Gregory cleared his throat. "So, what are you doing these days?"

"I own Mocha Joe's." He pointed up the street to a small café sandwiched between a beauty parlor and a pharmacy in a block of connected buildings. "We serve bagels, cappuccino, that kind of thing."

Gregory shook his head, smiling. "A coffeehouse? I thought I'd left all that back in California." He looked quickly at his old friend. "No offense."

Paul chuckled. "None taken." He smiled ruefully. "There's a lot of them out there, huh?"

"On every damn corner."

"I'm the only one in McGuane, and I still can't make a living."

Gregory looked up the street, toward the restaurant. All of the sidewalk tables were filled, and there was a line of people standing outside the door. "Looks like you're doing all right."

"Yeah. This weekend. But I can't live for a whole

year off the profits of three days. The rest of the year
this place is dead. McGuane is not exactly a mocha java
town, if you know what I mean."

Gregory laughed. "I do know what you mean."

They talked for a few minutes more, then Gregory
said he'd better catch up to his wife.

"I'm in the phone book," Paul said. "Call me."

"I will," Gregory promised. "Nice to see you again."

Adam and Teo came running up. Sasha following
them slowly and coolly, and Gregory introduced them
to his old friend.

Adam gave Paul a cursory nod hello before turning
back toward Gregory. "It wasn't even scary!" he said.
"It sucked!"

"It was a little scary," Teo amended, although Gregory could tell she'd thought it was much more than that.

"The stunt show's going to start in twenty minutes,"
Adam announced. "We have to go now if we're going
to get a good seat."

"Let's find Mom first." Gregory waved good-bye to
Paul and led the kids through the crowd. They found
Julia at the Molokan booth, and here were even more
faces that he recognized, but he did not feel like talking
to anybody, and he used Adam's Wild West Show as an
excuse to drag Julia away from the Molokans and across
the park to the grandstands.

2

Finished, Julia turned off the vacuum cleaner, started
wrapping up the cord. They'd been here for more than
two weeks, almost unpacked for the past three days, and
by now they were pretty familiar with the house, with
its boundaries and dimensions and idiosyncrasies, but it
seemed . . . different now than it had been when she
and Gregory had gone through it with the real estate
agent. Less hospitable. It was always dark, and while no
one else appeared to notice that fact, she almost certainly did. She knew the reason: the house lay at the
bottom of a steep outcropping of hill, which protected
it from the morning sun, and there were two few win-

dows facing west, making it gloomy even in the afternoon. She even understood why the house had been built this way: it was old, constructed before the advent of air-conditioning, and its owners had attempted to shield it from the desert sun as much as possible. But the end result was that their new home seemed odd and uncomfortable to her.

Spooky.

Spooky. It was a child's word, and she didn't know why she'd thought of it, but it described perfectly the atmosphere of this house. She had not been alone much the past couple of weeks, but the few times she had, she'd found herself listening for noises, peeking carefully around corners, being startled by shadows. There was an air of unease about their new home that seemed almost tangible to her, although it was apparently imperceptible to everyone else.

She wheeled the vacuum cleaner back to the hall closet. Of course, it was probably nothing, probably just stress. It was a shock to her system, moving from metropolitan Southern California to rural Arizona, and she was having a difficult time adjusting and this was just the way it was coming out.

But she was already wondering if they'd made a big mistake coming here—and that was not a good way to start a new life.

Julia went to the kitchen and poured herself a glass of sun tea from the pitcher in the refrigerator. With the vacuum off, the house was silent, and she popped a Rippingtons tape into the cassette player on the counter just to hear some noise. Sasha was upstairs in her room, brooding as usual, feeling sorry for herself, and Gregory's mother was in her room, taking a short nap. Gregory had taken Adam and Teo to check out the video store and see if they could find something to watch tonight. Their cable was still not hooked up, and antenna reception here was little more than wishful thinking. She'd always been one of those parents who decried the evils of television, but the fact was, now that they were deprived of TV, the kids weren't spending their time any more wisely. If anything, they were engaged in even more frivolous pursuits: Teo dressing and undressing and redressing her Barbie dolls; Adam reading superhero comic books; Sasha lying on her bed listening to the same bad rap songs over and over again. None of their children, she realized, ever read the newspaper, and with no television, what little exposure to current events they had was cut off.

She'd be glad when the cable was connected.

She walked back out to the living room. Her mother-in-law's crocheting project—a granny-square afghan—was lying over an arm of the couch, trailing onto the floor. Several skeins of yarn were piled on the coffee table.

As much as she hated to admit it, Gregory's mother was starting to get on her nerves. The old woman had already chided Julia for shopping at the Copper City Market when the Fresh Buy grocery store had a Russian butcher, and she'd insisted that Gregory buy gas for the van at Mohov's—even though it was five cents higher there than anywhere else—because the station was owned by a Russian.

"The Molokan Mafia," Gregory called it, and while Julia had always thought the idea rather humorous, she understood now why Gregory had never laughed. It was a particularly annoying form of cultural myopia, a prejudice that actually affected day-to-day life rather than merely an abstract belief with no real-world applications. Her own parents had been Molokan, but they hadn't been quite as strict, hadn't tried to so thoroughly purge all American influences from their lives, hadn't so circumscribed the borders of their existence that they lived in a completely Russian world.

But her parents had been born and raised in L.A. Gregory's family came from a more insular community, and their fear of the outside culture was greater. There was also a certain element of racism, a sense of superiority. Russians were better than Outsiders, and somehow businessmen and merchants who were of the same religion were regarded as more trustworthy.

Gregory had tried to explain to his mother that gasoline was not more holy because it was dispensed by a Molokan, and that the free-market principles that applied to every other aspect of life still applied here. "I buy gas wherever it's cheapest," he said. "If Mohov is cheapest, I'll buy from him."

His mother hadn't liked that, and her face had registered her harsh disapproval. She'd been uncooperative ever since, polite but obviously angry, and the atmosphere at home had been tense.

Julia sighed. She and Gregory had made a conscious decision to try and get along with his mother, to give in if need be during arguments, to put aside disagreements and differences with her in order to maintain harmony in the household, and Julia had not expected there to be a problem. She had always gotten along fine with her mother-in-law, and she'd actually looked forward to having another female voice of authority in the house. But seeing someone on weekends and talking occasionally on the phone, she discovered, was quite a bit different than living together twenty-four hours a day.

Of course, some problems were to be expected. They were all feeling their way, trying to determine the parameters of their new lifestyle and subsequently changed relationships, and it would be a while before all the kinks were worked out.

She herself felt somewhat lost, at loose ends, and while she had originally told Gregory after quitting her job at the Downey Public Library that she would like to write a children's book, she seemed to be completely unable to translate that dream into reality, to take the concrete steps necessary to accomplish the goal. At this point she was not even sure if that really *was* what she wanted to do.

This was all turning out to be a lot harder than she'd thought it would be.

Maybe she should volunteer at the McGuane library. Or at the elementary school, once summer ended.

The phone rang, and she answered it immediately. It was Debbie, and Julia found herself smiling as she heard her friend's familiar voice. "Jules!"

She was so grateful to have someone from the real world to talk to and Julia suddenly realized how much she regretted moving to Arizona.

Debbie was going to see a sneak preview of a new Steven Spielberg movie that night. She'd been walking

through Lakewood Mall on Saturday, had answered a
few questions from a canvasser, had obviously fit the
desired demographic profile, and had been given two
free tickets to an unnamed sneak. When she'd called the
phone number to confirm, she'd been told that it was
Spielberg's new film.

"I wish you were here," she said. "I don't have anyone to go with. John refuses to come with me. I'm going
to have to forfeit the other ticket."

"I wish I was there, too," Julia said.

They talked for another fifteen or twenty minutes before Debbie said she had to go and pick up Therese
from kindergarten.

Julia hung up reluctantly. The house seemed even
darker after she finished talking to her friend, and
though both Gregory's mother and Sasha were in their
bedrooms, the house felt deserted. A lone shaft of faded
sunlight fell on the half-finished afghan, and for some
reason the sight made the skin prickle on her arms.

Spooky.

Outside, she thought she saw a small shadow dart past
the front window. Teo, probably. Gregory and the kids
must be home. Grateful that the others had returned,
she walked to the window and looked out, but the drive
was still empty and there was no sign of the van out on
the street.

In the kitchen, the Rippingtons tape was playing, but
the house still seemed far too quiet, and she considered
going upstairs and waking Sasha to tell her that she had
to help with some of the housework, had to help clean
up.

She didn't want to be alone.

Stupid. She was being stupid again. The unease she
felt had nothing to do with the house itself; it was just
a by-product of culture shock, a perfectly ordinary psy-
chological response. There was nothing scary here, nothing frightening, nothing out of the ordinary.

But she could not assuage her fears with logic. They
were feelings more than thoughts, not subject to the arguments of rationality, and she wished that her mother-
in-law would wake up or that Sasha would come
downstairs.

She thought of that small shadow passing by the window.

Jedushka Di Muvedushka.

As embarrassed as she was to admit it, her mother-in-law's consternation over not inviting the Owner of the House had also affected her. It was ignorant, Julia knew, and she shouldn't let herself get sucked back up into that sort of superstitious claptrap, but as logical and modern and freethinking as she tried to be, somewhere deep within her she still retained a seed of belief. She wasn't that familiar with this particular legend, but she knew that Jedushka Di Muvedushka was supposed to protect them. He was the guardian of the family against whatever supernatural entities might want to infiltrate and interfere with their lives.

Gregory's mother had been visibly upset ever since she'd discovered they had not invited the Owner of the House, and that might also account for some of her irritability. Ever since they'd come to McGuane, she'd been praying and discussing God even more than usual, and while she no doubt found such talk reassuring, to Julia it was annoying and slightly disconcerting. All this emphasis on the unseen world, on the supernatural, religious, made her uncomfortable. It also kept such thoughts in the forefront of her mind, and, as ludicrous as it might be, she had to admit that she would be feeling better if they *had* invited the Owner of the House, if they had some built-in protection against ghosts and demons and . . . whatever was out there.

There was a crash from the kitchen, the sound of dishes shattering, and Julia jumped, her heart lurching in her chest. Catching her breath, she hurried to the doorway, expecting, *hoping* to see that her mother-in-law had knocked over one of the boxes of dishes that had not yet been unpacked.

There was an overturned box on the floor. And the linoleum was covered with broken china and broken glass.

But there was no one else around.

A chill passed through her. She scanned the shadowy kitchen, eyed the closed, dead-bolted door that led outside, saw nothing out of the ordinary.

"Julia!" Gregory's mother called from her bedroom. "Everything is all right?"

"It's fine!" she called back, grateful to hear another voice.

She walked into the kitchen, bent down, and righted the box. Quite a few dishes were still inside, and many of them, thankfully, appeared to be intact. She must've put the box on the counter next to the refrigerator and it had just fallen off.

No. She distinctly remembered setting it on the table in the breakfast nook—on the other side of the room.

That was impossible.

She opened the cupboard under the sink, took out a plastic garbage sack and began picking up the broken pieces of china. She looked up at the counter. Obviously, she'd moved the box to the counter and simply forgotten that she'd done so. And she'd placed it too close to the edge and it had eventually fallen.

She tried to gauge the angle of descent.

Yes, she told herself. That must have been what happened.

But she could not make herself believe it.

3

Babunya didn't like the *banya,* and Adam didn't either. There was something about the small adobe building that made him uneasy. It was what attracted him to the structure as well, though, and over the past few weeks he found himself returning to the abandoned bathhouse again and again.

Looking up from the shed snakeskin he'd been examining, he glanced toward the house, making sure that Teo had gone back inside, then took off, dashing around the carport and past the overhanging cottonwood tree. His sister had been hanging around him way too much lately, and while he didn't really mind, since neither of them had met any other kids or made any friends yet, it did get annoying after a while. Sometimes he just wanted to be by himself.

Besides, he liked to go to the *banya* alone.

He ducked under a tree branch and started down the path that led through the high, dry weeds. Their yard was massive, and the *banya* was not even within sight of the house. It stood alone on the other side of the property, almost around the curve of the hill, past a small copse of paloverde trees and a jumble of oversized boulders. Beyond the *banya,* the cement foundation of an old house emerged from the weeds, bits of blackened board dissecting the empty space between low irregular walls.

He and Babunya had been the first ones into the *banya,* the second day they were here, and both had had immediate reactions to the place. The moment that she stepped over the threshold, Babunya had staggered as if struck, grabbing the wall for support. She'd instantly turned around and exited the bathhouse, breathing heavily, but when he followed her out, asking what was wrong, she waved him away and said everything was fine.

Everything was not fine, though. He, too, had felt the oppressiveness of the atmosphere as he'd walked through the door, a sensation entirely unrelated to the darkness of the small building and the natural scent of mold and must. It was a creepy feeling completely divorced from anything physical.

It scared him, but he liked being scared, and as soon as Babunya had told him that she was all right, he went back in to explore.

He had been back several times since.

Now Adam passed under the thin green branches of a paloverde and headed up the slight incline to the bathhouse, feeling the familiar foreboding in the pit of his stomach.

The *banya* had obviously been abandoned for many years; the weeds that grew around it were almost as tall as the doorway. But inside, there were no spiderwebs as he'd first expected. The place was not crawling with bugs, and although it was not something that would have ordinarily occurred to him, he thought there seemed something ominous about the lack of pests. It was as if even insects were afraid of this place, and in his mind that only added to its exoticism and allure.

He had been in the *banya* many times now, but he had never touched anything, never moved or removed a single object, and all was exactly the same as it had been that first day. He stopped for a second in the doorway, peering in. There were bones on the rough wooden floor. Not skeletons but individual bones, although the impact was the same. They were clearly not chicken or beef but were from other animals—coyote or javelina, rodents or rabbits or pets or pigs—and there was one that looked like a femur from a human child.

That was the one that intrigued him the most. He'd learned most of the bones of the body in school last year, and that particular bone had jumped out at him the first time he saw it. It looked just like a femur bone, a small femur, and whenever he came into the bathhouse he always stopped to look at it.

He did the same thing this time, crouching down before it, once again trying to imagine where it had come from, how it had gotten here, feeling a delicious tingle of fear pass through him as he examined the yellowing object.

But the bone was only an appetizer.

He stood, turned.

At the back of the structure was the thing that really scared him, the thing that had sent him running back out into Babunya's arms that first day and had haunted his nightmares ever since. The thing that had made him break his promise to his grandmother never to go into the *banya* alone.

The shadow.

It hovered on the adobe wall above the broken benches, bigger than life. The profile of a man. A Russian man with a fat stomach and a full, chest-length beard.

It was not a stain or discoloration, was not imprinted onto the wall, but was an honest-to-God shadow, and there was about it the insubstantiality of something that was only a shaded copy of an actual object.

Only there was no object. There was no source within the *banya* or within the sight line out the doorway, no comparable shape that it was thrown by. The shadow existed in seeming defiance of the laws of science, and he'd thought about it and thought about it, tried to attribute its form to everything from the weeds outside to the wooden beams of the ceiling inside, but nothing worked. For one thing, the shadow was always there, clear sky or cloudy, its contours immutable and unchanging. For another, it was not an accidental resemblance. It was not a coincidental configuration of images that happened to form the semblance of a man but was a specific, definite figure that could not under any circumstances be interpreted as anything else.

There was something foreboding about the shape itself, about the man being portrayed, something stern and commanding about his thick body and the way his head was held so unnaturally straight, something intimidating about the figure that, combined with the shadow's unknown origin, lent to the entire *banya* an aura of dread.

Adam gathered his strength, looked up. He saw the silhouetted profile, the strong brow and thick beard, and he had to force himself not to turn away. His heart was pounding, and the air inside the bathhouse suddenly felt cold. The shadow seemed to deepen as he stared at it, the entire interior of the *banya* growing darker around it, and for a fraction of a second it appeared to have three-dimensional depth.

He thought he heard a sigh, a whisper, and, his pulse rate shifting into high gear, he bolted out of the *banya* and back into the sunlight, running as fast as he could, not stopping until he had reached the line of paloverdes.

It was the longest he had ever stayed in the *banya,* and he was proud of himself for that. He was getting braver. Always before, he had been out the door immediately after setting eyes on the shadow, but this time he'd been able to look at it for a moment before having to run.

He shivered, thinking of that sigh, that whisper, and quickly started back down the path toward the house.

Next time, he would borrow Sasha's watch and time himself, see if he couldn't stay in there a little longer each visit.

He slowed down and turned to look behind him, but the *banya* was already hidden behind boulders and trees.

He stood there for a moment, catching his breath, then continued on.

It was hard for him to believe that the bathhouse had ever really been used. Even if it hadn't been scary, he couldn't imagine himself going in there, getting naked, and sitting around with other guys while they whipped themselves with tree branches. Part of him felt embarrassed even to be *related* to people who did that.

But of course, that was not really anything new.

He'd often been embarrassed about his background.

Last year, they'd had an "ethnic pride" day at school, and it had been pure hell. They were all supposed to share the foods, clothes, language, and traditions of their families' cultures with the other members of the class, and he'd brought in some borscht his mom had made. Mrs. Anders had insisted on pronouncing "borscht" the way it was spelled, sounding out the silent "t," and no matter how often he said it correctly, she refused to vary her pronunciation. He had the feeling she was trying to correct him, as though she was hinting to him that *he* said the word wrong, and that made him feel even more embarrassed. It was as if she was making fun of him, something she did not do with Ve Phan or George Saatjian or any of the other kids in class.

He'd passed out the wooden spoons and small sample bowls of the Russian soup and had been expected to talk about the history of the Molokans as the class ate, to describe how they acted and what they believed in, and he'd said most of what he'd planned to say, but he'd been too embarrassed to bring up the pacifism. It was at the core of the Molokan religion, was what Babunya had drilled into his head since he was little, but it shamed him to admit to it. He honestly believed in those principles, deep down, but at the same time he didn't really want to. Babunya had always told him that it was in man's nature to kill, that Cain, the first truly human being in the Bible, the first made from the union of man and woman rather than by God, had killed his brother. It was an evil act, but after he had murdered his brother, he had been marked by God, protected from all human justice, and she said that this not only showed God's mercy and forgiveness but indicated that God did not

want humans to judge other humans, that He forbade
revenge, that only He could mete out punishment. It was
a prohibition against violence, against war, against the
death penalty, and Molokans took their pacifism very
seriously. They had left their mother country for it, and
they had refused to fight in any of America's wars because of it.

That was all well and good, and when he was in his
bed in his pajamas and Babunya was telling him Bible
stories, it was nice to hear, and he believed in it. But at
school those ideas seemed not only irrelevant but embarrassing. It was impossible not to want to hurt people
who hurt you, and more than once he had wished Jason
Aguilar or Gauvin Jefferson or Teech Sayles dead. Hell,
if he'd still said his prayers, he probably would have
prayed for God to strike them down. But he had stopped
praying several years back. He was not really sure why
that was, but at some point he had just felt foolish clasp-
ing his hands together and asking God for favors.

It was not something he would ever admit to Babunya, though.

The truth was, he was not sure if he even *was* a Molokan. His family didn't go to church anymore, and even
when they had gone, when he was little, they'd gone to
a Presbyterian church in Norwalk.

His parents also hadn't taught him Russian, and he
knew that was one thing Babunya was not happy about.
He knew a few words here and there—*popolk,* belly
button; *zhopa,* butt; *babunya,* grandma; *dushiska,*
sweetie—but he couldn't even remember the short Russian prayer his grandmother had made him say each
Thanksgiving when he was younger. Even Babunya herself spoke less Russian than she used to. When he was
little, his parents and his grandmother used to talk in
Russian all the time, especially when it was something
they didn't want him to hear. When his dad used to talk
to Babunya on the phone, his end of the conversation
was often entirely in Russian. But that had changed over
the years and now they almost always spoke English.

He walked past the cottonwood around to the front
of the house. His mom, dad, and Babunya were now
sitting on the front porch, his dad reading the newspa-

per, his mom reading a magazine, Babunya crocheting. Teo was playing with her Barbies on the steps. The sound of rap music blasting from one of the upper side windows told him that Sasha, as usual, was in her room.

He'd been planning to explore the front yard and see if he could find any more snakeskins, but the whole idea of all of them sitting around, doing family things together, made him gag, and he knew that he had to get away. His dad might be trying to get into all that small-town family-values crap, but on the off chance that a potential or future friend walked past on the road and saw them acting like rejects from the 700 Club, he needed to disassociate himself. He didn't want to be humiliated.

There was nothing more uncool than hanging with your parents.

He walked up to the porch steps, grabbed the railing and looked up at his dad. "Can I walk down to the store?" he asked.

"Which store?"

"Does it matter? They're both practically right next to each other."

"Why?" his mom asked.

"Jeez! Am I going to get the third degree every time I want to leave the yard? You let me and Roberto go almost everywhere. And that was in California. Now I can't even walk a couple of blocks in this crummy little town?"

His dad smiled. "Go ahead." He looked at his mother. "What's he going to do?"

"Be back in forty-five minutes," she said.

He nodded and took off running before Teo could say that she wanted to go too.

At the store he made a friend.

It was purely by accident. He was standing by himself, next to the comic books rack, glancing through the new *Spiderman,* when a kid about his own age came into the small market, causing the bell over the door to jingle. Adam looked up, saw a boy with longish hair, wearing torn jeans and a Smashing Pumpkins T-shirt, and then went back to his comic book without giving the kid a second thought.

The boy said something to the clerk, then walked over to where Adam was standing. Adam stepped back a pace, and the boy twirled the rack. "Where's *Superman*?" he said, turning back toward the front of the store. "I'm here to pick up the September *Superman*."

"Sorry," the clerk said, "we're all out."

"You said you'd tell me when they came in."

"Sorry. We've been busy."

"Shit."

"I have that one," Adam offered.

The boy looked at him for the first time. "Yeah?"

"Yeah."

"Who are you?"

"I just moved here," he said. "My name's Adam."

The boy thought for a moment. "You like comics?"

"No. I'm just looking at these for my health."

The kid smiled. "Superman fan?"

"Spiderman mostly. But I like 'em both."

"Me too." The kid nodded in greeting. "I'm Scott."

They were shy with each other at first. It was no longer as easy for Adam to make friends as it had been when he was younger, when every time he'd go to the park or go to the beach he'd make a new friend for the day, someone he'd never see again but who, for those few hours at least, was his best buddy in the world. Scott, too, seemed to be hesitant, unsure of how to proceed, how to tentatively approach the boundary of friendship without coming off like an asshole.

That was another thing they had in common.

But by the time they made their way around to the shelf of trading cards next to the candy, they were talking: Adam describing life in the big city, Scott explaining what a hellhole McGuane was for anyone who wasn't what he termed a "goat roper."

Like himself, Scott was going to be in seventh grade, and after they left the store, Scott took him by the school to check the place out. It was bigger than he'd expected and more modern than most of the other buildings in town. The two of them walked up to a drinking fountain on a wall adjoining the tennis court, and Adam got a drink while Scott took out a pen and began writing on the brown stucco above the fountain. He looked up as he wiped off his mouth and saw the word "Pussy" written on the wall—with an arrow pointing down to where he'd been drinking.

Scott burst out laughing.

They walked around the empty school, wondering where their classes were going to be, wondering where it would be safe for them to hang out so the eighth- and ninth-graders didn't beat them up. They took a shortcut across the field to Turquoise Avenue, and Adam invited his new friend to come over, thinking he could show him the *banya,* but Scott said he was supposed to have been home an hour ago and he'd better get back before his mom threw a fit.

"Where do you live?" Scott asked.

"Twenty-one Ore Road."

"What's it look like? Your house?"

Adam shrugged. "I don't know. It's white. Wooden. Two stories. Set back from the road. There's like a hill behind it and off to the right, and I guess we own that, too."

Scott's eyes widened. "The old Megan place?"

"I think I heard my dad say something about that."

"Cool. I'll cruise over there tomorrow. What time're you guys up and about?"

"Me? Early."

"What about your parents?"

"Everyone should be up and everything by nine or so."

"I'll be there." Scott started down the street, waved. "And have that *Superman* ready!"

"You got it!" Adam called back.

He started home, feeling good. He'd made his first friend, and that was a big worry off his shoulders. He'd been dreading going to school cold, knowing no one, being "the new guy," and he was grateful that he'd found a pal.

And Scott seemed pretty cool.

Maybe McGuane wouldn't be so bad after all.

It was getting late, and he could tell by the angle of the sun and the shadows in the canyon that he'd been gone more than forty-five minutes. He knew his mom would be mad, and he didn't want to end up being

grounded, so he broke into a jog. They'd wound their
way around from the store to the school, and though he
didn't know the layout of the town that well, it looked
to him like he could cut across a few streets and take a
shortcut around the hill behind their house and get home
quite a bit faster than he would if he went back the
same way he'd come.

He jogged down unfamiliar streets, following the land-
marks of cliffs and hills, and did indeed find a small dirt
trail that looked like it led around to their property.

The *banya*.

He'd known he would pass it returning this round-
about way, known he would have to see it in this dying
afternoon light, but he hadn't allowed himself to think
about it, had concentrated instead on getting home.

Now, as he ran between outstretched ocotillo arms
and irregularly shaped boulders, he could not *help* thinking about it.

And, suddenly, there it was.

He approached the bathhouse from the back, from a
direction he had never come before, seeing it from an
angle he had never seen. As expected, the *banya* stood
in shadow, past the ruined foundation of the old house,
while the tops of the trees behind it were still in sunlight.

Inside the bathhouse, he thought, it was probably
like night.

The adobe wall in front of him was the one opposite
the door, the one on which the shadow was projected,
and he increased his speed, trying not to look at it as
he ran by, feeling cold.

He looked at it anyway, though.

The *banya* stood there, door open onto blackness.

Waiting.

Shivering, he dashed past it and ran through the rest
of the huge yard into the house. Babunya was in the
kitchen chopping vegetables, and they exchanged a
glance as he came in the back door. She'd seen him
through the window, knew the direction from which he
had come, and though he saw the look of disapproval
on her face, she said nothing. He knew she felt guilty
because she had not blessed the *banya* before walking
into it, had made no effort to cleanse it of evil spirits,

and she considered herself partially responsible for the *banya* being the way it was. He didn't believe any of that, he told himself, not really. But she did, and that spooked him. It gave everything a bit more credibility and made his runs to and from the bathhouse seem less of a game, seem much more ominous.

"I didn't go there," he said in response to her look. "I just came home that way. It was a shortcut."

She said nothing, just continued chopping vegetables.

He walked out to the living room, where Teo was lying on the floor, watching TV, an open storybook on the carpet in front of her. Neither of his parents was around, and for that he was grateful. They hadn't seen him come in, and that had probably saved him from a grounding.

He plopped on the floor next to Teo, poked her in the side. She yelled and hit him.

He glanced over at her book. *Shirley Temple's Fairy Tales.* It had been his mom's originally, but it had been passed down to Sasha, then to him, then to Teo. In the center of the book, he recalled, was a two-page picture of Rumpelstiltskin, a cavorting dwarf with a sly, evil face, and he thought that that was what Jedushka Di Muvedushka must look like.

He dreamed that night of Rumpelstiltskin. It was the first nightmare he'd had in their new house, and in his dream the dwarf was naked in the *banya,* sitting in steam, the shadow wavering above him, hitting himself with leaves, grinning.

Four

1

Gregory walked with his mother to the Molokan church. She'd been wanting to go since the first day they'd arrived, but everything had been so hectic, they'd been so busy unpacking and rearranging and getting the long-neglected yard into some semblance of order, that he simply hadn't had the time to take her.

Today, though, she had demanded and he had acquiesced, and now the two of them stood in the dirt parking lot in front of the church, she leaning heavily on his arm. He'd wanted to drive down, but she'd insisted that they walk, like they had in the old days, and although it had taken nearly forty minutes to get here, with frequent rest stops, they'd finally arrived.

Gregory looked around: at the variety store, which began the block of businesses on the other side of the vacant lot to the left of the church, at the wood-frame house on the building's right flank that had been turned into a nursery. He looked up at the church itself as the two of them approached. He'd expected to have a better memory of the place—after all, his family had spent a lot of time here—but he must have blocked it out, because the church seemed no more familiar to him than the mine office or the town hall or any of the other buildings he'd seen as a child but with which he had had no real involvement. He recognized the church, but it was an impartial, impersonal recognition that contradicted the intimate acquaintance he'd had with the place.

They walked up the three short steps, went in. Like

the church in East L.A., it was simple. A wooden structure with one big open room and a small adjoining kitchen. There were benches stacked against one wall, and an old man with a white beard that hung down to his stomach was sweeping the hardwood floor.

"Jim?" his mother said, stopping. She squinted. "Jim Ivanovitch?"

The old man broke into a huge grin. "Agafia?"

The two of them hobbled across the floor toward each other, meeting somewhere around the middle of the room for a big bear hug. Gregory smiled. He didn't recognize the old man, but his mother did, and she was clearly delighted. He hadn't seen her this happy since they'd left California.

She turned toward him. "Gregory?" She spoke in Russian. "You may not remember, but this is Jim Petrovin, our old minister." She laughed a strangely girlish laugh he didn't recognize. "And my old boyfriend before your father."

The minister nodded and grinned, the expression on his face impossible to read behind the huge beard. Gregory stared at him, maintaining his own now meaningless smile. He suddenly didn't know what to say or how to act. It was childish of him, but he felt an instant antipathy toward the old man, a defensive rivalry on his father's behalf. The minister was ancient, practically on the verge of death, but it seemed somehow disloyal for him to accept the man, to feel anything positive toward him. He thought of his mother's laugh, that girlish laugh he didn't recognize, that laugh from an earlier time of her life, before he had been born, and he realized that there were a lot of things about his mother that he didn't know, whole segments of her life, whole aspects of her personality that were shielded from him and entirely unfamiliar.

He understood for the first time that he did not really know his mother.

"Jim followed my family to McGuane," she said. "Hoping to win me back."

The minister nodded. "I did not covet," he said. "But I hoped."

Gregory didn't want to hear this. "You two probably

have a lot to talk about." He was suddenly aware of
how rusty his Russian sounded, how long it had been
since he'd spoken more than a few words at a time in
the language. "I am going to walk around town. I will
come back in an hour or so and pick you up."

His mother nodded. "I will be here."

She smiled at him and waved, and he walked out of
the church, across the dirt, out to the street. He felt like
a child again, confused and conflicted, and though he
knew it was silly, knew that there was nothing going
on—and that even if there *was,* his mother had a perfect
right to resume a romantic life this many years after his
father's death—he felt uncomfortable. The fact that she
had known this minister before she had known his father
trivialized the life of their family, implied somehow that
this man was her one true love and that her husband,
his father, had been merely an impediment that had temporarily gotten in the way. It was a dumb thought, imma-
ture, but there it was, stuck in his mind, and he had to
force himself not to think it, to at least attempt to look
at the situation objectively.

He headed downtown to the shopping district. He'd
been too busy or too lazy to come down here sooner
and, despite occasional trips to the grocery store, he
hadn't seen the area up close since the Copper Days
celebration that first weekend.

The throngs of people were gone now, and the side-
walks were empty, only parked cars and an occasional
pickup or broken-down Jeep clattering up the canyon
roads to indicate that McGuane was anything other than
a ghost town.

He walked along the cracked sidewalk, peering into
the windows of the shops—some open, some closed—
that fronted the street in a series of connected rock and
brick buildings. There was a used bookstore, an antique
store, a pawnshop, a jewelry store, a shoe repair shop,
a pharmacy.

Halfway down the block, between the shoe repair and
a western wear shop, he came across a narrow building
with no windows and a dark, open doorway.

A bar.

He stopped walking.

The same bar he'd passed with his father all those years ago on the way to church.

He hesitated only a second before stepping inside.

He didn't know what he expected. Hostile rednecks gathered around the counter? The same men who'd insulted his father all those years ago, now grown old? He wasn't sure, but his muscles were tensed as he walked through the door.

He needn't have worried. The interior of the bar was neither threatening nor intimidating. It looked like a typical small-town tavern. Only a few patrons occupied the dimly lit room: a couple in a back booth, two uniformed sheriff's deputies at a small table.

And Paul.

His old friend was seated at the front counter of the bar, next to an older man, and he called out Gregory's name and happily waved him over.

"Hey," Gregory said, walking up. He sat down on an adjacent stool. "Didn't expect to find you here."

"I'm here most days." Paul grinned. "Where everybody knows my name." He motioned to the bartender. "A beer for my friend here."

Gregory shook his head. "No. Thanks. It's a little early for me."

"It's ten o'clock!"

Gregory smiled. "Coffee," he told the bartender.

Paul turned to the old man next to him, nodded in Gregory's direction. "This is Gregory Tomasov, my best friend from . . . hell, kindergarten through high school. He just moved back to town."

The man reached around, held out a weathered hand. "Howdy. I'm Odd Morrison."

Gregory smiled. "That's an odd name."

"Never heard that one before," the other man said dryly.

Gregory laughed.

"Odd's my right-hand man. Plumber, carpenter, bricklayer, carpet installer, and all-around fix-it dude."

"I get it," Gregory said. "He does odd jobs."

"You're a wit," the old man said. He sipped his beer. "Or at least half a one."

"He doesn't take too kindly to people making fun of his name. Especially strangers."

Gregory reddened. "I'm sorry. I didn't mean to offend you. I was just . . ."

Both Paul and Odd burst out laughing.

"Same old Gregory," Paul said. "Still afraid of hurting anyone's feelings." He clapped him on the back. "Insult Odd all you want. He doesn't give a shit."

"As long as I can do the same to you."

The bartender brought over a cup of coffee. Gregory thanked him, and Paul held up a finger, said, "My tab."

Gregory took a sip. Not bad for bar coffee. "That reminds me," he said. "Shouldn't you be working over at your coffeehouse?"

Paul waved his hand dismissively. "What do you think teenagers are for? Besides, the place is dead. The few customers we do have either show up before work or at lunchtime. The joint's not exactly jumping midmorning."

"What about nights, evenings?"

Paul shrugged. "So-so."

Odd raised an eyebrow.

"All right. Business sucks." He sighed. "You know, I was almost going to open up a health food store—"

"And a juice bar? Those are big in California, too."

"No, just a health food store. But it was too depressing. I thought of the health stores I'd been in, and I realized that no one in there ever looked healthy. They were always either skinny, ugly weirdos or dying old people looking for last-chance miracle cures. Normal people just weren't into health food. *Healthy* people weren't into health food. So I decided to try the café." He shook his head. "I just thought it would be cooler than it turned out to be."

"And more successful," Odd pointed out.

"And more successful," Paul agreed. He sipped his beer. "Let's get off this subject. It depresses the shit out of me."

"All right," Gregory said. "What ever happened to Larry Hall?"

"Larry Hall!"

They talked about old times, old friends, what had happened to everyone and where they had gone. Most people had moved away. The few who hadn't seemed to be walking country music clichés—unhappy under-achievers with an extraordinarily high divorce rate. Many of their old schoolyard enemies had turned out to have miserable, unhappy lives, and they both chuckled over that.

"You know," Paul said seriously, "friends come and go, but family's always there."

"You've sure changed your tune."

"What are you talking about?"

"Come on. Back in high school, when you couldn't get a date to save your life, you used to tell me that girls come and go, but friends are forever."

"I did not."

"Did too. You'd been watching too many buddy movies or something. War movies. And you had this asshole idea that even if you eventually got married, your friends would be more important than your wife."

"You a fag?" Odd asked, squinting up at him.

Gregory laughed.

"Very funny."

"All that male bonding crap is just Hollywood bull-shit," Odd said. "I've had a million friends, but I've only had one wife, and if I ever had a choice to make be-tween the two, it would be a damn easy one. I may like my friends, but I love my wife."

"Fuckin' A," Paul said.

Gregory grinned, shaking his head. "I can't believe it. You finally grew up."

"Blow me."

Gregory chuckled, sipped his coffee. He felt good. He and Paul hadn't hung out since high school, but there was none of the awkwardness between them that he would have expected. It was as though they'd picked up exactly where they'd left off all those years ago. They'd fallen into the old rhythms, the old patterns. They were comfortable with each other, perfectly at ease, and there was something nice about that.

"So how is Deanna?" Gregory asked.

"Still at her mom's. I pick her up Thursday. I called and told her you were back, but to tell you the truth, she didn't seem all that fired up to see you."

"Tell her I've changed, too."

"Yeah. Right."

They laughed.

Gregory motioned to the bartender for a refill. He glanced around the bar, saw neon beer signs, a few old mining photographs half hidden in the gloom, a dead jukebox and a Pac Man video game. In his mind, this place had always been demonized, the home of hate, an evil spot, and it was liberating to see that it was merely a typical small-town business, to recognize on an emotional level that his dread had been all self-induced and that none of the attributes he had ascribed to it existed anywhere outside of his mind. He finally understood what people meant when they talked about "a sense of closure." The phrase had always smacked of pop psychology to him, and he'd dismissed the word "closure" as yet another trendy, meaningless buzzword, but it was apt in this instance. It felt as though an open wound had been healed, and it made him think you *could* go home again.

The bartender poured him another cup of coffee, and Gregory smiled his thanks. "You know," he said to Paul, "I was thinking. You need some help at your café? I'd do it for free," he added quickly. "You wouldn't have to pay me a dime."

Paul frowned. "You won the lottery and gave up your high-paying job to become . . . a waiter in McGuane? Are you drunk or are you just insane?"

"I don't want to be a waiter. You have the only café in town, and I thought about all the ones back in California, and I figured I could help you out. You know, spruce it up, bring it up to California standards."

"How?"

"Do you have entertainment? Performers?"

Paul shook his head.

"There you go. That'd help draw people. I could help you book local singers. Or cowboy poets. Or, hell, maybe even some club acts that usually don't even hit this part of the state."

"Why?" Paul asked.

Gregory shrugged. "Call it an investment." He smiled.

"Or the whim of a bored rich guy. Well, rich-for-McGuane guy."

Paul nodded, looked over at Odd. "We *could* have entertainment. We could move back those chairs and tables on the east wall and you could put up a little stage . . ."

"I'd pay for the materials," Gregory said. He nodded toward Odd. "And your time. We could get a decent lighting setup, a mike and a speaker system."

The old man nodded. "It's doable."

"This has potential," Paul admitted, and Gregory thought he detected a hint of excitement in his voice. "No place else in town has live entertainment."

"Even if we just booked local talent, you'd get their friends and family coming in to watch. At the very least. Charge a two-item minimum, and voilà!"

"This could work. I might be saved from bankruptcy yet." He grinned, held his hand out to Gregory, shook. "Deal!"

Gregory wanted to go immediately over to the café, but both Paul and Odd had beers in front of them, and neither one was in a hurry to leave. They talked excitedly of the specifics of renovation, the mechanics of outfitting the café with a performance area, and Odd borrowed a pen from the bartender and started writing figures down on a napkin.

After ten minutes of increasingly grandiose plans that made Gregory mention the fact that they should have a budget, a limit, Paul excused himself and headed off toward the bathroom at the rear of the bar.

Gregory and Odd sat for a moment in silence, sipping their respective drinks.

"You've lived here for a while, haven't you?" Gregory asked.

"All my life."

"You wouldn't happen to know whatever became of the Megans, would you? The ones who used to own our place?"

Odd frowned.

"Did they move or—?"

"They're dead," the old man said.

Gregory stared at him and blinked.

"Bill Megan shot his family. Killed 'em all, then turned the gun on himself."

Odd answered his next question before he even asked it. "In their bedrooms," he said. "Murdered 'em while they slept."

He needed alcohol after that.

He ordered one beer, then another, and finally finished off a third before stopping.

"You're living in the old Megan place?" Paul said after he returned from the bathroom and Odd told him. He whistled. "Brave."

"I didn't know I was being brave. I didn't know anything had happened."

Odd looked disgusted. "Who sold you that house?" he asked. "No, let me guess. Call. Call Cartright."

Gregory nodded.

"It's against Arizona law to sell a place without informing the buyer that there's been a murder there, but Call'd sell his own sister to cannibals if there was a penny to be had, so it don't surprise me none." He squinted up at Gregory. "You could sue his ass, you know. Get out of the contract. You don't want that house, you can—"

"No, we want it, all right."

Paul frowned. "Why, in God's name?"

"Well, for one thing, we're all moved in, we just got settled. I don't want to have to look around for another house, move again, and go through all that stress. Besides, I don't believe in ghosts—"

"Who does?" Paul said. "But it's just the thought that all that shit happened where your kids are sleeping, where your wife takes a bath, where you eat breakfast. Hell, I'd be thinking about it all the time. I'm not superstitious or anything, but that doesn't mean I want to buy Jeffrey Dahmer's refrigerator and store my milk in it. It's sick."

Odd nodded. "Besides, that's why the last people moved out. They *heard* things."

"Things?"

"I don't know if it was their imagination or what, but the people said there were knocking sounds in the mid-

dle of the night. And voices. I don't know whether it
was real ghosts or just their own minds playing tricks on
them, but whatever the cause, they couldn't stay there."
He paused. "Sometimes the demons in your head are
worse than anything outside."

"We haven't heard anything," Gregory said.

"Yet."

He smiled. "Yet."

"Just the same . . ."

"I'll admit it's not something I really wanted to hear.
And I would've been much happier if no one had told
me. But I'm not going to panic and pull up stakes and
disrupt my entire life because of it. Hell, someone's
probably died in almost every old house."

"Just the same . . ." Paul said.

"Well, keep it to yourself," Odd suggested. "Don't
tell your family. That's my advice. What they don't know
can't hurt 'em."

Gregory nodded and thought of his mother blessing
the house before they could go in, cleansing it of evil
spirits. "Maybe you're right," he said. "Maybe you're
right."

2

The Molokan church hosted a welcoming get-together,
an end-of-the-summer barbecue with steak and shashlik.
Gregory was mingling and talking with people he hadn't
seen in years—mostly the parents of childhood church
friends, who seemed to be the only Russians who had
not moved away. His mother was in heaven, the center
of attention, laughing happily and talking loudly, more
animated than Julia had ever seen her.

Julia herself felt slightly out of it. She smiled and chat-
ted and pretended to be enjoying herself, but the truth
was that she had never liked these sorts of functions,
and the unwritten Molokan mandate that every shower,
wedding, funeral, or party put on by or for a church
member must be attended by everyone in the congregation had been one of the many things she had rebelled
against. Even as a child, even in L.A., she had not en-

joyed Molokan mixers, had always done her best to avoid them, and here in the boonies of Arizona, with people she didn't know and with whom she had no intention of socializing, the chore as even less pleasant.

The kids were not having a great time, either. There were no other children or teenagers, and Sasha, Adam and Teo stuck together, hovering on the edge of the small churchyard, eating from paper plates, talking among themselves and gazing longingly out toward the freedom of the street. In addition to being old, everyone here was speaking in Russian, and Julia knew her son and daughters were bored and desperate to leave. Especially Sasha.

She understood how they felt—she felt it herself—but this afternoon was not for them, it was for Gregory's mother, and the least they could do was be polite and put up with it. It would all be over in a few hours.

A huge copper samovar stood on the lonely picnic table in the middle of the yard, and she walked over to get herself some chai. She remembered as a child using sugar cubes to build a bridge across her cup, placing them in a row and wedging them in, pouring the tea over the bridge to dissolve it. It was an almost universal rite for Russian children, and she had taught her own children how to do it, though none of them had ever been big tea drinkers and the novelty had worn off fairly quickly.

Gregory sidled up next to her, nudged her with his shoulder. He poured himself some chai. "Having a good time?"

"Oh, wonderful," she said.

He laughed. "We'll bail as soon as other people start leaving."

She shook her head. "It's okay. Let your mother have her fun."

"You sure?"

"I'm willing to stay to the bitter end. Anything for the sake of family unity."

"Thanks." He gave her a quick kiss. "I owe you one."

She smiled. "You can pay me back tonight."

He grinned, gave her a quick squeeze. "Happy to."

Gregory downed his tea, poured himself another cup,

then asked her to come and meet Semyon Konyov, the man who had been his father's best friend. She accompanied him across the yard to a spot under the cottonwood tree where a group of old men stood around eating shashlik. Introductions were made, polite questions were asked, then the conversation turned to church matters, and she excused herself and walked back to the samovar. She didn't really want anything more to drink, but the picnic table was in a centralized location and offered her a perfect vantage point from which to observe almost everything that was going on. She saw three old women huddled together near the back fence, holding their hands over their mouths as they talked, gossiping. She saw one old man with a gray beard down to his waist, obviously drunk, loudly denouncing both the Russian and the American governments for perceived slights to himself and his family. She saw a group of men gathered around the barbecue, arguing vigorously over something she could not make out.

In the doorway of the church, Gregory's mother was emerging from the building, followed closely by Jim Petrovin. The two of them walked down the steps, over to the barbecue, and Julia watched the minister hover around her mother-in-law. Although she'd told Gregory that he was just being paranoid and overprotective, she found herself revising that analysis. He was right, she thought. The minister *was* after his mother and was making a concerted effort to rekindle the relationship that had ended all those years ago.

Julia understood how Gregory felt, but she had to admit that it was kind of cute, these two old people taking another stab at romance this late in the game. It was also kind of sad. It was clear that there had been no one else in Jim Petrovin's life all this time and that her mother-in-law's return was the fulfillment of a life-long fantasy.

Gregory's mother happened to glance over just at that moment, their eyes met, and they both looked instantly away, embarrassed.

Finally the party began to wind down. Couples started leaving, drunks were ushered into vehicles and driven home, leftover food was taken into the church.

Julia and Gregory stood with their kids, saying good-
bye, thanking everyone for welcoming them to McGuane. They were polite and everyone was polite to them,
but there was a reserved formality to the way in which
they were addressed, a definite distance between themselves and everyone else. She'd noticed it earlier, and at
first she'd put it down to her own aversion to such events
as this, but the truth was that the McGuane Molokans
were acting somewhat . . . secretive.

That was it exactly. They were acting as though there
were some sort of knowledge or plot that they were all
in on but had been forbidden to let her or her family
know anything about. Molokans were naturally secretive, she knew. It was an understandable by-product of
being an oppressed minority. Her own family had always
been suspicious and evasive when asked about their religion or ethnic background. But this was something different. There was an added dimension here, something
specific to these people and this place, and although it
was probably nothing, probably harmless, it nevertheless
made her uneasy.

Gregory went to get his mother. She was making ar-
rangements to get together with several other old
women to make bread and *lopsha* noodles, and for that
Julia was grateful. Maybe that would finally stop her
from moping around the house all day. At the very least,
it would do her good to get outside and see some of her
old friends.

Julia tried to look at it from that perspective, tried to
keep her mind on that aspect of the afternoon, but those
other thoughts kept returning, and she was silent as they
walked up the canyon road toward home.

3

Jolene started screaming at midnight.

Harlan was yanked out of sleep by the sound and
bolted upright in bed next to her. "Is it time?" he asked,
instantly awake. "Is it time?"

She could not even answer him. She continued to
scream—a high-pitched, nonstop, animal sound unlike

anything he had ever heard—and there was no break in
the noise, no rhythm to the cry. Something was wrong,
he knew. Labor was not supposed to be *this* painful, and
it was supposed to come in bursts, to ebb and flow, not
remain constant, not be so relentless.

She was thrashing around on the bed, her body twist-
ing and contorting with agony, the corded muscles of
her neck visibly straining, and he reached out to her,
tried to touch her, tried to feel her forehead, but her
wild movements completely rebuffed him. He reached
down and pulled off the twining, bunching covers, and
saw what he was praying he would not.

Blood.

He was up like a shot, out of the bedroom and into
the hallway. Grabbing the wall phone, he called 911,
screamed his address and said that he needed an ambulance. He slammed down the phone, then immediately
picked it up again and dialed Lynda. How in the hell
had Jolene gotten the wacky idea into her head that a
midwife was better than a doctor, that so-called "natural" childbirth was better than modern medicine? And
why had he been stupid enough to go along with it?
Women used to *die* during natural childbirth. For a lot
of mothers, giving birth had been a fatal experience.

Lynda was already pounding on their front door by
the time his call was on the second ring. She'd obviously
heard Jolene's screams and had rushed over on her own,
and Harlan dropped the phone and ran over to unlock
the dead bolt.

The midwife did not even look at him as she ran inside, racing straight through the living room down the
hall to the bedroom.

The sheet was covered with red. Jolene's legs were
spread, and her genitals were obscured by the copiously
flowing blood. From someplace far away, Harlan thought
he heard the faint sound of a siren.

"Get me some towels and hot water!" Lynda ordered.
"Now!"

He ran into the bathroom, turned on the tub's hot
water, grabbed the flattened pink plastic bucket that his
wife used to handwash her underwear. He filled up the

container, yanked two towels from the rack, and hurried back to the bedroom.

Lynda grabbed a towel, dunked it in the water, and started wiping off Jolene's pubic area. Harlan thought he saw, amid the flowing blood, a rounded object pushing out from her vagina.

"It's the baby," Jolene confirmed.

She shifted position, blocked his view. It was just as well. His palms hurt from digging his fingernails into them, and he did not really want to see any more than he already had. His heart was pounding, and the thoughts racing through his head were all worst-case scenarios.

Jolene was still screaming, had not stopped screaming the entire time, and as Lynda reached between her legs and started working, the screams intensified. He had not thought her cries could get any worse, but he'd been wrong, and it wrenched his heart and terrified him to the depths of his soul to hear the undiluted agony in her voice, the inhuman suffering to which her body was being subjected.

"Oh, my God," Lynda said, and though she spoke quietly, though her exclamation was little more than a gasp, he had no trouble hearing her over the sound of the screams.

"What is it?" he demanded.

She grabbed both towels, quickly wrapped them around her hands, then reached between Jolene's legs and pulled.

It was alive for only a second, but in that second he saw it squirm, heard a partial cry.

Lynda backed away, her face white, and dropped the baby.

He stared down at the bed. Lying on the bloody sheet was a small saguaro cactus, bits of vaginal flesh clinging to its oversized spines, green plant skin visible beneath the wet layer of red. The cactus had a face, and the face was frozen in a hideous, distorted grimace.

Lynda ran out of the room.

Outside, the sirens had arrived. Red light pulsed around the edges of the bedroom drapes, and he could

hear the crackle of two-way radios, the voices of para-
medics shouting orders.

Jolene had stopped screaming and she was propped
on her elbows, cackling crazily. She was still bleeding
profusely, and the red tide was covering the unmoving
body of the cactus baby. "It's your son!" she said. "It's
your son!" Her laughter spiraled upward in tone and
volume and became as nonstop and persistent as her
screams had been.

He slapped her once, hard across the face, then ran
into the bathroom to throw up.

Five

1

Sasha was grateful for the beginning of school.

Moving to McGuane had been a complete and total disaster, and not a day went by that she didn't wish she had followed through on her threats to run away. She could have gotten a job, found an apartment. She probably could've even stayed with Amy's family for a few weeks until she got settled. It was not as if she was still a child. She was a senior, almost eighteen, *an adult* for all intents and purposes, and she could easily have continued on, uninterrupted, with her existing life, sans parents.

And she should have.

But she was a "good girl," and the truth was that she didn't have the guts to disobey her mom and dad. In her mind, her future life had always unfolded in a series of orderly steps. She would go to college, then move out of the house and, with the help of her parents, find her own place to live, meet a man, get a good job, get married, and live happily ever after in Newport Beach or Brentwood or someplace like that. There'd been no disruption anywhere in her vision of the future, and this sudden uprooting had caught her totally off guard. She'd never prepared for it and didn't know how to react to it.

Now she was stuck in the armpit of America, in the middle of this stupid desert, in what was practically a ghost town.

God damn the lottery.

At least school had started, at least she had a chance

to meet some other people her own age, backward hill-billies though they might be, and while nothing could erase the horrible mistake her family had made, it did serve to lessen the impact.

Back in California, she'd always gotten good grades, had always hung out with the right crowd, and she didn't know if it was some type of subconscious rebellion against her family or an attempt to punish her parents for moving here but she now found herself aligning with a different group of students—the losers, the tokers, the sluts, the people who hung out on Turquoise Street, behind the gym. Part of it was practicality. This clique was looser, less organized, more open to new kids and outsiders. But part of it was also the fact that, emotionally, she felt more in tune with the outcasts. A newly developed disdain for play-by-the-rules goody-goodies had tainted her outlook, and she now viewed with scorn the type of perfect little teacher's-pet students who had until recently been her choice for friends.

She slammed her locker shut, walked alone through the crowd of students to the sidewalk that circled the school, and started toward the gym. On Turquoise, most of the kids were stubbing out their cigarettes and starting to wander off toward their classes, but Cherie Armstrong leaned against the side of the building, rummaging through her purse, showing no sign that she was planning to leave.

It was Cherie she had come to see, and Sasha walked over to her. "You going to PE?" she asked.

Her friend snorted. "What for? So that dyke teacher can check out my crotch while I'm changing? No way."

Sasha tried to smile. The thought of going to PE alone did not sit well with her, and although she knew she'd better leave now if she hoped to get to class on time, she hesitated for a moment.

She looked at Cherie, nonchalantly searching through the contents of her purse. She had never ditched class before, but she had always hated PE, and if she was going to skip a period, this would be a good one to start with.

The other girl finally found what she was looking for and pulled out a pack of cigarettes.

The bell rang, and there was a last-minute flurry of students running to their classrooms.

Cherie smacked the pack against her palm, withdrew a cigarette. "Want a smoke?"

Sasha hesitated only a second, then moved next to her friend and leaned against the gym wall, holding out her hand.

"Sure," she said.

2

Their new home still made her uncomfortable.

Julia lay awake, listening to the muted electric hum of the alarm clock on the dresser. It was the only sound in the room, the noise of its imperfect workings absurdly amplified against the silence, and she stared into the darkness, trying not to hear it. She still wasn't used to the quiet out here, the absence of nighttime traffic and city sounds, and these low, isolated noises seemed more intrusive to her than all of the cacophony of Southern California.

The electric clock was keeping her awake, making it impossible for her to fall back to sleep.

Well, that and the fact that her bladder was full.

But she was afraid to get up and go to the bathroom.

She was ashamed of herself. She was a mother, for God's sake. She was supposed to be the one reassuring her children that there were no ghosts or monsters, that the world was the same at night as it was during the day, that darkness hid no terrors.

But she could not even make herself believe it.

She did not understand what it was about the house that unsettled her so, that engendered within her this feeling of dread, but it was there, and it had not abated one whit since their arrival. If anything, it had grown stronger. There'd been no incidents since the dishes, no overt examples of anything unusual occurring, but as much as she tried to discount what she felt, as often as she attempted to ignore her feelings and write them off as the result of culture shock or emotional strain, she could not.

Which was why she was lying awake in the middle of the night, afraid to go to the bathroom.

Was their new home haunted?

It was what she kept coming back to.

She had never been superstitious, had never even been totally convinced of the existence of God. Anything beyond the physical world had been, to her, entirely theoretical and more in the realm of fiction than fact. But that attitude was changing, and, as ridiculous as she would have found it a month ago, she was now seriously considering the possibility that some sort of ghost or spirit was living in their house.

A ghost or spirit? Was she serious?

She sighed. Hell, maybe it *was* stress.

Earlier, she and Gregory had lain awake for a long time, talking. It was the only time they really got any privacy these days, and once they were in bed, they snuggled together to share the thoughts and feelings they did not want to discuss in front of Gregory's mother or the children.

When he started talking about the café and his plans to make it into a nightspot, an entertainment venue that would lure name acts to this little corner of the state, she suggested that perhaps she would find something to do, too.

"You want to help me out with the sound system?" he asked.

She shook her head, smiled. "No. I was thinking more like volunteer work."

"I thought you wanted to—"

"I'll get around to that," she said quickly. "But I need some . . . adjusting time."

"Volunteer work, huh? Let me guess. At the library."

"Or Teo's school," she said defensively.

He chuckled.

"I want to be here when the kids get home in the afternoon."

Gregory nodded, still smiling. He pulled her closer, kissed her forehead. "Whatever you want."

His condescending attitude annoyed her, and she dropped the subject, letting him drone on and on about the café before they finally made love and went to sleep.

Or rather he went to sleep.

She was still awake.

And had to go to the bathroom.

She remained in the bed, wide awake, and it was another half hour before she finally gathered enough courage to get out of bed and walk across the hall to the bathroom, "accidentally" waking Gregory up in the process so that he would be conscious should anything happen. It was another forty-five minutes before fatigue finally overcame her and she fell asleep.

At breakfast, Gregory's mother talked about angels.

She was telling Teo and Adam a story about how a guardian angel had saved her from falling off a boulder into a cactus patch, and between bites of cereal, the kids asked clarifying questions that indicated they believed every word. It was not the first time this had happened, and Julia felt a little uncomfortable having so much religious talk in the house, but she understood that if her mother-in-law was to live with them, this was something that she would have to learn to put up with. She and Gregory exchanged a look, and he shrugged resignedly.

Besides, who was she to say? Maybe there were angels. A completely separate race of beings existing on some other, higher plane. It was something that a lot of people seemed to believe in. But would angels take such an interest in specific individuals that they would monitor a person's every move? It didn't make any kind of logical sense, but perhaps angels sat around and discussed the impact of things upon people just the way people sat around and discussed animals and the environment. To a race of beings that advanced, humans would be like pets, like lower life-forms, and perhaps their intervention in human affairs would be the equivalent of saving redwoods or protecting the denizens of natural wetlands.

Sasha walked downstairs, poured herself a glass of orange juice, and quickly downed it. "I'm off," she announced.

Her grandmother frowned. "You need good breakfast. You eat breakfast."

"No time!" She was out the kitchen door and into the living room. "See you this afternoon!"

Gregory pushed his chair back and stood. "Come on," he told Adam and Teo. "Better get ready."

"How come you have to drive us?" Adam said. "How come I can't walk to school like Sasha?"

"Because she's in high school. Go brush your teeth and get ready."

"No good," his mother said, shaking her head. "Breakfast important."

"I don't want to brush my teeth!" Teo announced.

Julia pulled back her daughter's chair, lifted the girl out and set her on the floor. "You brush them anyway. Hurry up, you don't want to be late for school."

Ten minutes later, both children were in the car, and Julia waved to them as Gregory pulled out of the drive. She turned and walked back into the house, where Gregory's mother was already clearing the breakfast table and preparing to wash dishes.

Julia picked up her cup and sipped the still-warm coffee, sitting down at the table and glancing through first the Food, then the front-page sections of the *Los Angeles Times* that they'd received yesterday in the mail. They'd fallen into a pattern: she made breakfast and Gregory's mother did the dishes afterward. She and her mother-in-law took turns cooking dinner, and Gregory and the kids alternated with the washing. Which meant that she was only really stuck with cleaning the lunch dishes.

It was the one part of their new domestic arrangement that was an improvement on the way things had been before.

From out on the road, there was the sound of a rattly pickup truck passing by. Julia glanced up from her paper and over at her mother-in-law. They were alone, the old woman had just been talking about angels, and this was a perfect opportunity to bring up what she'd been thinking about. She sat there for a moment, finished off her coffee, then took her cup over to the sink. She placed the cup in the sudsy water and cleared her throat. "Do you believe in ghosts?" she asked.

Gregory's mother looked at her, but did not answer immediately. She rinsed the plate she'd been washing and placed it on the rack. "Why you ask?" she said finally.

This was her chance. She could come clean, tell her mother-in-law what she'd been thinking, what she'd been feeling, but her American attitude was too firmly ingrained for her to drop the facade, and she was disgusted with herself as she said, "I was just curious."

The old woman nodded, as if this was what she had been expecting. She looked at Julia. "There are *things,*" she said earnestly. She paused, thought. "Father, before he die, he saw brother George. He die long time ago, when he was ten years old. Poor ragged clothes. Father in bed, and brother George came to the room and he gave Father a key and disappear. Father dying and he told Mother, said, 'He give me the key, the door's open. I'm going to die.' And he did. He said brother George look exactly the same, same ragged clothes. So those things happen."

Julia felt a chill pass through her, though she could tell that her mother-in-law had meant the tale to be reassuring, not frightening.

Those things happen.

She thought about the uncomfortable darkness of the house and the uneasiness she'd felt here ever since they'd arrived, about the box of dishes that had fallen from a place where it had not been put, in a room that had no one in it.

There was the sudden sound of their van crunching gravel in the driveway, and Julia jumped, startled. Gregory's mother looked at her, and there was a knowing expression on her face, a look that said she knew what Julia had been thinking and why she had really asked about ghosts.

Julia turned away in embarrassment.

"Hey," Gregory said, walking into the kitchen and dropping his keys on the counter. "What're you guys talking about?"

"Ghosts, the afterlife, the usual stuff." Again, Julia was disgusted to hear the flippant tone of her own voice.

"I tell her about Father. How he see brother George before he die."

Gregory poured himself the last of the coffee. "What

about Aunt Masha's husband? He died when she was
really young, didn't he?"

A cloud passed over his mother's face. "That was no
good."

"Still, it happened. Tell Julia. It's interesting." He
smiled at Julia, and she suddenly hated that smug, superior look on his face, the same exact look she knew was
all too often found on her own. For the first time, she
saw things from the perspective of their parents, and she
thought that Gregory's mother had been uncommonly
patient with them and their intellectually snobbish attitude, far more patient than she herself could ever be.

She gently took her mother-in-law's arm. "Tell me
about it," she said.

The old woman sighed, nodded. She wiped her hands
on a dishtowel, then followed Julia back to the table,
where the three of them sat individually, like the points
of a triangle, facing each other.

"Masha's husband, Bill, see, he die. At thirty. She
took it too hard. She cried every single day. Was losing
her mind, she cry so much. Then she said she hear so
much noise from the back room. Always noise. But nobody was there. Then she call Father and say she saw
Bill in a black suit. When she told Father, Father said,
'We have to have prayer' "—she clapped her hands together firmly—" 'That's it.' They have a prayer, and she
never saw him, never dream, never notice him again.
Gone."

"He was a ghost?" Julia asked.

"No. No ghost. No such thing as ghost."

Gregory sipped his coffee. "Father told me, 'If I can
come back and let you know, I will.' "

His mother's expression was determined. "He's not
going to come back."

"So there are no ghosts?" Julia said. "Dead people
can't come back?"

"Sometimes they come . . . but in the form of angel.
Then you know it's not a devil."

"So when dead people come back, those are evil
spirits?"

The old woman nodded. "Yes. See, when somebody
dying, they always see someone. Like my father see

brother George. And when my grandmother's father dying, he said, 'There's your mother, standing by my feet.' 'Where?' 'Right there.' " She leaned forward intently. "He saw. Nobody else saw, but she *was* there. When you die, somebody's there with you. You don't die alone, but other people cannot see it."

"What if a regular person sees a ghost? What if someone who's not dying sees a ghost?"

She shook her head. "Ghost is nothing."

"I thought you said Masha saw her husband dressed in black. Wasn't that a ghost?"

"No." She shook her head. "It was evil spirit." She thought for a moment. "Devil like mean things. He want to disturb her more and more and more, see? That's why you have to *pray*. It happen to Sonya, my cousin. She live in San Diego and her mother die. She so close to her mother. She lost husband on account of mother. She take care of her mother, husband took other lady. So after her mother die, she said, 'My mother came and visit me and she talk to me.' When she told her father, he said, 'What you mean, you talk to your mother?' They have to have prayer, too. See, it wasn't her mother but the *form* of her mother. Because she cry too much. You don't cry. Well, you cry, but not everyday everyday everyday, you know?"

Julia felt chilled. "So when you have too much grief, they come back?"

"*Evil* come back. That's why when John die, I pray every single night. It's hard, but it's easy. If you say prayer, he not going to come in. When you pray, they don't like it. The devil will leave." She leaned back. "Those things happen."

Those things happen.

Julia was glad that Gregory and his mother were here, that she was not alone in the house.

"Anyway, that's what I believe. That's what I think happen." She gave Julia a meaningful look, then stood and walked back over to the sink. "Dishwater getting cold," she said.

Gregory drank his coffee and shrugged apologetically, but Julia ignored him, looking away, watching his mother's back as she began washing plates. She felt bad about the way they'd treated the old woman over the years, guilty for the manner in which they'd automatically dismissed her obviously deeply held beliefs.

Was Julia a believer now herself?

No, not really. She was spooked, yes, but she still thought that it was probably due to the fact that she was spending too much time in the house. That was what was at the root of the problem, not anything supernatural. She just needed to get out, meet some people, find something to do.

Maybe volunteering wasn't such a bad idea.

But she had a newfound respect for her mother-in-law, and as she walked out of the kitchen and back to the bedroom to change out of her pajamas and bathrobe, she vowed that she would no longer disparage the older woman's convictions. After all, this was her culture as well. She was American, but she was Molokan, too, and perhaps it was time she started honoring her roots.

She walked into the bedroom. The drapes were open, but it was still dark in here, and Julia shivered involuntarily as she quickly flipped on the light.

3

There was a letter waiting for him when he got home from school, a letter from Roberto, and Adam took it immediately into his bedroom and closed the door. He plopped down on the bed, tore open the envelope and read. Roberto had written a hilarious account of the first day of school, catching him up on what all of the other kids had done over the summer, how Sheila Hitchcock had ballooned up even more and now looked like a white whale, how the sixth-grade teacher, Mrs. Mejia, wiggled her butt when she wrote on the chalkboard and how Jason Aguilar stood behind her and did a killer imitation and then quickly sat down in his seat before she turned around. He'd included, as promised, a Spiderman card, a new one, and Adam immediately added it to his collection, placing it on the top of the rubber-banded stack on his dresser.

He reread the letter, then lay on the bed, looking up at the ceiling.

As much as he liked Scott, he wished Roberto was here instead.

He missed his friend.

He missed California.

But he was getting used to McGuane, and already his feelings of homesickness had faded from the peak intensity of that first week or so. He broke out his English notebook, ripped out a page, and wrote Roberto a reply, describing his own first day of school, what the kids were like here, Scott. He embellished and exaggerated, made everything sound a lot more exciting than it actually was. He considered telling Roberto about the *banya,* but he didn't quite know what to say or how to describe it, and he decided to save that for another time.

It cheered him up, writing, and he felt good as he addressed the envelope, slapped a stamp on it, and carried it up the drive to the mailbox. He popped up the little red flag on the box to signal the postman that there was outgoing mail, and then jumped as a hand smacked the back of his head.

"Loser," Sasha said.

She started down the drive to the house, swinging her backpack, apparently having forgotten that he even existed, and he was tempted to run after her and smack her in return. Maybe knock her backpack into the dirt, but even though she was a girl, she was still bigger than he was and could easily kick his ass, so instead he waited by the mailbox until she was halfway to the house before following.

He walked slowly, looking down at the ground, kicking small rocks ahead of him. His birthday was coming up soon, in a few weeks, and he found himself wondering what they were going to do about it. Ordinarily, his parents took him and a group of friends to Chuck E. Cheese or someplace like that, someplace with pizza and video games, but this year there were no friends to take. Scott, maybe, but that was it. He half hoped they'd simply ignore his birthday this year. The thought of going someplace with just his family depressed him, and he didn't want anyone from school to see him sitting in some crappy restaurant with Babunya and his parents and his sisters like . . . well, like a loser.

He'd rather not celebrate his birthday at all than be humiliated.

But his parents probably had something planned, and he thought that he'd better let them know he just wanted a quiet celebration at home before they went out and made reservations at some embarrassingly public place.

It was Friday, and although there were Fox shows he wanted to watch, when Scott called after dinner asking if he felt like hanging out, checking what was happening around town, Adam agreed to come over.

He knew his parents wouldn't want him to go, so he put the best spin possible on it as he presented the plan to them. "Scott asked me to come over," he said.

His mother frowned. "Now? It's getting dark."

"So?"

"I don't want you wandering around out there at night."

"I'm not a baby."

"Why don't you just stay home?"

"I thought that's why we moved here. So we could do things like this."

"There may not be gangs in McGuane, but there are coyotes, snakes, drunk rednecks, who knows what all."

"And perverted cowboys," Sasha said, grinning.

"Sasha," his father warned.

"Scott was born here. He knows this town. And, besides, we're not just going to 'wander.' I'm going to his house, we may walk down to French's and get a milk shake or something, and that's it. Then I'll come home."

"Why don't you have your father drive you?"

Adam grimaced. "Why don't you just hang a big sign on my back that says 'Mama's Boy and Wuss'?"

"We could do that," Sasha said agreeably.

Teo laughed.

"Knock it off," his father said. He turned toward Adam. "What are your *real* plans?"

"That's it! That's the plan! God!"

His parents exchanged a glance.

"Be home by eight-thirty," his mother said.

"That's only an hour and a half!"

"How much time do you need to get a milk shake?"

"It's that or nothing," his father said. "Take it or leave it."

"I'll take it."

His father grinned. "If you're five minutes late, I'll be out in that van looking for you, asking everyone I see, 'Do you know where Adam Tomasov is? His mommy wants him to come home.' "

Teo burst out laughing.

Adam kicked the sole of her tennis shoe as he walked by, pretending to be annoyed, but he was secretly pleased. Things had gone a lot smoother than expected. He grabbed his comb and wallet and was out of the house before his parents could change their minds.

Scott was waiting for him on the low wooden fence that encircled his yard. From inside the set-back house came the loud, angry voices of a man and a woman arguing, and Scott said, "Let's hit the road. My old man and old lady are going at it, and, believe me, you don't want to be around when that happens." He jumped off the fence and led Adam across the street and through the yard of a darkened home abutting a dry ditch.

They hopped into the ditch and followed it behind a line of houses and buildings, emerging in the field behind the high school. Scott led the way through the school grounds onto Malachite Avenue, and they walked down the sloping street toward the center of town.

"Can you believe this place is so dead?" Scott said disgustedly. "The whole town closes up at six. What a fucking hellhole." He looked over at Adam. "I bet it's not like this in California."

Adam laughed. "No, it's not."

But he went on to tell his friend how they wouldn't be able to walk around like this at night in Southern California. There were gangs and drive-bys, sickos and psychos.

Scott was incredulous. "You can't go out at night?"

"Well, you can if you have a car. I mean, my dad or my sister could drive us places like movies or malls or something. But you can't, you know, just wander around like this." He grinned. "This is bitchin'."

Scott nodded, smiled. "Yeah, it kinda is."

They reached the shopping district and walked down the intermittent sidewalk through the center of town. There were lights on in a few of the stores, but French's was the only business actually open, and even it was devoid of customers. They stopped by the restaurant, bought two Cokes and split an order of fries to go, then continued on, eating out of the greasy bag they passed back and forth.

At the park, Scott sat down on top of one of the picnic tables. Adam tossed the empty bag into an adjacent trash barrel and leaned against a chain-link backstop. The park seemed different at night, its contours changed, its boundaries expanded by the darkness. They were the only ones here, but while that would have been a plus back in California, where any gathering of two or more people at night signaled possible gang activity, in this place it only served to heighten the disquiet that Adam felt. Leaning against the backstop, he was facing Scott, facing the street, but the bulk of the park was behind him, and he didn't like having all that empty darkness at his back. Casually, he moved over to the picnic table, sitting next to his friend.

He hadn't planned on bringing it up, but Scott said, "This place is creepy at night."

Adam played it cool. "Yeah," he agreed.

"It's supposed to be haunted, you know."

Goose bumps popped up on Adam's arms.

"A long time ago, two miners were supposed to've gotten into a fight. One killed the other one, and before the sheriff could get out here, a lynch mob hung the killer from a tree." He gestured around. "Supposed to be one of these trees here in the park. Ever since then, people've said this place is haunted."

"You ever seen anything?"

"No. But I've never been here at night before, either."

There was a sighing in the leaves at the top of the closest cottonwood.

Scott leaped off the picnic table. "Let's get the hell out of here."

Adam quickly followed suit. "Wise decision."

They ran back out to the sidewalk and hung a left,

slowing down only when they were safely in front of
buildings again, past the periphery of the park.

Scott bent down, breathing heavily. He grinned. "I
didn't want to say anything," he said. "But you felt it,
didn't you? There was something there."

Adam nodded.

"I just wanted to test it. I was too chickenshit to go
there myself at night, but I figured with two of us . . .
well, I didn't think I'd get that scared. And I knew I'd
get an honest reaction from you, especially if I didn't
say anything about it." He looked over at Adam. "You
were freaked, weren't you?"

"Yeah," Adam admitted.

"Cool."

They remained in place for a few moments, catching
their breath. From somewhere far off came the sound
of a car engine, followed by the sequential barking of
dogs up the canyon. Adam felt good. This was more fun
than hanging out at the mall or going to a movie any
day. This was *exciting*. He thought that maybe he'd ask
his parents if Roberto could come and visit during
Christmas or Easter or next summer. He knew Scott and
Roberto would get along, and he knew that Roberto
would think this place was totally kickass.

He glanced over at Scott. "So what now? What's the
plan?"

"I don't know. We could—"

Scott broke off in midsentence, his head jerking to
the right, and Adam quickly followed the direction of
his gaze.

There was movement in front of the mining museum
across the street.

His heart jumped almost all the way up into his throat,
and his first thought was that it was a ghost, a vampire,
a monster, but he saw almost immediately that it was
only a group of high school students, hanging out.

There were no lights here, no streetlamps, merely light
from the moon and dim illumination from inside the
closed assaying office next to the museum, but that was
enough to see by, and he noticed now that a group of
tough-looking teenagers about Sasha's age were leaning
on the oversized mining implements arranged in the

small open space in front of the building. The four girls all looked the same: dyed black hair, black clothes, black lipstick, pale skin, broad white-trash features. Of the three boys, one had long, stringy hair and was wearing jeans and a T-shirt, one was bald and shirtless and heavily tattooed, with pierced ears and nose, and one had a spiky punk haircut and was wearing a creased leather jacket far too heavy for this weather.

He and Scott started slowly forward, moving up the sidewalk the way they'd originally been headed, away from the park, away from downtown, trying to be inconspicuous, trying not to attract attention.

A loud male voice rang out from the direction of the museum. "Well, well, well! What do we have here?"

Caught.

Adam looked at Scott, who stopped, turned around. They both faced the building across the street.

The bald pierced guy laughed loudly. "If it isn't the pussy posse!"

The rest of the high schoolers joined in the merriment.

"Get ready to run," Scott whispered.

Adam's mouth was suddenly dry, and panic threatened to rise within him. "What?"

"Just follow me."

Scott moved into the street, into the open, away from the shadows of the buildings, and held up a middle finger. "Fuck you!" he called. "And fuck your mama, too!"

He took off, dashing back onto the sidewalk and up the hill, darting into the small space between the hardware store and an arts and crafts shop. Heart thumping crazily, Adam chased after him.

There was the sound of running feet behind them, boots pounding on pavement.

"You're dead, fucker!" one of the boys yelled, and a girl laughed drunkenly. "I'll kick your ass so hard your fucking sphincter'll be pressing out your lips!"

Scott kept running, and Adam followed, moving as fast as he could, feeling the night air burn into his lungs, the muscles of his legs straining so hard they threatened to cramp at every step. He had never been this close to actual danger, had never physically pushed himself to this extent, and the irrational thought occurred to him that he might keel over from a heart attack.

But he knew he couldn't stop. He had to keep going, and he was right behind Scott as the other boy slid down the rocky slope that led from the back of the downtown stores to the dry wash at the bottom of the canyon.

There was no noise directly behind them anymore, but from the top of the slope came an angry male voice. "I'll get you, you little shit!"

The two of them scurried through the darkness of the canyon floor, occasionally bumping into rocks and brush but not slowing or stopping for anything. Scott was little more than a gray blur in front of him, and they ran for what seemed like an hour before reaching a road that crossed the wash and led up to McGuane's east residential district.

They waited for a moment, listening to discover whether they were being followed, but Adam could hear no noise above the ragged sounds of their breathing, and he sat down on a rock to rest. Scott plopped onto the sand.

"What're we going to do?" Adam demanded.

"What do you mean?"

"What if they see me walking home from school or something? What if—"

"They didn't see you at all. And they won't even recognize *me* in the daylight." He waved a hand dismissively. "I've done this a thousand times."

Adam wasn't sure he believed that, but he wanted to, and he was willing to let his friend have the benefit of the doubt. In his mind he went back over every second of the incident, and the more he thought about it, the more convinced he was that Scott was right. Hell, the high schoolers hadn't even chased them down the slope. They'd only run across the street and behind the buildings before stopping. It had been nothing more than a laugh for them, a joke.

Most of them were probably so high they wouldn't even remember it tomorrow.

Scott let out a wheezy, winded laugh. "Had enough exercise for one night?"

"I've had enough for a month."

They both laughed and sat there for a few moments longer, breathing heavily, not saying anything but remaining unmoving, looking back down the canyon floor to make sure no one was coming, until their breaths grew more shallow and finally faded into normal silence.

"What time is it?" Adam asked. "You got a watch?"

"No. Why? What time do you have to be home?"

"Now, probably." Adam stood. "Come on, let's head back."

Scott got up off the ground, brushed the sand off his pants, and the two of them started up the curving road toward the tiered rows of houses above.

"You heard about what happened to Mrs. Daniels, didn't you?" Scott asked as they reached the first home.

Adam shook his head. "Never even head of her."

"She was pregnant and she went into labor, and she was supposed to have a little girl." His voice lowered ominously. "But it wasn't a girl."

"What was it? A boy?"

"It wasn't even a baby." He pointed toward the next house up, a small wood-frame home with darkened windows. "It was right there, man. Right in that house."

"You're crazy."

"It was a cactus. She gave birth to a cactus."

"No way!" Adam said.

"That's what happened. They're trying to keep it secret and not let anyone know, but she had a saguaro instead of a baby. A little saguaro cactus with a baby's face."

"How do you know?"

"My dad's friend is a paramedic, and I heard them talking about it. He said it was the freakiest thing he'd ever seen."

"Was it . . . alive?"

"I guess not. But she was all cut up, and it came out of her, and it had, like, little feet and hands and a face."

"Jesus."

They were silent for a moment as they walked past the house.

"This whole fucking town's haunted," Scott said.

"Yeah?"

"Yeah."

There was a pause.

"Your house is haunted."

"No way."

"Way."

"Really?"

Scott nodded. "No one's been able to stay there more than a few months. The people who lived there before, the original people, were all murdered. The dad offed the rest of the family while they were sleeping and then wasted himself. Ever since then, people only last a little while. They get scared off."

"Why didn't you tell me this before?"

Scott shrugged. "Didn't think you could take it."

"So they, like, see things and hear things? Like ghosts and stuff?"

Scott nodded. "You ever see anything?"

Adam thought about mentioning the *banya,* but he didn't feel like talking about it right now and decided to save it for another time. He shook his head. "Not yet."

"You will. Take my word for it. Your house is haunted."

"You're lying."

"I'm not lying."

Adam looked at him, and the corners of his mouth slowly turned up in a smile. "Cool," he said.

Six

1

"**S**hit," Paul said softly.

The stage lights had fallen during the night, the troupers they'd spent all yesterday rigging. Not only had they fallen, but they'd broken—every last damn one of them.

They stood looking at the damage, the dented casings and shattered glass, the overturned tables and cushion-ripped chairs. Gregory bent down, picked up a bent bracket, examined it.

"You must've put them in wrong," Paul said.

Odd shook his head. "We installed those according to spec and added a few new specs of our own. There's no way this could've happened."

"Well, it did happen, obviously."

"Someone musta broken in."

"No one broke in." Paul kicked at the broken glass with his boot. "Jesus, it looks like a damn earthquake hit this place."

"A couple of these bolts sheared off," Gregory said. He held up the bracket and two bolt heads. "This might not have been the cause of it, but even if this bracket bent on its own, the bolts should've been able to handle the extra pressure. They're supposed to be designed for these things."

Paul sighed. "I don't need this crap."

Gregory forced himself to smile. "No problem. We'll just replace them. I'll drive over to Tucson and—"

Paul shook his head. "I can't let you do that. You've already wasted enough money on this. It's my place and my responsibility. I'm thinking we'd be better off to bag the whole project."

"Bullshit. You didn't let me finish. I'll drive to Tucson, explain what happened, show them what we have, and if they won't replace everything, *then* I'll buy new lights. The way I see it, this whole thing is the fault of poor workmanship on their part. We installed a faulty product. I'm going to emphasize that people could've been killed, tell 'em I'm going to report them to the Better Business Bureau and whatever other agency I can think of. I think they'll fork over a new set."

"But do we want a new set?" Odd asked. "You're right. I think this here's a faulty product. I think we should try to get our money back and buy something else."

"We could," Gregory agreed. "But the point is, we shouldn't overreact. This is only a temporary setback. It isn't the end of the world, and we shouldn't let it derail our plans."

Odd nodded. "Exactly."

"Of course *you* guys say that, but I'm the owner," Paul said gloomily. "I'm the one who pays the insurance bills, and it's my ass if someone gets hurt because of this."

"No one's going to get hurt," Gregory told him.

"By the time we're through," Odd promised, "kids'll be able to use this thing for a jungle gym and it won't even sway."

Gregory took a deep breath. "I could chip in for insurance if that's what you're worried about."

Paul waved him away. "I'm not looking for a co-owner."

"And I don't want to be one."

Paul picked up one of the broken spotlight casings. "Look, let's get this cleaned up, call the lighting company, and see where we go from there."

"All right," Gregory said. He went with Odd to get broom, shovel, and dustpan from the maintenance closet between the men's and women's rest rooms, and after taking Polaroids of the overall damage and close-ups of the broken bolts and bent brackets, the three of them spent the better part of the morning cleaning up. The outside tables and those closest to the counter and register weren't affected, and Paul cordoned off the area of damage with yellow rope so that the morning's customers would not be inconvenienced.

The place had potential, Gregory thought. The café's space was easily big enough to accommodate forty or fifty people, and Odd had done a great job of building the small stage against the wall to the left of the counter. Despite Paul's worries and reservations, they'd gone too far to turn back now, and he knew that his friend would not pull the plug on the project at this point.

Besides, Gregory had already been to the printer and arranged for a whole bunch of flyers to be made up. He was planning to slap them up around town—on the bulletin boards in both markets, in the office windows of the gas stations, in the windows of the bookstore and the hardware store and as many of the other shops as he could. He would put one up on the Community Calendar board in the post office and tack up the rest on various telephone poles around town. That *should* get the word out. If it didn't, he was prepared to buy a full-page ad in the newsless mixture of Chamber of Commerce PR, high school sports photos, and garage sale announcements known as the *McGuane Monitor*.

He had faith that people would come, though. They were going to start with a Talent Night, an open-mike evening in which anybody who wanted to could come up onstage and do anything he or she wanted. Singers. Guitarists. Storytellers. Bands. Comedians. From there, they'd offer slots to the better performers.

It was a seeding of the grass roots, an outlet for local talent previously denied an opportunity to perform in public, and it was precisely that alternative ethos that appealed to him. They were giving people a chance. Providing a potentially receptive audience for garage bands who until now had only annoyed neighbors with their noise and offering exposure to sensitive singer-songwriters who'd been practicing in front of mirrors in their bedrooms.

The café might be dead now, but he would turn that around. He'd build a clientele for this place, build an audience for these performers. This was an exciting opportunity, and he was determined to make the most of it. He had never really pondered what it would be like to have a "career" before. He'd always just had a "job." But he could see himself as a latter-day Bill Graham—booking name acts, performers on the way up or on the way down, discovering talent, managing careers. Eventually, the café might even have to expand into the hair salon next door. They would need some type of dressing room or backstage area if they were to lure professionals to their venue.

They finished righting the tables and sweeping the floor and taking the debris to the stockroom in the back.

Odd picked up a hanging socket. "I still say that someone did this. Vandals. There's no way these lights could've fallen on their own. Not after the way we set them up."

"I don't understand it either," Gregory admitted.

From behind them came the sound of footsteps, a clearing throat. They turned. Paul stood in the doorway, looking around at the tangled jumble of lights and cords and cables. He took a deep breath. "You think you can rig new lights that won't collapse and kill people?"

Odd answered, "Of course."

"By Saturday?"

"No problem."

Paul nodded. "All right," he said, turning away. "All right."

Odd looked over at Gregory. He grinned. "I guess we're back in business."

2

Julia stood in front of the library, not sure if she wanted to go in. She'd finally decided to volunteer, to assist in shelving or checking in books or whatever the library needed done, but she was having second thoughts. There was no rational reason, just a vague feeling of apprehension within her, but if a vague feeling was enough to scare her in her own home, there was no reason one couldn't just as legitimately steer her away from this.

No. She was neurotic enough as it was. She needed to set her mind to something and do it, follow through with the promises she made to herself and not just flit from one failed intention to another.

She grasped the handle, pulled open the glass door, and stepped inside.

The McGuane Public Library was big enough to be serviceable but small enough to be picturesque. In place of the impersonal bank of computer screens that had supplanted the card catalog in most Southern California libraries, there was an oak filing cabinet set against the far wall, between two open windows. Four reading tables adjoined the two racks of magazines and a glass display case filled with old photographs and mining tools. Fully stocked bookshelves took up the middle two-thirds of the well-lighted room, and a wooden bookcase marked BESTSELLERS AND NEW RELEASES was located just to the right of the checkout counter, where a friendly looking overweight woman was sorting through what looked like a stack of overdue notices.

There were two other women in the library. Patrons. A blond woman approximately her own age standing next to the best-seller rack and reading the dust flap of a new Stephen King book, and a gray-haired old lady sitting at a table with a stack of sewing magazines in front of her.

The library smelled deliciously of old books, the deep, resonant fragrance that had all but disappeared from the climate-controlled environments of most modern libraries. Breathing the familiar, half-forgotten scent took her back to her childhood.

This would be a good place to work.

She was glad she'd come, and she vowed to see it through. She *needed* to see it through. As much as she hated to admit it, she had not been prepared to win the lottery, and she understood now that she was one of those people who required imposed structure in her life, for whom adversity and necessity were motivators. Coming into money was the worst thing that could have happened to her.

She walked up to the front desk, and the overweight woman smiled up at her. "May I help you?"

Julia nodded. "I'd like to volunteer. I don't know if you need anyone to work here—"

"Honey," the woman said, "we always need volunteers." She stood up with some difficulty. "What's your name?"

"Julia. Julia Tomasov."

"Molokan, huh?"

Julia nodded, not sure if there was disapproval in the woman's voice or just simple recognition.

"I don't remember seeing you before."

"We just moved back to town. Or rather my husband moved back. He's from here. I was born in L.A."

The woman nodded. "I'm Marge Lindsey. The librarian. I have no paid assistants or aides, so everyone else here is strictly volunteer. You ever work at a library before?"

Julia almost gave the librarian her true résumé, but at the last minute she simply nodded and said, "Yes." She didn't want to appear to be competing or engaging in any sort of one-upmanship, and she had the feeling that in a place like McGuane, any prior experience would be seen as a threat. This was the woman for whom she would be working, and she was determined to remain on the librarian's good side.

"Good. We can use all the help we can get. As I said, I'm the only paid staff member here. The library's county-funded, and in addition to the money for my salary, we receive only a small stipend for purchases each year, so anything beyond that is strictly volunteer. Most of our acquisitions are from donations, and our volunteers are the ones who sort and catalog and index and repair the books. They also shelve, and sometimes check in and check out." Her eyes swept Julia's face to gauge her reaction, and Julia smiled pleasantly.

Apparently satisfied, the librarian called out to the two patrons, "Deanna? Helen? You're not in any rush, are you? I'm going to take our new volunteer back and introduce her."

Both the old woman at the table and the younger woman with the King book nodded their acknowledgment, and Julia followed Marge through the open doorway behind the front desk into a surprisingly large work area. There were two middle-aged women sitting at a long table in the center of the room, stacks of books piled in front of them, boxes of additional books on the floor under the table. A few volumes were arranged at one end of the otherwise empty metal stand-alone shelves behind them, and two handcarts were situated against the far wall, next to a small refrigerator and a sagging couch.

The women looked up as they entered.

"Alma?" Marge said. "Trudy? This here's Julia Tomasov, our newest volunteer."

The two women nodded, smiling.

"Alma here is in charge of acquisitions. She's been with us for six years now—"

"Seven," Alma said.

Marge looked surprised. "Seven? It's been that long?"

"Time flies when you're having fun."

All three of them laughed, and Julia smiled politely.

"Anyway, Alma's in every day, and she's sort of my right-hand woman. Trudy's been volunteering for about a year, and she comes in a couple times a week. I don't know what you had in mind, but we can use you whenever you're available. An hour a day, once a week, whatever."

"I was thinking about Tuesdays and Thursdays at first. Maybe . . . ten to two?"

"That'd be fine," Marge said. "That'd be great. As you can see, we're processing donations right now. We got a pretty big gift from the estate of one of our ex-mayors a few months ago, but we were in the middle of a remodeling project, and we haven't been able to get to it until now. We sort of let that slide. But processing these books is now our top priority." She looked at Julia. "Were you planning to start today?"

Julia nodded.

"Great, great. You said you worked in a library before, so you can probably pick up on this pretty quick." She motioned toward an empty seat next to Trudy. "The girls'll show you the ropes. If you have any questions they can't answer, just pop up front and I'll be more than happy to help you."

Marge remained a few minutes longer, helping her to

get settled, then excused herself and walked back out front to check on the patrons.

"Molokan?" Alma asked, handing her a stack of blank accession cards.

Julia nodded.

"My first husband was a Molokan. Drunk bastard."

She remained silent, not sure where this was going.

"Your husband Molokan?"

"Yes," Julia said.

"He ever beat you?"

She laughed. "No."

"You're lucky."

"They're not all wife beaters," Trudy said.

"I know."

"And not all wife beaters are Molokan."

"You don't have to tell *me* that."

Trudy smiled sympathetically at Julia, giving her a quick she's-not-so-bad-when-you-get-to-know-her look.

Julia smiled back, understanding, and the conversation soon settled into the usual biographical chitchat. Alma had indeed had a hard life, and Julia was amazed by the soap-opera quality of her troubles, from her string of marriages to various losers and layabouts to the recent arrest of her eldest son on drug charges. Trudy, by contrast, had been married to the same man since she was sixteen, an insurance salesman and an elder in the Mormon church. Both women seemed simple and honest and refreshingly free of pretensions, and when Julia thought about what her day would have been like had she remained at home, in the house, she was very glad that she'd come here this morning.

After that, the conversation took a turn for the worse.

It was Alma who steered the talk away from the personal and toward the political.

"The government's lying to us again," she said.

Trudy did not respond, and Julia followed her lead, saying nothing and continuing to fill out the accession card on the book in front of her.

"There's a comet that's going to crash into the earth, and the government knows about it, but they're keeping it a secret."

Julia could not help smiling. "Where did you hear that?"

"Joe Smith."

"Who's Joe Smith?"

"He's on the radio. From midnight 'til four on the Wilcox station. Last night, he said that there's a comet heading directly for Earth that's going to crash somewhere on the West Coast and kill millions of people but they're not telling people because they don't want them to panic."

Julia shook her head. "Don't you think if that was true, we would've heard about it before? We would've seen it on the news or read about it in the paper?"

"That's because the government's keeping it a secret."

"And even with all the big news organizations and everyone who has a telescope, no one's heard of this except the nighttime radio guy in Wilcox, Arizona? Sorry. I don't buy it."

Alma squinted, looked at her suspiciously. "You're not some kind of *liberal,* are you?"

"Alma's right," Trudy said. "Joe Smith tells the truth the government doesn't want you to hear. Joe Smith's not even his real name. It's just the one he uses so the government can't track him down."

She had considered Trudy an ally in this, but now she looked at both of them as though they were crazy.

She was reminded, absurdly, of *American Graffiti,* where the characters all invented elaborate stories surrounding the Wolfman, their favorite disc jockey, some claiming that he was broadcasting from a ship in the ocean in international waters, others believing he was illegally broadcasting from Mexico into the United States, when the truth was that he was a local guy working in a cramped studio at the edge of town.

She didn't feel like continuing the discussion, and she made the decision to ignore it, let it slide, and concentrate on the work before her. She was being arrogant and elitist, she knew, reverting to her old ways, but she put their opinions down to ignorance and a lack of sophistication. She assumed that the fundamental differences of opinion and diverging worldviews were due to the fact that Alma and Trudy had grown up here and had, at the most, high school educations, while she had grown up in Los Angeles and graduated from college. In her mind, she agreed that they would disagree and vowed to avoid the subjects of politics and religion entirely.

"You'll see," Alma said firmly. "When the comet hits California, then you'll believe it."

Julia refused to respond.

"The government lies to us all the time. They didn't tell the truth about Oklahoma City or the bombing of Flight 800. They won't even acknowledge helping to train the UN troops."

Trudy nodded. "The government's like that. That's why we need our own militias, to protect America."

Julia couldn't resist. "A militia's not going to do much good against a comet," she pointed out.

Alma squinted at her. "What are you? A traitor? Can't ever tell with you Russians—"

"Leave her alone," Trudy said. "It's not her fault. She's just been brainwashed by the media."

Marge walked through the door into the back room. "Girls, girls, girls . . ." She smiled tolerantly. "We can hear you all the way out front. I came back to tell you to keep it down. You're disturbing the patrons."

"Sorry," Trudy said.

The librarian's voice dropped. "Also, I heard what you all were talking about, and I couldn't just let it slide. Julia, believe it or not, our country does face some mighty big problems and some serious choices about the future. There are threats confronting America that our government just will not or cannot respond to. The United States is a country of the people, by the people, and for the people, and sometimes the people just have to take matters into their own hands. That's why we have the Second Amendment. So that we *can* form militias, so that we can respond when America's freedom is threatened."

Julia met Marge's eyes. "Who's threatening our freedom?"

The other woman backed off. "I'm not going to get into a political discussion here. I just came to tell you all to keep it down. After all, this is a library." She smiled, but there was no humor in it. "Come on, now. Back to work. You may be volunteers, but I'm in charge here, and there's a lot that needs to be done."

Julia watched the librarian walk through the door to the front of the library.

They were all loonies, she realized.

She returned to the pile of donated books in front of her, not looking at either Alma or Trudy. Silently, she filled out another accession card.

She left at lunch.

She did not return.

3

Jim sat on the edge of the unmade bed, head in his hands, elbows on his knees. He was tired, fatigued, and his head was pounding. He'd been sitting like this for nearly twenty minutes, wanting to get up, intending to get up, but for some reason unable to do so. It felt like a hangover, the pain in his head and the lethargy in his body, but he had not gotten drunk in a long time, and he knew that could not be the cause.

Ordinarily, he would have been at the church hours ago. It was nearly midmorning, the sun hot and high in the sky, and he should have already finished sweeping out the dust and cleaning the kitchen, and started preparing his sermon for Sunday. But he just hadn't been able to do it.

Perhaps he was sick.

No. It was not his body that was troubling him.

It was not even his mind.

It was his heart.

It was Agafia.

He did not know why, not specifically, but his heart ached when he thought of her. This should have been the happiest time of his life. His prayers had finally been answered, and Agafia had returned to him free and unencumbered. She had apparently forgiven and forgotten, and she seemed more than willing to take up where they'd left off.

But . . .

But something was wrong.

She'd changed.

Yes, she had. That was to be expected, of course. Only saints and fools walked through life without reacting and adjusting to the circumstances of their surroundings, without learning from their mistakes. But in Agafia's case, it was different. She hadn't changed all that much in her attitude or outlook, and on the surface she seemed to be the same as always, only older. But there'd been a subtle shift in the core of her being, and there was now something about her that made him uncomfortable.

He did not like being around her.

That was why his heart was so heavy. The woman he loved, the woman of his dreams, frightened him.

Frightened him?

Yes.

The thought occurred to him that it might not be her doing. She might be under the influence of an evil spirit, a *neh chizni doohc.*

Jim sighed. He was overreacting, obviously worked into a state by his concern for her, by his love, and by his inability to understand the ambiguity of his feelings. Agafia was the same religious woman she had always been. She was a good Molokan, and it was beneath him even to think otherwise.

Wasn't it?

He thought of what had happened in Russiantown all those years ago, and he closed his eyes, shivering.

He'd always assumed—no, he'd always *known*—that everything God did was good. God was *all* good and was incapable of doing something that was *not* good. So the Bible, God's word, was inherently pure, supremely incorruptible, the closest thing to perfection on this earth. Yet when he'd gone over to Agafia's home yesterday, when he'd looked at the big family Bible on top of the bureau in her dining room, he'd felt a vague sense of unease. He tried to tell himself that it was the room, the house, but that was not true. It was the Bible itself that was wrong. The black-leather binding looked ominous, the gilt lettering garish and almost obscene. There was about the volume a subtle air of decadence and corruption. He never would have thought such a thing possible, but the Good Book did not seem at all good. It seemed bad. Evil.

He was afraid of it.

He was a man of God. How could he be afraid of a Bible? He didn't know, but he was, and as Agafia talked, he had gently urged her into another room, away from the horrid book.

The Bible a horrid book?

Maybe it wasn't her at all, he reasoned.

Maybe it was him.

Maybe it was the house.

That was the most likely explanation. After what had happened at that location, it was more than realistic to assume that evil lived at that address. He had not yet asked Agafia whether she knew what had transpired in her house, and though he had not wanted to bring it up before, had not wanted to taint her homecoming, he now thought the time had come to tell her of the massacre, assuming she did not already know.

If she had not said the proper prayers, perhaps all of the church members could go over to her home and attempt to cleanse it. If she *had* done everything correctly, then they could still put their heads together and, with the combined power and goodness of all their wills, drive out whatever had taken root at that spot.

And if it wasn't the house?

He didn't know. But whatever the problem, whatever the cause of his unease, he still loved her.

He would always love her.

His head was still pounding and he felt like going back to sleep, but he forced himself to stand. He walked into the bathroom, wet a comb, and ran it through his tangled white hair. He rinsed with Listerine and grabbed yesterday's pants and shirt from the top of the hamper, putting them on before going into the kitchen and grabbing a handful of crackers to snack on.

He walked down to the church.

And sensed immediately that something was wrong.

He walked slowly through the open room, his footsteps echoing on the dusty wooden floor. The windows were shut, the doors securely locked, nothing appeared to have been touched, but he could tell that he was not alone. He could *feel* it. The church looked empty, but it wasn't, and it was with trepidation that he approached the darkened doorway of the kitchen.

"Zdravicha!" he called. *Hello.*

There was no answer.

He tried to tell himself that kids had broken in or that he was worried about robbers and vandals, but there was no sign of a break-in, there was nothing to steal, and nothing had been vandalized.

And the truth was, it was not human intruders that concerned him.

It was *neh chizni doohc.*

He flipped on the kitchen light, looked quickly around. Nothing.

There were only the stove, the sink, an empty counter, and the metal rack holding pots, pans, and various cooking utensils. At the opposite end of the room was the closed door of the storage closet, and Jim said a quick protective prayer as he walked across the kitchen and yanked the door open.

Again . . . nothing. Only brooms and tools and buckets and cleaning solvents.

He closed the closet door. That was it. There were no other rooms or spaces inside the church. He had looked everywhere and found nothing. He sighed heavily. He should have been able to relax, his fears allayed, but the feeling was still there, as strong as ever, that he was not alone, that someone—

something.

—was in the building with him.

He thought for a moment, then decided to get out his Bible and walk through each square inch of the church in order to drive out any demons or evil spirits that might be lurking. He did not understand how *neh chizni doohc* could even enter the blessed house of God, but he thought of his experience at Agafia's and reminded himself that just because he did not understand something did not mean that it could not occur.

He walked back through the kitchen, out the doorway, and across the dusty open floor to the wall against which the benches were stacked. Next to the piled-up benches was the small chest of drawers where he stored his Bible. He pulled open the top drawer—

And his Bible screamed at him.

He leaped back, startled, practically tripping over his feet in his instinctive haste to get away from that horrible noise.

There was another scream—high-pitched, loud, short, strong—and the Bible shot up, out of the drawer and into the air, as if it had been thrown. Jim continued to stagger backward, praying out loud, as the Bible turned in midair and flew toward him, its pages flapping. It looked like some sort of hideously deformed bird, not like a book at all, and he ducked, losing his balance and falling to the floor, as it dove at his head.

He was shouting now, Molokan prayers against the devil and his minions, as the Bible flew up to the top of the ceiling, then dove at him again. This time it smacked hard against the top of his head before he could move out of the way. He grunted with pain at the force of the blow and tried to grab the Bible as it bounced off his head and hit the floor, but it shot up between his grasping hands, closed hard on the tip of his beard and pulled away, yanking out hair.

There was laughter accompanying the attack, a close relative of the screams, a hideous high-pitched cackle that sounded like nothing he had ever heard.

He had never been so terrified in his life. None of this made any sense. He did not know why this was happening or even what was happening. He knew only that his church had been invaded, that he was being attacked, and that his prayers seemed to be having no effect.

Agafia's Bible.

Was this some sort of plague afflicting Russian Bibles, some type of evil that could only manifest itself in this manner? Or had this originated with Agafia? He did not know. All he knew was that he loved her, loved her with all his heart and soul, loved her almost as much as he loved God, and the thought at the forefront of his mind was that he needed to get out of here, needed to get to her, needed to protect her.

The Bible was circling in the air above the benches,

and Jim clumsily scrambled to his feet and started across
the church toward the front door.

He was not fast enough, however, and before he had
gone even one-fourth of the distance, the Bible swooped
down and slammed into his back, knocking him over.
He tried to get up, but this time it did not fly back into
the air. Instead, it remained on top of him, its weight
unnaturally heavy, pulling itself up his body toward his
head with a series of thumping pulses. He rolled over,
trying to throw it off, but he only managed to get himself
turned onto his back. The Bible was not knocked off his
body but was still on top of him, now open on his chest
and slowly, steadily creeping upward toward his face.

He grabbed the book with both hands, but it was
stronger than he was, and with a suddenness he could
not hope to match, the heavy volume jerked hard to the
left, hard to the right, and forced his hands off. There
was the sound of cracking bone as the weight of the
Bible broke his right wrist.

Jim screamed.

And the open Bible plopped onto his face.

He was fighting for his life. He knew it, and he was
doing the best he could, but he was old and not in the
greatest health, and he was battling something that had
the strength of hell behind it.

With his one good hand, he grabbed the leather spine
and tried to pull the Bible off him, but it would not
budge. Beneath the binding, each page seemed sentient,
thin individual sheets of bound printed paper suddenly
strong and sinewy, competing with each other for supremacy as they tried to force their way into his mouth.

He tried to fight off the book, biting with his teeth,
clamping shut his jaws, but the pages turned, shifted to
the side, pulled down, paper cuts slicing into his lips until
he opened his mouth to cry out.

The pages shoved themselves into his mouth, sliding
into the narrow spaces between his teeth and cutting
into his gums, slitting the soft delicate flesh of his tongue.
The flapping page in front of his eyes whipped back and
forth, back and forth, and the movement of the words
made it look like an animated cartoon, several lines
printed in corresponding locations on double-sided

paper forming one blasphemous, incongruous message
before him: *God is dead. Thou art evil. The Lord thy
God is a glutton and must be stoned.*

His good hand grabbed the book's front cover, tried
to rip it off, but the Bible lurched again, hard to the left,
and there was another crack of bone as his left arm
went dead.

He was not going to win, he realized. He was not
going to make it. He did manage to get his mouth shut
again, but then a page of the New Testament sliced
across his right eye, cutting into the cornea, and as he
screamed in agony, the Book of Ruth shoved its way
down his throat.

4

It had been a long time since either of them had gone
to a Molokan funeral—and if they had been in Southern
California they probably would have skipped this one,
too—but they were here and they felt obligated, so
Gregory and Julia dutifully put on their traditional garb
and, leaving Sasha in charge of Adam and Teo, took his
mother from the church, where she'd been staying with
the body, to the Molokan cemetery on the ridge above
the mine.

Gregory glanced in the rearview mirror as he drove.
In the backseat, his mother stared straight ahead, looking at nothing, her gaze focused not on Julia or himself,
not on the scenery outside, but somewhere in the middle
distance. She looked old. She'd aged several years in the
last two days, and the lines on her face seemed suddenly
more prominent, the vicissitudes of life more pronounced in the defeated cast of her features.

She was taking Jim's death much harder than he
would have expected.

Harder than his father's?

He didn't know, but he resented her feelings, found
himself angry with her for caring so much. She hadn't
seen the guy in thirty years, had gotten reacquainted
only a few weeks ago, and now she was acting as though
she'd lost the love of her life.

The love of her life.

He didn't want to think about that.

He knew he was being petty and childish. After all, she had a right to be sad and shocked, depressed and upset. One of her old friends had died—been killed—and it was selfish and inconsiderate of him to ascribe motives to her feelings, to feel betrayed because she was experiencing an understandable human reaction to an incomprehensibly horrific event.

Was she supposed to be cheerful and happy, to feel nothing at all and act as if murder were an ordinary everyday occurrence?

Of course not, and Gregory chided himself for his suspicious self-centered thoughtlessness.

But he still felt it.

Jim Petrovin's death was the talk the town. Everyone in McGuane was stunned by what had happened, and there were rumors flying every which way. It was truly bizarre, like something out of one of those Vincent Price movies where the villains were dispatched in ironically appropriate ways. A minister killed with his own Bible? It was an unlikely murder weapon, to say the least, and Zeb Reynolds, the lead detective, was in the process of interviewing all church members, trying to find out if anyone had had a grudge against the old man. He had already spoken to Gregory's mother, and she had answered all of his questions and pretended to be cooperative, but her English became a little worse when she talked to him, her already thick accent a little more pronounced, and Gregory could tell that she didn't want to involve herself with the police.

She did not think they could solve Jim's murder.

And that was why the minister had not been left alone since his death, why someone had always been with him. His mother and a bunch of the other men and women from the church had taken turns and remained with the body around the clock, saying special prayers of protection even as they said traditional prayers for Jim's soul. The assumption was that his death was not caused by the hand of man but was the work of demons or spirits, and there were hints that the minister had battled with a devil and lost, that he had died a martyr trying to protect the church. While Gregory didn't believe that, the idea of it still gave him chills. He was not as divorced from the religion as he liked to pretend, and being back here in McGuane, being once again among his people, brought it all back and made him feel like a boy again, afraid of things that in California would have seemed to him like silly superstitions.

The dirt road wound up to the crest of the ridge, disappearing at the top, and Gregory drove across the rocky, ungraded ground to the spot where other vehicles were parked, outside the wrought-iron fence that surrounded the cemetery. He slowed the van as he approached, feeling odd as he looked at the open gates of the graveyard. It was where his father was buried, and it had not changed one whit. The land, the sky, the fence, the headstones were exactly as he remembered them. It was as if time had stood still, and he licked his suddenly dry lips as he pulled to a stop behind a Ford pickup.

He had not been here since the day of the funeral, all those years ago, and he felt guilty and ashamed, acutely conscious of his filial neglect. His father had often been in his thoughts—not a day had gone by, in fact, when Gregory had *not* thought of him—but he had never made the effort to visit the gravesite. Until now he had been able to rationalize his actions and not face the fact that his avoidance was the result of a childish and selfish inability to confront his father's passing. He'd always told himself that there was no reason to visit the grave, that his father was gone, that what was lying buried in the coffin was a husk, an empty shell. And he believed it. But the truth was that he also didn't want to have to think about it. He had chosen the emotionally easy way out, preferring not to experience emotions that would make him uneasy or uncomfortable.

Now they were flooding over him.

He glanced at his mother in the rearview mirror and realized for the first time that she had never returned to McGuane either.

And she had not asked to visit the gravesite since they'd moved back.

She was unaware that he was watching her, and her

face was set in what looked like a grimace. Her back had been hurting for the past few days, and he would have attributed the look on her face to the physical pain but for the fact that he recognized her expression: it was exactly the same one she had worn at his father's funeral.

He remembered the way she'd broken down, sobbing, wailing, falling to her knees in the dirt next to the open grave; remembered that he'd been embarrassed and had looked away, looked over the side of the ridge, down at the ugly open pit of the mine; remembered that when he turned back to look at the group of mourners his mother was no longer crying but was grimacing as if in pain.

Precisely as she was now.

He couldn't help wondering: was this face for his father or the minister? It was wrong of him to be so judgmental, but he couldn't help it. He didn't like the fact that his father and Jim Petrovin would be buried in the same cemetery, and he hoped their graves were far apart.

Where would his mother be buried? he wondered. Between them?

Of course not. She had already purchased a plot right next to his father's, had already planned out her funeral to such an extent that he knew where her burial clothes were and what style of casket she wanted. She was sad because an old friend of hers had died, and he was just being an insensitive asshole.

He and Julia got out of the van, Julia unfolding a sunscreen over the windshield so the inside of the vehicle wouldn't be an oven when they returned. He opened the sliding side door, and his mother stepped out slowly, pressing one hand against her aching back. "Oy," she groaned.

He took her arm as she straightened. "Come on," he said kindly in Russian.

And flanked by his wife and his mother, he walked through the gates, across the rocky ground, past his father's final resting place, to the open gravesite near the edge of the cliff.

5

Just as he'd thought, just as he'd known, his parents wanted to take him out for his birthday, and though he'd begged them not to, though he'd specifically requested that they celebrate alone, at home, his mom and dad had made reservations at the Mining Camp restaurant, the most popular eatery in town, and invited Scott to come along.

Adam just hoped to God they hadn't told anyone at the restaurant about it and that all of the waitresses and busboys weren't going to come over and sing "Happy Birthday" and embarrass the hell out of him.

He'd never be able to live it down.

At least he had gotten his family to agree to open the presents at home, so he didn't have to sit at the table with a pile of wrapped boxes in front of him and open them while everyone stared. Two girls from his class were at the restaurant tonight, Liz and Livia Stanson, the blabbermouth sisters, and he knew that anything occurring here this evening would be all over school by Monday. If he had had to unwrap a package of underwear from Babunya in front of them, he would have been humiliated all the way through junior high.

Actually, things weren't turning out as badly as he'd feared. The Mining Camp's one banquet table had already been occupied when they'd arrived, so their party had had to spread out over two tables. Since he was the birthday boy, he got to sit alone at one with Scott, while the rest of the family sat together in a booth.

So, all things considered, it wasn't too embarrassing.

Not as embarrassing as it could have been.

He'd been told by his dad that he could order anything on the menu, but there wasn't a whole lot to choose from, and both he and Scott decided on bacon double cheeseburgers and Cokes. Over at the other table, his parents were having a difficult time getting Teo to order anything. She was in one of her non-eating moods, and they read off the menu items to her one by one, trying to entice her, but she continued to shake her head.

"I'm not hungry," Teo said.

"Zdohcly!" Babunya admonished her.

"What's that mean?" Scott whispered.

Adam shrugged, embarrassed. "I don't know. She always says it when we don't want to eat. I think it means, like, 'puny' or something."

"You can't speak Russian?"

"No," he said, and now he was embarrassed about *that.*

The waitress came and took everyone's order, and his stomach sank as he saw his father motion her over and whisper something in her ear. He knew what that meant. The old candle-on-the-dessert-while-everyone-sings-"Happy-Birthday" routine. Great. He had told his parents he didn't want that, had threatened to walk out if they did it, and he'd thought they understood. They'd acted sympathetic, had promised there would be no singing, but apparently they had no intention of honoring his wishes. He should have known by the smirk on Sasha's face when he'd talked to his parents that they had something planned.

"Looks like there's going to be singing," Scott said. He grinned. "But don't worry. I won't participate."

"Yeah, that makes a big difference."

He looked toward his family's table and happened to glance over just as Sasha was shifting position. The booth bench seats were slightly higher than his and Scott's on the floor, and he saw, between her legs and up her skirt, a flash of white that was her underwear.

His breath caught in his throat.

And he was instantly erect.

It was a completely unexpected reaction. He had never before thought of his sister in that way, had never really seen her as anything other than his older sibling, a bully and a pain in his ass, but that galvanizing look between her legs had stirred him, and he casually glanced that way again, but her knees were together and he could see nothing.

This was wrong. She was his *sister,* for God's sake. He wasn't supposed to be aroused or sexually stimulated by her. He never had been before this, and he didn't know why it was happening now, but today he was a teenager, and maybe that was the cause of it. Maybe some kind of hormone kicked in when you turned thirteen and you just couldn't help thinking about sex.

He wanted to tell Scott about it, wanted to share what he'd seen, but something held him back. It was not guilt or embarrassment. Not exactly. It wasn't any respect for his sister or her right to privacy.

It was the fact that he didn't want his friend to see her.

Jealousy and possessiveness? The waitress brought their drinks, and Adam took his glass and downed a huge swallow of Coke. There was something wrong with him. This wasn't normal. He wasn't supposed to be having these . . . Thoughts? Feelings? Urges?

He didn't know what they were, but he knew they weren't supposed to be there.

He'd seen Sasha in a bathing suit before, of course, but somehow this was different, and as much as he hated himself for doing it, he kept looking over as they waited for the food to arrive, hoping to catch another glimpse. It was the fact that it was her underwear that made it so exciting. The ugliest, unsexiest panties were more intimate than the tiniest bathing suit—their sole purpose was to shield the most private of areas, to protect a girl's secret spot. It was something boys weren't supposed to see, and it was the fact that he *had* seen that was so forbidden and nasty and sexy.

He had a difficult time concentrating on the rest of the evening. They did bring a chocolate sundae with a lit candle and everyone did sing, but he was not that embarrassed. He was too distracted to object, and he went along with everything without too much fuss.

Later, after opening the presents, after going with his dad to drop Scott off at his house, he pretended he was tired and retreated to his room.

He sat on the bed, replaying the scene in his mind. He saw again the way she'd shifted in the booth, moving her legs, and how for a few brief seconds he'd had that perfect view of white cotton-covered crotch. He'd had a boner for half the night, although he'd been able to successfully hide it, and now he was once again hard.

Sasha's bedroom was right next to his, and he thought about drilling a hole in the wall between the two rooms so he could peek at her, so he could watch her getting dressed and undressed, but he knew that was not realistic. It was also not right. As he kept telling himself, she was his sister, and when he even *started* to think about her in that way, he should immediately try to focus on some other unrelated topic. That was unhealthy, perverted.

Still, he could not stop thinking about it, and the thought that there was only a wall between them, that she took off her clothes in there in order to put on her pajamas, aroused him.

He wondered what she was doing now. He wondered if she was naked. He placed his ear against the wall, listened. He could hear her, moving around, and he quietly pulled down his pants and leaned back on the bed. He began stroking himself, imagining she was walking around her room without any clothes on. He had never seen a naked girl before, not a real one, only pictures in magazines, but he could easily conjure up the picture in his mind.

He thought of her secret spot, covered only by thin, snugly fitted cotton material.

It was getting close, he could feel it reaching the fever pitch, and he began stroking faster, harder. He knew it was wrong, knew it was sick, but he wanted to hear her voice, wanted her to talk to him as he climaxed.

He closed his eyes, thought about that glimpse of white cotton panty.

"Sasha?" he called.

"What?" she said from her bedroom.

"Sasha?"

"What?" she yelled.

And he came.

Seven

1

Julia needed the van to buy groceries, and after lunch she offered to drop Gregory back off at the café, but he said he'd rather walk off the calories, and he gave her a quick kiss and started up the drive.

He was looking better since they'd moved to McGuane. The middle-age spread that had been overtaking his midsection for the past few years had receded somewhat, and he looked fitter than he had in quite some time. All the walking on those hilly streets was doing him good. He seemed happier, too, than he had back in California, and he'd made the adjustment to small-town life quite easily.

She was getting used to McGuane herself. After her disastrous attempt at volunteering, she'd retreated back into her home and actually started to write her children's book. So far it was going surprisingly well. She was pleased with what she'd accomplished.

There'd also been no new "incidents," as she called them, and her fear and dread seemed to have disappeared as quickly as they had arrived. She could still not truthfully say that she felt comfortable in the house, but she was not afraid of it anymore, and while Gregory's mother continued to say a quick prayer each and every time she entered the place, a hurried blessing muttered half under her breath, she'd always done that, and it didn't bother Julia at all.

She walked back inside the kitchen, picked up the grocery list she'd made, and invited her mother-in-law to accompany her to the store, making it clear that she was planning to go to the Molokan market, but the old lady declined, claiming she was tired. She'd been tired ever since the funeral, and both Julia and Gregory were worried about her. She seemed to have lost something after Jim Petrovin's death, some spark of animation, and she seemed to be just existing these days, exhibiting little or no interest in . . . well, in anything. It was as if she had simply disconnected herself from life and was biding her time, waiting to die.

This could not go on. Julia knew that she and Gregory were going to have to sit her down and talk to her, but Julia did not feel qualified or comfortable enough to do it alone, and she did not press her mother-in-law to go on the trip to the market. She simply nodded, accepting the old woman's decision, and said that she'd be back in twenty minutes or so.

Julia took the keys out of her purse, walked outside, and got into the van, starting the ignition and immediately turning on the air conditioner. They had discussed buying another vehicle—they could certainly afford it now—but one seemed to be enough at this point. Sasha had been pressuring them for her own car, and while she and Gregory had adopted a "we'll see" attitude in front of their daughter, they were planning on getting her a jeep for graduation.

She drove down to the market, parking in the dirt lot on the side of the building. She grabbed a shopping cart and looked up at the painted butcher paper in the window that advertised this week's specials. Bell peppers were on sale, as were whole chicken fryers, and she mentally adjusted her planned menu, deleting ground beef from her list. They would have fajitas tomorrow instead of burgers.

She'd finished most of her shopping and was in the canned-food aisle picking up some diced green chiles, when a woman next to her said, "Excuse me, don't you work at the library?"

Julia looked up, confused. "Uh, no."

"Really? I thought I saw you there a couple of weeks ago."

"And you remembered me?"

The woman smiled. "It's a small town."

Julia examined her fellow shopper more carefully. Approximately her own age, with short blond hair and clothes that seemed far too hip for McGuane, she was not someone Julia recognized, yet she did seem vaguely familiar.

"I was thinking of volunteering a few days a week," Julia explained. "But I changed my mind."

"The reason I ask is because I used to work at the library myself." The woman paused. "How . . . did you like the other volunteers there?" she asked carefully.

"They were loony. That's why I quit. Alma was talking about some comet that was going to hit Earth and they were all into bizarre conspiracy theories."

The woman wiped her brow in a melodramatically exaggerated expression of relief. "Whew! I was hoping you'd say that. But you can't be too careful in this town." She smiled. "My name's Deanna Matthews."

Julia blinked. "Are you related to Paul Matthews?"

"He's my husband."

"This *is* a small town. My husband is Gregory Tomasov."

Deanna laughed. "Gregory's wife and a normal person to boot! It's my lucky day. Are you Molokan, too?"

Julia nodded.

"I'm not, but I grew up here."

"So you knew Gregory when he was little?"

"Oh, yes."

"I take it you were all friends—"

Deanna laughed. "Well . . . Not exactly. To tell you the truth, he was kind of a . . ."

"Jerk?"

"Thank you. I was trying to think of a polite way to say it."

"I think he's changed since then."

"I hope so." Deanna chuckled. "Although, to be honest, Paul was just as bad back then. Maybe even worse. They were both typical teenagers, but in a place like this that means asshole." She moved her cart aside to let another shopper pass. "Listen, Paul's really grateful for everything Gregory's doing. He's not the kind of guy who'll express it, but I can tell you that he's really excited about everything that's happening down at the café. We were just barely keeping our heads above water, and you guys've been a godsend. He seems to think the place actually has potential now." She smiled. "Your winning the lottery's having a sort of trickle-down effect on us, and since he probably won't tell you, I thought I would. We're really glad you're here."

"Thank you," Julia said, genuinely touched. "Gregory'll be happy to hear that. He's pretty excited about the café himself."

"Paul's also glad Gregory's back just for personal reasons. As you can probably tell, this isn't exactly the hub of cultural activity, and we don't really have a lot of friends here in town. Paul hangs around with that Odd guy, and I occasionally see some of my old friends from high school, but . . . Well, I guess what I'm trying to say is that I hope *we* can become friends. It'd be nice to have an intelligent conversation once in a while."

Julia laughed.

"You think I'm joking?"

"No. Not after my experience at the library."

"Comet conspiracies are just the tip of the iceberg."

"What are you doing this afternoon?" Julia asked.

"No plans. Why?"

"Would you like to come over?"

"Sure." She nodded at her half-filled shopping cart. "Just let me take this home and get it put away."

"You know where we live?"

"Of course."

Something about Deanna's tone of voice, her surprise at the fact that the question had been asked at all, set off Julia's internal alarm. " 'Of course'?" she repeated.

Deanna frowned. "You live in the old Megan . . ." She trailed off, realization dawning in her face. "Oh, my God. You don't know, do you?"

"Know what?"

"About your house. What happened."

A chill crept down Julia's spine. She didn't want to hear what was coming next, but she knew she could not turn back. "No," she said. "I guess not."

"It was a while ago, and several people have lived

there since, but . . ." She shook her head. "I don't exactly know how to put this."

Julia felt cold. "What?"

"A family called the Megans were living in the house.
They'd been there for . . . well, for years. They'd lived
there for a long time. And one day the father, Bill
Megan, just snapped. He woke up in the middle of the
night and . . . killed his family. His wife, their kids. He
shot them all. Then he killed himself. No one knows
why. He hadn't been fired from his job or anything.
Nothing traumatic had happened. He just . . . he went
crazy."

Julia licked her suddenly dry lips. "How many kids
were there?"

"Three."

All at once her fears and worries didn't seem quite so
silly—all at once the dread she'd felt was understandable, made sense.

"I wondered why you two would live there." Deanna
shook her head. "I can't believe no one told you."

"Who *could've* told me?" she said, but at the instant
she said it she thought of the Molokans at the picnic. "I
don't really know anyone in town."

Deanna laid a hand on her arm. "You do now."

Julia nodded, forced herself to smile, though inside
she felt like ice. "Yes," she said. "I do now."

She confronted Gregory the minute he came home.
Deanna had left only a few moments before, and Julia
was still putting away cups and dishes when Gregory
walked through the door.

She told him everything: Deanna's story and the
fleshed-out details her new friend had provided, her own
uneasy feelings about the house, the mysterious box of
dishes that had fallen for no apparent reason. She threw
it at him angrily, getting in his face, but he seemed neither surprised nor particularly upset by her behavior. He
was calm, rational, and his unflappability only increased
her anger.

"What do you want to do?" he said. "Move?"

She met his eyes. "Yes."

"Come on."

" 'Come on' what?"

"You think our house is haunted? You think the ghosts of that murdered family are harassing you and breaking your china?" He shook his head. "Jesus. You sound like my mother."

"Maybe she's smarter than you give her credit for."

"Even if she is, even if there are such things as ghosts, this house is safe because she purged it of evil spirits and she blesses it every time she walks through the god-damn door!"

"Keep your voice down. She's in her room."

"We're not moving because you got a sudden attack of superstition."

"It doesn't bother you at all that people were mur-dered in the room we sleep in? In the rooms our kids sleep in? That doesn't bother you at all?"

"It didn't bother you until you found out about it."

"It's not as if we have all of our money tied up in this place. We—"

"All our money *is* tied up in this place. All our money for this year, at least. We're not going to get another lottery payment until next August. So unless we can mi-raculously sell this house, which is pretty doubtful, con-sidering its pedigree, we're stuck here."

She stared at him, blinked. "You knew," she said. "You knew about this."

"Paul and Odd told me. I thought it would be better if you didn't know. I didn't want to worry you."

"What gives you the right to make that decision for me? Who are you to censor my information like I'm some goddamn child?"

"Why don't you keep *your* voice down?" he said.

"It's my house, and I'll yell if I want to!"

"Where are the kids?"

"School," she said, but she couldn't help glancing at the clock. Three-ten. They'd be home in twenty minutes.

"Look, I admit it's not the most comforting thought in the world, but we're stuck here—for the short term, at least—and we're going to have to make the best of it. I suggest we don't tell the kids—"

"Of course we're not going to tell the kids," she snapped. "But since our family seems to be the only one in town that doesn't know what happened here, I'm sure someone, sometime, will tell them."

"And when they ask, we'll explain that there's nothing to be afraid of."

"Isn't there?"

Gregory looked at her. "You honestly believe Bill Megan's ghost is going to try to murder us in our sleep?"

"I don't know what to believe."

He wiped his forehead. "Jesus," he sighed.

"What's that supposed to mean?"

"Nothing."

"Oh, I'm just a stupid little backward Molokan girl, huh? Let me remind you, mister, that *I'm* the one from L.A. You're the one from Hicksville here. So don't try to pull any more-sophisticated-than-thou crap on me."

"Just shut up," he said.

"What?" she demanded.

He turned away. "We'll talk about this when you're more rational."

"We'll talk about it now!"

"No," he said levelly. "We won't."

"Fuck you!"

"Fuck you."

"Go to hell!" she said, but he was already walking down the hallway toward the bathroom. She turned her back on him and stormed into the kitchen. She was shaking, with fury and frustration and some emotion she could not identify, and she poured herself a glass of water and sat down at the kitchen table, breathing deeply, drinking slowly, trying not to think about Gregory, trying not to think about the house or the murders, trying to calm down before the kids came home.

2

Sasha stood on the corner of Malachite Avenue, finishing her cigarette before turning onto her own street. She might be an adult, but she still didn't want her parents to catch her. Her father would shit a brick if he ever caught her smoking, and while she wasn't afraid to stand up to her parents, she didn't want to go through all the hassle. It was better to avoid any conflict with the family and just pretend that things were going along the way they always had.

She took one last deep drag, then dropped the butt and ground it into the gravel with the toe of her shoe.

She popped a couple of Tic Tacs into her mouth and headed up the street toward home.

Adam assaulted her the moment she walked through the door. "What's twelve base six?"

"What?"

"We're doing base six in math. What's twelve base six?"

Sasha pushed past him. "I don't know."

In the living room, her father put down his paper and looked coldly at her. "I thought I told you to be nice to your brother."

"I am being nice. I just don't know the answer to his question."

"You were short, brusque, and rude. I told you before, you may be almost eighteen, but as long as you are living in this house I expect you to abide by our rules. I expect you to treat your family with decency and respect. And that includes Adam. Now I want you to help your brother with his homework."

"Why don't you help him, Father? Or don't you know how?"

He stood up, his already red face growing livid. "I will not be spoken to that way in my own house!"

She thought he was going to hit her, and she stepped back, suddenly afraid. Neither of her parents had ever hit any of them before, aside from small slaps on the bottom when they were younger, and this new, threatening authoritarianism took her by surprise.

"You . . . help . . . Adam . . . with . . . his . . . homework," her father said evenly.

Sasha glanced at her brother, and he seemed just as unnerved as she was.

That little shit Teo started laughing, but Sasha silenced her with a look.

"Do you understand me?" her father said.

"Yeah," Sasha told him, but she did not stay around to prolong the discussion. She stomped up the stairs to

her bedroom, half-expecting to hear her father's footsteps following behind, but no one came after her, and
she walked into the room and boldly slammed the door.

She threw her books on the bed. Everyone was acting
fucking weird these days. Her father was all pissed off,
her mother was all silent, Babunya seemed like she was
getting ready to die. Everyone was freaked.

They should never have moved here.

She herself was behaving strangely—she certainly
wasn't the same person she had been back in California—but while she recognized that fact, she did not
really care. She was happy with the new Sasha, happy
with the way things were going, and if she *had* to live
here in this dumpy little rathole of a town, at least she
would do it on her own terms.

There was a tentative knock on her door, and she
heard Adam's voice. "Sasha?"

"Go away!" she said.

"You're supposed to help me with—"

"Fuck off!" she yelled.

"You're in trouble now." Her brother's footsteps receded down the short hallway and retreated down the
stairs.

Sasha moved over to the door, locked it, then sat
down on her bed.

And waited for her father.

3

The storm hit an hour out of Tucson.

Gregory had picked up replacement relays for the
café's soundboard at an electronics warehouse on the
south side of the city, loaded them into the van, and
headed immediately back toward McGuane, hoping to
stay ahead of the weather, but the storm caught up to
him just past the turnoff to Cochise Stronghold. There
was only rain at first, and wind, but by the time he'd
gotten off the interstate and was driving down the two-
lane McGuane Highway, there were thunder and flashes
of far-off lightning.

He sped up. Save for an occasional saguaro or paloverde tree, his vehicle was the tallest thing on this stretch of desert, and as he saw a jagged flash of lightning touch ground a couple of miles to his left, he increased his speed. The seconds between the increasingly deafening thunderclaps and the slashing blue-white bolts of lightning were steadily shrinking, and he wanted to make it to the mountains before the full force of the storm reached him.

Ordinarily, he would have been able to see for untold miles in every direction, but clouds and rain hemmed in the horizon, and though the lightning illuminated specific sections of desert, the land for the most part remained dark. Darkest of all was the highway before him, and though he knew the mountains were close, he could see nothing ahead save swaths of gray.

A whipcrack of thunder exploded nearby, so loud that it sounded as though a cannonball had shattered the van's windows, and Gregory jumped, unintentionally swerving to the left. He saw no accompanying lightning, but his ears were still ringing and he knew that the hit had been close. The road was slick and dangerous, but he pushed the van up to eighty, wanting just to get out of this flat area before lightning hit the van.

Directly ahead and off to his left, a bolt of lightning so perfectly defined that it looked like it had been digitized by some Hollywood special-effects house hit a paloverde tree. The paloverde exploded, flying limbs on fire as they fell to the ground and bounced in the roadway. A deafening peal of thunder sounded at the precise instant of the hit, and it was the suddenness of the sound as much as anything else that caused Gregory to swerve out of the way and avoid the burning debris.

Then the cliffs were surrounding him and the highway was snaking through a canyon, into the mountains, and his van was no longer the tallest thing on the desert floor, no longer a moving target, and he slowed down as he rounded the second curve.

Already the thunder was fading, moving farther away, and ahead there were no flashes of lightning.

There were dark clouds over McGuane, but no rain, and when he pulled into town some twenty minutes later, the van's windshield had already dried off and his heart rate was finally back to normal.

Gregory drove directly to the café, parking in the middle of the steep back alley. Paul was over in Safford, taking care of some personal business, and the café was empty save for a newly hired teenage busboy and a minimum-wage female clerk, who were standing with their heads together at one end of the counter. They jumped apart as if struck the second he entered the room, and he could not help smiling at their obvious guilt as he asked, "Where's Odd?"

"Mr. Morrison went home," the girl explained. "He told me to tell you to call him as soon as you got back."

"Thanks." Gregory walked into Paul's office and dialed Odd's number. He told the handyman he'd gotten the relays, and Odd promised to be by "in two shakes of a lamb's tail."

Gregory walked out and poured himself a cup of regular, straight coffee before going back and unloading the van. The clerk and busboy were now in entirely different parts of the café, she wiping down the counter and he sweeping out a windowed corner, and if Gregory had not known better he would have thought they did not even know each other.

Odd arrived soon after he finished unloading, and they got to work. They finished putting in the relays, then tested everything, running the lights and checking the sound system, Odd croaking out an old Jimmie Rogers song as they tried out the mikes. Everything worked, everything was in order, everything was ready to go, and as a few late-afternoon patrons trickled in, the two of them began putting away their tools.

"I guess that's it, then," Odd said, wiping the sweat from his forehead with a blue bandanna.

Gregory nodded. "I guess so."

The grand opening of the new and improved Mocha Joe's Café had been postponed twice already due to what they were euphemistically calling "technical problems," but it looked like the third time was the charm, and if no disasters struck, they should be ready to roll tomorrow night. A local band, Montezuma's Revenge, was now scheduled to be the inaugural act, but there was still going to be an hour of open mike between sets, and the sign-up sheet Paul had posted on the wall next to the stage had fifteen wannabe performers listed.

Gregory would call Paul later, tell him everything was ready, and tomorrow they'd go through the last-minute preparations, and then it would be showtime.

He was excited. There was a twinge of disappointment that the physical work was over, but that was more than balanced by the fact that, starting tomorrow night, Mocha Joe's would be McGuane's only legitimate entertainment venue.

And it was all his doing.

He had come up with the idea, bankrolled it, seen it through, and now he would get to see the fruits of his labors. For the first time in his life, he felt a sense of professional accomplishment.

And it felt good.

Odd shut and locked the door of the maintenance closet. "Got any plans?" he asked.

"Not to speak of."

"Wanna get a quick drink?"

Gregory smiled. "You read my mind."

"Come on. I'll buy."

"No. I'll buy."

"Deal."

They went out through the back door, got in the van, and Gregory drove the half a block to the bar. On the way, he described his close encounter with the lightning.

"I'm glad I was in a car when it happened," he said. "I read that it's supposed to be the safest place in a lightning storm because the rubber tires ground you."

Odd snorted. "Tell that to Bill Daniels."

"Who's Bill Daniels?"

"He was driving that same stretch of road in a lightning storm four or five years back. A lightning bolt hit his windshield, smashed the glass, tore off his damn head and melted his neck to the car seat. Those sonsabitches are powerful. Pure energy. And if they can crack a tree like you saw, a windshield ain't nothing to it." Odd grunted, shook his head. "They had to identify Bill by his wallet. Only, his wallet was soaked with his own

blood and shit. Sure wouldn'ta wanted to be the one to
do that."

Gregory was silent, thinking about how close he'd
come to death.

"I wouldn't worry none about it, though. Chances of
something like that happening are astronomical. And if
it already happened once on that stretch of road, the
odds of it happening again are—"

"About the same as being hit by lightning?"

Odd grinned. "There you go."

He parked the van in front of the bar, and the two of
them walked inside and ordered beers.

"I didn't know milk drinkers were allowed in here."

The voice came from the darkness next to the rest
rooms, and the hackles rose on Gregory's neck as he
squinted into the gloom, trying to will his eyes to adjust.
A harsh laugh spat out from the cowboy-hatted figure
emerging into the dim light. It was Chilton Bodean.
Gregory hadn't seen Bodean in decades, but he recognized him immediately. Two years ahead of him in
school, the bully had made his first year of junior high
a living hell.

"Long time no see, Tomasov."

Gregory felt a pacifying hand on his arm. "Ignore
him," Odd said. "The guy's nothing but a drugstore cowboy, a fucking Rexall ranger."

But Gregory didn't want to ignore him. In his old
enemy's terminally belligerent face, he saw the expressions of the men who had made fun of his father all
those years ago, and he turned to face Bodean. "Are
you talking to me?"

The mocking smile faltered. Clearly, the bully had just
wanted to goad him, make fun of him, had not intended
for it to escalate beyond that, but Gregory wasn't about
to back down. There were a lot of old scores to settle
here, and he was in the mood to dispense with them
once and for all.

Bodean quickly regained his equilibrium. "How goes
it, milk drinker?"

"Chil," the bartender warned.

"Ignore him," Odd repeated.

"Say that one more time," Gregory told him flatly. "And I will kick your fucking ass."

The other man clearly didn't know what to do. He remained in place, smiling, but the smile had been on his face for too long and was already well past strained. Gregory did not look away, did not blink, kept his eyes on Bodean's face.

"You have anything else to say to me, *Chilton*?"

Bodean backed down. He looked away, strutted up to the bar, attempting to retain what little dignity he had left, gave the bartender a bill, and said, "Keep the change." He did not look at Gregory as he pushed open the barroom door and walked into the light.

Gregory felt good. He exhaled, his muscles relaxing, and he sat down on the stool next to Odd and took a long swig of beer. He'd dreamed of fighting back against that bully every day of seventh grade, and now that he'd confronted him, he experienced a strange sort of peace, an easy, calming sensation that was not quite like anything else he had ever felt. It was for his father as much as for himself that he'd pushed back hard when Bodean tried to make fun of him, and though his father had always remained philosophically opposed to even the threat of physical violence, Gregory felt good about what he'd done and told himself his father would approve.

Odd shook his head. " 'Milk drinker.' That's one you don't hear too often anymore."

"Good," Gregory said.

"Not many Molokans left here, are there?"

"Not really." Gregory finished off his glass, motioned for another. "Most of the younger ones moved away, and the old ones are slowly dying off."

"I remember when this town was chock full of Molokans and Mormons. And miners." He grinned. "Lotta *m*'s there, huh?"

"Yeah."

"Town had an identity back then, though. Now who knows who lives here? It's all kinda generic." He finished his beer. "I miss the old days. Guess that means I'm gettin' old, huh?"

"*Getting* old? You *are* old."

Odd laughed. "Don't remind me." He stood. "I gotta get going. My wife'll kill me if I'm late."

Gregory nodded. "See you tomorrow, then."

Odd waved low as he headed toward the door. "Later."

Opening night.

Not only was the inside of the café full but all of the sidewalk tables were taken, and there was a line of waiting people snaking up the street past the closed hair salon all the way to Ed's Variety Store. A photographer from the paper was covering the event, and the paparazzi-like flashes from his camera added to the excitement and gave a show-biz aura to the proceedings.

He and Paul and Odd had been working all day, preparing for the big event, and they were still going over last-minute details even as the band was setting up. Montezuma's Revenge had their own sound guy, but Paul would be working the lights, and Gregory would take over the soundboard for the open mike set. Even above the din of conversation, the three of them could hear the almost constant ringing of the cash register, and Gregory thought it was that more than anything else that accounted for the big grin that seemed to be permanently etched on Paul's face.

Julia and the kids showed up a little after seven. Alice, the senior server, tracked him down in the back, and Gregory met his family at the door and took them to the table he'd reserved, telling them to order whatever they wanted, it was all on the house.

He gave his wife a quick, grateful kiss. He and Julia seemed to have put their argument over the house behind them, but it had still been a relief when she'd arrived smiling. Her moods were tough to call these days, and he had given up trying to predict what she was feeling or why.

Adam and Teo were excited, honored to be treated like adults even if only for this one evening, but Sasha was her usual disagreeable self, and Gregory was thankful for small favors. There were a lot of single guys on the prowl here tonight and the four young men in the band were pinup quality themselves. He didn't want Sasha to make a good impression on any of them. There were also a lot of slutty-looking redneck girls hanging around the fringes of the café tonight, and he certainly didn't want his daughter falling in with that crowd. Let her stick to the boys at school.

Odd said that his wife was feeling a bit under the weather and wouldn't be able to make it, but Deanna showed up soon after and sat next to Julia at their table. The two of them immediately started talking, and Gregory and Paul left them together as they went back to the makeshift control booth to go over the light and sound boards.

The night was perfect. Everything ran like clockwork, and even Gregory's miscues and Paul's clearly novice manipulation of the stage lights did not detract from the triumph of the evening. The audience was more than kind, applauding wildly for even the most raggedly amateurish open mike acts, and the consensus of everyone, even the *Monitor* photographer, was that the night had been a rousing success.

After they came home, Julia checked on his mother, he made sure the kids went to bed, and the two of them met in the bedroom. They hadn't had sex in a while, not since the fight, but she gave him a long, slow kiss, massaged him through his pants, and told him he'd better stay awake while she took her shower if he knew what was good for him.

He took off his clothes, turned on the TV and got into bed, and she was clean and freshly shaved when she crawled under the covers with him fifteen minutes later. They waited a little longer, just to make sure everyone in the house was asleep, then she climbed silently on top of him. He was already hard, and he slid it in and began pumping, grabbing her butt the way she liked, and she muffled the sounds of her pleasure by screaming into his mouth as she kissed hm.

4

The bar closed at one, and except for Jimmy, the owner, Lucinda was the last one to leave. She hung up her apron, counted her tips, and shouted out "I'm leaving!" as she walked out the front and locked the door behind her. Jimmy's response was muffled and incomprehensible, but it didn't matter. She knew all of his standard smart-ass replies, and she double-checked the lock before heading up the street toward home.

It had been warm in the bar, but it was chilly outside, and she shivered as she walked along the gravel shoulder. She should've brought a jacket. The days were still summer, but the nights were edging toward autumn, and pretty soon she'd have to start driving to and from work.

When she'd first come to McGuane after traveling across the country from Sarasota, when she'd ended up here after Joel had dumped her and moved on to California, leaving her with an empty pocketbook and an unpaid motel bill, it was May and it was hot as hell. She'd assumed that the temperature would remain that way year-round. After all, this was the desert. But desert sand did not hold heat, and the winters here were surprisingly cold. She'd found out that rough first year that she needed sweaters, long pants, and long-sleeved blouses to supplement her shorts and T-shirts and tube tops.

She smiled to herself. It was a dry cold, though.

From somewhere up the canyon came a coyote's cry, and Lucinda rubbed her arms as she quickened her pace. That was one desert sound she'd never gotten used to. It still frightened her, and it seemed to her that the coyotes had been howling a lot more lately.

Closer in, a dog barked, and other dogs took up the cry, a chain reaction passing through the backyards of houses on several parallel streets.

She turned into Azurite Lane. The narrow road wound along the floor of the upwardly sloping side canyon, and the temperature seemed to drop even lower as she headed up the dirt street toward her house.

The buildings here were few and far between, and it was so late that most of the house lights were off, only an occasional lit porch lamp indicating that anyone lived in this section of town. The dogs had quieted, the coyotes were silent, and behind her she heard a noise she had not noticed before, a rough and ragged scraping that

sounded like someone wearing boots was coming up behind her.

She hadn't seen anyone out, hadn't passed anyone
along the way, and she tried to tell herself that it was
merely someone walking home from a friend's house
and that it was purely coincidental that the two of them
happened to be walking along this section of road at this
time of night, but she was afraid to turn around and
look to make sure.

The sound seemed louder now that she was listening
for it, and it conjured in her mind stalking scenes from
a thousand old monster movies. The horrific image she
tried to focus on was that of the shambling, slow-moving
mummy, but she could not sustain that fiction against
the reality of the noise behind her. There was a sprightliness to the strange step, a hint of quickness and agility
in the identifiable sound of movement.

On impulse, she stopped, froze in place, listening.

The sound stopped as well.

It resumed the second she started walking.

Someone was following her.

She began walking faster.

Striding quickly, she rounded the last curve before
home. The road grew even darker, if that was possible,
the high canyon walls effectively blocking out all but the
narrowest segment of sky. There was a full moon tonight, but the moon was still low in the east, and its light
was not yet able to penetrate down here.

A full moon.

She knew there was nothing to that. It was just a
bunch of superstitious hogwash, but the power of myth
was greater than the power of facts any day of the week,
and now it was not only the fictional terrors of Hollywood that took up residence in her mind, but the more
believable bogeymen of serial killers and psychopaths.

Gathering up her courage, she whirled around.

And there was no one there.

She scanned the shadows and the dark, searching for
signs of movement, a person or an animal, but visibility
was too limited, the night too black and inky to be able
to tell whether someone was hiding behind a rock or a
bush. The only thing she knew for sure was that no one

was on the road behind her. The dirt street was lighter
than everything else, and even in this dimness she would
have been able to see the smudged outline of anyone—
 anything
—on the road.

Maybe it had been an animal making the noise, she
thought. A jackrabbit. Or a bobcat.

Maybe.

But she didn't think so.

She broke into a jog. Her little cottage was only a
couple of hundred yards ahead, and if she hurried, she
could be home and safely inside in a matter of moments.
A motion detector switched on the sharp fluorescent
beam of a driveway spotlight on the house to her right,
and her attention was automatically captured and pulled
in that direction. There was no sign of any person or
animal on the gravel in front of the house, but in the
diffused glow of peripheral illumination, she saw movement on the cliff wall above the residence, a white, mis-
shapen figure that clambered down an impossibly steep
slope at an unbelievable rate of speed.

She started running toward home as fast as her legs
would carry her.

The road was rough, the hard-packed dirt filled with
rocks and ruts, and several times she nearly stumbled,
but she never fell and she kept moving forward, frantic
to get as far away from the freakish form as she could.
She was not at all sure that home would provide any
protection, but she could at least lock herself in and call
the police and let them take care of the problem.

She kept her eyes focused on the street in front of her
and on the darkened square at the end of the lane that
was her cottage, but the ultraquick movement of the
thing on the cliff remained at the edge of her vision and
the forefront of her consciousness, and as it dropped
past the roof level of the house and she lost track of it,
she increased her speed.

Or tried to.

For she was already running as fast as she possibly
could, her leg muscles aching and breath coming in harsh
gasps that were so loud in her ears they would have
drowned out even the sound of a scream.

She didn't know what was happening, didn't know what that figure was, but she knew that it was not human and she knew that she did not want to come in contact with it. At this point she was not even sure if the creature was aware of her existence. If she had imagined the noises behind her on the road, if that had been entirely unconnected and the monster on the cliff had been concentrating on the rock wall it was descending, maybe it had not spotted her. She prayed for that to be the case, and it was only the hope that she had not been noticed that kept her from screaming.

She reached her gate and pushed it open as she ran forward, already fumbling with her keys as she dashed up the wooden steps to the cottage door.

A loud, sharp thump on the roof of the porch did make her scream and startled her into dropping her keys. She heard them hit the rock between the open steps.

She looked up to see the source of the thump.

And saw it peeking over the edge of the roof at her.

The figure grinned, its teeth abnormally long in its too-skinny face.

She cried out, but this time no sound emerged, and before she could adjust her brain to rectify that, its cold, gelatinous hands were around her mouth.

Eight

1

It was the first time he'd been alone in the house.

And Adam was scared.

He didn't know why, but he was. He sat there watching TV, and after a while he had to go to the bathroom and realized that he was afraid to do so—afraid to go upstairs to his parents' bathroom, afraid to go to the bathroom by Teo's room, afraid to leave the living room, period.

He crossed his legs, held it in.

The house was dark. Even in the daytime it was dark, and after all this time he still did not feel comfortable in it. Part of it was no doubt due to what Scott had told him about it being haunted, but the truth was that he'd felt this way even before he'd known anything about that. It was an instinctive reaction, a response to the place that had nothing to do with stories or rumors or third-hand accounts, and now that he was here alone, he found that he was not quite as nonchalant about it all as he had been with his friend.

He thought about the *banya*.

He tried *not* to think about the *banya*.

Babunya was doing Molokan things, and his parents and Teo were out shopping, buying groceries and picking out videotapes: a Russian film for his grandmother and a Disney movie for Teo. Sasha was over at one of her friends' houses. Although his parents had invited him to come along with them, he had declined, explaining that he had some math homework to catch up on, and they'd left him here alone.

He'd been waiting for just such an opportunity to sneak into Sasha's room and do a little exploring, but now he was afraid to go upstairs at all, and his sick impulse would have to remain unacted upon until some other time, until he became braver.

Jesus. What the hell was wrong with him? Something sure had happened since they'd moved to Arizona. He'd turned into a complete wuss, for one thing. Jumping at every little sound, afraid of his own shadow. And he'd become some sort of pervert, stalking his own sister and trying to peek up her skirts, trying to catch her naked, wanting to examine the contents of her room in hopes of finding . . . what? A diary?

Yes. A diary.

In his sickest and most elaborate fantasy, he found her diary and discovered that she had intentionally flashed him on his birthday, had purposely allowed him to look between her legs and see her underwear as part of his birthday present. She had been waiting ever since for him to make a move and had put down all of her sexual thoughts about him in her diary.

It was ridiculous, of course, but he grew hard just thinking about it, and for a brief moment he forgot that he was alone in the house and afraid.

Then he heard what sounded like something heavy being dropped on the floor upstairs, and he jumped, spilling the sack of potato chips on his lap. He moved the potato chip bag aside, listening carefully, ready to run out of the house if he heard any other sounds, but all was quiet save for the lame jokes and canned laughter of the rerun on the television. He waited a few more minutes, but there was nothing else, and he put it down to the settling of the house—his father's all-purpose excuse for unexplained noises—then reached for the remote and turned up the television volume.

He and Scott had stopped by Dan Runninghorse's house on the way home from school yesterday. Dan lived at the edge of the reservation, and his dad was the chief, but even though the other Indian kids were always kissing his ass, they didn't much like him, and the feeling was reciprocal. They were nice to him, but only because of who he was and what he could do for them, and Dan resented that. He and Scott, though, had been pals since kindergarten, natural outcasts who had banded together, and they shared a relaxed, easy camaraderie that reminded Adam of himself and Roberto and made him feel a sharp pang of homesickness.

Adam, too, liked Dan and found the Indian boy easy to get along with. There was a calm sort of confidence about him, and an emotional and intellectual openness more common to metropolitan Southern California than small-town Arizona. Both Scott and Dan were different from most of the other kids here, more like himself, and he was grateful that he had found them.

He didn't know what he'd expected to see at Dan's place. Not a tepee, certainly, but also not the rather mainstream-looking house with its potted palms and wicker patio furniture. They'd gotten Dr Peppers out of the refrigerator and sat around in Dan's bedroom, talking a bit about scary stuff—haunted houses and mysterious deaths and cactus births and eerie occurrences. Dan said it was the mine that had drawn evil to McGuane. Adam assumed he meant that the town was built on a sacred site and that the gods or spirits or whatever had cursed the place, but Dan said no, not exactly.

The earth was their mother, he explained, not just their home. It was the source of all life. It was also a living entity, made up of dirt and rock, plant and water, and the mine was like a big open sore on its body. It hurt here, and it sent out the equivalent of antibodies to fight the disease—ghosts and spirits, demons and monsters.

"It is trying to protect itself," Dan said. "That's why this place is haunted."

The day was warm, but Adam shivered. There was a logic to Dan's argument that made it seem not only believable but likely, and he imagined increasingly powerful supernatural entities being sent to McGuane until the town was entirely overrun. The other boy seemed totally serious, it was clear that he was not goofing around or playing with them, and there was something about the gravity of his bearing that lent weight to his words.

Adam was acutely conscious of the fact that he was on a reservation, in the house of a chief, and it was

a strangely disorienting experience. He felt suddenly as
though he was in a foreign country, a place that was
geographically part of America but where American
laws and beliefs did not apply.

He'd lived with, gone to school with, been friends
with, people from a lot of different minority groups back
in Downey. There were Russians, Salvadorans, Guate-
malans, Mexicans, Armenians, *India* Indians, Chinese,
Japanese, Koreans, Vietnamese. But Native Americans
had not really been represented in the multicultural
melting pot of Southern California, and their ways were
unfamiliar to him, what little knowledge he had having
been filtered through the distorting prism of movies and
television. They were exotic but indigenous, and their
ghost stories, their folklore, their superstitions, seemed
scarier to him than others because they'd been here for
so long. They were an old people, the first residents of
this land, and he found that spooky. It gave their beliefs
greater credence in his eyes, and he had no trouble buying Dan's theory.

"You don't really believe that," Scott said.

"Of course I do," Dan replied. "It's common knowledge. At least among my people. And it explains why
all of that weird stuff happens here. Besides, do you
have a better theory?"

Scott shrugged.

Adam looked at Dan. He was impressed by how comfortable the other boy was with his heritage, with his
religion. Dan wasn't embarrassed by it, didn't try to
apologize for it or explain it away, and that made Adam
feel a little better about his own background. He suddenly didn't feel so ashamed about being a Molokan,
and for the first time he experienced a sense of . . . not
pride but . . . acceptance.

He cleared his throat. "I know a place that's haunted.
A *really* spooky place."

"Where?" Scott said, interested.

"It's on our property—"

"I knew it! After all those murders . . ."

"It's not the house. It's not even near the house. It's
on the opposite end of our property. It's a . . . a *banya*."

He felt good as he said the Russian word. "A bath-house."

"What's that?"

"It's a place where they cleanse themselves," Dan said, and Adam was reminded of the fact that Indians had *banyas* too. Or their version of it. "It's like a steam bath, right?"

"Yeah," Adam said.

"And it's haunted?" Scott asked.

He nodded. He described the bones and the shadow, told them of his grandmother's refusal to go in the building. They both wanted to see it immediately.

They'd walked over to his house, and he'd taken them out to the *banya* and shown them first the bone he believed to be the femur of a child and then the shadow of the Russian man.

The shadow.

They'd both seen it. Scott found it cool and exciting and thought they should call the *Enquirer* to take a picture of it, or at the very least charge admission to see it, but Dan's response was more serious and subdued. He would not speak while inside the *banya*, and when he was once again outside he told Adam that he agreed with his grandmother, and he suggested that Adam stay as far away from the *banya* as possible.

Adam had half thought that coming here with a group of people would dissipate the oppressiveness of the atmosphere, would lessen the dread he felt, but it did not. He was just as scared being here with Scott and Dan as he had been when he'd come by himself. More scared, perhaps, because he now had verification that the shadow of the man was real, was a concrete apparition and not some misinterpreted wall stain or trick of light.

And Dan's warning sent chills down his spine.

They'd left quickly after that, and on the way back his friends asked him if there was anything creepy about the rest of the property or the house itself, and he had told them no.

But that wasn't true, and he wished they were here now to confirm what he was feeling as he concentrated on the television and tried not to hear any other noises. The air in the house felt as heavy as the air in the *banya*, and there was that same sense of apprehension, that feeling that something bad was about to happen.

There was another thump from upstairs, and on the wall above the steps he thought he saw the quick dart of a wild shadow.

He ran out of the house.

He did not turn off the television, did not even close the door behind him. He simply dashed outside and kept running until he was halfway up the drive.

His heart was pounding, and he had a difficult time catching his breath, but that heavy dread was gone, and he turned around to look at the house. What was it? he wondered. What was in there? One of Dan's earth-sent spirits? Or the ghosts of the murdered family Scott had told him about? He didn't know, but either way he was scared, and he wished Babunya was here. She seemed to know how to handle this kind of stuff.

The front door of the house was wide open, and he knew flies were getting inside, but he wasn't about to go back and shut the door. He thought of leaving, walking over to Scott's or something, but he was supposed to stay home, and his parents would be ticked if he left. He'd probably be grounded for a week. So he sat down on a large rock, facing the house so he could watch it, prepared to haul ass at the slightest hint of anything strange.

He still desperately had to take a leak, and after a few minutes passed and there was no sign of movement, he stood, glanced around to make sure there was no one coming, and moved behind a paloverde tree to relieve himself.

He'd just zipped up when he heard the sound of an engine on the road behind him. He turned as a car pulled into the drive. A dusty old Plymouth rattled down the gravel trail, and he saw Babunya in the passenger seat and another old lady driving. The car braked to a stop next to him, and Babunya got out. She closed the car door, waved to the other woman, said something in Russian, and the old lady said something in reply before backing up.

Babunya's smile disappeared as soon as the car hit the road. "Why you outside?" she asked, and something in the set of her face told him that she suspected what was wrong.

He told her.

He described his strange feeling, the fear he'd felt being alone in the house, the sounds he'd heard, the shadow he thought he'd seen.

She nodded, seemingly unsurprised.

"What are we going to do?" Adam asked. He looked back toward the house, shivered as he saw the open door. "Should we wait for Mom and Dad?"

"No," she said firmly. "Don't tell parents. Better they not know for now."

"But they have to know!"

She shook her head. "I take care of it."

She grabbed his hand, and he was grateful for her strength, reassured by both her attitude and her apparent conviction.

"I already bless house," she said. "No evil spirit here. This only minor thing."

They walked up to the house, and Babunya continued to hold his hand as she stood in the open doorway, bowed her head, and said a quick Russian prayer.

He didn't know if it was the prayer that did it or if whatever had been in the house had already left, but he felt no trepidation as he looked into the house now. For the first time since his parents had left to go shopping, he was able to breathe easy.

"It gone," Babunya told him. She smiled at him as she squeezed his hand. "Close door," she said. "We go inside."

2

Gregory sorted through the screws and bolts in the metal bin at the rear of the hardware store, feeling better than he had in weeks. He'd just dropped his mother off at Onya Rogoff's, and while she wasn't quite her old hardheaded, judgmental, opinionated self, at least she had finally snapped out of her funk and was resuming some semblance of her normal life. She had not yet gone back to church, but she was meeting once again with

other Molokan women, planning times to get together
to make bread and borscht, and Gregory was grateful
that the rather frightening apathy into which she had
fallen had somewhat dissipated.

Somewhat.

She was still far more listless and uninvolved than
usual.

He wondered what the Molokans were planning to
do about Jim Ivanovitch's murder. His mother had not
mentioned the minister since the funeral, but his death
had been an unspoken subtext in her words and attitude
ever since, and he knew that those old women were
discussing a lot more than food preparation when they
got together. It was clear that they believed some sort
of demon or evil spirit had killed the minister and that
his mother, at least, was staying away from the church
for that reason. She was not avoiding the building because she did not want to be reminded of Jim—she
thought that the building was cursed or haunted, and
she would not set foot in it until it was cleansed and she
was sure it was free from evil influences.

He was not able to be as sarcastic and skeptical about
that as he wished.

Nikolai Michikoff had apparently taken over the reins
of the ministry—he had both wanted to do so and Vera
Afonin had had a dream that he should, which cemented
it—but Gregory was not even sure that *he* had returned
to the church since the funeral. Every time he walked
or drove past it, the building looked empty, deserted,
and he had to admit that the church looked a little
creepy even to him.

The other woman who had been killed last week bothered him as well. The barmaid. Her murder seemed to
bother a lot of other people, too, and the concern now
was that there was a serial killer in McGuane. The prospect had everyone nervous. In a town where the crime
rate was perpetually low and most arrests were for disor-
derly conduct and drunk driving, violent crime and the
potential for repeat violence set everyone on edge.

He just hoped that it *was* a killer.

Killers could be caught.

But the things his mother worried about . . .

Gregory pushed the thought out of his mind.

He finally found the size of bolt that he was looking for, put six of them into one of the tiny paper bags provided, and walked up to the front counter to pay for his purchase.

3

Teo sat in the *banya* and cried.

Today, once again, she'd been pushed down by Mary Kay and Kim at morning recess and this time she'd had to go to the nurse's office and get a Band-Aid for her scraped elbow. Later, as usual, she'd had to eat lunch all by herself because no one would sit with her. She hadn't even *gone* to afternoon recess but had asked Mrs. Collins if she could stay in the classroom and read, and her teacher had let her.

Another typical school day.

She hadn't said anything to Adam or Sasha about any of this—and definitely not to her parents—but she'd considered talking to Babunya about her troubles. She needed to talk to *someone*.

She was miserable.

She hated school. All of the kids were dumb and mean, and none of them liked her. She knew her parents wouldn't understand, though. They would pat her on the head, tell her everything was going to be all right, and suggest that she make an effort to talk to other kids and make friends. Adam and Sasha would just make fun of her.

She wasn't like the rest of them, though. She didn't know how to make friends, and no matter what she did, the kids in her class would continue to make fun of her.

Babunya might understand, but Babunya had been acting weird lately, and Teo figured it would be better just to wait and talk to her later.

She rubbed her eyes with a finger, wiped her nose on the back of her sleeve. She'd been forbidden to go to the *banya* by herself, but she felt like being alone today and the bathhouse was the only place she could be sure of not being bothered. So she told her mom that she was going to play in the backyard and immediately headed over to the far side of their property, to the *banya*.

Now she sat on one of the broken bench boards and looked up at the stick ceiling. She liked the bathhouse; she enjoyed coming here for some reason. Babunya, she knew, didn't like it at all, but she felt relaxed in the *banya*, at home. It was cool inside, and there was an aura of peace and tranquillity that made her feel cozy and comfortable despite the run-down condition of the place.

She wiped away one last tear. She could cry in here and no one would hear, she could talk to herself and no one would know. The *banya* was a place where she could escape from the problems of the world outside and just be by herself. It was nice to be alone sometimes, and this was the perfect place to do it. No parents around, no brother, no sister, no other kids, no other adults.

Just her.

She looked around the bathhouse—at the rubble strewn all over the floor, at the picture of the Molokan man on the far wall. If this place was fixed up, it could be like a little fort or a playhouse. If she had friends, she could bring them here and they could pretend this was a home or a castle or a secret hideout or . . . anything. They could clean up this junk and bring in some toys and make this place decent.

If she had friends.

That was the problem.

"Teo."

She heard the voice, a whisper, coming from somewhere within the bathhouse. The sun was going down, and the room was filled with more shadows than light, but it was still too small to hide another person, even a child, and she was getting ready to dismiss the voice, to assume she'd imagined it, when it came again.

"Teo."

The shadows shifted, moved. Nothing passed in front of the door, nothing moved outside, but the darkness within the bathhouse flowed clockwise, like a scene in a film using time-lapse photography, and shadows swirled slowly over the rubble in the center of the room before dispersing and once again flattening out on the walls and ceiling.

There seemed something different about the picture of the Molokan man on the far wall, but Teo couldn't quite figure out what it was. She knew she should probably be scared, but for some reason she wasn't, and she adjusted her butt on the board but did not stand up. This was weird, but it was not frightening, and the *banya* still felt friendly to her.

"*Teo.*"

It was the bathhouse itself that was talking to her, she realized now, and, hesitantly, tentatively, she said, "Yes?"

"*I'm hungry,*" the *banya* whispered.

Into her mind popped the image of a dead animal. A small dead animal, a rat or a hamster. She didn't know what made her think of such a thing, but she knew with a certainty she could not explain that that was what the bathhouse craved. It *was* hungry, and it had not been fed in a long time, and it had somehow recognized in her a kindred spirit. It wanted to be her friend.

"*Friend,*" the *banya* whispered, agreeing.

And again: "*I'm hungry.*"

There was the slightest hint of desperation in the voice, and Teo thought for a moment. She'd seen a dead rat somewhere recently. Somewhere nearby.

No. A bird. It was a bird she'd seen, on the side of the path on her way over here, and she stood up and hurried out of the bathhouse and back down the path the way she'd come. Sure enough, there it was, lying in a small tuft of dried brown weeds, several dead cottonwood leaves having blown against its unmoving form, one covering its feet like a blanket, one next to its head like a pulled-over pillow.

She crouched down next to the weeds and examined the bird. It looked like a baby. It was small, and there was something innocent and delicate about its little body. Usually, things like this grossed her out. Adam was always pushing dead bugs on her, holding up worms and dried beetles in front of her face, forcing her to look at flattened frogs in the road. And she supposed that was why she had passed it by on her way to the *banya*.

But it did not gross her out now, and while she felt sorry for the little birdie, she realized that it still had a function to perform, that even though it was dead it was still useful. Everything had more than one purpose, and it made the birdie's death seem not so sad when she understood that it could help maintain the life of the *banya*.

She wished she had a shovel, but it was getting late and even if she ran all the way back to the house to get one, it would be too dark for her to find this spot again. Already the light was fading and the bird's body had started to blend in with the weeds and leaves on the ground. She reached out and picked up the bird, scooping it up using both hands. The lifeless body felt surprisingly stiff and cold, and instinctively she curled her hands around it, trying to warm it up. It was not disgusting to her at all, and she wondered why she had once been afraid of things like this. Death was perfectly natural, and there was nothing scary about it. After creatures lived, they died. That was the way it was supposed to be.

She carried the dead bird back to the *banya* and placed its body on the pile of small bones in the center of the room. Immediately, she felt the play of cool wind on her face, light, soft breezes that came in from all directions, caressing her skin with a feathery touch and then disappearing into the dark. It was like nothing she had ever experienced before, the most sublime form of thank-you she had ever known.

There was a pause. A hush.

She sensed that the *banya* was grateful, that it was anxious to satisfy its hunger. But it did not want her here while it ate—she sensed that as well—and so she retreated, walking back outside.

She turned, once she was through the doorway, but the body of the bird was already gone, swallowed by shadows.

From inside the building came the whisper of air against her face: *"Thank you."*

She smiled back into the darkness. "You're welcome."

4

Julia and Deanna sat at the small table on Deanna's back porch, sipping iced tea.

"I love what you've done here," Julia said.

Her friend smiled. "Thank you."

Julia really was impressed. The yard looked like something out of *Country Living* or one of those kinds of magazines. A rustic birdhouse emerged from an overgrown patch of pink Mexican primrose, and a narrow dirt path wound between purple-blooming sage and a host of wildly growing desert plants. She and Gregory hadn't had time to get their yard in shape—they'd cleaned it up a bit, but they hadn't started planting—and looking at Deanna's backyard gave her quite a few ideas, making her eager to start working on her own garden. Maybe this weekend, they'd go over to the nursery and buy some seedlings.

"Paul told me that Gregory had a run-in with our old pal Marge."

"Well, I wouldn't exactly call it a run-in. He went in the library to use their computer and she put on a big fake smile and told him that they all missed me."

"Kind of creepy, isn't it? I stayed away from that place the first couple of months after I quit because I didn't want to face Marge or her gang, but then I thought that was stupid. This is my town, too, and I'm not about to go around being afraid to do something or go somewhere because of them.

"So I started going to the library once a week. At first I was militant about it. I'd just go in there and grin at her as she checked out my books for me, but gradually things simmered down, and now I'm just like a regular patron. We sort of peacefully coexist."

Julia shook her head. "Strange."

"There's something to be said for the anonymity of a big city. There, if you have a problem like this, you just go somewhere else. You pick another library."

"Or talk to that person's supervisor."

"Exactly. But here, you're bound to see that person again. You have to deal with her. It's tough."

"I take it McGuane has a lot of . . . 'militia sympathizers,' for want of a better word."

"You're right about that," Deanna said.

"Why do you think that is?"

Deanna shrugged. "Who knows? My theory is that these people are basically dissatisfied with their own lives, unhappy with their marriages or their jobs or whatever, and they need someone to hate. For some reason, hating someone else makes them feel better about themselves. And with the Soviet Union gone, they have no real enemy anymore. No organized enemy, that is. No one they can blame all their conspiracies on."

"So now they hate *our* government."

"Pretty much. I mean, these are the same people who were so pro-American back in the eighties that they wanted to bomb Libya and bomb Iran and bomb Iraq and bomb Russia. Now they want to bomb abortion clinics and government offices."

Julia smiled. "Maybe they just like to bomb things."

"Maybe. But it seems to me that if everyone would just live their own lives, would just concentrate on themselves and not worry about what everyone else is doing, we'd all be a lot better off. Happy people don't march in protests or spend their weekends playing soldier. These guys are losers, and if they'd just try to fix their own lives rather than dictate to everyone else how they should think and what they should do, we'd all be a lot better off."

"I agree." Julia looked out at the garden and sighed. "The frightening thing is not just how paranoid and cynical these people are, but how stupid. They don't trust the government. Fine. But they don't trust anything else, either. Except their own loony little network of people. Researched, verified stories from newspapers they don't buy, but some anonymous posting on the Internet they accept as gospel. Some disgruntled janitor from Kentucky comes home after work, eats his Hamburger Helper and starts ranting on the computer, and they believe him more than they do the trained journalists who work for legitimate news-gathering services. It's scary."

Deanna laughed. "I knew I liked you."

"You know, Gregory wanted to move back to McGuane

because he thought it would be a better place to raise the kids. Southern California's so full of drugs and gang violence and everything that it didn't seem like a great environment for Adam and Teo to grow up in. He wanted to come back here because he thought a small-town atmosphere might be better. I thought so, too. Originally."

"And now?"

"I don't know."

Deanna smiled.

"What's so funny?"

"Nothing . . ."

"What?"

"It's just that it's still hard for me to think of Gregory Tomasov as someone's dad, as a middle-aged guy worried about where to raise his kids. In my mind, he's still that obnoxious teenager who tried to sneak into the girls' locker room."

"Gregory?"

"Him and a couple of his friends. The coach caught them and gave them the choice of being suspended or joining the track team. At the time, McGuane High didn't have enough boys to even *have* a track team. Gregory, Tony, and Mike pushed them just above the minimum limit."

Julia laughed. "So tell me about Gregory back then. I can't even *see* him trying to sneak into a girls' locker room."

"Oh, he did more than that, let me tell you. A lot of those Molokan boys were hell-raisers. I don't know if they were trying to rebel against their background or what, but they were holy terrors back then."

"Same thing in L.A.," Julia said. "I even dated some of those boys."

"Then you know what I'm talking about. And Gregory was one of them. He was smarter than most of the other kids, more . . . I don't know . . . modern, I would say, but outside the classroom he was just as bad." She grew thoughtful. "Although he seemed to change quite a bit after his dad died. He wasn't here that long afterward—he and his mom moved to California—but there was a big difference in the way he acted. It was like he

suddenly turned into an adult or something. He was
quiet, serious, seemed to have lost his sense of humor."
She met Julia's eyes. "I guess I *can* imagine him as a
middle-aged man. I'd almost forgotten about that
Gregory."

"Every time I ask his mother about what he was like
as a boy, she tells me what a perfect and well-behaved
child he was."

Deanna laughed.

"I always suspected she was whitewashing the truth."

"Or she didn't know the truth." Deanna leaned forward. "Let me tell you what he was *really* like . . ."

"I talked to Deanna today."

Gregory shifted his pillow against the headboard,
opened his *Time.* "Yeah?"

"About you."

He laughed. "I'll bet she had some stories to tell."

"And tell them she did." Julia pushed down his magazine. "Did you really put red dye in the school swimming
pool and then claim it was from girls who were having
their period?"

"I didn't put the dye in."

"But you were there."

"I plead the Fifth."

"And you told the gym teachers that it was from
girls' periods?"

He grinned. "Yeah. I guess I did."

She hit his shoulder. "You were a brat!"

"I probably was," he admitted, laughing.

"That's it!" she said. "That's it!" She started tickling
him, and he dropped his magazine to defend himself.
She got in a few good underarm shots before he grabbed
hold of both her hands.

She gave him a quick kiss even as she struggled to
escape. "So what was Deanna like?"

He shrugged. "Stuck-up bitch."

She stopped struggling. It had been clear from what
Deanna said that she and Gregory had not gotten along
as kids, but there hadn't been any maliciousness in her
descriptions, any resentment in her retelling of old stories. These were things that had happened long ago, and

she obviously viewed them as simply humorous anec-
dotes from childhood.

There hadn't been this pettiness in her voice, this
flat meanness.

Julia pulled her arms free. "What did you say?"

"I said she was a stuck-up little bitch."

"That's what I thought you said."

"And she was."

"She's not now."

"Maybe," he said. "Maybe not."

She moved away from him. "I don't believe this."

"I know you're friends and all, and I'm glad you've
met someone you like, but that doesn't mean I have to
like them."

He reached for her, but she pushed him back. The
mood was shattered, and though she'd wanted to make
love tonight, she rebuffed his advances and turned away,
pulling the covers over her, as he picked up his *Time*
and resumed reading.

5

Jesse Tallfeather dropped the empty Mountain Dew
can on the ground at his feet and kicked it into the pile
next to the kiln. He walked slowly through the statuary.

Business sucked.

If things didn't improve—and fast—he was going to
have to declare bankruptcy. He wished he could get out
from underneath this, but he'd looked at it from every
angle possible, and he just didn't see a way. He sure as
shit wouldn't be able to sell the business. No one on the
reservation had the cash. Hell, no one in McGuane had
the cash. Most of the other shop and store owners were
barely hanging on themselves. Unless he could somehow
convince that Molokan who won the lottery to either
purchase the place or come in as a partner—and the
chances of that were pretty damn slim—he was going to
go down with the ship.

The ironic thing was that he hadn't even wanted to
get involved with the statuary in the first place. His father had started the business, and his brother Bill had

been set up to follow in his footsteps, but then Bill had up and run off with Hank Wilson's teenage daughter, hightailing it out of town, and Jesse had sort of ended up with the statuary by default.

In his father's day, things had been good. The family had made a decent, comfortable living. But times had changed, and there wasn't much call for statues any more. No one put them on gravesites these days, and even decorative driveway figures and lawn ornaments were not much in demand. He still sold some small stuff—an occasional fountain or birdbath or those little cement quails and ducks that old ladies liked to put in their gardens—but he'd been barely making a living for the past several years, and, unless there was a miracle, it looked like he was soon going to have to shut down completely.

He sighed. If McGuane had a casino he wouldn't have any of these problems. He'd wished many times that their tribe would jump on the casino bandwagon. Up north, the Navajos had nixed the idea, but a lot of other tribes throughout the Southwest had gotten rich off gambling, and there were no casinos at all in Rio Verde County. It was virgin territory, and since theirs was the only reservation in this particular corner of the state, they would have a virtual monopoly.

It was an enticing idea but, so far, not one that had caught on.

Although reservation casinos were almost universally successful, he was consistently surprised by the hostility they generated among politicians and the media. The idea that Indians were actually making money and succeeding on their own seemed to really tick them off. Even the so-called activists who were always raising money for reservation doctors and social services were unhappy about casinos.

Of course, he knew, they were supposed to be all noble and natural because they were what white America now called "Native Americans." That meant that their job was to live in hogans and tepees and look picturesque for the tourists driving by in their BMWs. They were *not* supposed to want anything better or more modern for themselves. They weren't supposed to run casinos but were supposed to squat in the dirt in native attire grinding corn in metates. They were supposed to live up to their media image, to be one with the land or some such bullshit and if they *were* to succumb to commercialization, it was preferred that the method be crouching on blankets by the side of the road and selling turquoise jewelry.

That whole aspect of contemporary American culture made him sick. The obsession with appearances. It was okay to build roads through sacred land but not to drop a McDonald's wrapper on the road. Hell, give him a whole sandstorm's worth of windblown trash in the desert rather than new development. Did people really believe that a beer bottle left on the ground by a camper was more harmful to the environment than a new subdivision?

It was this focus on neatness and cleanliness and a false antiseptic order that bothered him so. Nature was not clean, nature was not orderly. It was not like a suburban lawn, with everything carefully arranged and perfectly placed, and if these well-meaning people were really interested in nature they would abandon their cosmetic attempts to prettify its appearance and concern themselves with substantive issues.

He himself didn't even like nature.

Give him a nice new casino any day.

He imagined himself walking through an air-conditioned lobby, dressed in a suit and tie, nodding familiarly to the high rollers. Around him were video slots, computerized blackjack, wall-to-wall carpeting, and piped-in music. It was a new world, a different world, and one that he would be more than happy to join.

But for now, this was home.

Jesse looked around the yard at the statues. *Winged Victory*, sandwiched between two anonymous Roman-style pedestal busts, stared back at him from a slightly raised section of ground to the left of the kilns. A trio of Michelangelo's *David*s looked coyly toward a pair of *Venus de Milo*s. He started walking slowly through the yard. He stretched out his hands, let his fingers slide over the smooth figures as he passed by. The statuary reminded him of a junkyard. There were the same

crowded narrow aisles, only the objects flanking the dirt
paths were new cement and plaster rather than wrecked
metal.

He liked the cool feel of the statues against his skin,
liked the feel of the hot sun on his face. He had walked
this walk so many times that he could do it blindfolded.
He knew where everything was, and he remembered that
last year when he'd actually sold a major piece to one
of the Copper Days tourists it had thrown him off for a
while. The yard had not seemed the same, and he'd
found that he missed the sold statue.

Missed it?

Yes, he had, and he realized for the first time that,
despite his initial resistance, he would miss this entire
place if he had to give it up. He would honestly regret
losing the statuary, would be sad having to say good-bye
to all this. It had grown on him, incrementally, become
a part of him over the years and, as much as he hated
to admit it, it was now his home.

He reached the chain-link fence and turned around.

At the far end of the aisle, *Winged Victory* was staring
at him.

He frowned. That wasn't possible. The large statue
had always faced the sales office. Hell, he'd just walked
past it and it had been facing the opposite direction.

But now it was facing him.

He looked around, scanned some of the nearby figures. Hadn't that one's head been facing another direction? Hadn't that one's arm been positioned differently?

Chills spread over his skin, down his body. He turned
to his right and saw that several of the statues appeared
to have moved. The sun was still hot, but he felt suddenly cold.

There was something going on here.

Na-ta-whay, he thought.

Uninvited guests.

The idea frightened him. They were indeed living on
desecrated land, and though he didn't like to think about
that kind of stuff, he believed it, and he knew in his
heart of hearts that there had been and would continue
to be things going on in this area that were unexplainable, that were part of the Other World, not this world.

Why was he being picked on, though?

He didn't know, but it was clear both to him and to a lot of other people that things were escalating, that things were out of balance, that something had happened to change the status of coexistence in McGuane. He didn't know what it was or where it was going, but he knew that it now involved him, and he didn't like that at all.

It frightened him.

He thought he saw movement out of the corner of his eye, and he whirled left to see what it was, but all was still. He could not remember if the statue he was staring at had been posed differently or had always been this way.

Na-ta-whay.

He looked down that long, long aisle toward the sales office, thought for a moment, then climbed the chain-link fence, hopped over, and walked around the outside of the yard and back to the front.

Nine

1

In her dream, Agafia was walking through the Molokan cemetery toward the edge of the cliff. It was a cold day with a dark monsoon sky, and only occasional indistinct flashes of lightning illuminated the otherwise gloom-shrouded ridgetop.

She did not know why she was walking toward the cliff, but she was striding with purpose. She desperately wanted to see what lay over the edge, at the bottom of the mine—even though she knew that whatever was down there was evil and would destroy her.

There were no other thoughts in her mind, only that simple, instinctive desire to look into the pit, and she pressed forward with the single-mindedness of the obsessed.

She walked over her husband's grave.

Walked over Jim's.

The ground beneath her feet suddenly shifted, and in the second's worth of illumination provided by a flash of double lightning, she saw a hand emerging from the rocky soil. She managed to avoid it, but another one grabbed her right ankle and held tight, cold fingers digging into the skin of her leg with death-grown nails. She kicked at it, stomped down as hard as she could, and got away, but in another flash of lightning she saw that hands were coming up everywhere.

She was still walking, making a beeline for the cliff, but she glanced quickly around and saw that there were no hands coming up from either Jim's or her husband's graves. The ground above their burial plots remained completely undisturbed.

That energized her for some reason, and she increased her speed, lifting her legs high and stomping her feet down hard in order to crush any hands that might be trying to grab her.

As the rain started to fall, she reached the edge of the cliff.

And looked into the pit.

Where, climbing up the slippery slope from a black pool of mud at the bottom, she saw Gregory, dressed all in red, his face painted white, grinning up at her.

Agafia awoke feeling cold, her hands shaking as they pulled up the covers she had kicked off during her dream. Her heart was pounding. She forced herself to remain unmoving and stare up at the ceiling as she took a series of deep breaths. This was the second nightmare that she'd had about her son in as many months, and that worried her. What did it mean? she wondered. This was not coincidence, not chance. It was not the random workings of her brain that had brought on these nightmares. They had been *shown* to her. She had been *allowed* to see them.

There was a reason she was being led in this direction, but although she could think of many possible explanations, none of them felt right to her, and that left her feeling not only frustrated and angry but afraid.

She sat up, took a drink of water from the glass atop the nightstand next to her bed. There was a lot going on that she could not explain, and she wished her father were here. Father would be able to make sense of this. He knew a lot about both this world and the next world.

About evil.

There was no one around now with that same level of knowledge and comprehension. Jim might have been able to understand what was happening, but she herself did not and there was no one else she could rely on.

One thing she knew for sure—one thing they all knew—was that the police were wasting their time conducting interviews and looking for fingerprints on the Bible and footprints in the dust. There was no murderer. Jim had not been killed by anything human. It was some type of evil spirit, and though they were not yet sure exactly how to proceed, they knew a Cleansing was in order.

She was still not sure who would take charge of that. Nikolai Michikoff was a well-meaning man, but he was not deep. He saw only the surface, repeated only what he'd been taught. He was not a seeker, not a thinker, and she did not think he had the leadership qualities necessary to see them through something like this.

They would do something, though. Vera Afonin was still alive and kicking. She seemed sharper than she ever had, and with Vera around, they could be sure that a Cleansing would occur.

Whether it would be the right one or not remained to be seen.

Agafia rubbed her eyes. Her breathing had returned to normal, her heart had stopped pounding so furiously, and already she was feeling sleepy again. She took one more sip of water, replaced the glass on the nightstand, and lay down, adjusting her body so that her feet, hands, and everything except her head were situated safely under the blanket.

She closed her eyes, sank quickly back into sleep.

She dreamed of the grave.

And Gregory.

Ten

1

It was cold and breezy on his walk home from school, the sky overcast, the sun low in the west. Multicolored leaves skittered along the sidewalk, snapping and crackling beneath his tennis shoes. There was the smell of burning wood on the wind. Fireplaces, Adam assumed. A warm, comforting smell that reminded him of movies that took place in big colonial mansions in New England.

He would not have expected the desert to have seasons—Southern California didn't—but both Scott and Dan had told him that it got pretty darn cold here during the fall and winter, and he could tell that they were right.

He walked down the canyon road, past the high school, intending to cut through the football field and hit his street without having to go through the downtown area. He reached the school and was halfway across the field when he stopped, shifting his books from his right hand to his left. Ahead of him, he could see a group of slutty-looking girls, lighting cigarettes as they walked slowly around the left side of the gym, and he hesitated for a moment. Were these girls part of the pack he and Scott had met up with that night?

He thought of the way the boys who'd chased them had promised to hunt them down and beat the hell out of them.

"I'll get you, you little shit!"

He still worried about that sometimes. Scott was right, there was no way those assholes could identify them—and as the weeks passed, it became less and less likely that they would—but, still, the possibility existed, and it never hurt to be too careful.

He squinted. The girls were too far away to see clearly, but they could easily be the same ones the two of them had run into that night.

And they were taking exactly the same route he had planned.

He didn't want to meet up with them, but it was getting late, and rather than backtrack and have to go two streets out of his way in order to get home, he changed his course and made his way toward the right side of the gym rather than the left. There was another exit from the campus by the office, and while it would take him a block out of his way, it was a short block and he thought it safer.

He reached the gym and walked along the right side of the windowless building toward the center of campus. The school grounds were quiet, empty save for himself and the girls, and he could hear the diffused, muted sounds of their voices bouncing off the walls of the other classrooms. He came to the end of the building and started across the open blacktop toward the office. The acoustics changed here, and now he could clearly hear several female voices behind him.

And one of them sounded very familiar.

He stopped, looked back, but the girls were not in front of the gym. They were either still on the other side or had walked out to the street, and he hesitated only a moment before hurrying back and making his way past the closed double doors and along the gym face. The voices were muffled again, but he knew what he'd heard, and he reached the far end and carefully peeked around the corner to make sure.

It was Sasha.

He ducked back behind the wall. She and the other girls were standing next to the school fence, looking out at the street, smoking.

He moved as close as he could to the edge of the building without being seen and stood there, listening.

"Have you ever—you know—done it?" one girl was asking.

Sasha laughed, and though he recognized the sound

of his sister's voice, the cadence of the laugh seemed odd, unfamiliar. "Of course."

His heart was pounding. He was doing something wrong, eavesdropping on a private conversation like this, and though she was doing something even more wrong, he felt guilty. And frightened. It was his sister standing around that corner, but he was just as afraid—no, *more* afraid—of being caught by the girls now than he had been before. He didn't know what Sasha would do if she caught him, but he didn't want to find out.

"I like 'em long," Sasha said.

The other girls giggled.

Adam's heart was pounding. He could not believe this was his sister. If their parents ever found out . . .

He thought of that time at the restaurant, his birthday, when he'd seen her panties, and as sick as he knew it was, he was suddenly hard. He moved his books down, pressed them against his growing erection.

The light was fading, the afternoon disappearing. He should have been home by now, but he and Scott had stayed late in the library in order to finish a report that was due and they'd forgotten the time.

He wondered what lie Sasha was going to give for her lateness, what she would tell their parents she'd been doing.

"I always make 'em lick me first," one of the other girls said, between puffs on her cigarette. "Otherwise, I might not get to come at all." She laughed huskily. "And after they sniff me and taste me down there, they're usually hard enough that I don't have to suck them."

"I like to suck them," Sasha announced.

"Do you let them come in your mouth?"

"Every time."

There were squeals and laughter.

Adam was suddenly nervous. He'd heard too much, and he was filled with the absurd certainty that he would be caught, that the girls would decide to walk around the corner to where he was hiding and find him. It made no sense, but it was a feeling that was impossible to shake, and, moving in the shadows, he retreated back along the front of the gym until he reached the far side. Looking over his shoulder to make sure that neither

Sasha nor one of her friends was following, he sped across the open center of the campus and past the office, emerging onto the street.

He ran two blocks out of his way just to make sure he wouldn't be seen.

He thought about Sasha all the way home.

So she'd had sex. She was doing it. He imagined her naked, with her legs spread wide and her most private area open to the world, and he wondered if she was hairy down there.

He desperately wanted to share this with someone, wanted at least to be able to tell Scott what had happened, what he'd heard. And he would have, had it involved anyone other than Sasha. But he could not present his sister like that to other people. He did not know if it was because he wanted to protect her or because he considered anything that involved a member of his family a reflection on himself, but he did not want Scott to discover that Sasha was . . . the way she was.

Back in California, it would have been hard to imagine Sasha even talking about sex, let alone doing it. She'd been a bitch sometimes, yeah, but she'd also been kind of a goody-goody, and the type of girls she was hanging out with now were the type she and her friends had made fun of then.

But something had happened to her since they'd moved to McGuane. She was even bitchier—if that was possible—but there'd also been a deeper, more fundamental change. A change in the things she liked, the way she acted, the people she hung around with—her entire outlook on life. It was as if she was purposely trying to be exactly the kind of person their parents did not want her to be, as if all of her upbringing had suddenly been tossed out the window.

He was ashamed to say that he liked the new Sasha better.

Adam thought of that quick glimpse up her skirt.

I like 'em long.

He kept his books pressed hard in front of him as he walked.

He got home well before his sister did and explained to his mom why he was late. He'd been expecting a big

lecture—she usually freaked out about stuff like this—
but apparently she'd lost track of time, too, and she
hadn't really noticed he was not on time until he told
her. He took advantage of this rare occurrence, apologized and said it wouldn't happen again, and quickly
ran upstairs.

Sasha's door was closed, as usual, but he decided to
take a chance and tried the knob. Locked. It was what
he'd expected, but he was disappointed nonetheless, and
he was turning back toward his own bedroom when he
saw, on the hall floor next to the hamper that stood
beside the bathroom door, what looked like a pair of
panties.

Red panties.

Sasha's panties.

He hurried over and, sure enough, his sister's underwear had spilled out from the overflowing hamper and
was lying wadded up next to the plastic container on the
uncarpeted hardwood floor.

He didn't even think about it but looked quickly
around, bent over, scooped the panties up and retreated
into his bedroom.

2

The tyranny of a small town.

If he had been a writer, he could have used it as the
title of a book. As it was, it would go the way of most
ideas and observations, becoming nothing, not even a
memory, forgotten after a few moments of considera-
tion.

But it was a valid concept, Gregory thought as he
watched a trio of almost identically clad men emerge
from the cab of a pickup. All of the men were wearing
Wrangler jeans, with a telltale white circle on the right
rear pocket, indicating where they kept their cans of
chewing tobacco. All had on western shirts. Cowboys.
They even walked with a similar swagger, and he
watched as they entered the bar, laughing together at
some private joke.

He remembered, all during his childhood, wanting to

be like everyone else, feeling the pressure to fit in, wishing his parents talked with a Texas twang rather than a Russian accent. There had been a lot of Molokans in town then, and almost as many Mormons, but while there had not been a lot of overt prejudice, he had still felt the desire to blend in, to not be different, to assimilate into Arizona culture.

And things seemed to have gotten worse since then.

He supposed it was because McGuane was becoming more homogeneous, the diversity of its past fading into history as younger Molokans moved away in search of better jobs and better lives. The residents here now seemed somehow less tolerant, even though examples of overt bigotry were much rarer than before.

But conformity was all-important. Yesterday, he'd seen a young woman picking out baby clothes at the store. She'd intended to buy a red jumpsuit with the flags of different nations printed on both the front and the back, but when two of her acquaintances had stopped by and ridiculed her choice, she had instantly put the jumpsuit away and picked one that they liked.

And it was not only such superficial aspects of life as fashion. The tendency toward conformity ran far deeper than that. For example, the bumper stickers that were so ubiquitous in California, trumpeting a driver's support for a political candidate or cause, were nowhere to be found on McGuane vehicles because no one wanted to call attention to the fact that they might hold views and opinions different from those of their neighbors.

Was that going to happen to his kids? Had he uprooted them for nothing, merely exchanging the pressures of being hip and trendy for the pressures of conforming to the dictates of small-minded small-town rednecks?

The thought depressed him.

He sighed, staring at the door of the bar where the cowboys had walked in. He wondered what was wrong with him. He'd felt out of sorts lately, vaguely dissatisfied, though there was nothing he could put his finger on.

He'd spent the better part of the afternoon wandering around, doing nothing. He could have gone home and asked Julia to come with him, but he wanted to be alone, and he passed from shop to shop, stopping in at the mining museum, walking over to the chamber of commerce, peering down at the pit, sitting for a spell on a bench in the park. He didn't know what he was looking for, but whatever it was, he didn't find it.

He walked back up the street to the café. Or the coffeehouse, as it had been unofficially rechristened. The sign outside, the menus inside, and all of the ads still read "Mocha Joe's Café," but their new patrons had attempted to bestow big-city sophistication upon themselves, and nearly all of them now referred to the place as "the coffeehouse."

Wynona, the teenager working behind the counter, nodded at him as he walked in. "Hey, Gregory."

"Hey," he said.

It must be later than he thought. Wynona didn't get off school until three, didn't start her shift until three-thirty. He looked up at the clock above the counter.

Four-ten.

He'd been out wandering, wasting the day, since just after noon.

But was he really "wasting" his day? Would anything else he might have done been any more worthwhile?

No.

He looked toward the small stage, saw Tad Pearson, a local would-be folksinger, pulling the cover off one of the microphones and starting to set up for tonight's performance.

Was he glad they'd moved? Was he happy here? Gregory was not sure. He was glad he'd quit his old job, and he certainly had plenty of things to keep him busy, plenty with which to occupy his time, but if he were to be totally honest with himself, the life of unending joy that he'd always thought would be his if he ever came into a large amount of money had not really materialized.

The shine on his Bill Graham Jr. dream had also faded. He had indeed contacted some nationally known touring acts, but McGuane was so far away from any major center of population, that unless Mocha Joe's was willing to fork over big bucks, it would be too cost-prohibitive for any of the acts to play here.

So he was stuck with local bands and local musicians, and since he'd seen just about all of them now, even a few from as far away as Wilcox and Safford, he thought he could safely say that he wasn't going to be discovering the next Beatles or even the next Hootie and the Blowfish. There was still his plan to feature poetry, to try and find some legitimate cowboy poets to read their work, but even his hopes for success there had been considerably muted.

Odd emerged from Paul's office, carrying a section of sawed-off board and a toolbox so heavy it weighted him to the right. Odd always cheered him up, and he smiled as the old man twisted his body and walked sideways, grunting his complaints, in order to make it past the counter.

"You could've just taken it out the back," Gregory said. "It'd be a lot easier."

Odd looked up at him. "I've had about enough suggestions for one day. My truck's out front, and that's where I'm going."

Gregory met Wynona's eyes, and she shrugged, moving to the opposite end of the counter.

Gregory laughed. "You're a bitter old buzzard, aren't you?"

The old man sighed, put down his toolbox. He put the wood on top of it and wiped the sweat from his face with both hands. "I suppose I am," he admitted. "But you try working in that unair-conditioned little office for three hours and see if it don't make you crabby as hell."

"Where's Paul?"

"Took off early today. Said he had some personal business to take care of. I think he's coming back tonight, though. Why?"

"Nothing. I was just wondering." He walked over, picked up the wood from the top of the toolbox. "What kind of 'personal business'?"

Odd shrugged. "Not my place to wonder."

Gregory nodded, and the two of them walked through the café and outside to Odd's dented old pickup.

"You hangin' around for the show?" Odd asked.

Gregory shook his head. "I just thought I'd stop by for a second, see what's happening before heading home."

The old man looked back toward the open door of the cafe then leaned in closer. "Between you and me, I don't think that Pearson boy's got much of a future in show biz."

"I'd have to go along with you there."

"What do people like him do it for? Get up there and humiliate themselves like that? You know his buddies at the title company are bound to be talking."

"Some people just feel the need to express themselves, I guess."

"Well, I express myself in the shower. And it's not gonna go any further'n that."

Gregory laughed.

Odd walked around to the driver's side of the pickup. "I guess I'm off," he said.

"I'm heading home, too. Want to give me a lift?"

"Sure. Hop in."

"Just a sec." Gregory hurried back into the café, told Wynona he was going home and told her to ask Paul to call him if he came in.

The teenager nodded. "Will do."

He went back outside, got in the truck, and had barely closed the door before Odd was speeding up the road.

"You're supposed to take me home," Gregory pointed out.

The old man grinned. "I know a shortcut."

Sure enough, it was a shortcut, and not nearly as hair-raising a route as Gregory had feared. Odd drove down the drive, swung the pickup around, and left him off right in front of his door.

"You want to come in?" Gregory asked.

Odd shook his head. "Lurlene'll have supper made already. She gets pretty riled if I'm even half a second late. I'll take a rain check on that."

"Why don't you two both come by sometime?"

Odd nodded. "I'd like that. You never did have no housewarming party or nothing. We could get a few people together, see if we can't get 'em to bring gifts." He paused. "Only, I doubt they'd be too expensive. You're the lottery winner after all."

"Maybe *I'll* buy the gifts. Bribe people to come."

Odd grinned. "There you go. You can count me and Lurlene in."

Gregory slammed the cab door. "Later."

He could not tell if Odd bade him any form of good-bye; the pickup took off so fast that he instinctively jumped back so his feet wouldn't get run over by the right rear tire. He saw a hand poke out of the driver's window and wave, a silhouette in the dust.

In the kitchen, Julia and his mother were talking about planting flowers. In Russian. They'd all been speaking a lot more Russian since they'd arrived here, and he was not really sure why. Regression on his part, he assumed. A combination of living with his mother again and being back in the town where he'd grown up. But he wasn't sure about Julia. Was she doing it for his mother's sake, merely to be polite, or was she trying to keep in practice in order to . . . what? Maintain her heritage? It didn't make sense. None of it made sense, and he decided to let it slide and not worry about it.

He gave Julia a quick, perfunctory kiss, got a glass of water, and, ascertaining that the conversation was not yet over and that neither of them wanted him involved in it, retreated into the living room.

He sat down, turned on the television and flipped through channels until he found a tabloid news show. Setting the remote down on the coffee table, he kicked off his shoes and settled in on the couch to watch. The features were ostensibly human interest stories and were delivered in upbeat cheerleader tones by the pert female anchor, but they all involved murder, betrayal, and the worst sorts of human activity. A man tracked his ex-wife across country to a small town, where he attempted to run her down with a car: she leaped out of the way to safety while he crashed into a tree and was killed. A woman went from being a high-priced lawyer to being a high-priced call girl and was killed by a john on the same day she had written to her mother that she was quitting the prostitution business. A ten-year-old girl who had her arms chopped off by the father who'd molested her since she was three had learned to paint pictures with her feet.

Halfway through the show, his mother came into the

living room, sat down in her recliner and watched the
rest of the program with him. In the kitchen, he heard
the rattle of pots and pans as Julia started dinner.

The tabloid show ended, and a promo for the upcom-
ing news came on: a Phoenix youngster was missing and
police had found a body buried in the desert that might
be his.

Gregory turned toward his mother, speaking in Russian. "Makes you wonder sometimes about the goodness
of man, doesn't it?"

"People," she reminded him, "are a combination of
the dust of the earth and the breath of God. God created
man from the dust, but He breathed life into him. That's
why people may be base and animalistic in many ways,
but they still desire and keep reaching for the spiritual
and godly." She smiled at him. "I liked the girl painting
with her toes."

Gregory smiled back. Sometimes his mother surprised him.

He underestimated her, he thought. Her ideas were
nowhere near as simple, knee-jerk, and one-dimensional
as he sometimes believed them to be, and he should
know by now that despite the strict doctrine and rigid
culture, most Molokans were at heart good, decent,
moral people. They were also intelligent spiritually
minded individuals who gave a hell of a lot more thought
to metaphysical and philosophical matters than he ever
did. Despite his college education.

He might not believe the same things as the churchgoers, but it was wrong of him to dismiss their beliefs as
somehow intellectually inferior to his own.

His mother looked around the room, as if to make
sure Julia and the kids were not nearby, then got out of
her chair and came over to the couch, sitting next to
him. "I've been having dreams," she said.

Gregory said nothing. He knew where this was leading. Throughout his childhood, his mother had foisted
her supposedly prophetic dreams upon them, always in-
sisting on the inevitability of their outcomes. She wasn't
revered like Vera Afonin, but her dreams were still ac-
corded respect in the church, and that had given her far
too much confidence at home. His father, he knew, had

invented scenarios similar to her dreams in order to get
her off his back, and Gregory had long since learned
to do the same. There was no statute of limitation on
prophecy—it was what kept fortune-tellers and psychics
in business—and he knew that if his mother predicted
some sort of disaster for him, she would be on pins and
needles until something bad actually occurred. It could
be a year later and completely dissimilar to the event in
her dream, but if something happened to him, she would
claim credit for it. She could dream about him cracking
his head open, and if he injured his toe playing football
six months later, she would pull an I-told-you-so and
rest secure in the knowledge that she had successfully
predicted it.

This time, she told of dreaming about the Molokan
cemetery and seeing him crawling up the ridge from the
mine below, dreaming about him being trapped in the
banya and unable to escape, dreaming about him being
attacked by the shadow of a dwarf.

It was slightly unnerving, the sheer number of nightmares she'd had recently that involved him, but he still
didn't put any stock in their veracity, and he tried to
think of some way to put her mind at ease.

"I don't think any of those things are going to happen," he said in Russian.

"No," she admitted. "But they mean that *something*
bad will happen to you. I worry."

He looked into her eyes. She'd grown so old, he
thought. She had not regained her former sprightliness
after the minister's death, and she looked weak to him,
frail. He found himself wondering how much time she
had left.

He tried to push the thought out of his mind.

She met his gaze. "Just be careful," she told him.

He smiled, patted her hand. "Don't worry, Mother.
I will."

3

Saturday morning, they let Gregory's mother take care
of the kids and met Paul and Deanna at the Country

Kitchen for breakfast. They could have gone to the café, but both Gregory and Paul said they'd been spending far too much time in that place and were getting sick of it, so they took a break and went out for a real meal instead of Mocha Joe's bagels and coffee.

Paul and Deanna were already at the restaurant, and they waved the two of them over as soon as she and Gregory stepped through the door. The Country Kitchen smelled richly of bacon and sausage and buttermilk waffles, and to Julia there seemed something good and wholesome about that. Eateries in California were so trendy and health-conscious these days that far too many of them had the bland scent of a refrigerator filled with fresh fruit. It was heartening somehow to smell these old-fashioned breakfasts, and in a weird way she suddenly understood why Gregory had wanted to move back here.

They greeted their friends, sat down, ordered.

Gregory and Deanna were still a little wary of each other, both of them acting more polite than either of them did normally, and Julia had to smile at that. All these years later, those teenage dynamics were still in place, and the patterns of behavior that had been laid down in childhood had not changed one whit.

Julia wondered if she would act the same way if she encountered some old acquaintance from her high school days. She had not attended her ten-year reunion, but her twentieth was coming up and she was halfway considering going to it. There weren't a whole lot of people she was interested in seeing, but there were a few, and she figured she was successful enough and had kept herself up well enough that she could lord it over a few former rivals.

But would she still feel intimidated by the girls who had intimidated her back then? Would she still feel close to the girls who had been close to her?

She looked at Gregory and Deanna and wondered.

After breakfast the four of them walked off their calories. They paired off oddly—she and Paul were in the front, Gregory and Deanna behind them. Paul seemed to know quite a lot about the town's history and heritage, as well as its architecture, and he pointed out the boardinghouse that had once been a house of prostitution and the bookstore and thrift shop that shared what had been a Masonic temple. He knew who used to live where, and he told stories of land grabs and claim jumpers, cuckolds and adulterers as they walked up and down the winding, narrow streets.

Julia was curious about the Molokans, wanted to hear about them from an outsider's perspective, but Paul and Deanna both said that since they'd grown up with a lot of Molokans around, they hadn't paid much attention. Molokans had been an accepted part of everyday life. There'd been problems in the past, though, Paul admitted. Like the Mormons before them, Molokans had been relegated to a certain section of town at the outset, and he led them through the narrow drive lined with abandoned shacks that had once been Russiantown, recounting stories of several anti-Molokan attacks and beatings.

"Do you remember this?" Julia asked Gregory.

He shook his head. "Before my time."

Back in the Country Kitchen parking lot twenty minutes later, Gregory stopped in front of their van, taking out his keys.

"It's been fun," he said. "Thanks for the invite."

Paul grinned, nodded toward Julia. "You got yourself a good one, bud."

Gregory looked over at Deanna, then offered a half-hearted grin of his own. "I guess you did too."

"Tough admission," Deanna teased.

"Yeah," he said. "It is."

Julia hit him.

They all laughed.

4

He didn't tell anyone about it at first. It was embarrassing, for one thing. And it was weird, for another.

His belly button was growing.

If he'd been married, he could've talked about it with his wife. If he'd been a kid, he could've talked about it with his mom. But he was a grown single man, living alone, and this wasn't really something that he could bring up with his buddies down at the bar.

Chilton Bodean turned off the shower and rubbed his washcloth gingerly over the not-so-small nub protruding from the bulging mound that was his belly. He'd always had an "outie," but in the past week it had seemed to become more prominent. At first he'd thought it was just his imagination, but overnight he'd had to throw that theory out the window.

It was now more than an inch long.

He got out of the shower, used a towel to rub the steam off the mirror, and looked at his body in the glass. The pinkish belly button was now hanging down, like a small second penis, and the thought occurred to him that maybe his umbilical cord was growing back.

That was what it looked like, and the thought scared him. Years ago, he'd taken a wart off his knee with Compound W, and the medicine had indeed worked, but years later the wart had returned in exactly the same spot.

Was something like that happening here?

The mirror was fogging up again, and once more he wiped it with the towel. He knew he didn't eat right, drank too much, didn't exercise, didn't take care of himself, and he'd been worried for several years that he might get cancer or have a heart attack or something. Not worried enough to do anything about it, but worried enough that the thought concerned him. Skin cancer was the most likely, he figured, and for quite a while now, he'd kept a close watch on any moles or pimples or changes in skin tone on his body.

Which was how he'd noticed his belly button.

Which was why he'd thought at first that he might be overreacting.

He touched the protruding piece of flesh, squeezed it between two fingers. He felt nothing. He squeezed harder. No pain. No sensation at all.

He could go to the doctor—he *should* go to the doctor—but he was afraid of finding out that it was something serious. Or, as he really feared, something unknown. He had never heard of anything like this happening before,

and it was possible that it was the first time it had occurred, that it had never happened to anyone else. Ever.

He might be the very first victim.

He combed his hair, shaved, brushed his teeth, and
got dressed.

He went to work, tried not to think about it.

He kept hoping it would go away, but as the days
passed, the umbilical cord grew. From one inch . . . to
two . . . to three. He knew that it *was* an umbilical cord,
and that was what frightened him. It was regenerating
itself, but he was no longer inside his mama's body and
there was nothing for it to connect to. It hung down at
first, but then it started to curve to one side, following
the contours of his stomach. Would it just keep growing
forever, trying to find his mama? He prayed that it
wouldn't.

The thought occurred to him that he could cut it off.
After all, his first umbilical cord had been cut off after
he was born and there hadn't been any side effects.
What if he just got himself some shears and lopped that
sucker off?

But the truth was, he was afraid to do that. There was
still no feeling in it, but it was a part of him nonetheless,
and whacking it off would be like chopping off a finger.

It grew.

Six inches.

Seven.

And then it moved.

This was not just a shift in direction of growth, like
before, an unobservable change that occurred over a
long period of time or during his sleep. He felt it *wiggle*,
and he practically screamed when it happened. *Would*
have screamed had he not been in church at the time.
He glanced quickly to his left and right, making sure
that no one had seen any movement or noticed his reaction, and was gratified to see that everyone's gaze was
focused on the preacher up front.

The umbilical cord was cold, he noticed now, though
that was not something that had registered before. It felt
like a worm or a snake, and it slithered beneath his
white church shirt, the slimy tip of it pressing against his
right nipple.

He was filled not only with horrified disgust but with a sudden sensation of panic. What could he do? It felt as though it was growing even now, beneath his shirt, and he half expected it to pop out from the top of his shirt, whipping out from underneath his collar like some overlong pecker.

The cord moved to his left nipple, started down the side of his stomach.

He'd had enough, he couldn't take it anymore. He stood quickly and excused himself as he passed in front of Jed and Travis and Maybelle, trying not to step on their feet as he made his way out of the pew and into the center aisle. He didn't know if they could see the outline of the umbilical cord beneath his shirt, and at this point he didn't really care. It might even be a relief to have his secret discovered. But despite the overwhelming feelings of fear and panic within him, despite the sheen of sweat that draped his head and was soaking through his cotton whites, everyone apparently assumed that he'd had a sudden attack of the runs or something and let him pass without even looking at him.

He rushed out of the church, threw up in the bushes outside.

His truck was parked on the street, but he ran all the way home, the umbilical cord sliding slowly and methodically over his upper torso, exploring.

He ripped the shirt off the second he was inside his house and the door was closed safely behind him.

The umbilical cord whipped out straight, practically pulling him off balance, then, like a tape measure being called back and rewound, slipped faster than the eye could see down his pants. He felt it slide through his underwear and press against his leg before tapping his knee and coming to a stop.

Chilton fell into his recliner, crying, tears coursing down his cheeks and great hiccuping sobs of fear and frustration issuing involuntarily from his uncooperative mouth. He couldn't remember the last time he'd cried— he must have been a baby then—and he didn't want to be crying now, but he just couldn't help himself. He didn't know what the hell was going on, his own freakish body was attacking him, he was embarrassed and terrified and all alone, with no one to talk to. Everything was crashing down on him at once, and he knew that he was cracking under the pressure like some pathetic little pantywaist, but he just couldn't help it.

He crossed his legs, trying to trap the umbilical cord in place, and sucked in his gut as he unbuckled his belt and then pulled it as tight as it would go, rebuckling. It was uncomfortable and chafing, but he figured it would keep the cord from moving around, and he slumped back, feeling drained. He was still crying, could not seem to stop, but he knew he had to do something about this and he tried to think of something, tried to come up with a plan. His brain seemed fuzzy, though, his thought processes muddled, and the only thing that made any sense to him was to stay here, in the recliner, and wait for it to go away. It *wouldn't* go away, he knew that intellectually, but remaining here felt right, and he curled up and doubled over, and was grateful that he felt no movement in his pants.

He cried himself to sleep.

He awoke unable to breathe, his windpipe choked off by the umbilical cord that was now wrapped around his neck. The recliner was all the way back, and he was stretched out. His belt was still tight, his waist hurt from the leather digging into his skin, but the umbilical cord had escaped.

And it had grown.

He flailed around, attempting to suck in air but unable to draw breath any deeper than the back of his mouth. His whole head was hot and it felt as though the entire world was pressing in on his body. His feet kicked out at the elevated footrest, and his thrashing hands knocked over a lamp and an ashtray on the table next to him before his fingers curled around a pair of scissors.

He fumblingly tried to fit his fingers through the holes, but he couldn't seem to work the scissors and was afraid he would drop them and his last and only chance would be gone. His vision was getting fuzzy, and he knew time was running out, so he held the scissors tightly and stabbed at his belly button, but he missed the umbilical cord and the pointed steel sank shallowly into his flesh.

His body jerked with the pain, and he screamed . . .

only he couldn't scream. The attempt seemed to deplete what little air remained in his lungs, and his vision darkened. He was dying, and he pulled out the scissors and stabbed at the cord wrapped around his throat and was gratified to feel movement. He still could not breathe, but the cord was sentient and it wanted to save itself, and it tried to move away from the knife without letting up on its grip.

He succeeded in stabbing the umbilical cord, but he also hit his own neck, and blood was streaming down his shoulder, down his back. He was growing weaker, his brain fogging, and he sensed that his last resort was to get at the source.

He gripped the scissors hard and plunged them into his stomach.

He'd been aiming for his belly button again, but again he'd missed, and the scissors sank blade-deep into his flesh. The pain was unbearable, unlike anything he'd ever experienced before, and he was glad to feel himself passing out from lack of oxygen so he wouldn't have to experience the agony of the stab wound any longer.

He just hoped the umbilical cord died with him.

Eleven

1

"I found something really cool," Scott said.

They were at lunch, and Adam had just traded his apple for half a Twinkie. He bit into the creme-filled snack cake. "What is it?"

"I can't tell you."

"If you can't tell me, why'd you bring it up?"

"I mean, I have to show you." He grinned. "It's so cool."

Adam finished the Twinkie, wiped his hands on his jeans. "At least give me a hint."

"I can't."

"You're really annoying, you know that?"

"We all know that," Dan said, sitting down on the opposite side of the table and opening his lunch sack.

"Where've you been?" Scott asked.

"The office."

Scott leaned forward excitedly. "What happened? What did you do?"

"Nothing. I forgot my lunch and my mom brought it." He shook his head. "I could've just bought my lunch at the cafeteria."

"Nothing more embarrassing than having your mom come to school," Scott agreed.

"Is there anything good in there?" Adam asked, looking over.

Dan pulled out a sandwich. "Salami," he said.

"That's it?"

Dan smiled. "A lot of trouble for just a sandwich, isn't it?" He shook his head. "My mom . . ."

"I found something really cool," Scott said. "I was telling Adam about it."

"He wasn't telling me anything."

"I'm going to show you guys after school. Do you have to go home right away?"

Dan shook his head.

"I could call my parents," Adam said.

"Call them. You won't regret it."

"What is it?"

"I can't tell you."

"Come on!"

Scott smiled mysteriously. "You'll see."

They met on the basketball court after school. Scott was the last to arrive, and as soon as he rounded the corner of the locker room, Adam and Dan stopped talking about who would win in a fair fight between Batman and Spiderman and walked over to their friend.

"So?" Adam said. "What is it?"

"Not what. Where." He started across the asphalt toward the field. "Come on, I'll show you."

"Not even a hint?" Dan said.

"Nope."

They left school, walking past the rows of old houses, through downtown and out to the highway. Several cars were traveling in both directions, and all three of them remained safely on the dirt shoulder as Scott led them up the road toward the tunnel at the end of town. Just before the diner, he dashed across the highway and stopped before a steep sandstone cliff practically covered with hanging succulents—green, cactusy plants that looked to Adam like the ubiquitous ground cover used to abut California freeways.

He looked around. "So?" he said.

Scott smiled. "Follow me." He used his foot to push a clump of plants aside, and Adam saw a narrow dirt path leading slantways up the cliff.

"Cool," he said.

"I hid the entrance so no one else would find it."

"Where does it lead?"

"You'll see." Scott started up. "I discovered it when I was walking back from the diner. I'd never really noticed it before, but I spilled my Coke on the ground and I stopped to pick it up and saw this path."

"And you took it?"

"I wanted to see where it led."

"Was it night?"

"No. It was yesterday at lunch. I tried to call you doofuses when I got back, but neither of you were home." He looked over his shoulder at Adam. "Thanks for calling me back, by the way."

"What are you talking about?"

"I left a message with your sister, and she told me she'd have you call me back."

Sasha.

"She never told me," he said.

"Bitch."

The path was steep, and they were grabbing strings of succulents as though they were ropes, using the plants to help pull themselves up the trail. Adam looked to his right and saw that the highway was already a couple of stories below them. He stopped for a moment, looked ahead. The path continued sloping upward until it was above the diner's tiny back parking lot, then switch-backed and returned in this direction farther up the cliff.

Dan poked him in the back. "Come on. Get moving."

They followed Scott up.

Around the curve, three-fourths of the way to the top of the bluff, the path sank down a little, behind a low wall of sandstone and succulents, before suddenly dead-ending into the cliff face. Adam stopped. They were at a spot that couldn't be seen from the road. Looking up from below, the cliff face had appeared to be even, with no indication that there was anyplace where people would be able to stand. The path itself was invisible from the bottom, but this little open space was completely unexpected. It was like a little secret clearing, a smuggler's hideout, and he looked over to see Scott sitting on a chunk of rock and grinning hugely. "What'd I tell you?"

"It *is* cool," Adam admitted.

Dan was looking around. "Who do you think made it?"

"No one. It's natural."

"I doubt it. And even if it was, do you think you're the first person to find it?"

"Looks that way. I don't see signs of anyone else up here."

"There's a path," Dan pointed out. "That means someone had to make the path at least."

"But that was a long time ago. Look around. I'm telling you, no one's been here but us in . . . God knows." He stood. "Now this is the really cool part." He shoved his hand into the draping plants behind him, but instead of hitting rock wall, his arm went in up to the elbow. He pushed the plants aside, like a curtain.

Behind the succulents was an indentation in the cliff large enough to walk inside.

A cave.

Scott grinned. "Bitchin', huh?"

It was. Even Dan had to admit it. They walked over, peeked behind the hanging strands. It was small enough that they could see the back wall, even with the afternoon shadows, but large enough that all three of them could have easily fit inside with room to spare.

It was like something out of a movie, and Adam took in the high ceiling, the sandy floor, the irregularly eroded sides, before heading over to the opposite end of their little clearing and peeking over the edge. The highway looked very far below, and he could not believe they had come up this high.

"This place is like a secret hideout," Scott said behind him. "We can spy on people down there and they can't see us. We can check out what's happening at the diner and they won't even know."

Adam nodded. He wished Roberto was here. Roberto would think this place was kickass. Maybe he'd take a picture of it, send it to him.

"It's like something out of *Tom Sawyer* or *Huck Finn*," Dan said.

Scott nodded.

"But what're we going to do with it?" Adam asked.

Scott grinned. "Don't worry," he said. "We'll think of something."

*   *   *

On the way home, he could not help wondering about that little space halfway up the cliff: how it had gotten there and who had made it. Dan was right. Even if the cave and the flat little section of ground behind the sandstone wall were natural, the path was not. It had been made by somebody, worn by the passage of feet, and for some reason that made him nervous. *Why* was it there? What was the purpose?

The shallow cave had reminded him of a shrine. There was something primitive and ritualistic about it, but since Dan had not mentioned anything, he assumed its origins weren't Indian.

Was it older than that?

Younger?

Either way, the idea was creepy, and he could just as easily imagine a group of identically dressed townspeople trudging up the path to perform some sort of human sacrifice as he could a primitive tribe.

Dan was wrong. It wasn't like something out of *Tom Sawyer* or *Huck Finn*.

It was like something out of a horror movie.

Suddenly the place didn't seem quite so cool.

And Adam thought of the *banya*.

Before they'd parted ways at the foot of Ore Road, Scott had brought up the bathhouse again. He'd been harping on the subject for over a week, and he honestly seemed to think that they would be able to sell a photo of the *banya* to one of the tabloids and make a fortune. Although Dan had remained silently disapproving, Adam had finally agreed to let Scott go in there and take pictures.

"But I get half the cash if you sell them," he said.

"Fair deal," Scott told him.

Dan had said nothing but shot him a look of warning, shaking his head, and while Adam had not responded, the Indian boy's reaction concerned him. He believed Dan, cared about what he thought, and despite his facade of California cool, he trusted Dan's instincts far more than his own—and ten thousand times more than Scott's.

Maybe it was a mistake.

He himself had not gone back to the *banya* since he'd

shown it to his friends, though he'd felt the lure, felt the pull. He'd dreamed once of the femur bone, and in the dream he'd taken the femur and polished it and kept it on his dresser for a good-luck charm. It had seemed so real that when he awoke, he'd checked the top of his dresser to make sure the bone wasn't there.

And he'd wanted to go out to the *banya* and make sure it *was* there.

But he'd managed to resist the temptation.

At least he hadn't agreed to go with Scott. He'd half thought that that would dissuade his friend from going through with it, but Scott had acted as if he hadn't even heard that provision, and he told Adam that he'd be by on the weekend.

"We're gonna be rich," he said.

Adam merely nodded as Dan walked on ahead.

The van was gone when he arrived home, and he assumed his dad was off somewhere, but it was his mom who was gone, and the house was totally silent when he walked inside. His dad was in the living room, reading a magazine.

"Hey, sport," he said.

Adam nodded.

"Have a seat. Come and visit with me."

He'd been intending to go straight to his room, but he recognized that tone in his dad's voice and knew the suggestion was more mandatory than the words made it sound.

He sat down on the couch. "Where's Teo?" he asked.

His father shrugged.

Adam frowned. His dad didn't know? There was something strange about that. Both of his parents had always kept very close tabs on their movements. *Too* close a lot of times. He and Sasha—Sasha in particular— had often been embarrassed in front of their friends by the strictness of their parents' monitoring.

Of course, it was just as strange for him to be inquiring about Teo. His sister was usually a pest and he was more likely to want her to leave him alone than to seek out her company, but he felt awkward being by himself with his dad, uncomfortable, and he thought it might be a little less tense to have Teo around.

Awkward? Uncomfortable? Tense? He had never felt that way about his father before, and he was not sure why he felt that way now, but he did, and it bothered him.

He sat there for several moments in silence, staring at the wall, before finally picking up a *TV Guide*.

"This is nice, isn't it?" His dad smiled, looking over his magazine. "Just us men?"

Adam nodded, forced himself to smile back. "Yeah," he lied. "Yeah, it is."

2

They performed the Cleansing on a Monday, the Lord's first workday, and the ten of them prayed in unison as they marched through the church, each carrying and clutching his or her own Bible.

Agafia would not have believed a house of God could be this tainted, particularly not one so small, but evil hung thick and heavy over the building, the scent of corruption so strong they could practically taste it. A cathedral she could understand. One of those old medieval churches with labyrinthine chambers and endless corridors. But their plain little house of worship did not seem as though it had room for such powerful and concentrated energy.

It was here, nevertheless, and as they walked in unison over the dusty floorboards, over the dried blood spots that marked the location where Jim Ivanovitch had been murdered, Agafia felt the pressure of its presence. Her sadness and anger at the loss of her old friend had been entirely supplanted by fear.

Was the specific spirit responsible for the minister's murder still here? It was impossible to tell. *Something* was here, but whether that something was the actual entity that had killed him or whether it was merely related to that being remained to be seen.

It was Nikolai who had chosen the ritual to be performed, and it was he who had chosen the ten to participate. The entire congregation had met yesterday morning in the park for an abbreviated service, and Ni-

kolai had finally preached his first sermon. He was not
a great speaker, but he led them in the hymns, led them
in the prayers, and there was even some jumping as a
couple of the devout were overtaken by the Holy Spirit.
A crowd had gathered, and there'd been laughter from
some of the people in the audience. She was reminded
of the old days, but she forced herself to ignore the
onlookers, like the rest of them, and they conducted
their service as if they were alone and in church. Afterward, at the time they should really have been eating,
Nikolai called out the names of the chosen ten and had
them all gather around the bench table on which he
stood.

He had picked them, he said, to help him perform *Vi
Ha Nyuch Neh Chizni Doohc.*

The Cleansing.

They had all been selected for logical reasons, and the
reasons sounded good, but she was not sure that logic
had anything to do with this. She glanced over at Vera
Afonin, but Vera didn't seem to have any problems with
the selection, and that made her feel a little better.

The minister had decided upon the Cleansing ritual
used to dispatch and exorcise murderous spirits, and they
all felt that that was appropriate.

They'd met at Nikolai's house this morning in order
to practice and prepare. The ceremony was unfamiliar
to all of them, but none had any trouble memorizing
what they were to say. It was as though the words the
minister had written out merely served to remind them
of something they already knew, and she took that as a
good sign. Nikolai had chosen correctly, and God was
with them.

They reached the front of the church, stopping before
the chest of drawers Jim had used to store his Bible and
his papers.

There was a rumble beneath the floorboards. In the
kitchen, a pot fell to the ground, clattering loudly.

How could the police not have felt this presence? No
Molokan had been inside the church since Jim's burial,
but the police had been all over it, searching in vain for
clues that they might have overlooked, and she marveled
that they could be so dense. Hadn't they sensed in the

unnatural air the existence of the entity within the building? The aura of evil was so strong that even a nonrelig-
ious man could not have helped noticing that it was here.

They began reciting the final prayer, the entreaty to
God to banish the spirit from this site—

—and spiders fell from the ceiling.

Not just a few, jarred from their perch by the rum-
bling, but a tremendous number of them, an intentional
concentration of hundreds of the creatures that dropped
from the rafters and onto their heads, onto their shoulders, onto the ground. She could see them, feel them,
running over her skin, scrambling into her hair, darting
under her clothes, the terrifying tickle of their horrid
little legs moving over intimate areas of her body, and
she wanted to scream, wanted to run away and rip off
her clothes and beat the spiders off her, but she knew
this was the devil's doing, and though it was all she could
do to maintain her concentration, she continued repeating the words of the Cleansing.

She closed her eyes, clasped her hands tightly together
as she finished the prayer. *"Svetomou, Amien."*

A wave of cold air passed over them, the spiders were
gone, and Agafia thought she saw a black, shapeless
shadow pass over the room when she opened her eyes.

They immediately started singing. A hymn. A song of
praise and thanks to the Lord, an addendum to the
Cleansing that Vera had suggested.

There was wind. Not the sort of wind that blew, but
more of a vacuum, as though the air in the church was
being drawn rather than pushed.

The breath was practically sucked out of her body.

And, as quickly as that, whatever had been here was
gone.

She breathed deeply, trying to keep on singing. Next
to her, Semyon and Peter were coughing, Semyon practically doubled over.

They finished the hymn as best they could and began
the physical cleaning of the building, the five men breaking out mops and brooms, the five women each using
individual washrags but sharing a bucket of Lysol water.
When they were through, the church looked the way it
always had when Jim was finished with it, and although

she didn't want to, Agafia started to cry. She felt
drained, both physically and emotionally, and the brief
sense of purpose that the Cleansing had given her had
fled, leaving her feeling alone and adrift. There was an
emptiness within her, and she did not think it was an
emptiness that could ever be filled or alleviated.

Nikolai put an arm around her, patted her shoulder.
"It's over," he told her.

He had no idea why she was crying, but she did not
want to tell him, and she grasped his wrinkled hand,
squeezing. "I know," she said.

But . . .

Something was wrong.

She looked around, met Vera's eyes, the eyes of the
others. The church was clean, free of spirits, but nothing
had really been accomplished and they all felt it.

All of them except Nikolai.

Whatever had killed Jim was still here—not in the
church, perhaps, but in McGuane. It had been forced
out of this building, but had taken up residence somewhere else. Rather than killing it or banishing it, they
had merely driven it out, forcing it to find a new home.

Now they didn't know where it was.

The knowledge seemed to come to them all at once,
and Vera gently explained it to the minister.

Outside, in the yard where they'd had her welcome-
home party, in what seemed a lifetime ago, they stood
next to the fence and talked in low tones. Cars and pickups passed by on the street outside, but it was as if
those things belonged in another world and they were
separated from that world by an invisible barrier.

There was no consensus on what they should do or
how they should do it. Finally it was Nikolai who said,
"We must visit Vasili."

Agafia's breath caught in her throat. "Vasili?"

The minister nodded.

The others were silent.

Vasili.

The *pra roak*. The prophet.

"Is he . . . still alive?"

This time, it was Vera who answered. "Still alive,"
she said.

Agafia shivered. If that were so, the *pra roak* would be nearly two hundred years old now. He had been well over a hundred when she was a child, supposedly over eighty when he first left Russia. He'd had a life-changing vision when he'd arrived in Mexico, and though he had spent all of his previous life as a farmer, he never picked up a plow again. He became a prophet, devoting his life completely to God, eschewing physical labor and the work of the soil for solitary contemplation of the words the Lord revealed to him. It was a hellish existence by every account, and there were many who said that he had been driven mad by having God's glory revealed to him, but the common wisdom was that this was what God *wanted* him to do, that it was for this mission that he had been born, and for generations Molokans had gone to him when there were problems in the community and questions that no one could answer.

And he had always answered.

And he had always been right.

She had met him only once, as a child, and he had terrified her so much that she had had nightmares about him for weeks afterward. It was not an experience she would ever forget.

It was not an experience she wanted to repeat.

There'd been a severe drought, and all of the crops had died. Money was low, and the Mexican government was once again threatening to take their land back. So they'd all marched out into the desert outside Guadalupe to consult the *pra roak*. They'd entered the prophet's cave, and when the old man smiled at her, wiggling his fingers, she'd screamed in terror and burst into tears.

She'd spent the rest of the time hiding behind her mother's skirt, praying for God to deliver her from this devil, and after what seemed like an eternity, they'd finally left.

The next day, the rains started.

Agafia took a deep breath, looked over at Nikolai. "Do we all have to go?" she asked.

"I think it would be best."

"I don't want to see him," she said.

The minister was understanding. "I know."

"I don't either," Vera admitted, and there was something in her voice that made Agafia's blood run cold. "None of us do." She paused. "But we have to."

They left early the next morning, Peter driving, all ten of them crammed uncomfortably into David Dalmatoff's passenger van. Peter was the youngest of them, and the best driver, but even so, his glory days were far behind him, and though she had her seat belt on, Agafia gripped the armrest tightly as the vehicle chugged up the narrow dirt road that wound up the cliff to the top of the plateau. She could see McGuane stretched out below them, through the twin arms of the canyons, sloping toward the giant, gaping pit of the mine, and the sight made her nervous. She looked away, focused for a moment on Nadya in the seat in front of her, but she could still see the passing scenery in her peripheral vision and she closed her eyes.

Once they reached the top of the plateau and were on flat ground it was better, but she still silently prayed for their safety. Peter kept wandering from side to side on the narrow lane as it wound through a series of hills, apparently oblivious to the rules of the road, and she could only hope that they did not meet up with any others on their way out to the prophet's.

Pra roak.

The prospect of seeing him again filled her with a strange, heavy dread. He was a good man, she knew, a holy man, but he scared her. He was part of the same world of the supernatural that they were fighting against, and though he was on their side, on God's side, he was still different from everyone else, still not *of* them, and he frightened her.

He was also, quite possibly, the oldest person on earth.

That scared her too.

She had no idea where Vasili was living now, but she'd assumed that it would be closer to town than it was. They drove for another full hour through barren, uninhabited desert before finally reaching the small series of rocky hills that housed the cave where he made his home.

They hadn't seen a single other vehicle since leaving

McGuane, and Peter parked the van in the center of the dirt road, confident that no one else would be coming by.

There was a walk from the road to the cave, but luckily it was short. The sun was hot and they were old, and even under the best of circumstances most of them could not climb. Thankfully, the path wound along flat ground, between saguaros and ocotillos, before sloping gently between two boulders and disappearing into a crevice in the hillside.

They walked slowly into the cave.

It opened up beyond the entrance, but though the chamber was wide, the pathway was narrow. It was a strip of sand running through piles of bones and skulls and discarded animal carcasses, and they were forced to walk single file between the piled remains, toward what looked like a campfire at the far end. None of them had thought to bring a flashlight, and they moved slowly through the middle of the chamber, each of them holding into the shoulders of the person in front as they passed through the dark area that lay between the entrance, lit by outside sunlight, and their destination, lit by the *pra roak*'s fire.

The path widened, and they could finally walk two abreast, the bones and carcasses disappearing as they approached Vasili's sleeping quarters.

Agafia's heart was pounding.

She didn't want to be here.

They did not see the prophet until they were almost upon him. He sat crouched by the fire, naked, his beard so long it covered his genitals. He was mumbling to himself, and when they drew closer, she could hear that it was scripture from the Bible.

There were all sorts of Molokan prophets. Most, over the years, had lived among them, had been normal, productive members of the community. But God had told Vasili to live alone in a cave and be naked, and so that's what he did. The ways of God were mysterious, unknowable to man, and who were any of them to judge?

The prophet kept mumbling. There were ten people standing before him, but he did not seem to notice them, or at least was not willing to acknowledge their presence, and they looked at each other uncertainly, no one quite sure how to approach the *pra roak*.

Finally, Semyon cleared his throat. "We need your help," he said loudly.

Vasili grew silent. He remained crouched, did not stand, but he looked up at them, his gaze flicking over the face of each. Agafia shivered as his eyes met hers, and he smiled at her. He still had all of his teeth, she saw, and seeing strong teeth in his wrinkled head was disturbing somehow.

On the sand next to the *pra roak* was what looked like a small village made out of sticks and stones and bits of dried cactus. Looking closer, she saw that it was McGuane. Not McGuane as it was, but McGuane as it used to be, when they'd first come here. There was a hole at one end, representing the mine, and from it stretched the other buildings, leading all the way up to Russiantown.

Nikolai took over. "We're here—" he began.

"I know."

And Vasili began to recount the story of Jim's death. It was a detailed description, filled with specific incidents none of them could have known. It had happened much the same way they'd assumed, but hearing it spelled out like this was sobering in its horror.

The prophet's Russian was hard for her to understand. Despite his appearance and reputed origins, the old man spoke in a higher-class dialect than that of the other Molokans. It was closer to Brezhnev's educated speech than Krushchev's peasant dialect, and she had to listen carefully and reorder the accented syllables in her mind before she could tell what he was talking about.

As he described the agony of Jim's last moments, she wished she could not understand him at all.

"What is causing this?" Nikolai asked when he was through. "And what can we do about it? We have performed a Cleansing— "

"There is not only one," Vasili said, and they were silent, listening to him. A distorted shadow of his crouched form flickered on the rock wall behind him in concert with the flames of the fire. "There are *many* evil

spirits in McGuane. And more are coming. The dead do
not rest well there.''

Agafia shivered. The *pra roak* looked up at her, and
she felt more than saw the unfettered intensity of his
gaze.

She heard the voice in her mind: *You have invited
them.*

She looked quickly around, but none of the others
were reacting, none of the others had heard.

This was meant only for her.

It is your fault. You have invited them.

The fact that the prophet was communicating with her
in this way, that he *could* communicate in this way, did
not surprise her, but it frightened her. No less frightening than the nature of the communication were the ideas
behind it, and she tried to think of what he meant, of
what she could possibly have done to invite these sorts
of . . . beings to McGuane.

Invite.

The word triggered an association in her mind. Perhaps she had not *invited* these spirits, but by *not* inviting
one, she had inadvertently allowed them entrance.

Jedushka di Muvedushka.

That could not be it. They had forgotten to invite the
Owner of the House when they'd moved to McGuane
and that would account for any unusual or unexplainable
events at their new home, but all of the other Molokans
had Owners protecting their houses, and there was no
way that their own lack of protection could be affecting
the entire town. The *pra roak* had to mean something
else—but she could not for the life of her figure out
what it was.

"No!" he suddenly screeched. "No!"

They jumped, all of them, Katsya letting out a little
gasped cry and clutching a hand to her breast.

Vasili was holding his ears and grimacing with pain.
It looked like he was trying to keep his head from
exploding.

Suddenly he slumped forward, toward the fire, then
seemed to catch himself. He shook his head as though
just waking up from a long nap.

"They must be stopped," he said, looking up.

"That is why we are here," Nikolai explained patiently. "We do not know what to do. Are we supposed to pray? Perform more Cleansings? What do we do?"

"God will show you."

"Has he shown *you*?" Nikolai asked. "If so, tell us. We are lost."

"God will show you," he repeated. "You will know what to do."

"What if we don't know what to do?" Agafia got up the courage to ask. She faced him. "What if God shows us, but we are too stupid to figure it out? What will happen then?"

The prophet grinned, the translucent skin of his face pulling tighter, his too-strong teeth giving his head the look of a skull. "All gone," he said, and with one sweeping arm flattened the makeshift town on the sand next to him. His beard swung to the side as he moved and she saw his wrinkled, shriveled genitals. "All gone."

They were silent on the trip home, each of them thinking individually about what Vasili had said, about what his words and warnings meant.

That was the trouble with prophets. They had to be interpreted.

Agafia closed her eyes, thought about the meeting.

The McGuane he had destroyed with his hand was already gone.

All gone.

Had he meant by that that the Molokan community in McGuane would be destroyed, the community that had been born when the town really had looked like his model? Or had he meant that the *existing* town would be somehow turned to rubble? Had he meant that there would be some sort of earthquake or disaster, or that spirits would somehow bring about the destruction?

It was impossible to tell, and that's what was so frustrating. She considered asking Vera, seeing if the old woman had any ideas or any feelings about this, but Vera was already dead asleep in the back of the van.

Agafia was tired, too. Tired not just physically but mentally, spiritually. Living seemed like such an effort, the energy required to get through a single day almost

too much to bear. Would she had felt the same way if
she was still back in California, she wondered, if she had
not agreed to leave L.A. and come with Gregory? She
did not know, but Los Angeles seemed far away now,
part of another life, and she could not imagine leading
that life again.

Was she ready to die?

She might have been, but it was her grandchildren
that kept her going, that supplied what little spark of
meaning she had in her life. She sensed that they needed
her, and though there was no evidence of that, she felt
it in her bones and knew it to be true, and that was
what enabled her to keep on living.

It is your fault. You have invited them.

She'd been avoiding that, trying not to think about it.
Vasili had said no more to her, either verbally or in her
head, and the entire meeting, the entire experience, had
been so strange and dreamlike that already the reality
of it was fading, the sharp edges blurring in her mind.

But the emotional impact of it had not lessened. And
that was how she knew it was real, that was why she
knew it had actually happened. The fear she'd felt was
still inside her and could be recalled at any time.

Had he spoken to the others that way as well? Had
they all heard voices in their heads? She didn't know,
but somehow she didn't think so. She'd looked around
at that moment, and everyone else's attention had been
focused on the external reality of the old man crouched
next to the fire. None of them appeared to have been
hearing any inner voices.

Why had she been chosen?

Was it really her fault?

She didn't know. She glanced around the van at her
fellow passengers, her fellow parishioners, her friends.
She felt guilty for not telling them everything, for not
telling them about what the *pra roak* had said, but she
felt guiltier for what she'd done, for forgetting to invite
the Owner of the House, and now she was too embarrassed to tell them the truth. Especially at this late date.
If she'd been honest with Jim from the very beginning,
perhaps he could have thought of some way to counter-
act or counterbalance her mistake, perhaps it all could

have been avoided. He had known a lot more about
rituals and traditions and ceremonies than anyone else,
and it was possible that he could have come up with
an idea.

But it was here and it was now and all they could do
was deal with it.

Besides, when it came right down to it, despite what
the prophet had told her, she didn't really believe that
it was because they had not invited Jedushka di Muvedushka that all of this was happening. The Owner might
have been able to protect their house from evil spirits,
but that had no bearing on what was happening elsewhere in McGuane.

It wasn't her fault, she told herself again.

But she could not make herself believe it.

3

Scott woke up early on Saturday and had two cold
cinnamon Pop Tarts for breakfast, washing them down
with the dregs of his dad's coffee. His parents were gone
already, off on their usual weekend rounds of McGuane
garage sales, and he was once again on his own.

He watched cartoons while he ate, then dumped his cup
and plate in the sink and took his dad's 35-millimeter camera from the closet where it had been gathering dust
since their last trip to Disneyland. It still had film in it,
but the counter had broken and he didn't know how
many pictures were left.

One would be enough if everything went perfectly,
but things hardly ever did, and he hoped there was at
least half a roll to go. He pressed the "Test" button on
the attached flash. It worked, and he turned off the TV,
locked up the house, got his bike out from the backyard,
and pedaled over to Adam's place.

Their family's van was gone when he arrived, and
though the house looked empty, he checked to make
sure anyway. He knocked on the door, waited, knocked
on the door, waited, but there was no answer, and after
the sixth round of knocks he gave up. He'd told Adam
ahead of time that he was coming over this morning,

but obviously his friend wasn't home. Maybe he'd been corralled into some family outing, suckered into going on a hike or a shopping trip or something.

Maybe he really *hadn't* wanted to help him.

Scott hadn't actually considered that before. He knew *Dan* was uncomfortable with the idea of taking photos of the bathhouse, but he hadn't taken Adam's mild objections seriously, and now he found himself wondering if *both* of his friends weren't afraid of the small building.

No, he told himself. Adam went there all the time. Alone. It was spooky, but it was cool, and there was a slight prickle at the back of his neck as he hopped back on his bike and pedaled around the side of the house and across the property toward the hill.

The bathhouse.

He saw it against the background of the old burned-out home as he emerged from the copse of paloverdes and stopped.

The day was bright, the sun high in the sky, but suddenly he was not so sure he wanted to go through with this. The idea was a winner, and he had no doubt that he would be able to sell any pictures he took, but he thought that maybe he should wait until Adam was here or at least someone was home at Adam's house before trying to take any photos.

He did not want to go into the bathhouse alone.

That's what it came down to.

He leaned his bike against a tree trunk and walked slowly through the jumble of boulders toward the small adobe structure. There were no birds here, he noticed. This area was completely silent, the only sounds the crunching of his tennis shoes on the ground. He took the lens cap off the camera as he walked, turned on the flash. Maybe he could just take the pictures quickly and then get out of here as fast as possible.

He approached the bathhouse, feeling nervous. He'd been too glib before, too flippant in his attitude. Dan was right. There *was* something here.

Of course there was something here. That's why he'd come to take pictures.

But it was evil, he thought now. It was not merely weird and interesting and *X-Files*-ish. It was not just a freakish occurrence to be exploited. There was something wrong and profoundly unnatural about what lay inside that little building, and he was suddenly cowed, intimidated by its presence.

Maybe he should just forget about the whole thing.

No, he'd come this far, he might as well go through with it. Because, after this, he certainly wouldn't be brave enough to come back and try it again.

After this, he didn't plan *ever* to come back here again.

He shivered as a tingle of fear shot down his spine, but there was something exciting about it. It was exhilarating as well as frightening, and that extra rush of adrenaline gave him the courage to walk across the last few feet of ground and up to the bathhouse.

He stood in the doorway, aimed the camera. It was too dark inside the building for him to see anything— the scene in the viewfinder was completely black—but he pointed the camera toward where he knew the shadow of the man was and pressed the shutter. There was a blinding overwhelming strobe of light, then darkness once again.

He stepped back. He thought he'd seen something in the flash. Movement. It had been quick, almost too quick to see, but it had been there. He was sure of it. A quicksilver flow of shadow from one place to another.

Heart pounding, he leaned forward, took another picture.

Again, movement.

Movement and flesh.

Yes. This time he'd seen skin. Someone naked, sitting on a bench.

Someone waiting for a steam bath.

He should run, he thought, leave, get the hell out of here. It would take only a few seconds to reach his bike, then he'd be gone, speeding away. He already had two pictures. He'd gotten what he came for.

But he had to know what was in there. He could not leave without seeing this through.

This'll make a great story at school, a foolishly brave part of him thought.

It gave him the strength to go on.

He took another picture.

Once more, something was illuminated by the flash. Something he could not see on his own. The scene was more complicated this time, and he had the impression that there were several people in there.

People?

No. Not people.

It was completely silent in the bathhouse, and the phrase "the silence of the grave" popped into his mind. He didn't know where he'd heard it before, but he backed slowly away from the door, peering into the darkness, trying desperately to make out any shapes inside the room, but the light seemed to die immediately after crossing the threshold, and nothing could be made out.

He wanted to take one more photo, give it one last shot, but this time he stayed away from the door and pointed the camera in the general direction, not bothering to look through the viewfinder.

He saw flesh and shadows, movement more fluid than anything on this earth, and, overseeing everything, on the back wall, the figure of the Russian man.

He ran.

He'd reached the end of the film anyway, and the camera's automatic rewind was whirring. Several long strides brought him to the paloverde tree against which he'd leaned his bike. He hopped on it and took off, not looking back.

I got it! he thought as he pedaled furiously, leaping the ruts and holes in the path. *I got it!*

He did not slow down until he was off Adam's road and downtown. He took the film out of the camera and dropped it off at the 1-Hour Photo next to the video store.

He went back home and put the camera away, turning on the television and watching *Scooby Doo*, trying desperately not to think of what he'd seen and waiting in vain for his fear-accelerated heart rate to slow.

After an hour that seemed like a day and a series of cartoons that seemed to make no linear sense, Scott raided the sock drawer where his dad stored the loose change he collected, snagged five dollars' worth of quarters, and hoping that would be enough, took off on his bike for the 1-Hour Photo.

He waited until he was outside the store and alone on the sidewalk before ripping open the package and sorting through the pictures. Disneyland . . . Disneyland . . . Disneyland . . . the beach . . .

The bathhouse.

He stopped, looked at the photo.

The picture began to slide through his suddenly sweaty fingers, but he gripped it tighter as he stared at a scene that did not exist. He recognized the door frame at the top of the photograph, but inside he saw neither the abandoned, neglected wreck that Adam had taken them through nor the creepy world of moving shadows that he'd almost seen in the flash illumination.

He saw a bunch of fat old people sitting naked on benches.

It was nothing he had expected, and he flipped to the next photograph.

Same thing.

The next.

The same.

He frowned at the last picture. The creepy ambiguity of the half-illuminated flash scene was nowhere in evidence. There was nothing remotely mysterious about the shot. About any of them. The scene was clear and well lit—two fat old couples, the men with towels around their waists, the women with towels around their waists and upper bodies. They were all sweating, though the photos showed no steam, and they appeared to be tired, the two women leaning back, eyes closed, the men leaning forward, with grimaces of discomfort on their faces. The back wall, he noticed, was clear. No ghostly shadow.

Maybe these people were ghosts.

Maybe. But somehow that didn't seem right. They seemed too . . . real. These people were not spirits. They were flesh and blood. He could see the ugly mole on one man's thigh, the sagging arm muscles of the heavier woman. It was too concrete, this scene, too specific. It was as if he had taken a photograph of a real event—only that event had not been the one before the camera in real life.

What had happened?

He'd taken pictures of the past!

It was the only logical explanation, and he quickly sorted through the bathhouse photos once again. He saw now the anachronistic hairdos and somehow old-timey faces of the women, the way the men looked more foreign than any Molokan he'd ever seen.

These were not just pictures of a spooky shadow. This was a miracle. These photos were worth way more than he'd ever hoped they could be. He shoved them back into the package and hopped on his bike, pedaling straight home. He was no longer scared. He was excited, tremendously excited, more excited than he had ever been in his life, and the first thing he did was immediately call Adam, but though he let the phone ring twenty times, no one answered.

Could they repeat this? he wondered. If they took more pictures of the inside of the bathhouse, would they get other scenes of other people, other times? He was eager to try it out, and he picked up the package and opened it up again, taking out the photos.

They were different.

His heart jumped, and he suddenly felt like he was back at the bathhouse, the fear in him so strong it was almost overpowering.

The people were seated in different spots, facing different directions. They were the same fat old men and women, but whereas before they'd been sitting together like husband and wife, now the two men were seated next to each other and the two women were on the opposite bench.

One of the women was smiling into the camera.

She no longer had a towel on.

He could see everything and it was gross. She was hairy and disgusting, and there were rolls of fat hanging down almost everywhere.

He dropped the photos, scared.

Even on the floor, the pictures creeped him out. All but one of the bathhouse photos had fallen facedown, but in that one he could still see the old lady's inappropriate smile. He backed away from them.

He was still clutching the package, and on impulse he

opened it and pulled out the negatives, searching quickly through them.

The ones from the bathhouse were blank.

He was having a hard time catching his breath. Something was going on here that he did not understand but that frightened him to the core. The near-euphoria he'd experienced only moments before at his discovery had curdled into terror, and he wanted nothing more than to be through with all this, to be safe and secure back in his normal old life. He would give up money and fame forever if he could just get rid of these pictures.

He considered leaving them where they were and letting his dad take care of them when he came home, but he knew he could not do that. He wanted to protect his parents from this. He did not want them to know anything about it. He wanted to keep it from Adam and Dan, too. He didn't want *anyone* to know about what had happened.

He stared down at the photos on the ground. He was afraid to touch them, afraid to be anywhere near them, but he knew he had to get rid of the pictures, and he reached down, scooped them up, and ran to the kitchen sink, where he dumped them in. Their vacation photos were mixed up in there, too, but they were probably contaminated as well, and if he got rid of all the evidence, his parents would never miss them. They'd probably forgotten they still had film in the camera anyway.

He dumped the negatives into the sink as well.

He half expected the photographs to leap up, to start moving, to try and escape, to make noises, to do something in order to stop him, but nothing unusual happened as he pulled open a drawer, took out a soup ladle, and used the big spoon to herd the pictures over to the drain mouth and shove them into the garbage disposal.

He turned on the water, turned on the disposal.

A sense of relief coursed through him as he heard the grinding, as he saw the little flecks of paper that spit out from the drain mouth as the disposal chewed up the pictures.

He turned off the garbage disposal, took the 1-Hour Photo package in which the pictures and negatives had come, and shoved it down there as well.

He turned the disposal back on.

"Hey," his mom said behind him. "What're you doing?"

He turned to see his parents walking in, carrying sacks of junk they'd bought at the garage sales. He flipped off the disposal switch. "I was going to clean the breakfast dishes," he lied. He was aware that his voice sounded too high, and he knew that he was sweating profusely. His heart was still pounding crazily in his chest.

"You don't have to do that," his mother told him. "I'll get them."

"Okay," he said, backing away.

His dad frowned at him. "Is something wrong? You look a little funny."

"No," he said. "I'm fine. Everything's fine."

Twelve

1

They were alone at the bar. Paul had just left to pick up his car from Henry's Automotive, where Henry Travis had charged him an arm and a leg for simply flushing out the cooling system, something Odd told him he would've done for free, but Gregory and Odd had decided to stay for an extra round of drinks.

There were no other customers today, and even the bartender was keeping his distance, giving them privacy, pretending to be wiping glasses at the far end of the counter.

Gregory had had three beers already and was feeling pretty good, but when he glanced over at Odd, his mood faltered. The old man was looking into his beer, not drinking, and the expression on his face made Gregory feel uneasy.

"What is it?" he asked.

Odd shook his head.

"What?"

"Nothing."

"Something."

"You don't want to—"

"Yes, I do," Gregory told him.

There was a pause. "People are talking," Odd said finally.

"About what?"

"You. Your family."

Gregory could feel his face tighten. "What about us?"

"These . . . deaths didn't start happening until you all moved into town."

"That's ridiculous." But his heart was pounding.

"I know it is, I know it is. But the timing's there. And you know how superstitious these yokels are. Someone noticed that Loretta Nelson's murder over at the realty office happened about the same time you bought your place in town, and it probably spread from there. And Chilton Bodean was the capper. Everyone knows you two weren't exactly pals and that you threatened to beat the shit out of him." He lowered his voice. "Hell, the bartender saw it."

"Come on. I saw him that one time since I moved back. And you were with me."

"I know."

"Besides, he stabbed himself."

"But he stabbed himself because he had another peeder growing outta his belly button. That's not a normal everyday occurrence."

"And that's my fault, too?"

"I'm not saying it is. All I'm saying is that people are talking. They're saying that even if you didn't do anything on purpose, maybe you brought this weird shit with you. Part of it's probably those old anti-Molokan feelings creeping out. But you gotta admit that there's some strange stuff been happening here lately."

Gregory's face felt flushed.

"I debated whether to tell you or not, but I figured you wouldn't hear it from no one else . . ."

"Paul's not—" he began.

"Hell, no!" Odd looked at him. "Your friends are your friends. You can count on that. And this is probably nothing. It's probably just a few people and it'll blow over before long." He took a long drink of beer. "Maybe I shouldn't've even opened my stupid mouth."

"No," Gregory told him. "No, I'm glad you did."

"Just forget about it."

"So they don't think me or my family did anything. We didn't murder anybody. We're just . . . the cause of it somehow."

"I told you they're superstitious."

"But why blame us? What about the Megans?"

"There's talk about that, too. Maybe it's your house. Maybe you activated it or it activated you or something.

Some type of chemical reaction." He shook his head. "I told you you should've gone after Call, gotten a new place instead. Hell, maybe you still can. I'm not sure what the statute of limitations is on something like that, but if he sold you your home under false pretenses—"

"No."

"Well, just forget about it, then."

"What do *you* think?" Gregory asked.

Odd squirmed in his seat. "Don't matter what I think."

"Odd . . ."

The old man sighed. "I seen a lot of things over the years. This ain't no murderer or serial killer. I know that."

"But do you think I'm involved? Or my family?"

"Oh, hell, no. I know better'n that. But . . ." He took a deep breath. "It ain't inconceivable that your house is somewhere down in the mix." He downed the rest of his beer in one huge gulp. "McGuane's a funny place. Not funny ha-ha, but funny strange. I seen things myself over the years, heard about a lot more. But lately it's sort of . . . turned nasty. People are getting killed, and that scares me. There's probably not one reason for it all, no single thing that's the cause of it, but it's happening, and I understand why people are looking for easy answers."

"You don't think there's an easy answer."

"I don't know if there's a hard answer. I don't know if there's any answer. You know that saying, 'Shit happens'? That's kind of how I look at it. Shit happens, and the best thing to do is just stay out of the way." He took a five-dollar bill from his pocket, placed it on the bar. "That's why I'd get out of that house if I were you. A lot of people died there, and that can't be good."

Odd got off his stool, patted Gregory's shoulder. "I gotta go," he said. "Lurlene'll kill me if I'm late. We'll talk about this tomorrow."

Gregory nodded, watched the old man walk out of the bar. He picked up Odd's five, then took out some bills of his own and walked down to the end of the counter to pay the tab. He handed the money to the bartender, but he didn't like the look on the other man's face. It reminded him of the nearly identical expressions on the faces of the men who had berated his father outside this very building—

Milk drinker

—and he considered taking back the tip he'd included, but he knew he was probably reading meanings into things that weren't there because of his conversation with Odd, and so he just smiled, nodded, and left.

He walked back to the café, where his van was parked.

When he got home, Gregory headed straight into the kitchen, found the bottle of aspirin in the cupboard next to Julia's vitamins, and popped two tablets. He had one big bastard of a headache, and he closed his eyes against the pain, willing the aspirin to work faster. It seemed like he had a headache every time he walked into this damn house lately, and he wondered if he wasn't allergic to something in here. Maybe there was something wrong with the insulation, or the cleanser or furniture spray they used was affecting him. Maybe it was one of Julia's new drought-resistant plants. He didn't know, but the headaches were starting to become a pattern, and that was a pattern he wanted to break.

The stress from what Odd had told him could not have helped, and maybe that was why the headache today was so much stronger than usual.

He walked into the living room, flipped on the TV, lay down on the couch, and closed his eyes.

The headaches made him irritable, and he realized that he'd been a little hard on Julia and his mother and the kids lately. He didn't mean to take anything out on them, and he vowed that tonight he would be cheerful. He wouldn't let any headache or allergy get the best of him, would not get angry with anyone for anything.

But later that evening Teo started fighting with Adam, playing with the remote control and speeding through television channels, running back and forth between the living room and the kitchen, and he ended up yelling at her and sending her to her room. Julia thought he overreacted, but she didn't say anything until they were in bed, and then *they* wound up getting into a fight. They'd been having a lot of fights lately, and he was getting tired of it, and then they started fighting about *that*.

Julia finally refused to respond to his increasingly angry arguments, and she pulled the blanket up around her neck and turned away from him, facing the other direction.

He was sorely tempted to go downstairs and sleep on the couch. That would teach her a lesson. They'd never slept apart in all the years they'd been married, had made a pact after their first fight that they would always try to resolve their differences before bedtime and never sleep separately, but tonight he would have moved down to the couch had his mother and the kids not been here. It would be too difficult to explain to them, though, and he pulled up his own side of the blanket, turned away from her, and closed his eyes until he finally fell asleep.

2

Julia wandered through the ruins of Russiantown.

She did not know what had compelled her to come here, why she had walked all this way to look at a bunch of abandoned shacks, but ever since Paul and Deanna had led them on the walk through McGuane she hadn't stopped thinking about this place.

She peeked into the open doorway of a one-room house with no roof, saw a collection of rusted tin cans lined up in what remained of an open cabinet, saw clumps of dead dried weeds poking through missing sections of floor. There was no furniture in the tiny shack, just as there'd been no furniture in most of the abandoned houses she'd looked through, and she chose to believe that families had taken their belongings with them when they'd moved to better homes.

Several of the buildings were no longer standing, were nothing but cement foundations and stumps of charred beam, and she could not help wondering when the fires had occurred. She'd asked Gregory's mother about Russiantown, but the old woman had not wanted to talk about the subject. There was an element of denial or cover-up in her refusal to speak, even after all these

years, that made Julia think that something bad had happened here.

What was it that Paul had said? There'd been problems in the past? That was vague enough to cover a
multitude of sins.

She was surprised that Gregory wasn't more conver-
sant with the specifics of Molokan history in McGuane,
but she knew how secretive her own parents had always
been about their past, and she understood how it could
happen. She'd had a friend in college, Janet Yoshizumi,
whose parents had been interned at Manzanar during
World War II, and she recalled how Janet had said that
they never discussed their internment, that they refused
to talk about it and chose to pretend that it hadn't
happened.

Was that what had happened here? Something so bad
that no one wanted to talk about it?

She was probably romanticizing what was no doubt a
very ordinary, very prosaic chapter in local history, but
unanswered questions invited that sort of speculation.

She could go to the library, she thought, see if she
could find some information about Russiantown.

No. She'd rather not know than have to see Marge
and her pals again.

She stepped over a small prickly pear and walked over
to the next empty house.

It was strange how interested she'd become in not just
Russiantown but all things Molokan since they'd moved
here. She'd never understood the fascination some people seemed to have for their roots, their ethnic background, and she'd always dismissed as trendy and self-
absorbed those women who tried to track down distant
relatives in distant lands or who spent money on classes
to learn the languages and cultures of the nations their
ancestors had left behind. But she was beginning to understand that connection to the past. She herself had
been feeling more Russian since they'd moved here. She
was not sure if it was because Gregory's mother was
living with them, or because everything was so personal-
ized and community-conscious in a small town compared
to the anonymous individuality of life in a metropolitan

area, but it was as if her American veneer was cracking, gradually revealing the Russian beneath.

Maybe the fact that she wasn't feeling as close to Gregory as before had something to do with it, the fact that their relationship was no longer there to support her against the influences of the outside world.

She couldn't sustain her lifelong rebellion against Molokan culture knowing she did not have him to lean on.

They'd been fighting a lot lately, and sometimes it felt as though they were two strangers living in the same house rather than a couple who had been together for eighteen years. She'd never believed those dire warnings that money could ruin a person's life, attributing their origin to the rich who wanted to keep the poor content with their lot by pretending that it was *better* not to have money, that poverty was somehow morally superior to wealth.

And, truth be told, it wasn't money that had changed their lives.

It was moving to McGuane.

Although they'd been able to move to McGuane only because they'd won the lottery.

She peeked in a back window of a big house, saw the rusted skeleton of an old bed, the rotted wood of what had probably been a vanity. On one remaining wall hung the top three sides of an empty frame, glittering shattered glass visible in the pile of dirt and dust beneath it.

Deep down, she wished they'd never left California. Or at least that they'd moved somewhere else. New England, perhaps. Or the Pacific Northwest.

Anywhere but Arizona.

She did not like this house, and rather than peek in one of the other windows or walk inside, she headed up a rocky path behind it, past the crumbling walls of a *banya*, to a building that looked like it had once been a store or a place of business. She stood for a moment with her hands on her hips, sizing it up. It was definitely not a house, and though there were cracks and rock holes in the dust-covered windows, the glass was still there for the most part, and she cupped her hands on the sides of her eyes and peered inside. She saw a lean-

ing desk, an overturned chair, what looked like a broken safe.

She was in the approximate center of Russiantown
right now, and she took the opportunity to look around
at the empty shacks, the burnt and crumbling buildings.

There were ghosts here.

The thought came unbidden. She tried to tell herself
that she was thinking of ghosts in the most mainstream,
literary sense—as a synonym for memories or history—
but that was not true and she knew it. She was thinking
of literal ghosts, real ghosts, and even though it was
broad daylight and she could hear the sounds of children
playing at the grammar school, could see down the canyon the roofs and top stories of the business district, she
felt isolated enough that the thought frightened her.

Ghosts.

She looked around, aware all of a sudden how many
rooms there were in the empty structures surrounding
her, how many places there were to hide, how many left-
behind relics of lives remained in the abandoned husks
of these buildings.

Was that why she was here?

Had she been *lured*?

She thought of the noises at night, the box that had
fallen in the kitchen. Ghosts had been in the back of
her mind ever since that first week. She was surprised
that she had not thought about this earlier, when she'd
first arrived. After all, this was a ghost town. Wasn't it
logical for ghosts to be here?

There was nothing logical about ghosts, and for all her
vaunted rationalism and intelligence, she found herself
spooked, no pun intended. The fact that she'd been
thinking about Russiantown, that she'd felt herself
drawn here, was more than a little disturbing, and, as
much as she hated to do so, she started to see a pattern
in what before had seemed to her merely a series of
random coincidences.

She was reminded of the tag line for a movie.

Out here, she thought, no one could hear her scream.

Of course, that was not strictly true. She could hear
the voices of children from the school, and she could
probably be heard down there as well, but she knew that

even her loudest scream would be only a muffled chirp
to anyone downtown.

If, that is, they were listening.

She could die here and no one would know.

Julia shivered. She was no longer quite so interested
in exploring the empty buildings of Russiantown, and
she turned and started back down the path the way
she'd come.

There was movement to her right, and her attention
was drawn in that direction, but whatever it was had
already disappeared behind a *banya*. She told herself it
was a cat or a dog, *hoped* it was a cat or a dog, but she
knew that the figure she'd caught in her peripheral vision
was bigger than that.

Movement again. This time ahead and to the right.

She saw a child dash from one shack to another, heard
it laugh . . . but the laugh was that of an old man, not
a young kid, and the juxtaposition was shocking.

Heard *it* laugh?

Yes. For she'd sensed even in that moment, even with
just that brief glimpse, that it was not a boy, not a girl,
but . . . something else.

Her skin was covered with goose bumps, her pulse
was racing. She was afraid to go forward, afraid to return
down the same path on which she'd come. She decided
to take a detour, an alternate route back to the road,
glancing frantically about all the while to make sure that
the child—or whatever it was—did not pop out at her.

She passed a shack with a detached and dilapidated
front porch, heard a strange scuttling noise from inside.

Her heart lurched in her chest.

A little face peered out at her from a broken, dirt-
smeared window.

She screamed, and the face faded, disappearing into
the darkness of the shack.

There was the laughter again, the old-man laughter,
and she backed quickly but carefully away, keeping her
eyes on the window. The face did not reappear, but the
sight stayed with her. The features had been unclear
behind the dirty glass, but she had the impression that
the eyes, nose, and mouth were scrunched too close to-

gether, that there was something horrid and aberrant about the small figure.

Again, she was acutely conscious of how far away from the occupied part of McGuane Russiantown was.

It was playing with her, she thought, whatever it was, it was after her. She took off running, no longer looking for the figure, no longer trying to hide from it, but prepared to knock it over or run around it or even jump over it if it popped out at her. She would do whatever she had to in order to avoid it, but she was determined to get out of Russiantown as fast as possible, as quickly as her legs would carry her.

She thought she saw the figure again, in a hole in the adobe wall of a *banya*, but the face looked older, and she did not stop to think about or acknowledge it but simply kept running, finally reaching the dirt road and jumping over the small ditch, running toward downtown McGuane.

Behind her, again, the laughter.

Her chest hurt and she could not seem to suck in enough air to fill her lungs, but she forced her legs to keep pumping and did not slow down until she reached an occupied neighborhood, where an old woman watering her roses outside, smiled at her and told her to slow down before she had a heart attack.

3

She sat in the *banya* with the body of the cat on her lap.

"Teo."

She felt warm and tingly as she heard the *banya*'s voice. It seemed to echo through her, the words being absorbed into her body, into her bones.

"Teo."

"I brought you a present," Teo said. She looked down at the tabby's matted fur. She had killed it herself. She'd found it wandering through their yard yesterday and had picked it up. She'd petted it, talked to it, carried it down the path—and then thrown it down as hard as she could onto a boulder, smashing its head.

She'd poured dirt into the wounds to stop the blood and had hidden the cat under some leaves so it could dry.

She'd come back today and picked it up.

It was the biggest thing she'd ever brought here, and she knew that the *banya* would be grateful. The *banya* had devoured everything she had brought so far—the bird, the mice, the chipmunk—and it had grown stronger as a result. There was a new energy in here now, and even though the building still looked abandoned, it had started to clean itself up. The benches were fixed and set up against the wall the way they should be. The bones were mostly gone.

She had always liked coming here, but she enjoyed it even more now. She felt at home in this room. Accepted, wanted, appreciated.

The *banya* was her friend.

The *banya* was her *only* friend, and she did not know what she would do without it. She could let out all her frustrations in here, describe all of her problems, scream, cry, throw a tantrum, and it was always there for her. It never told her what to do, never made judgments, never bossed her around.

It listened.

And understood.

Teo took the cat off her lap, set the stiff body down in the dirt. "Here you go," she said.

She watched the cat's body with anticipation. She no longer had to leave while the *banya* ate. It let her watch now, let her see it devour food, and she felt a thrill of excitement pass through her as the shadow came down from the far wall, as it broke up into long, swirling segments and the familiar cold-yet-pleasurable wind began to blow. The body of the cat lifted almost imperceptibly off the floor, swathed in shadow, and then it began to disappear. In pieces. The left ear was gone. The right rear paw. The tail. A section of stomach. The head.

There was no noise—it was like being in a place where sound could not penetrate—but there was a lot of movement, and as the shadows touched her skin, her arm, her cheeks, she laughed. It tickled.

In less than a minute, the cat was gone.

"Good," the *banya* said. *"So good."*

She smiled, feeling pleased.

She was glad she could do something for the *banya*—because the *banya* had done so much for her. It had promised to help her, and help her it had. She still had no friends, the other kids still refused to talk to her, but no one was making fun of her anymore. The *banya* had given her . . . something, and the other kids in her class seemed to sense it. They stayed away, afraid of her, and that was good. She no longer had to spend her recesses in the classroom with the teacher, hiding. She strode bravely and proudly through the playground, doing whatever she wanted, and though she had to do it by herself, she didn't really mind. Just knowing that she was not alone, just knowing that she had the *banya*, gave her the confidence to be herself, allowed her to shrug off criticism and not worry about what other kids said or thought or did.

Of course, Mary Kay and Kim hated her more than ever. They did not trip her or push her down like they used to, but she sensed the hatred and resentment building in them, and she thought that eventually they would probably try to get back at her somehow, do something to her.

If only she could get them first. If only she could beat them to the punch.

The *banya* seemed to know what she was thinking, because it gave her a comforting breath of warm, sweet-smelling air.

She smiled.

"It is time," the *banya* said.

She blinked. "What?"

She thought she heard the sounds of a playground, thought she heard Mary Kay's voice singing, "I see England, I see France, I see Teo's underpants!"

"It is time," the *banya* repeated.

And she understood.

Going out to morning recess, Teo was bumped by Kim, but when she said, "Watch it!" Kim just kept running, pretending it was an accident.

She stared after the other girl. Apparently whatever

immunity her newfound confidence had given her had worn off and she was once again in for some teasing and torture.

She walked out to the playground. That's okay, she thought. The *banya* would show them.

But how? she wondered. Was she supposed to lure the girls over to the bathhouse, trick them into going inside?

The thought came to her, unbidden, that she was supposed to present the girls to the *banya* the way she had the bird, the mice, the chipmunk, the cat. As an offering.

Was she supposed to kill them?

The idea stopped her cold. There was no way she would do that, no way she *could* do that, and for the first time, it occurred to her that maybe the *banya* wasn't really her friend, that there was something wrong with it. It was trying to make her do things she shouldn't do, things she didn't want to do, and in a burst of clarity, she understood that it was not normal, not right, for her to sit in a bathhouse and talk to it, to bring it dead animals.

She thought about what had happened. She had not just picked up the bodies of dead animals and fed them to the *banya*. She'd actually killed a cat herself, had murdered a little kitty, and tears welled up in her eyes as she realized what she'd done. It was as if she'd been hypnotized or something and had suddenly awakened, and she looked back at what had happened and was horrified.

Now the *banya* expected her to bring girls home and kill them?

She heard its voice, faintly, as if carried over a distance.

"No," it said smoothly. *"No, Teo."*

The voice made her stop, pushed all those negative thoughts out of her head. She stood there listening to the faint words of the *banya*, and her doubts fled, her faith was restored. The *banya was* her friend, she realized, and it told her that it was going to punish the girls who had tormented her, that it was going to make them pay.

But they would simply be taught a lesson, the bathhouse told her. No one would be seriously hurt.

And then the birds came.

They swooped down from previously clear skies, a living black cloud. They were the same type of bird that she'd fed to the *banya*, and they buzzed the heads of the kids on the playground. Boys jumped out of swings and off slides, girls fled hopscotch and tetherball courts. The birds were shrieking, and it was like a scene out of that old movie. The teachers monitoring the playground were simultaneously trying to scare off the birds and yelling for the children to head for cover.

The birds were followed by mice and chipmunks.

The birds were still there, above, but on the ground chipmunks and mice raced out from the field, swarming beneath the playground equipment, dashing between the feet of the panicking students and the screaming staff.

Teo looked around, searching out faces she knew. Kids were crying, running, not just heading back to the classrooms but darting about in all directions, trying to avoid the birds and get away from the rodents on the ground. She finally found Mary Kay, and a thrill of vindication coursed through her as the bratty girl stumbled and fell, sobbing while other kids tripped over her and fell on top of her. She also picked out Kim and two of Kim's friends and was gratified to see them stranded atop the monkey bars, swatting their own heads as they tried to keep the birds away.

A tabby cat walked through the melee, oblivious. It ignored the mice, making a beeline for her. Teo looked down at the animal, and the cat looked back at her. It meowed softly, rubbed against her legs.

She picked the cat up, petted it.

Standing alone, next to the drinking fountains, untouched by everything, Teo smiled.

Thirteen

1

Sunday.

It was the third week in a row that they'd tried to perform a Cleansing for the entire town, one that would exorcise once and for all the unseen beings that had invaded this place. They stood in the empty church, the ten of them, holding hands, praying. All of the other parishioners had gone home, and the pots and pans and dishes and cups and spoons had all been washed and put away, the leftover food placed in the refrigerator. All of the tablecloths and napkins were in Nikolai's car, ready to be taken to the laundromat and washed.

The dying sun shone orange through the west windows, creating long shadows in the empty room. They continued the ceremonies, but no matter how many words they repeated, no matter how earnestly they wanted this to work, their efforts were in vain. The church remained clean, free of spirits—they had successfully cleared and protected it—but though they once again prayed and sang, performing virtually every Molokan exorcism ritual known, it seemed to have no effect on the rest of the town. There were no accompanying signs of either success or failure as they worked, not even a slight drop in temperature, and if Agafia had not known better, she would have thought that McGuane was clean, that there was nothing here.

But there was.

The *pra roak* had been right. There were spirits everywhere, demons all around. They could all feel them, could sense their growing presence, and periodically one of their own would be provided with proof:

Vera Afonin. She came home after last Sunday's services to find that all of the furniture in her house had been rearranged, placed in its opposite location, so that it looked like she was walking into the mirror version of her home.

Peter Potapov. For a full day, all of the taps at his house disgorged urine rather than water.

Alexander Nadelashin. Control of his car was wrested from him, the steering wheel in his hand turning of its own accord, forcing him to bump into and damage six other cars on his way down the street.

The attacks had all been relatively harmless, mischievous even, but outside the church, outside their circle, in the rest of the town, that had not been the case. No one had been killed recently, and there'd been no specific news of anything in the paper, but rumor had it that the man who owned the auto parts store had died of a heart attack after seeing something in his store, something that had subsequently disappeared, leaving behind only a gelatinous puddle in the middle of the floor.

Things were going on that nobody could explain, and no one knew how to defend against such an assault. Agafia and the other Molokans hoped that faith would protect them, that the Lord would keep them safe from harm and put a stop to it all, but so far their prayers had not been answered. It was a distinct possibility that they were being tested, that God was allowing this to occur in order to see their reactions. Which made it doubly important for them to maintain their faith.

That was Nikolai's position, and Vera's, but Agafia was not sure she believed it. Not only did she not believe God would be so deliberately cruel and unfeeling, but there was a seriousness in all this that made her think it was more than just a test, that it had a definite purpose and goal. She did not know what that could be, but she did not believe it involved God's complicity. She was frightened, but she vowed to do everything within her power to put a stop to it and to prevent the catastrophe that the prophet had predicted.

The *pra roak*.

It is your fault.

She did not believe herself guilty, thought that that part of the prophecy was wrong, but she bought into the rest of it and was willing to take responsibility for fixing the problem. And even the remote possibility of her involvement made her that much more determined to find an answer—and a solution.

They stopped praying, let go of each others' hands, began singing a hymn, but there was no real enthusiasm for the music, no feeling put into the song. They knew already that this Cleansing had failed too, and their discouragement was audible in their singing.

Afterward, they did not even address the subject, did not even mention it. They were all frustrated and disheartened, and, saying good-bye, they took their leave.

It was Semyon who drove her home, and she was afraid that he would want to talk about the old days, would bring up things she did not want to discuss, but they were mercifully silent with each other on the trip back to the house, and they parted with polite, formal farewells.

That night she dreamed of Jim.

The minister was young, the way he'd looked when she first met him, and he was kneeling before a statue of what looked like Jedushka Di Muvedushka. He was mumbling to himself, praying, but it was not Russian, was not English, was not Spanish, was not any language she could understand. He was wearing a short-sleeve shirt, and his slender arms were unwrinkled, without age spots.

She was young too, and she was overjoyed to see him, but the statue frightened her, and she was afraid to come any closer.

"Jim!" she called. "Jim Ivanovitch!"

He turned, looked over his shoulder at her, and she saw that he had no face. There were no eyes, no nose, no mouth, only blank skin, and he gestured at her, waving his arms, obviously attempting to communicate, but she had no idea what he was trying to say, and behind him the statue started laughing. His gesticulations grew more wild, and the statue's laughter increased. The rest of its form remained completely stationary, only its mouth opening and closing, and soon it was laughing so hard that tears streamed down its cheeks from its cold stone eyes.

2

"You look terrible."

Julia nodded, glanced at her reflection in the window of the antique store. She had not slept well since her visit to Russiantown, her dreams disturbed with images of dwarves and shadows, the sounds of old laughter.

"Is anything wrong?" Deanna asked.

Julia shook her head. "No. I'm just tired."

She had not said anything to her friend about what had happened up there, though she was not sure why. She'd told Gregory, in bed that night, away from the kids, but he either didn't believe her or didn't care—it was hard to tell which. He offered vague, ineffectual reassurances, the kind of bland platitudes they told the children when they had nightmares, and his attitude so infuriated her that she simply shut up, closing down, unwilling to even try and make him understand what she had gone through.

She would have told his mother, talked to her about it, but her mother-in-law was all churched-out these days, spending most of her time with her old Molokan friends rather than the family, and Julia didn't especially want to drag the entire church into this.

Although sometimes she thought that might be the best thing that could happen.

Deanna would have been the natural person for her to discuss this with, but something kept her from it. She did not know why, but she did not feel comfortable telling her friend what had happened. It could have been her own natural reluctance to believe in anything beyond the material world and the fact that her friends had always shared her opinions on that subject, it could have been that she did not yet feel close enough to Deanna to open up to that extent, to expose herself to possible ridicule, but she had the feeling that it was something else, something . . . outside, that was dictating her behavior. It wasn't overt and she had no proof to back it up—her feelings, in fact, felt perfectly natural, as though they were an organic part of her being—but intellectually she sensed a skipped beat, an emotional response on her part that should have been there but wasn't.

Such a thought almost made her want to confide in Deanna just to prove to herself that she could, that it was her decision, that nothing was keeping her from it.

Almost.

But her reluctance to speak of the events in Russiantown was stronger than her desire to break free of that reluctance, and she kept quiet, not knowing whether it really was her own decision or one that had been imposed upon her.

They stepped into the antique store and spent about twenty minutes looking through everything. Deanna bought a pink dogwood plate and a Homer Laughlin gravy boat from the old lady behind the counter.

The two of them walked up the sidewalk, past Dale's Heating and Plumbing, and stopped in at the used bookstore, where Deanna bought an old Phillip Emmons novel and Julia picked up a Paul Prudhomme cookbook. By the time they finished, it was almost time for school to get out, and Julia had her friend drive her home so she could be there when Adam and Teo arrived.

"What are your plans for tomorrow?" Deanna asked.

Julia smiled guiltily. "I really should get back to work on my book," she said.

Deanna laughed. "Too much playing lately, huh? The old work ethic kicking your brain in the butt?"

"Yeah. Something like that."

"Have fun, then. I'll call you Thursday. Maybe we can go out for lunch."

Julia nodded. "Sounds good."

She waved as her friend drove back up the drive, then stepped inside the house.

Gregory's mother was home, taking a nap in her room. With some quiet time at her disposal, Julia did break out her notebook and spent a good half hour writing a possible ending for her children's book before Adam and Teo got home.

And she didn't think of scary things once.

They ate dinner together that night, all of them. It was the first time in a while that the six of them had been seated around the dining table at the same time. Usually Adam and Teo were hungry and Gregory was late, so she fed the kids first and saved their own dinner for later.

Or Sasha was off with her friends, eating at the diner.

Or Adam was over at Scott's house.

But today they were all here. She wished she could have known ahead of time because all they were having was leftover borscht. She would have made something better, something special, had she known.

She was acutely conscious of how awkward they all seemed with one another, how stilted and uncharacteristically formal, and it occurred to her that their family was breaking up. The democratically even relationships that they'd shared with each other in the past were giving way to fractured, specific, individual relationships within the overall family framework. They were not all equal anymore, and while she had a relationship with everyone here at the table, those relationships were different. It was as though they were diverse and separate people being held together only by force of habit and authority.

It was a disturbing thought, and she wanted it not to be true, but the dynamics of their family had changed and such a judgment seemed inescapable.

Perhaps this happened with all families as the kids grew older and grew up. It was impossible to remain static, to run in place forever. Maybe this was just part of the natural process, the evolution of parent-child-sibling relationships.

Maybe.

But she didn't recall it happening with her parents when she was growing up. They had never gone through such a stage. Their family had remained intact, their relationships stable and unchanged, up through her father's and then her mother's deaths.

Maybe she and Gregory just weren't good parents. Or, more likely, they were setting the tone for everyone else.

God knows, they weren't exactly behaving like June and
Ward Cleaver these days. They were barely speaking,
and when they did talk, it usually ended up in an argument. The reasons always seemed specific, unique to
each conversation, but the pattern was definitely there,
and she thought that maybe they should be making more
of an effort to get along. Family relationships didn't just
happen, they needed to be nurtured and worked at, and
they'd all been taking each other a little too much for
granted, allowing things to get out of control and not
setting them straight or correcting their course.

It was up to her to make the first move, and so she
smiled at Gregory as she passed around the wooden
Russian spoons. "How was your day?" she asked.

He looked up at her, and though it had been meant
sincerely, though she'd been trying to indicate concerned
interest, under the circumstances it came off sounding
snide and sarcastic, and the expression on his face was
one of annoyance. He frowned at her, didn't answer.

That annoyed *her*, and she spent the rest of the meal
talking to the kids, ignoring Gregory completely.

3

There were noises outside in the middle of the night,
but Gregory didn't think much about them. He heard
some bumps and scratches and muffled thumps when he
got up after midnight to take a leak, but he assumed
they were animals or put them down to the wind,
crawled back into bed, and once again fell asleep.

In the morning, however, when he walked outside to get
his weekly copy of the *Monitor*, he saw that the noises
had not been animals, had not been wind.

He stopped walking, stared at the house.

There was graffiti spray-painted on the walls to either
side of the door: MOLOKAN on the left side, MURDERERS
on the right.

MOLOKAN MURDERERS.

Gregory felt both angry and impotent as he stared at
the epithet, filled with a rage that made him want to
tear down the entire wall in order to remove the words.

He felt violated. He'd been planning to repaint the house anyway, but the fact that he had been forced into it, that some punk kids or asshole adult had defaced his home, infuriated him. They had been on his property. They had sneaked into his sanctuary in the middle of the night and defaced it, defiled it. It was an invasion of his privacy, an invasion of his home, an attack on his family. No one had been hurt, but the potential was there, and as he looked at the words—

MOLOKAN MURDERERS.

—he knew it was only a matter of time.

A gun. A shotgun. That's what he needed. Julia and his mother might go crazy, but goddamn it, they needed to be able to protect themselves. Even if he just filled it up with salt and pepper, or pellets, instead of buckshot, at least he'd be able to fend off any intruders. Next time it might not be just graffiti. Next time someone might try to hurt one of them. Nationally, hate crimes had been on the increase for years, and it usually took only a small incident to bring out old resentments, to allow hatred and prejudice to bubble to the surface.

And a series of murders in a small town?

People were going to be looking for scapegoats.

And that would be them.

With a gun, he would be able to protect himself. Himself and his family. Anyone who tried to harass them? He'd shoot the bastard's legs out from underneath him.

He felt guilty at the thought—he was the only Molokan he knew who had ever even considered buying a gun—but it was a pleasurable sort of guilt, and he imagined those self-righteous old fucks at the church shaking their palsied hands and wetting their pants when they learned that he'd armed himself.

He stared at the spray-painted vandalism. What would his father have done?

Nothing, a small, mean part of him said.

Turned his other cheek like a Christian, Gregory supposed—

like a pussy

—and not overreacted, not gone off half-cocked, not automatically planned how he could permanently injure and physically incapacitate the culprits. His father was a calm man, a peaceful man; there was no way he would ever have stooped to buying or using a weapon.

But those were different times and these were different people and, most important, he was not his father. He was not religious, not pious, and he did not believe it was wrong to fight fire with fire. There were times when a man had to stand up and be counted. He would not, for example, have allowed those losers outside the bar to insult and ridicule him in front of his family. He would have done something about it. He would have fought back. He might have been outnumbered, but he would have made the effort. He would not have allowed his wife and children to witness his weakness.

Weakness?

His father, he knew, would have considered it weakness to give in to the base desires for revenge and retribution. Those were privileges reserved only for God, and it was a sign of man's transcendent potential that he could recognize this, that he could rise above the level of the animal and abide by God's laws and wishes.

Gregory knew this, and he understood that his father had shown strength in that encounter, not weakness, that he had tried to set an example.

But he'd wanted him to do something different.

Gregory walked into the house, immediately called the police. Two officers arrived ten minutes later, and the rest of the morning was wasted answering questions, watching as photos were taken of the "crime scene" and an exhaustive search was conducted on and around the drive.

After the police left, he took his own photos for reference, then put on his crappiest clothes and walked back outside. Paint and brushes were in the storage shed, and while he didn't have time to redo the whole house today, he painted over the words, leveling off the repainted segment just above the door so it would at least be slightly symmetrical.

Tomorrow, he would borrow a ladder and a paint gun from Odd and try to finish the rest of the house. If he started at dawn and worked until dusk, he might just be able to get one coat on.

If he was lucky, Odd would offer to help.

He took a shower, scraped the paint off his skin with a soapy fingernail, then put on clean clothes.

"We need some milk and sugar!" Julia called when he opened the bathroom door to let out some steam. "Do you want to go to the store?"

No, he didn't want to go to the store, but he ran a comb through his hair and yelled, "Yeah, I'll go!"

He walked out of the bathroom, grabbed his wallet and keys from the dresser. He met Teo in the hall. "Can I come too?" she asked.

"No," he said. He rubbed the top of her head. "You stay here and be a good girl."

He realized how patronizing he sounded, how dismissive, but he wanted to be alone, wanted some time to think, and he felt guilty for only the briefest second as he walked out to the kitchen, double-checked what he was supposed to buy, and left.

At the Fresh Buy he recognized several faces, but he made no effort to be friendly and simply picked up the groceries he'd come for. The other people seemed to be ignoring him anyway, giving him the cold shoulder, and he pretended he didn't notice and didn't care.

People are talking.

All of that changed at the counter.

Both checkstands were open today, but he picked the left one because the girl working the register was attractive and friendly and had already smiled at him when he caught her eye. He'd seen her before, at the café, and he seemed to recall that she'd made an effort even then to meet him. He was pretty sure that she'd told him her name, but he'd met a lot of new people lately, and he could not remember what it was.

"Kat," the name tag informed him when he finally got close enough to see.

He placed the plastic milk carton and the sack of sugar on the checkstand's conveyor belt.

She was a trainee, he noticed. Which was probably why he hadn't seen her here before.

The checker smiled at him shyly. "Hello, Mr. Tomsaov."

"Gregory," he told her.

She tallied up his items on the register. "I just love

what you've done to the coffeehouse. This place was so
dead before you got here. You've really made a
difference."

That was exactly what he'd wanted to do, make a
difference, and he smiled at her gratefully. "Thanks."

"No, I really mean it. There was nothing to do in this
town except rent videos or watch TV at night. Now we
finally have some real entertainment."

He nodded. "Glad you like it."

"That'll be four-twelve."

He turned around and looked at her after leaving the
market, and he reddened and walked quickly away after
she caught him and smiled back. How old was she? Sasha's age? She had to be. Or a little older, maybe. It
was wrong for him even to look at her, much less allow
the sort of fantasies that were starting to creep into his
mind.

He'd had to park a few doors up the street, and he
started toward the van but saw that one of the store-
fronts he'd passed on his way into the market was a
gun shop.

He stopped in front of the store, looked in the window. There were handguns and rifles, even what looked
like a crossbow displayed behind the barred glass. It
couldn't hurt to take a peek, he thought, to check on
prices.

MOLOKAN MURDERERS.

His heart pounded as he walked inside. His entrance
rang a bell somewhere in the back of the shop. He felt
like a child, a child doing something wrong, something
of which his parents would not approve, but there was
an illicit thrill in the feeling, and when an overweight
man wearing military fatigues emerged from the darkened room behind the back counter, Gregory smiled at
him.

The man looked at him suspiciously. "Anything I can
do you for?"

Gregory wanted to browse, and he had a lot of questions, but the milk was getting warm, and he had to
get going.

"You sell shotguns here?" he asked.

The shopkeeper gestured around. "All kinds of guns. You want 'em, I got 'em."

"What are your hours?"

He pointed toward the window. "Like the sign says, eight to six, every day except Sunday."

Gregory smiled, nodded. "Thanks." He backed out of the store, aware that the suspicious expression had never left the man's face.

Did the shopowner know who he was? Was the man involved in the vandalism of his house or did he know something about it? This was the type of closed-minded guy who probably went in for things like that, and Gregory no longer felt like he had done something slightly naughty. Instead he felt as though he had inadvertently crossed an invisible line and attempted to enter a world in which he did not belong, in which the inhabitants hated him and were out for his blood.

He walked directly to the van without looking back, placed the grocery sack on the passenger seat next to him, and made a U-turn in the middle of the street.

He drove.

He knew there was cold milk that he needed to get into the refrigerator, but instead of going straight home he headed up to the Molokan cemetery. He had not consciously intended that to be his destination and was not even fully cognizant of the fact that that was where he was heading until he was on the narrow road winding up the ridge.

Gregory parked in front of the gates and got out of the van, not bothering to lock it. Although he could not see the huge, gaping pit of the mine from this far back on the cliff, he could see, beyond it, part of the town— buildings and houses snaking up the opposite canyons in paths determined by the roads.

He walked slowly through the gates into the cemetery.

MOLOKAN MURDERERS.

Did people really believe that he and his family were responsible for what was happening in McGuane? It didn't seem possible, but he was reminded of books and movies in which innocent newcomers were blamed by superstitious townsfolk for bad things that occurred and were attacked and lynched or beaten as their homes were burned to the ground.

Such a thing was not going to happen here.

He would make sure of that.

He walked over the rocky ground, around and between old headstones, until he was standing before his father's grave. He looked down at the weathered stone and the slightly sunken gravesite. He didn't know why he had come here. He was not one of those people who talked to the dead, who remained next to a grave attempting to communicate with someone who had passed on. He stood there silently, staring, thinking not of his father's death but his life, not of where he might be or what might have happened to him after dying but of what had happened to him while he was alive.

He thought about the rednecks outside the bar.

"Milk drinker."

He felt sorry for his father, he realized, and somehow pity seemed a sadder thing to feel than anger. He felt unaccountably depressed, and he wished he could believe that his father would hear him if he talked, but the truth was that he thought that sort of one-sided conversation was for the living, not the dead. It made the survivors feel better. The dead were dead, and whether they went on to Nirvana or heaven, or whether their brains simply stopped and they rotted into nothing, they were not here, they could not understand, they did not care.

He stared at the headstone, wiped a tear from his eye. The engraving was so faded that if he had not already known what it said, he would never have been able to read it.

He took a deep breath, walked past a series of newer tombstones, and stopped in front of Jim Petrovin's grave. He stared at it for a moment, then looked around. The milk was getting warm and he needed to get home, but he scanned the ridge for signs of anyone else.

There was no one here, and he hesitated only a second before unbuckling his belt, unbuttoning his Levi's, taking out his pecker, and pissing on the minister's grave.

Fourteen

1

Adam lay on his bed, listening to tunes while he read through the new *Spiderman*. His parents' friends Paul and Deanna Mathews were over tonight, and after dinner he and Teo had been sent off to their rooms so the grown-ups could talk. Sasha, as usual, was out with her friends somewhere—

I like 'em long

—and she probably wouldn't be back until . . . well, whenever.

Teo had tried to hang with him, but he'd kicked her out of his room, closed and locked the door, and put on his Walkman headphones so he couldn't hear her whining.

He wished he had a television in here. Even a black-and-white one. They'd won the lottery, they were supposed to be rich, but his parents didn't seem to be doing anything with the money except spending it on themselves. He still didn't have a decent stereo or a computer . . . or a television.

The television was a necessity. Especially for nights like this. Hell, Scott had his own TV. Even Roberto had had one. But his mom had some bee up her butt about limiting the amount of time kids watched television. She'd made him read an article about some group that was sponsoring an "Unplugged" week, a week where everyone was supposed to turn off their TVs and do something else. The woman who was president of the organization said that since giving up television viewing,

she'd had more time for knitting and reading and playing Scrabble.

He'd thought that meant that their TV viewing was
going to be curtailed, but luckily for him and Teo, their
dad had weighed in on their side, laughing at the woman
in the article and saying that she could learn a lot more
watching PBS than she could sitting in a silent house
and knitting.

"Her 'reading' must consist of romance novels," he
said.

Their parents had gotten into an argument after that,
and the upshot of it was that their father had granted
them unlimited viewing privileges rather than the two
hours a night they'd previously been allotted.

But, meanwhile, he still didn't have a TV in his room.

He finished *Spiderman*, picked up a *Hulk* that Scott
had lent him, but then he finished that comic book and
the tape in his Walkman ended.

He was thirsty and bored, and he tossed the comics
aside, took off his headphones, and walked over to the
door, opening it slowly. He hadn't exactly been exiled
from downstairs or banned from going out to the
kitchen, but it was more exciting to think he had, and
so he planned a route that would enable him to sneak
out and snag a can of Coke without his parents or their
friends seeing him.

Adam looked up and down the hall, made sure there
was no sign of Teo, then walked to the edge of the stairs.
He could hear the mumbled buzz of adult conversation
but could see no sign of anyone, and he crept down the
steps. They were all in the living room—he could see
the side of his mom's head at the close end of the
couch—and he considered trying to sneak into the
kitchen that way, but he would have to pass through a
corner of the living room and then through the dining
room, and detection was almost certain. Even crouching
down and scuttling behind furniture, there wasn't
enough cover.

So he settled for the easy route, going into the kitchen
from the hall doorway.

He could tell from their voices that the adults had had
a little too much to drink, and he made it successfully

across the kitchen to the other side, moving past the open entryway of the dining room without being seen. A plate of leftover tortilla chips and an empty salsa bowl were on the breakfast table, and he popped a couple of chips into his mouth, sucking on them instead of biting so that they wouldn't crunch, not wanting to give himself away.

He opened the refrigerator, took out a can of Coke, and started back the way he'd come, grabbing a few extra chips for the return trip. He paused for a moment at the edge of the dining room, listening to the conversation, hoping to hear something about himself or his sisters.

"Well," his father was saying, "my first wife, Andrea, absolutely loved the idea of living in a small town. She wanted to move to Oregon or Washington—"

Adam felt as though he'd been punched in the stomach.

His father's *first* wife?

His parents' friends were talking now, but Adam had no idea what they were saying. The conversation had become background noise to his thoughts, which were coming fast and furious, tumbling over each other in his head. The overwhelming feeling was one of betrayal, and the idea that kept repeating in his brain was that this man, his father, was a stranger to him, was not the person he'd thought he was, was not the person he knew.

Adam practically jumped out of his skin when his mother passed by, walking into the kitchen.

She saw him before he had fully recognized her, and she smiled at him. "Thirsty, huh?" She motioned toward the table. "Want some chips?"

He shook his head dumbly, though he still had quite a few tortilla chips in his hand.

"Well, you'd better go back to your room and get ready for bed. It's getting late and tomorrow's a school day."

He nodded, walked out the way he'd come in, but instead of going back upstairs, he made his way down the short hall to Teo's room. Her door was closed, but it wasn't locked, and he let himself in, shutting the door behind him. Teo frowned and was about to yell at him to get out, but he put a finger over his lips, indicating that she should be quiet, and her annoyance disappeared instantly, replaced by curiosity.

He crossed the room noiselessly, sitting down on the bed next to his sister. He looked at her, came straight to the point. "Dad was married before."

"What?"

He held up his Coke can. "I came down to get something to drink, and I heard them talking. Dad said he was married before. To someone else."

"Nuh-uh!"

"Uh-huh. Mom's his second wife."

There was silence as he let the revelation sink in. Teo looked like a ghost. All of the color had drained out of her face, and she blinked rapidly, her lids and lashes the only movement on her otherwise still features. She looked like she was about to cry. He felt a little like crying himself.

"He said her name was Andrea."

"He was married to someone named Andrea before he married Mom?"

"I guess."

Teo still looked like she was about to cry, and for the first time since she'd been a baby, Adam felt like reaching over and giving her a big hug.

"Does Sasha know?"

Adam shrugged. "Maybe. You think she'd tell us if she did?"

"But how come . . . ?" She looked up at him. "Does Mom know?"

"Of course. She was there too, and she wasn't surprised about it or anything."

"How come no one ever told us?"

"I don't know," he admitted.

He stayed in Teo's room for over half an hour, the two of them talking, analyzing what had happened, going over and over the few sentences he'd heard, until their mother came in, intending to make sure Teo was in bed, and found him there. She was surprised to see him, but she did not overreact. She simply told him to go upstairs, it was time for both of them to go to sleep.

He half expected Teo to bring it up, to ask their

mother about it, and he purposely lingered, wanting to hear what was said, but Teo kept it to herself, and he and his mother left the room at the same time.

"Now go to bed," she told him sternly. "You have school tomorrow."

He nodded, went upstairs.

Teo was obviously very upset. Normally, it was impossible for her to keep her mouth shut, especially when something was bothering her, and the fact that she was not willing to ask their mom about this indicated that its magnitude was off the scale.

He was pretty shaken up himself, and he wished he hadn't been so stupid, wished he'd listened in on more of the conversation, but he told himself that they were probably talking about something else anyway and the subject of his father's first wife had come up only in passing.

His father's first wife.

It was an idea he still could not seem to get his mind around.

He did not even check to see if Sasha's door was unlocked but went immediately into his own room, slamming the door behind him and plopping onto the bed. He tossed the Walkman and the comics on the floor.

His father had been married before.

It devalued everything, he thought. Mom was not his first choice for a wife. They were not his first choice for a family. They were the runners-up, the ones he'd had to settle for.

It occurred to him for the first time that Babunya knew all about this. She'd been someone else's mother-in-law before his mom's. She could have been someone else's grandmother.

Was she someone else's grandmother?

No, they would have known about that, they would have heard of it before.

But which wife did she like better? he wondered. Had she liked the first wife more? Had she wanted his dad to stay married to her?

He felt betrayed by Babunya too, although the feeling wasn't quite as strong.

What if his mother had been married before?

He stared up at the ceiling, ashamed of his next thought: what if Sasha was her daughter from the first marriage and was not really his full sister? It wouldn't exactly be incest, then.

He shouldn't even be thinking about that. He'd just found out that his mother was not his father's first wife, and he was horned out over his sister? What kind of sicko loser was he?

But what if she *wasn't* his sister?

He reached under the bed and pulled out Sasha's panties. He knew it was wrong, knew it was especially inappropriate now, but just thinking about Sasha had turned him on, and without any preamble, he did what he always did: unbuttoned, unzipped, and pulled down his pants, stretching out.

He grasped his penis firmly and began stroking it.

He closed his eyes. His door was unlocked, and in his fantasy Sasha came home early and walked in on him just as he was reaching his climax.

That moment was already getting close, and he used his left hand to pick up her panties. At the last second, he wrapped them around his erection, poking the head of his penis against the cotton panel where he knew her vagina had been.

He looked down and watched the explosion of white wetness burst against the confines of the cotton crotch as he came.

Afterward, he lay there for a few moments, breathing heavily, before tossing the panties back under the bed.

He pulled up his pants, went over and locked the door, lay back down on the bed, and began to cry.

2

There was nothing for him to do.

Gregory awoke late, the sun shining through slatted slits in the window shades, and realized that he had nowhere to go.

Oh, he could putter around the house, do yard work, fix up the storage shed, but those things weren't necessary. And the truth was that things at the café were running themselves. He wasn't needed. Shows were booked through the end of the month, there was no problem with any of the equipment, procedures were in place and working smoothly, and everything ran like clockwork. He didn't have to be there.

In fact, he *hadn't* been there for a while. He'd hung out, helped Paul and Odd with a few menial tasks, but he hadn't been to a performance in over two weeks, and he hadn't even bothered to check with the café's other employees to find out how the shows had gone. He assumed that if there was a problem, someone would tell him. And since no one had told him, that must mean everything was fine.

Gregory sat up in bed. His work was done and he had nothing to take its place.

He didn't know how to react, how to use this unstructured, unrestricted free time. He supposed he could try to think of other projects, but the truth was that his short burst of ambition and drive seemed to have fled, leaving in its place a disconcerting lethargy. He recalled, years ago, reading an interview with Pete Townsend, one of his idols. It had been a long interview, wide-ranging, and Pete had responded thoughtfully to all of the questions, but there was nothing he seemed excited about, nothing he seemed interested in, nothing he wanted to do. He and his wife had just had a baby, and he didn't even seem interested in that. It was as if he'd seen everything, done everything, and there was nothing new. He was just putting in his time, waiting to die.

At the time, the interview had depressed the hell out of him, and he had not been able to understand how someone so rich, so famous, so talented, with so many things going for him, could have such an attitude. But he thought he understood now, because he felt the same way. He'd won the lottery. He no longer had to work, he could do whatever he wanted to do—and there *was* nothing he wanted to do.

He'd thought moving to McGuane would change his life, and it had. But not for the better. Things were not working out well here. He was not happy. He was not satisfied. He was not content. He was just . . . lost. And he didn't know what to do about it.

He found himself wondering what his life would have been like had he remained with Andrea. She was completely different from Julia: flamboyant where Julia was subdued, spontaneous where Julia was thoughtful. He had loved her, he supposed—even though she was an outsider, as his mother had never ceased reminding him—and it had hurt him to break up with her, but it was the aftereffects of the breakup that had been hardest to deal with: having to explain to the family what had happened, having to adjust to seeing friends without her by his side, having to meet people by himself instead of on equal footing, as part of a couple. He was not meant to be alone, was not the kind of guy who did well by himself. He wasn't clingy, but he needed a woman, and socially he worked better if he was part of a team.

It was why he'd gotten married again so quickly.

He had never thought of it that way before, had never even considered that the life he had now, the family he had now, had not sprung from a foundation of love and romance but had resulted from his unwillingness to be alone and his need to be married.

Did he love Julia?

He'd always thought he did, but now he wasn't sure. They seemed to be drifting apart, and he didn't think it was simply a temporary downturn on the graph that measured their relationship. They had moved to a small town in another state, basically cutting themselves off from their friends and their previous life. It was a sink-or-swim scenario, and they were sinking. They were not drawing closer together in this pressure-cooker situation—the test of true love in his book—but were coming apart. It pained him to think that the only reason their marriage had survived for so long on such a relatively even keel was because he had a life, she had a life, and they saw each other only on nights and weekends. Now that they were together so often, now that they had more of a life *together*, things were not working out.

And lately he'd been thinking about other women.

That was a shock to him. He'd never had any respect for those wealthy older men who dumped their longtime wives for some young chippie, had never had any use for married losers who looked elsewhere for sex and were unfaithful to their spouses, but now he could understand where they were coming from.

He thought of the checkout girl at the market.

Kat.

She seemed to like him. She always talked to him when he came through the line, always smiled at him when she saw him come in for groceries, and she had mentioned more than once that she was not married and had no boyfriend. She was a regular at the café as well, and Wynona had even joked that she only came to the concerts to look for him—which meant that he wasn't the only one who had noticed her interest, that it wasn't all in his mind.

Kat was a nice girl, and he had the feeling that she was more understanding than Julia, more open, more willing to compromise within the context of a relationship.

Not that he necessarily wanted a relationship with her.

But sex would be nice.

The last time he and Julia had had sex, it was the checkout girl he'd visualized as he pumped away between his wife's thighs. He'd imagined a tighter vagina, slimmer hips, perkier breasts, and he had come much more quickly than usual.

He had been to the store only once since then, but in line he kept thinking of how Kat would look naked, how she would behave in bed.

She was probably wild.

She would probably let him do whatever he wanted.

"Gregory!" Julia called from downstairs. "Are you up? I'm going to do the breakfast dishes! This is your last chance!"

He groaned, rubbed his eyes.

"Gregory!"

He kicked off the covers, got out of bed. "I'm up!" he yelled as he walked into the bathroom, and there was a touch of anger in his voice. "I'm up!"

The kids were at school—a friend had picked up Sasha, Julia had driven Adam and Teo before she even tried to wake him up—and Julia was in the den, working on her children's book. His mother, as usual, was at church or doing some other Molokan thing.

He was the only one at loose ends, and he found himself wandering around the house before finally drifting upstairs into the attic.

The attic was one of the old kind that he'd seen before in movies but never in real life. The entrance was not a small square hidden in the ceiling of the bedroom closet, as the attic in their California house had been. It was a large rectangle in the ceiling at the end of the upstairs hall, and when he unfastened the chain from its hook and pulled on it, a fold-out wooden ladder slid down. The attic itself paralleled the hall below and was slightly wider, tall enough for him to stand up in the center. They'd used it so far to store some of the boxes that had formerly been in their garage, and Julia had made him get a lock for the entrance so that the kids couldn't play in there. He could reach the lock standing on tiptoe, but everyone else in the house needed a chair. He kept the only key on his ring.

He'd thought her precautions a little excessive at first—after all, the kids weren't babies anymore—but now he was glad of them.

Gregory unlocked the lock, pulled on the chain, walked up the ladder.

Once inside, he pulled the ladder up and shut the trapdoor behind him. Walking to the end of the room, he reached up to a shelf above the small dormer window and took down the gun case.

He opened the case, took out his revolver.

He touched the cold metal, hefted the gun's weight in his hand. He'd bought the revolver yesterday, and though he hadn't told anyone about it, already he felt different, more confident. There'd been no more graffiti, no more vandalism, but he was ready if there was. He pointed the unloaded weapon at the opposite wall and pretended to fire. Any criminal who violated the sanctity of his home had better be prepared to face the consequences.

He'd wanted to tell Paul and Odd about his purchase, thought about telling them, but in the end he decided to keep it to himself. He'd been brought up in a household and a culture of pacifism, and for the most part those beliefs had taken. He felt right now like a little boy sneaking behind his parents' backs to smoke behind the barn. He was doing something he shouldn't, something he knew to be wrong, and on some level, he supposed, he was embarrassed about it.

But it gave him a sense of empowerment, and because of his background, because of his upbringing, he also felt like a pioneer, a rebel paving the way for others to follow.

He'd brought the gun into the house in a brown paper bag, and when Julia asked him what it was, he'd merely smiled and said nothing. The kids were still at school, and shortly afterward, she'd taken the van to drop something off at Deanna's. His mother was asleep in her room.

So he'd taken the gun and its case out of the bag and brought it up to the attic. He'd originally planned to keep it under his bed, but he knew Julia might see it there, and so he decided on the attic instead. No one else ever went up there, and he could be assured that his purchase would remain a secret. He would not be able to get to it quickly, would not be able to stop a home-invasion robbery in progress, but that was not the kind of crime that happened too often in McGuane, and it was not the situation for which he was preparing. He was after the people who had defaced his home, the bigoted redneck assholes who blamed him and his family for the recent deaths and problems in town.

He looked down at the revolver in his hand and there was a sense of soothing satisfaction as he imagined the scenario: waking up in the middle of the night after hearing a noise, getting his weapon and going outside, surprising the intruder, the vandal dropping his spray can, going for his gun, and then clutching his chest as Gregory beat him to the draw and blew him away.

"Gregory!" Julia's muffled voice called from downstairs.

He quickly slipped the revolver back into its case, shoved it back on the shelf, and quietly opened the trapdoor, hurrying down the ladder.

"Gregory!" Julia called.

"What?" he replied, and he smiled to himself as he closed the attic door, locked it, and headed downstairs.

3

Though it was cold, Gregory had left the van at home today, walking to work in order to burn off some of his fat. Julia drove down to the café around noon, thinking the two of them could have a pleasant little lunch together.

But the young woman grinding coffee behind the counter for an elderly man told her that she hadn't seen Gregory all morning.

That was strange. Before leaving home, he'd specifically mentioned that he was going to the café today because the sound system needed some fiddling. Her first thought was that something might have happened to him. She hurried back to Paul's office and found him going over invoices. Alone.

"Have you seen Gregory this morning?" she asked.

He frowned. "Gregory? He hasn't been here all week."

"He said he was going to work on the sound system today."

"There's nothing wrong with the sound system."

She didn't know what to say. Obviously, he had lied to her. Which meant nothing had happened to him and he was off doing something else, something secret, something he didn't want her to know about.

She wondered if he was seeing someone else, if he was having an affair.

"Odd!" Paul called out. He smiled at Julia. "Don't worry. We'll track him down."

From the alley in back of the café came a "Wait a sec!" and a moment later, Odd walked into the office, wiping greasy hands on an equally greasy rag. "Yeah?"

"Have you seen Gregory today?"

The old man nodded. "Sure. He was sitting on one of the benches in the park reading a magazine about twenty minutes ago. I think he was going to go over to the bar afterward. The Miner's Tavern." He looked sideways at Julia. "He don't drink much, but he seems to have some kind of feeling for that place, although I don't rightly know what it is."

She smiled thinly. "Thanks."

Odd nodded. "That all, boss?"

Paul grinned, waved him away. He turned toward Julia. "You going over there to get him?"

She shook her head. "I was going to meet him for lunch, but I guess I'll just go home."

"You're welcome to join me," Paul said. "I was getting ready to eat myself."

She thought for a moment, then smiled. "Thanks," she said. "I'd like that."

"Grab yourself a table out there. I'll just wash up and join you."

She walked out of his office to the café proper, sitting down at a table near the window. Paul joined her a moment later. "Our lunch menu isn't too extensive. How about a pizza bagel?"

"Sounds delicious," she told him.

"And coffee?"

"Iced cappuccino?"

"Iced cappuccino it is." He walked over to the counter, spoke to the girl, then returned and sat down across from her.

"I don't mean to pry," he said. "And I'll understand if you don't want to talk about it, but how are things with you and Gregory?"

She shrugged noncommittally. "Okay."

"Lying to you? Not telling you where he's going?" He held up a hand. "I know it's none of my business, and you can tell me to buzz off, but that doesn't sound 'okay' to me."

"I'm sure there's a reason for it. I'm sure there's less here than meets the eye."

"Maybe." He nodded. "Maybe. But like I said, he hasn't stopped by all week, and the last few times I've seen him, he's seemed a little distracted, a little . . . I don't know. Lost."

Lost. It was a good word, and it described her take on the situation perfectly. She was tempted to talk to Paul, to tell him everything—about Gregory's increasing coldness toward her and the kids, the trouble they were all having adjusting to McGuane, even her little adventure up in Russiantown. But Paul was Gregory's friend, not hers, and while he seemed sympathetic, she knew where his loyalties lay.

On the other hand, she'd already opened up enough to tell him that Gregory was MIA today, and perhaps if they talked he could shed some light on what was happening, offer a different perspective. He *was* Gregory's friend, and perhaps that meant he was as concerned about Gregory as she was.

She took a deep breath. Started talking.

She left out the supernatural stuff, the hints of weirdness and suspicions of hauntings—she needed all the credibility she could muster here—but she ran down everything that had happened since they'd won the lottery. They had changed, she said, drifted apart. And it wasn't the money, she emphasized. It was . . . this place. Sometime in the middle of the conversation the girl arrived with their food and coffee, but Julia didn't stop, didn't pause, just kept going, until, finally, drained, she leaned back in her chair.

Paul was silent for a moment. "I . . . I don't know what to say," he admitted.

"That's okay." She smiled at him. "I think I just needed to get it off my chest. I needed a sympathetic ear more than helpful advice." She took a bite of the now-cold pizza bagel, a huge sip of the coffee.

"I can't help but think that if you told Gregory this, sat him down and explained it to him exactly the same way you explained it to me, he would understand. I mean, he's not a bad guy. And he's not a dumb guy. And I'm sure he realizes something's wrong. I know it sounds corny and clichéd, but maybe the two of you just need to communicate. If you sit down without the kids and the grandma and just talk to each other—"

"That's the problem. We don't seem to be *able* to talk to each other lately."

"He's going through something, and I don't think either of us knows what it is." Paul finished his coffee, motioned for more. "I don't want to sound like some pop psychologist, but I can tell you that he got a lot more secretive, a lot more withdrawn, after his dad died.

There wasn't a big personality change or anything, but he went through some kind of head trip, something that he didn't tell any of us about, any of his friends. Maybe coming back here—and living with his mom again—brought some of that back."

Julia nodded. "I've thought of that," she agreed. "And I'm hoping that's all it is. I'm hoping he just needs a little space, a little time to get himself together and sort things through. And I'm trying to give that to him. But life doesn't stop just because you have a few problems to work out. And, besides, I'm his wife. He's supposed to be working them out with me. It's not as if I've ever been uncaring or unsympathetic. I think he knows he can come to me with anything, that I'll always be here for him. We're partners here. Or at least we're supposed to be."

"Give it a little more time," Paul suggested.

"I have no choice. What else can I do?"

They were silent for a few minutes, Julia finishing her food, Gregory getting a refill on his coffee.

"No relationship's perfect," Paul said finally. "There are always problems."

Julia waved him away. "You think I don't know that by now? As long as we've been married?"

Paul took a deep breath. "You know, Deanna and I are having some problems too," he said. He held up a quick hand. "Nothing serious, nothing we haven't been through before, but in the peaks-and-valleys scenario we're in a valley right now."

She smiled. "Maybe it's catching."

"Maybe," he said. But he did not smile.

She leaned forward. "What's wrong?"

"You're Deanna's friend. I was hoping you could tell me. I know she talks to you—"

"Yeah, but not about that. I was under the impression that everything was fine between you two."

"Maybe it is," he said. "Maybe I'm reading more into this than I should. I hope I am. I love Deanna more now than I ever have, but lately she's been kind of bitchy."

"PMS?" Julia suggested, joking.

He reddened. "No, it's not that."

She was immediately sorry she'd mentioned it. "I didn't mean to make light of—"

"Don't worry," he assured her. "I know you're not serious."

"Is there anything I can do?" she asked.

He sighed. "I suppose we could spy on each others' spouses, report back to each other."

"Is *that* a joke?" she asked uncertainly.

"Yeah. That's a joke."

"If you'd like me to talk to her, I will."

"No. I was just kind of curious if she'd said anything to you."

Julia shook her head. "Like I said, I had the impression that everything was fine."

"She hasn't seemed bitchy to you?"

"Nope."

"Maybe it's all in my head. Or maybe she's jealous because she's been hanging around you so much lately. After all, you're a very attractive woman." He tried to laugh it off, but the humor fell flat and she felt slightly uncomfortable.

She pushed her chair away from the table, stood. "Well, I'd better get going."

He nodded, his face red.

"If you do see Gregory this afternoon, you might mention that I stopped by, looking for him."

"I'll do that," Paul promised.

"Do I owe you anything for . . ." She gestured toward the table.

"On the house," he said.

She smiled. "Thanks."

He looked at her, and once again she felt uncomfortable. "You're welcome."

Adam and Teo confronted her that afternoon.

She picked them up from their respective schools, and they were both unusually silent on the ride back. The temperature was stuck somewhere in the mid-fifties and, though the heater was on in the van, neither of them bothered to take off their heavy jackets.

It was Teo, sitting in the back, who brought it up.

"Dad was married before, wasn't he?"

She'd known this day would come sometime, but it still threw her for a loop. She managed to remain on an even keel, to show no surprise, and she nodded. She and Gregory had decided years ago that they would handle this matter-of-factly, and so she said, "Yes, he was."

In her peripheral vision, she saw Adam turn in his seat and look back at his sister, giving her a meaningful glance that Julia could not see to interpret.

She stuck to the party line, the tack they'd decided to take. "Your father was very young, and he made a mistake. He realized that early, and he got a divorce, and we met after that."

"Her name was Andrea, wasn't it?" Adam's voice was hostile.

"Yes, it was. But, like I said, he realized his mistake early. Which just goes to show you why you should not rush into things and why people should not get married too young."

"How old was he?" Teo asked.

"About twenty."

"How old were you when you and dad got married?" She took a deep breath. "About twenty-three."

"That's not much difference," Adam said.

"You and Teo are three years apart. You don't think there's any difference in maturity there?"

"No!" Teo announced from the back.

"I guess so," Adam admitted grudgingly.

They were all silent. Julia knew there were more questions they wanted to ask, but she did not want to volunteer any information. She waited to see what they would come up with.

The next question, from Adam, was a surprise.

"When did Sasha find out?"

She looked back at him. "I'm not sure she knows. She's never asked about it."

That brought him back into her corner. The hostility was gone. He was shocked and disturbed to find out that his father had already been married and divorced before starting their family, but the fact that he knew something his older sister did not almost made up for it.

"Does Dad like you better than that other woman?" Teo asked.

That other woman. Julia liked that. She smiled. "Yes, because he divorced her and married me and we had you children and we've been together now for almost twenty years."

"Did you have another husband before Dad?"

"No," she said. "Your father is my only husband."

That seemed to satisfy them. There were no other questions immediately forthcoming.

She pulled into the drive. "We'll talk about it some more with your father when he gets home."

"Do we have to?" Adam asked.

"Well, he can explain better—"

"I don't want to!" Teo announced.

"He was the one—"

"Can't we just pretend like we don't know?" Teo whined.

"Yeah." Adam looked at her. "I'm sorry I found out. I didn't mean to."

They were both upset, upset and a little frightened, and she thought of Gregory's recent behavior. She pulled to a stop, turned off the van's engine. "It's okay," she said softly. "You don't have to discuss it with your father if you don't want to."

They needed time to adjust, she decided. They needed to think about it a little more before they felt up to talking.

She would bring it up with Gregory herself tonight, when they were alone in bed, and tell him not to let on that he knew they knew.

Adam fixed her with a look so adult and sincere that it almost broke her heart. "Thanks, Mom."

"Yeah," Teo echoed, "thanks, Mom."

The phone began ringing the instant she walked through the door, and she tossed her purse and keys on the coffee table in the living room as she ran to answer it.

Adam and Teo raced each other to the kitchen to find some snacks.

She kept her eyes on the phone across the room, wondering who was calling. She was suddenly aware of how rare an occurrence this had become. Back in California, the phone had rung constantly—calls for Sasha, mostly, but also quite a few for herself. Here in McGuane, however, very few people called. The telephone was seldom used, and what had been an ordinary part of everyday life had become almost an event. It brought home to her how much her social circle had shrunk and how much she missed her old life.

She answered the phone on the third ring. "Hello?"

It was Debbie, and Julia's heart lifted as she heard her old friend's voice. "Greetings from sunny California. How goes it, stranger?"

Debbie had called for no specific reason, just because she was bored and wanted to shoot the breeze (and she wanted to annoy her miserly husband by calling in the daytime instead of during the cheaper evening hours), and that touched Julia more than anything else. Adam and Teo emerged from the kitchen with Cokes and cookies in their hands, and she waved them away, motioning for them to stay out of the living room so she could talk in private.

Debbie always liked to work from the generic to the specific, so they started out talking about movies, making Julia realize how long it had been since she'd had a serious movie discussion with anyone.

"I watched *Singin' in the Rain* last night," Debbie told her. "It was on AMC."

Julia smiled. "A classic."

"Yeah, but don't you always wonder about the movie they're supposed to be making? The Lockwood and Lamont costume epic that's turned into a musical? I mean, what kind of movie could include 'Broadway Melody' *and* 'The Dancing Cavalier'? And 'The Dancing Cavalier' is supposed to be part of a dream sequence, while the rest of the story is contemporary, but 'The Dancing Cavalier' ends the movie! Does that mean the movie ends with a dream?"

Julia laughed. "God, I miss you."

Debbie's voice, which had been righteously serious, softened. "I miss you too, Jules. That's why I called. How are things going there?"

She shrugged, but the shrug could not be heard over the phone. "Okay, I guess."

Debbie had always been able to read between the lines. "That bad, huh? What is it? Mother-in-law troubles?"

"Not exactly."

"Local hillbillies?"

She laughed. "No. It's just that . . . it's taking us a little longer to adjust than we thought."

"Gregory, huh?"

"How do you do that?" Julia asked.

"Do what?"

"See through whatever I'm telling you and guess the truth."

"It's an acquired skill," Debbie said. "So spell it out for me."

This time, Julia kept nothing back. She even talked about the box of dishes and her feelings about the house and her trip to Russiantown.

"You want my advice?" Debbie said when she was finished.

"What?"

"Get the hell out of Dodge. Pack your things and go. Stick your little tails between your legs and come running back here to the real world."

"You really believe me about our haunted house?"

"I believe that you believe, and that's enough for me. Whether it's ghosts and creeps or simple dysfunction, things aren't working out the way they should, and it sounds to me like it's time for you to bail."

Julia smiled, already feeling better. "This is your totally objective opinion?"

"The fact that I'd like my friend back here in California in no way compromises my impartiality."

"Well, I'm stuck here for a while. For this school year at least."

"But you're thinking about coming back?"

"Every damn day."

They both laughed.

There was a long pause, and it was Debbie who spoke first. "You're really spooked, though, aren't you?"

"Yes," Julia admitted.

"I didn't think you were the type to believe in ghosties and ghoulies and things that go bump in the night."

"I didn't either."

"I've always kept an open mind, myself. I don't believe or disbelieve. But the fact that you think you saw

something scares the shit out of me. I trust you more
than I trust my own eyes."

"That's reassuring."

"Jules?" Debbie's voice was serious.

"Yes?"

"Be careful."

A shiver passed through her, but Julia managed not
to let it reach her voice. "I will," she said.

"I mean it. I don't want anything to happen to you."

"I know."

The conversation ended on an up note, with a return
to movies.

Debbie was the one to finally say good-bye, and she
hung up promising to call soon. Julia put the receiver
back in its cradle and stood there next to the phone until
her vision started to get blurry. She wiped her eyes before the tears overflowed onto her cheeks.

Teo emerged from the hallway, walked over to her.
"What are we having for dinner?" she asked.

Julia looked at her daughter, felt her strength return.
"I don't know," she said. She smiled. "But let's go into
the kitchen and see what we can figure out."

4

She had not been to the *banya* in a long time and it
was mad at her.

Teo peeked out at the bathhouse from behind a boulder. It even *looked* angry. There was something cross
about the defiant darkness staring out of the open doorway. The small building looked better than it ever had
before—the adobe seemed new, the roof no longer appeared to be caving in on one side—but it also looked
sore, although that was something she sensed as much
as saw. It knew she was here, it could see her, it could
sense her, but it was refusing to speak to her, and Teo
could feel the rage behind its silence, the anger within
its darkness.

She wanted to leave but dared not, was tempted to
walk closer but was afraid to do so. She was trapped

just where she was, and the thought occurred to her that that was exactly where the *banya* wanted her to be.

It had called to her, and though there'd been no words, no explicit commands, she recognized the summons. It was one of those feelings that didn't need words, that her brain understood without having to translate into language. She'd ignored it at first, pretended she didn't notice, tried not to think about it, but the calling had grown increasingly insistent until it no longer seemed to be something outside that was beckoning her but a part of herself, a need.

So she had come.

But she was not brave enough to go all the way, and indeed the need within her seemed to have lessened—which was why she was beginning to think that this was exactly where the *banya* wanted her.

She'd been trying to think of ways to explain why she had not been by, things she could tell the *banya* that would explain her absence: the weather was getting too cold; she'd gotten in trouble and was grounded; her parents had found out about her coming here and had forbidden her to come again. She liked the weather idea the best. Being grounded was only a temporary excuse, and her parents had already banned her from coming here and she'd done it anyway. But it was definitely fall, and it was a lot colder fall than she was used to, and she could always say that she'd *wanted* to come but it was just too darn cold out. In fact, the idea of being inside the warm house, sitting on the living room floor, doing her homework and watching TV, sounded mighty good to her right now.

But she'd been called and she'd come, and it was as though she was helpless to refuse. She was a puppet. She thought of the animal attack at school and knew with dreadful certainty that the *banya* had done something for her and now it expected her to do something for it.

She already had, Teo told herself. She'd brought it food.

But she knew that was not enough, and that was what scared her.

The *banya* was still not speaking to her, and as scary and angry as it looked, she told herself that if it did not say anything in the next five minutes, she was going to leave.

At that thought, there was movement within the darkness, the sense of something *shifting* inside the bathhouse. She sucked in her breath.

And a horde of mice streamed out of the *banya* door toward her.

It came completely out of the blue, was not something she had thought about or could ever have expected, and she remained rooted to the spot as hundreds of the tiny rodents, far more than could possibly have fit inside the bathhouse, sped in a living wave over the rocky ground, the brown bodies so close together that they looked like a carpet being unrolled.

They stopped three or four feet in front of her, instantly, at the same time, as if they'd run into an invisible wall. They were in rows, she saw, lined up perfectly, like little army men. It was the orderly unnaturalness of it that frightened her the most. She wanted to run, but something kept her from it, and she could only hope that that something came from inside herself.

There was an exhalation of warm air from the door of the *banya*. She could see it rustling the fur of the mice, could feel the outer edges of it touching her face. It brought with it a foul stench that reminded her of rotting cucumbers, and she wrinkled her nose, turning away, finally freed from her immobility.

The mice stood up on their hind legs and smiled at her.

It was a frightening sight. A mouse's mouth was not meant to smile, was not built to move in those directions, and seeing hundreds of them doing it at once, all facing her, made her blood run cold.

As one, the mice screeched, and the sound coming out of their mouths was her name:

"Teo!"

She ran.

Crying, screaming at the top of her lungs, finally able to make her body obey her mind, she sped back down the path toward home as fast as her legs could carry her.

She could not be sure, but behind her she thought she heard the sound of the *banya* laughing.

Fifteen

1

Scott carried the flashlight as the three of them made their way up the hidden path to the secret spot on the cliff. They should have all brought flashlights, Adam knew, but Scott was the only one who'd thought to do it, and the going was slow because he and Dan were forced to stand in place until Scott climbed up each section of trail, then turned around and illuminated the way so the two of them could follow.

It was an arduous journey, the ascent at least twice as difficult at night as it had been in the daytime. When they stopped to rest at the curve in the switchback, Adam looked over the edge at the road below. To the left, he could see the diner, the shape of its roof defined by the lights around the building, two lone pickups in the parking lot. To the right and down the sloping highway, he could see some of the lights of town, the ones not hidden by the cottonwoods or the canyon dropoff. The highway itself was empty, not a single vehicle on it.

Adam turned toward Scott. "What if there aren't any cars?" he asked, secretly hoping that there wouldn't be.

"Don't worry," Scott said. He motioned with the flashlight. "Come on. Let's go."

They continued up the trail.

This section of the path was shorter, and ten minutes later they were at the clearing.

It was freezing out tonight, but Adam was sweating from the climb, and so he took off his jacket. The cold air felt good against his skin, and he stood there enjoying it, looking down over the wall at the still silent highway, as next to him Scott sat down hard in the dirt. "Whew!"

"The tough part'll be going down," Dan said from behind them.

Scott snorted. "You're crazy. We can slide down on our asses if we have to. Piece of cake."

Adam checked out what he could see of the town, getting his bearings and trying to find his own house, but it was blocked from view by a low hill. He wondered what he would do if he looked down and saw their van pull into the diner's parking lot. He'd told his parents that he was spending the night at Scott's, and they said that was okay as long as the two of them remained at his friend's house and didn't go anywhere. He'd lied and said they were just going to watch the *Star Wars* movies on video.

To be honest, he was surprised that his parents had even let him stay overnight. They knew Scott, but they had never met Scott's parents, and though he'd falsely portrayed his friend's mom and dad as kind, caring, loving, happy Mike and Carol Brady clones, he was still surprised they had let him go. Back in California, they never would have been so lax, and while part of him was happy for this change, another, more responsible part was worried by it. He tried to tell himself that it was nothing, that they were acting this way because they believed this was a better, safer environment, but he could not make that rationalization stick. Deep in his heart he believed that they did not care as much about him as they used to.

His sweat had dried, and now he could feel the cold. He slipped back into his jacket and sat down next to Scott in the dirt. Dan remained standing, looking over the edge. Above them, a half-moon turned everything into silhouette.

"So what's the plan?" Dan asked.

"You know what the plan is. Keep a lookout." Scott turned toward Adam. "You take over when he gets tired."

Adam nodded.

There was something different about Scott lately, too, although once again it was not anything he could pin down. Like his parents, his friend had seemed preoccupied recently, as though something was worrying him. And while Scott's interests and actions were the same as they'd always been, a cruelty and harshness had crept in where before there had been playfulness.

None of them spoke as they waited. Adam picked up the flashlight between them and shone it on the dirt around him.

"What are you doing?" Scott said.

"Looking for spiders," he explained. "I want to make sure there are no bugs here."

"Don't worry. If there are, you'll feel them."

The light played over the small indentations made by their feet before settling, near the wall, on an object with a red-and-gold pattern that he immediately recognized. He leaned forward for a closer look, not believing what he saw.

There in the dirt, half hidden, chipped and cracked with age, was a wooden Russian spoon.

The hairs on the back of his neck bristled. He scooted forward, picked up the object. He could not have said what about the spoon so unnerved him, but finding it here seemed somehow—meaningful. That was stupid, he knew. There'd been a lot of Russians in McGuane over the years, and finding a piece of discarded trash like this was perfectly natural.

But it did not *feel* natural. It felt preordained, as though it had been left here specifically for him, as though he was *supposed* to find it. He could not help thinking that the fact that it was a Russian spoon and *he* was Russian and he had found it way up here in their little secret hideout had some deeper, hidden meaning.

"What's that?" Dan asked, walking over.

He handed the other boy the spoon as though it was nothing to him. "A Russian spoon."

"What's it doing up here?"

"You got me."

"Somebody keep an eye on the highway," Scott said.

Dan handed the spoon back to Adam, and they returned to their original positions.

They lapsed back into silence, and Adam found himself wondering how this little clearing had come to be,

who had constructed the path up to it. Its origin still
seemed suspect to him, and the spoon made him think
that maybe Molokans had built it.

But for what purpose? He looked at the low sandstone
wall that separated Dan from the cliff drop-off. It was
almost like a fort, like someplace built to be defended.

He had avoided thinking about the cave until now,
had not even looked at the hanging succulents covering
its entrance when they'd arrived here, but the image of
that alcove in the cliff, with its hint of ritualism and
unknown purpose, was imprinted permanently on his
brain, and he could not get away from it. Even in avoidance, it dominated his thinking about this place, and he
was acutely conscious of the fact that the cave was facing
his back. He was tempted to turn around, to look at it—

to make sure nothing was coming out of it

—but he remained facing forward, willing himself not
to give in to temptation and fear.

Fear?

Yes. There was something scary about the hidden cave
behind them. He was reminded of the *banya,* and when
he thought about the cave he imagined the shadow of a
Russian man burned into the rock of the back wall.

He wished he hadn't come here. He had a bad feeling
about this.

The spoon suddenly felt strange in his hand, and he
tossed it over the edge. Dan ducked, thinking it was a
rock, and turned on him. "What the hell was that?"

"The spoon."

"What did you throw it at me for?"

"I wasn't throwing it at you. I was just throwing it."

Dan looked at him, and Adam knew he understood.

Adam stood. "I don't like this place," he admitted.
"It's creepy."

"It's haunted," Scott said.

Adam looked at him, and he shrugged. "I told you.
There are a lot of haunted places in McGuane."

"And you think this is one of them?" Adam asked.

"You said it yourself, didn't you?" Scott stood, walked
over to the wall. "I don't like the cave."

Full-fledged chills rippled over nearly all of Adam's
body. His mouth felt dry.

"Let's get out of here." Dan's voice was low, quiet, as though he didn't want to be overheard.

"Nah, we'll be all right." Scott looked down on the empty highway. "Let's give it another ten minutes."

"I don't like the cave either," Adam said.

"I don't know what it is, but it didn't seem that scary to me in the daytime."

"I thought it was scary."

"You didn't say anything."

Adam looked at his feet. "Yeah, well . . ."

"I'm bored," Dan said. "Let's go."

Scott smiled. "Bored? You're scared."

"So am I," Adam told him.

"Another ten minutes." He looked at the two of them. "Come on. You know we're not going to be coming up here again. This is our only chance." He bent down, picked something up out of the dirt. "Here. I got a rock."

Adam took a deep breath, avoided looking at the succulents hanging over the cave entrance. "Ten minutes," he agreed. He looked at Dan. "It's a long walk down."

The Indian boy didn't say a word, started picking up his own rocks.

"Did you ever take a picture of the bathhouse?" Dan asked a few moments later.

Scott paused for a moment, as if deciding what to say. "Yeah," he admitted finally.

Adam looked at him. "Why didn't you say anything?"

Another pause. "The pictures turned out . . . weird."

"Weird?"

"There were people in them. Fat old Russians taking a steam bath. The bathhouse looked all new, and . . ." He trailed off. "I think I took pictures of the past, pictures of something that happened before."

Adam's mouth was dry again. "What did you do with them? Did you send them off to the *Enquirer*?"

"I threw them away. Destroyed them, actually. In the garbage disposal. They were . . . starting to change."

"Why didn't you tell us?" Dan demanded.

"I don't know," Scott admitted.

"That's it," Adam announced. "I'm going."

"You said ten minutes."

"I changed my mind."

"Just wait. You don't want to go down by yourself."

Adam stopped. He was right.

"Besides, I have the flashlight."

Adam glared at his friend.

Dan cleared his throat. "Don't you think there's been a lot of . . . scary stuff going on lately?"

Scott snorted. "There's always scary stuff. You know this town."

"But doesn't it seem more . . . active?"

The two of them shared a look, and Adam glanced from one to the other. "What's that about?" he said.

Dan shook his head. "Nothing."

The look again.

"Tell me."

Scott moved closer. "There are a lot of people who are saying it's your fault. Not you personally. I mean your family."

"What are you talking about?"

"I think it's an anti-Molokan thing." Dan shrugged. "It's a rumor."

Adam backed up, his heart leaping into his throat. "You guys brought me up here to kill me! You're going to push me off the cliff!"

Scott blinked, genuinely startled, then burst out laughing. Dan started laughing, too.

"You're . . . not?" Adam asked hopefully.

"Hell no!" Scott could barely get the words out. "Where'd you come up with a loony idea like that?"

"It's not that loony," he said.

His friends' laugher trailed off. "No," Dan said. "I guess it's not. Not these days."

Scott punched his shoulder. "Even if you were the cause of it, I wouldn't rat you out. We're buds, bud. And any fan of *Spiderman* is a friend of mine."

"It's not your fault," Dan said. "We know that."

"Then why's—"

"Who the fuck knows?" Scott shook his head. "Most people are dipshits."

Adam thought he heard a rustle behind him, and he picked up the flashlight and shone it around the clearing, but there was nothing there. Behind the succulents, he could see the blackness of the cave.

"Did you hear that?"

The other two nodded.

"What do you think it was?"

Dan's voice was quiet again. "My people call them *Na-ta-whay*. Uninvited guests."

"Ghosts?"

"Some of them. Demons mostly, though. My father says they're homeless and they're looking for a place to stay, and sometimes they invite themselves over to someone's house or a store or a building."

Scott walked back over to the edge. "I thought it was the mine that attracted them."

"That too."

"You need to get your stories straight."

Adam shivered. "Let's get the hell out of here."

"Wait a minute!" Scott was looking over the edge of the sandstone wall. "Cars! Two of them!"

"Places!" Dan said, hurrying over and picking up some rocks.

This was wrong, Adam thought. But it was also cool. And exciting. And he picked up a rock of his own and looked over the edge at the highway below. Off to the right, coming up the road toward the diner, he could see two sets of headlights.

"On my count," Scott said.

The vehicles drew closer, closer.

"Heave 'em!"

Adam threw his rock, and was filled simultaneously with horror and elation as he saw it tumble into the darkness, heard it hit, heard the shatter of glass, the thunk of metal, and the squealing of tires as the driver of the first car slammed on his brakes and jackknifed into the opposite lane. Behind him, the other driver swerved to miss the first vehicle, and one of the other rocks hit *his* car.

The three of them ducked behind the wall, crouching on the dirt. Scott was giggling, but Dan was silent, and Adam assumed that the other boy already felt guilty about what they'd just done. Adam's own heart was pounding so loud that even the noises right next to him sounded muffled. He had not expected there to be an accident. He'd known what they were planning to do, of course, but somehow the outcome of it had been softened in his brain. His focus had been on the action rather than the result.

But he had to admit that there was something vaguely gratifying about the sneak attack. His mind told him that it was in the same category as drive-by shootings or other acts of random violence, that he was no better than the vandals who had spray-painted graffiti all over his house. But emotionally it was a kick, and he'd gotten from it the same sort of thrill that he got from a roller-coaster ride, the thrill of the forbidden and dangerous.

Scott ventured a peek over the side, quickly ducked back down. "They're looking up here," he said.

Dan's voice was worried. "Did they see you?"

"No. It's too dark."

Adam licked his lips. "I hope they don't come up here."

"They'll never find the path."

"But how'll we get down?"

"We'll wait 'til they're gone."

There was a loud sound behind them, and Adam stood, turned—

And a policeman grabbed his arm.

Adam looked up into a cold, hard face, and his heart stopped as he heard a deep, grave voice intone, "You're under arrest."

2

Julia was in the passenger seat next to him, crying, and Gregory wanted to hit her. They were both wearing today's wrinkled clothes that they'd grabbed from the floor after being awakened by the phone call. He was angry at Adam and annoyed at being roused from sleep, but she was devastated, taking it personally, taking it hard, wailing that it was her fault, that she'd been a poor mother.

Her whining irritated him, and he was tempted to shout out, "Yes! It's your fault! You *are* a poor mother!" But he gripped the steering wheel tighter, gritted his teeth, and said nothing.

Her sobs had been reduced to sniffles by the time they reached the police station and got out of the van.

They'd been given no details over the phone, had been told merely that their son had been arrested for malicious mischief, but the sergeant behind the desk who made them sign the release papers said that Adam and two friends had been up at the old lookout above the highway near the diner, throwing rocks at cars. One car had a dented trunk, and another had a cracked front windshield, a shattered rear windshield, and a damaged hood.

The station lobby was empty save for them. There was no sign of the car owners, and obviously the other boys' parents had not yet arrived.

"It's pure luck we caught 'em," the policeman said. "A patron at the diner noticed a flashlight moving up the old lookout trail, and he told Sam Wright, who called us. We intercepted the boys by coming up behind them, off the topside trail. We surprised them at the lookout, but not before they had thrown the rocks and damaged the cars.

"There'll be no criminal charges pressed," he concluded. "But Mr. Redfield and Mr. Robson, the drivers of the damaged vehicles, have the option of filing a civil complaint in order to collect damages."

"Give me their names and numbers," Gregory said. "I'll contact them. I'll make it right."

The policeman smiled thinly. "You're the one won the lottery, aren't you?"

Gregory looked at Julia, nodded.

"Ought to spend a little less time counting your cash, a little more time taking care of your boy, maybe."

Gregory nodded, not wanting to argue. Next to him, Julia started quietly crying again, and though he still wanted to hit her, he put his arm around her and pretended to be comforting.

"Charlie'll bring the boy out." The desk sergeant nodded toward a metal door with a small window of mesh-reinforced safety glass. He wrote down the names and telephone numbers of the victims on the back of a business card, handed it to Gregory. "Here you go." He smiled. "And good luck. The way those two were talking, you're going to need it."

Gregory led Julia away from the desk, over to the door. They stood, waiting for Adam to be brought out.

Behind them, the door to the station opened, and a couple who were obviously the parents of one of the other boys came in, the woman crying, the man angry. Gregory turned away, not wanting to face them, not wanting to talk to them. He didn't know if this stunt had been Adam's idea or one of the other kids', but it didn't really matter. He intended to concentrate only on his family and let the other parents handle theirs.

The lookout.

He knew exactly where it was, though he had never been there. He was surprised that it was still referred to as "the lookout" after all these years. He was also surprised that the cop was so nonchalant about finding kids up there.

He remembered what had happened at the lookout before.

Gregory shivered as he recalled hearing the news for the first time. It had been his sophomore year in high school. A group of seniors—guys on the football team and a couple of cheerleaders—had gone up there to party after one of the games. According to what he'd heard afterward, things had gotten rough. And crazy. One of the girls had volunteered for a gang bang. The other had refused to put out, and the girl had ended up dead, sacrificed on the sand, her body staked down with miner's pikes, her head severed and tossed into the shallow cave.

There'd been rumors of drugs, LSD-laced snacks, enhanced beer, but as far as he knew, none of that had ever come up in the trial, and though the trial had taken place up in Phoenix and they'd received only newspaper and television reports, since the kids' families had all moved away and out of town, coverage had been pretty thorough, and for that year people had talked of little else.

The boys had all received life sentences, and the feel-

ing around town was that they'd been lucky they hadn't
gotten the death penalty.

After that, the town council had voted to seal off the
cave, to destroy the path and the little outcropping that
was the lookout itself. That hadn't happened—it would
have been too difficult, and the lookout was right above
the highway, which could have caused problems—but for
Gregory's remaining years in McGuane, just the memory
of that incident had scared everyone away from the spot.
He'd assumed that that sort of self-prohibition would
last forever, growing into the kind of local myth that
tainted a locale in perpetuity, but obviously that had not
occurred, and it seemed to him ironic that it was his son
who had committed another crime at that location.

Although Adam and his friends probably weren't the
first. The desk sergeant had not seemed especially
shocked or angry about the matter, and he hadn't mentioned anything about it being unusual. Maybe the location's past had been forgotten.

No. That was too hard to believe.

Maybe the story hadn't been passed on to the younger
generation because it was too brutal, despite its obvious
use as a cautionary tale.

That was possible.

But there'd been . . . something else. Something about
the incident with the cheerleaders and the football play-
ers that had made it seem even stranger and scarier than
did the details he could recall. He couldn't remember
what it was, though, and he wondered if Paul or Deanna
might. It was on the tip of his brain, nagging at his consciousness, but it would not be made clear, and he found
that frustrating. It was like trying to remember the name
of a specific song or a character actor in a movie and
not being able to fall asleep because of it.

What was it? What was he thinking of?

A statue. That was it. There'd been some sort of
statue. They'd been worshiping it, holding some kind of
ceremony. It hadn't just been a party, it had been a
ritual, and the cheerleader had been killed not in some
drug-induced frenzy but deliberately, purposefully, as
part of some twisted religious service.

It all came back to him now. The statue had been of

a dwarf. Neither he nor any of his friends had seen the statue before it had been seized as evidence for the trial, but they'd heard about it, and it was the word "dwarf" that had really fired up his imagination, lending the entire business an eeriness that made the situation even more morbidly fascinating than it had been already. He'd imagined the statue in its alcove, in the shallow cave, a small, forbidden god, and just the idea of it had led to nightmares.

He hadn't remembered any of this when he'd first decided to move back to McGuane. The town had seemed a lot more innocent in his memory than he now knew it to be, and he marveled at how the mind glossed over events from the past, remaking them in a nicer image.

Julia turned toward him. "What are we going to do?" she asked.

He looked at her, annoyed.

"Are we going to talk to him? Ground him?"

Gregory felt his anger rise again. "Oh, I'll do a lot more than that."

"What are you talking about?"

"You heard me."

"We've never hit any of the kids."

"Maybe it's about time we did."

"Knock if off," she said. "We have to decide how we're going to handle this before he comes out."

"I've already decided."

"Gregory—"

"I'm going to beat some sense into him. Like I should have done a long time ago."

"You are not." Her voice was deadly serious and filled with a conviction he had not really heard from her before. "You are not going to lay a hand on that boy."

He had not been entirely serious about his stated course of action, had said it more to irritate her than because he had any intention of doing it, and he found himself backing down in the face of her determined opposition. "We'll ground him," he conceded. "And we'll give him a lecture and make sure he understands what he's done."

She nodded. "Okay."

Behind them, the woman's crying grew louder as the

desk sergeant talked to her, and another couple walked into the station, an Indian man and a white woman, obviously the third boy's parents.

Before them, the metal door opened, and a uniformed officer ushered a sick-looking Adam out into the lobby. The boy stared at the floor and would not meet his father's eyes. Something about his son's cowed, guilty passivity irked Gregory. Next to him, Julia started crying again. Adam seemed to shrink even further into himself.

He grabbed his son's arm, squeezing hard, but though Adam grimaced, he did not cry out or complain. That was one point in the boy's favor.

He looked down at his son, tried to rein in his anger. "Come on," he said evenly. "We're going home."

3

He'd actually sold something today, and Jesse Tallfeather was feeling pretty good. Two hundred and twenty bucks for a combination birdbath-fountain in which the water cascaded down a rocky hill from the top of a cement saguaro cactus. It wouldn't stave off the inevitable, but it might buy him another week or so. And at this point, that was about the best he could hope for.

He locked up the yard fence, then walked back into the statuary office to close out the register. The sun had passed over the mountains, and though the sky above was still blue, it was dark down here, and he flipped on the light in the office as he walked through the door.

The statue was standing directly in front of the cash register counter.

He stopped, feeling a sickening lurch in his stomach that he recognized as fear.

It was the statue of a man. A small man. A dwarf or a midget. In addition to its mysterious appearance, there was something disturbing about it, some irregularity in the features of the face that made him feel uneasy, and he thought of that day in the yard when the statues had moved. He'd successfully concentrated on the here and now since then, had not allowed himself to dwell on what he thought he'd seen that day, and had almost succeeded in convincing himself that it had not happened.

Na-ta-whay.

The statue had not been here five minutes ago, the last time he'd walked through. He looked around the small room, glanced out the windows, hoping to see someone running away, some practical joker who had placed the statue here, but there was no one.

He knew that already, though, didn't he? No *person* had brought that statue to the office.

His first instinct was to run, to get away from the statuary as quickly as possible. He could leave, lock the door behind him, taking a chance that no one would break in and steal from the register in the middle of the night. Hopefully, in the morning, the statue would be gone. But even if it wasn't, it would be a lot easier to deal with in the new light of day. And he would have the night to try and formulate some plan.

But what if he awoke at 3 A.M. to see the statue standing at the foot of his bed?

He shivered, feeling cold. He would lock up, he decided, then go talk to the chief and the council, tell them what was happening, bring them over to see—

The statue moved.

He sucked in his breath, holding it. It was only a wobble, a slight rocking of the pedestal base, but the movement was visible and unaided, and in the silence of the office, the creak of weighted cement on wood sounded as loud as a shotgun blast.

Jesse was frozen in place. He wanted to run, but fear kept him from it, and in a quickflash image, he saw in his mind an army of statues moving through the yard toward the office, where their leader waited. A glance out the window told him that was not so, but the feeling lingered, and the sky was getting dark, and he decided that the best course of action would be to get the hell out.

Behind him, the office door slammed shut. He had not closed it after walking in, and he was near enough that it hit the pinky edge of his left hand, the force of the contact making him cry out.

The statue laughed.

It wobbled again.

Jesse fumbled behind him for the doorknob, unwilling to take his eyes off the statue for even a second. The doorknob would not turn, and the statue lurched forward. There was no movement in its legs or stubby arms, no change in the cast expression on its disturbingly peculiar face. The entire object pushed itself across the wooden floor toward him, almost as though there were a person encased inside who was attempting to maneuver despite the limitations of cement imprisonment.

He looked around for some sort of weapon.

Nothing.

He had a toolbox behind the counter, and there was a hammer in it that he could use to smash the shit out of this damn thing, but the statue was between here and there, and though its movements were slow and jerky, he was afraid to go around it.

Logically, there was not much the statue could do to him even if it did reach him. It stood slightly higher than his waist, so he was much bigger than it was, and it could not move its arms. He could knock it down and it would not be able to get up.

But there was nothing logical here, and that reasoning did not apply.

Na-ta-whay.

He tried the door again. Still locked, still closed.

The lights went off.

In the darkness, he heard the squeak of movement and the subtle lilt of laughter.

He jumped out the window.

Or rather he tried to. In his mind, during the second in which he'd come up with the idea and acted upon it, he'd seen himself leaping heroically, jumping out amid the broken glass, rolling on the dirt outside, running away to safety. But it was a double window, divided into two by a metal frame that slid open and shut on the right side. Even in his skinniest days, he'd been larger than the space it afforded him, and he jumped headfirst, hands out, feeling the pain in his fisted knuckles as they broke through the glass and were sliced, followed a split second later by even more excruciating pain as the glass cut into his face.

And then he stopped, his midsection denting the metal of the sliding right window but not breaking it. He was halted in midleap by the too-small frame digging into his gut and forcing the air out of him. The remaining shards of glass cut into his sides, slicing open skin and muscle, as his head and upper torso flopped over and smacked the outside office wall beneath the window.

From the stomach down, he was still inside the office.

And he felt the statue shove itself between his spread legs.

The wind had been knocked out of him and he could not scream, but the force of the cement smashing into his groin tripled both the pain and the need to express his agony verbally, and he gasped like a fish, feeling like he was suffocating as the contradictory impulses that made him need to both scream and breathe collided somewhere in his airless lungs and throat.

His survival instinct was strong, however, and though he was still gulping air and exhaling it too quickly, his chest feeling as though it was about to burst, he marshaled enough of his senses to move his arms and legs. He kicked out at the statue at the same time he tried to position his hands against the bottom of the windowsill.

At least the statue was limited in its movements and could only lurch forward or backward. At least it was not truly sentient.

He tried to wiggle out, using his hands as leverage against the outside wall of the office.

And then he felt cement hands grabbing his feet and pulling him back inside. He kicked, struggled, tried to grab hold of the windowsill, but it was no use.

His death was slow.

Very slow.

And bloody.

4

It was the first concert she'd attended in nearly a month, and Deanna picked a seat that was near the front so she could see the performers, but next to one of the wooden posts so she wouldn't have to share a table with

anyone. Paul was going to be working the soundboard—
the kid he'd hired part-time had called in sick—and she
didn't want to sit with anyone else.

The concert tonight was by a singer from Benson, an
older woman heavily into Patsy Cline. She'd never really
been a big Patsy Cline fan, and she doubted that she
would like this woman all that much, but Paul had been
so loving, caring, and attentive the past few days that
she wanted to reward him, and when he'd asked her to
come and help fill out what was sure to be a less-than-
sellout crowd, she had happily obliged.

Besides, she didn't want to break this mood, and she
figured the best way to keep it rolling was to spend as
much time as possible with him.

They'd had a little makeout session in his office before
the singer and her band showed up. Paul had wanted to
do it on the floor, but she'd drawn the line at that. The
floor was filthy, and despite their desire, they weren't
the hormone-enraged adolescents they had been in high
school. They could wait until later to consummate their
evening. It had been a hot and heavy petting zoo in the
office, however, and they'd both come out feeling high.
Even though they *were* adults, it still got the juices flowing to be doing something slightly forbidden, and she
was already planning what would happen when they
got home.

Around her, the seats began filling. Either the singer
or Patsy had a bigger fan vase in McGuane than Paul
had thought, and pretty soon nearly all of the chairs and
tables were taken. Only two waitresses were working
tonight, and they were earning their pay, taking and filling orders that would have kept four girls running.

Deanna sipped her coffee. She was glad things were
back on an even keel. It had been a rough couple of
weeks. She didn't know what was wrong, didn't know
what had happened between them, but there'd been a
chill, a kind of emotional estrangement, and they'd
fought a lot, for no reason, though it never seemed to
be the fault of either of them.

Julia had seemed somewhat distant lately, too, and it
occurred to her that the problem lay with herself, not
her husband or her friends. She was the nucleus around

which this was occurring, and it was only logical to assume that she was somehow the cause.

But she knew that was not the case. She seldom listened to gossip or rumor, and almost never believed it,
but she was not deaf, and she knew that there were a
lot of problems in McGuane right now. Interpersonal
problems as well as . . . other things.

And she was not the cause of that.

She didn't know what was.

But it made her uneasy.

The lights dimmed, and Deanna looked over her
shoulder, saw Paul at the soundboard. She gave a little
wave, and he smiled and waved back.

The stage lights clicked on, and to the applause of the
audience a slightly overweight woman with a lined but
pretty face led a group of guys along the open aisle next
to the wall and onto the stage.

"Howdy!" the woman announced. "I'm Linette Daniels, and this here's my band, the Crazies!"

There was a guitarist, a bass player, a drummer, a
fiddler, and a pedal-steel player, and they immediately
ripped into a typically turbocharged version of "Orange
Blossom Special." Linette did a little buck dance, to the
delight of the crowd, and then the musicians downshifted
into "She's Got You" and she started singing.

The woman did a fair Patsy Cline impression, Deanna
thought, but it was precisely because of that that her
interest began to wander. The monotonous whining and
yelping was as off-putting coming from this woman as it
had been from Patsy herself, and Deanna found herself
reverting to crowd-gazing. There were quite a few people here that she knew, but an equal number that she
didn't. She watched a grossly overweight man awkwardly
attempt to dance with a lithe little teenager who looked
like his daughter but was obviously his wife or girlfriend.
A small section of the café had been cleared and set
aside for dancing, but they were the only two on the
floor. Her attention wandered to a skinny cowboy sitting
alone next to the stage who had what was without a
doubt the longest neck she'd ever seen on a human
being. He made Audrey Hepburn look like Stubby
Kaye, and his head was rocking back and forth in time

to the music, flopping around on that huge neck like a plum on the end of a bendable straw.

It was a peculiar-looking crowd, and she was having fun just watching the offstage show when her gaze alighted on something that made her heart skip a beat.

A shadow.

It was short, squat, almost simian, and she watched it scuttle along the edge of the crowd toward the side of the stage. It was not flat, like an ordinary shadow, but seemed to be three-dimensional, as though it was a being in its own right, which was appropriate, because there seemed to be no original source to which it corresponded.

The shadow started to climb up the metal rigging to the right of the stage, and she saw that it *was* a self-contained entity. There were no ties to anything else. Its form ended at its feet.

The figure climbed hand over hand until it was at the top of the rigging near the ceiling, but no one else seemed to be looking at it. Even those audience members who weren't intently watching the singer and her band had not noticed the shadow. Deanna looked quickly around, checked out the waitresses. They were busy running back and forth between the tables and the counter, and they had not spotted it either.

Couldn't anyone else see it?

She scooted her chair to the left, saw the small figure crawl along the rigging pipes until it was directly above the stage. There was something unnatural about it, a deformity visible even in its silhouetted shape that marked it as inhuman. That made no logical sense, but she knew it to be true, and though she wanted to look away, she did not.

The shadow began fiddling with the center spotlight.

Deanna stood, pointing and screaming, as she realized what it was trying to do, but the concert was too loud, and though a few of the people around her saw her pointing and looked in the direction of her finger, no one seemed to hear her.

The light fell.

It crashed on Linette, the huge, blocky casing landing corner-down on the singer's bleached-blond head, crushing her skull and shearing off the entire right side of her face. Blood was everywhere—spurting, spraying, misting—and the song ended unnervingly, not with a scream but with a quiet "uh" that cut off Linette's voice as the musicians continued obliviously for a few more bars.

The shadow was jumping up and down on the rigging in a furious assault, and seconds later the entire thing collapsed, lights and pipes, wires and metal bars falling forward onto the audience.

People were screaming, scrambling to get away. Screeching feedback from the speakers drowned out even the screams, and it was as though the entire scene was taking place in some overloud movie. Deanna's mind focused on and absorbed individual events, recording them with a clarity she had never known before: the musicians, covered with spraying blood, dropping their instruments, stumbling back; a stray light swinging from an attached cord and smashing into the face of the long-necked man, knocking him flat; an intact section of rigging falling onto one of the big tables, crushing several couples beneath it; a stray bar of metal spearing through the foot of an older woman, pinning her to the floor as she tried to run.

Where was the shadow?

At the same time she was backing up, trying not to be knocked down by the surging, panicked crowd, Deanna was scanning the ceiling above the stage for any sign of the dark figure.

There it was.

She saw it swinging through the rafters like an ape, and then she was knocked to the ground by a screaming old man who did not even stop to see if she was all right but continued running over her.

She struggled to her feet, leaned back against a post for protection and scanned the ceiling for the figure. Her eyes found the place where it had been, but it was not there, and her eyes darted back and forth, searching.

She found it.

In the rafters directly above.

It was looking down at her, and for a split second she saw glowing white teeth grinning in its dark shadow face.

And then a speaker came crashing down on her head.

Sixteen

1

Julia walked home from the funeral alone, declining to ride with Gregory in the van. She held her breath as a pickup passed by, trying not to breathe until the agitated dust settled.

Moving to McGuane was the biggest mistake they'd ever made.

If she'd thought it once, she'd thought it a thousand times, but it was truer now than it had ever been. As she walked down the dirt road from the American cemetery, she thought of Deanna's death, thought of Adam at the police station, and knew that it was time for them to admit defeat, give in, call it quits, and head back home to California. Their noble experiment had been a failure from day one, and it was time to get out while the getting was good.

She would have a hell of a time convincing Gregory of that, but she was set on this course of action and nothing could dissuade her. She'd go without him if she had to, although she didn't think it would come to that. His mother and the kids would jump at the chance to move back to California, and the pressure of all five of them would hopefully be sufficient to convince him to leave.

Because it was getting dangerous here.

That's what the alarm bells inside her head were saying, and it was not something that she would dispute. She had always felt danger here, from the first day in that dark house, and though she'd tried to rationalize it, explain it away, deny its existence, it had been the one underlying constant in her experience here. She had never felt at home in McGuane, and she knew now that she never would.

It was time for them to cut their losses and run.

Another vehicle passed by—the preacher's car, she thought—and she moved aside and held her breath until the dust had started to settle. She looked over her shoulder, saw the backhoe filling in Deanna's grave behind the iron gates at the end of the road, and was consumed with a profound sadness and sense of loss. Deanna had been her only friend in town, and that, of course, had amplified her feelings, but the truth was, Deanna had been a *real* friend, a person she'd liked immediately, to whom she'd grown close in an extraordinarily short time. Next to Debbie, in fact, Deanna was probably her best friend in the world.

She'd had a tough time maintaining her composure during the funeral service. She'd cried the entire time, but the crying had constantly threatened to erupt into hysterics, and she'd had to hum some goofy old Monkees song in her mind in order to keep from dwelling too intently on the fact that her friend had died.

Been murdered.

She didn't know that, she told herself. She didn't know that for sure.

But she did. She did.

These things happen.

Gregory's mother had not gone to the funeral, had stayed home with the kids instead. She had wanted to come, had wanted the children to go, but Julia did not want Adam or Teo to attend. She remembered her own mother dragging her to church funerals all during her childhood. It was a Molokan tradition, and her parents' generation thought nothing of it, considered it normal and appropriate, but she had hated spending so many weekends in graveyards, had had nightmares and resulting fears and worries that she swore even back then she would never inflict on her own kids. She still considered it unhealthy to spend so much time glorifying and thinking about death, and she had refused to budge on her funeral prohibition for the kids.

Her eyes were so swollen they hurt, and the dust was not making things any better. She wondered if she should have ridden home with Gregory after all, but when she thought of his blank, expressionless face at the graveside service, she knew she had made the right decision. If they'd been trapped in the van together all the way home, they would have been fighting by now. She needed this time away from him, needed this time to herself.

Maybe she wouldn't go home at all for a while. Maybe she'd just wander around, walk, think. Give herself the opportunity to really feel what she needed to feel, to sort out her emotions, to dwell on Deanna's passing and mourn her friend. Alone. In private. Where she could indulge her own feelings and not have to worry about the needs and feelings of others.

She deserved at least that much.

Yes, she thought. She would walk around town for a while.

She'd just make sure to stay far away from Russian-town.

She and Gregory had not made love in weeks. No, that was not true. They had not had *sex* in weeks. They had not made love for months.

That record was not broken tonight. She didn't really want sex, but she wanted someone to hold and hug, a shoulder she could cry on, and Gregory, the bastard, ignored her completely, sitting up in bed and reading his damn *Time,* the blankets pushed into a little wall between them.

She'd gotten home just before dusk to find that Gregory's mother had already made *nachinke* for dinner. They'd all eaten separately—Gregory in the living room in front of the television, Adam and Teo in the dining room, Sasha in her bedroom. Her mother-in-law had sampled as she'd cooked and wasn't hungry, but Julia was famished, and she grabbed four of the pastries and ate them over the sink in the kitchen.

After dinner she'd taken a hot bath, and by the time she was finished, the kids were all safely ensconced in their separate bedrooms. She had the feeling that either

Gregory or his mother had told them to leave her alone, not to bother her, and while she would have preferred some noise, would rather have heard the sounds of talking and laughter and life in the house, she was too tired to make the effort to set things right.

She did not bring up the idea of moving back to California until she and Gregory were both in bed because she did not want to fight in front of the kids, and she knew this would provoke a confrontation. She also wanted a little lag time, a little breather so she could marshal her emotional forces and build up some strength. It had been a long and draining day.

It was an ultimatum she intended to deliver, but she did not want to phrase it as such, and on her first pass the approach was light. "What do you think about moving?" she said.

He looked up from his magazine. "To a different house?"

"Back to California."

She saw his face harden, saw the stubbornness settle over his features, and her own anger rose in reaction. "It's not working out here," she told him. "We tried it, we all followed your dream, but it's turned into a nightmare."

"Still afraid of our haunted house, huh?" He looked like he was sneering.

"Our son was arrested, our friend is dead, there's been a string of murders that somehow we're supposed to be responsible for!" She glared at him. "This fucking town is practically ready to lynch us, and you're obliviously going on like nothing's happened! Well, something has, and it's affected our ability to live here, and it's time we left!"

He looked at her levelly, and he put on his calm, rational, explaining voice, the voice he used when he was going over something with one of the kids or when they were in the middle of an argument and he really wanted to get her goat.

Once again, it worked perfectly.

"I have put a lot of money into this house and into the café, and we will not be getting another lottery check until next summer," he said. "We—"

"We can get jobs!" she interrupted him. "And in case

you haven't noticed, your precious stage collapsed! It killed Deanna and three other people and—"

"Paul has insurance," he said calmly.

"Stop that!" she told him. "Stop playing these fucking games and talk to me like an adult. We're not competing to see who wins this argument here. I'm telling you that we are going to sell this house and move."

"And I'm telling you we're not."

"Well, the kids and I are. Your mother too, probably. We're getting out of here. We're moving back to California—"

"No, we're not." His smile stopped her. There was something strained and artificial about it that frightened her. She was reminded suddenly of an old friend from college, Teri Yu, who, for a brief period of time, had been involved in an abusive relationship. Her boyfriend, Todd something or other, had hit her and beaten her, but Teri always gave the usual unprovable excuses that she'd tripped and fallen, hit her head on a piece of furniture or twisted her arm on the stairs. One evening, however, they'd double-dated, gone to a Jethro Tull concert at the Forum, and in the parking lot afterward, Teri and Todd had gotten into some kind of argument. Todd had slapped her, and he would have done more had not Julia stepped between them and faced him down. His expression at that moment had been terrifying: he was smiling, yet filled with anger, filled with hate.

And he'd looked, at that precise second, exactly like this.

She stared at Gregory. He stared back. She knew they'd been drifting apart, but the thought came to her that they did not know each other at all. She had no idea who this man was anymore, and that frightened her more than she could say.

Then the expression was gone from his face, and her feeling with it, and Gregory just seemed to deflate. The stubbornness was gone, the anger, the hatred, and she saw the fear beneath his bluster, the confusion and vulnerability behind his macho mask.

She saw her husband again.

"I'm sorry," he said. "I'm sorry." There were tears pooling in his eyes, and for the first time she saw how hard all this had been on him. He was stressed out too, and instinctively she reached over to him, put her arms around him, hugged him. They'd drifted so far apart that they'd been unable to read each other's moods. Maybe that was at the root of their problem—lack of communication. They were both the same people they'd always been, neither of them had changed, and she thought that maybe their recent adversarial relationship had arisen from the strangeness of circumstance rather than any true differences between them.

"I didn't mean for it to turn out this way."

"I know," she told him.

"I've failed all of you. I didn't want to—"

"Shhh," she said. "Shhhhh. It's all right." She held him, felt the familiar contours of his body beneath her fingers, the ridges of his collarbone, the muscles in his back, and for the first time in a long while, she felt close to him, truly close to him. They were going to see this through, she thought, they were going to make it, they were going to survive.

"I love you," she told him.

"And you were going to leave me?"

"I couldn't leave you."

"Then give it one more chance," he said. "A month. And if things haven't changed, things haven't improved, we'll sell the house and move somewhere else. Back to Downey . . . wherever you want."

She wanted to argue, knew that she should stick to her guns. This wasn't a problem between them, it was something else, something bigger, and the need to leave seemed imperative. It made no logical sense, but she felt as though the chance to move was a rare window of opportunity that was being offered them, a window that soon would close, and close forever.

But he was asking her, begging her, pleading with her, and she owed him at least that much. It had been his dream to come here, it meant a lot to him, and it was only for a month. Besides . . . maybe she was overreacting, letting her emotions dictate her thoughts.

"I swear. One thing more and we're out of here. Packed and gone. McGuane in our rearview mirror."

There was something about his voice that rang false

to her, and she had the sudden desire, the sudden *need*,
to look at his face and see if the deception she thought
she heard was really there, but he was still hugging her,
holding her tight, his head on her shoulder, her head on
his, and she decided to give him the benefit of the doubt.

"All right," she said. "Okay. One month."

2

The café was closed, as it had been for the past three
days, but Paul's car was parked in the alley, and Gregory
used his own key to unlock the front door. He walked
inside. "Paul?"

There was no response. He shut the door behind him,
looked around. Nothing had been touched since that
night. Yellow police ribbon still circled the mangled
mess of lights and rigging that littered the better part
of the room. Even from here, Gregory could see dried
bloodstains on the floor and on the smashed tables and
chairs.

He had not spoken to Paul since the funeral, and then
it had been merely a generic "I'm sorry," that echoed
the words of the people in line in front of him. He felt
bad that he had not called, had not made more of an
effort to be there for his friend. He'd sent a condolence
card, but that was even more impersonal, and he knew
he should have talked to Paul, but the truth was that he
did not feel close enough to him to do that. Sure, they'd
been hanging together for the past few months, but before that it had been nearly twenty years since he'd seen
him, and Paul had to have friends who were closer to
him than Gregory, had to have formed relationships with
other people in the intervening years.

Gregory felt strange being here alone like this. He
should've called Odd first, brought him along. He had
no idea what to say or do, but he'd already committed
to this course of action, and again he called out, "Paul?"

There was noise in the back.

"It's Gregory!"

Paul emerged from the office area, looking bad. He
obviously hadn't shaved since the funeral, and although

he had changed out of his suit, his clothes were wrinkled, dirty, and disheveled. "What are you doing here?"

Gregory shuffled his feet awkwardly. "I just . . . I came to find out how you were doing, see if you need any help with anything."

"How I'm doing? How I'm doing?" Paul strode across the floor toward him, fists clenched. "How the fuck do you think I'm doing? My wife is dead."

Gregory licked his lips. "I thought you might need some help with the cleanup—"

"Cleanup? What am I supposed to clean up? This place is history. After the victims finish suing my ass, I'll be lucky to own the fucking clothes on my back." He shoved a finger in Gregory's chest. "I never would've done any of this if you hadn't bullied me into it!"

"Bullied you?"

"You think I wanted to have concerts in my café? I never even thought of that before!"

Gregory felt himself being drawn into the argument. "You were complaining that you were barely making enough money to survive. I was just trying to help you out."

"You were on an ego trip. You were bored and rich and looking for something to do, and you thought you'd come and lord it over the people you used to know. And now Deanna is dead because of it."

"Wait a minute—"

"You never liked her anyway, did you? Are you happy now? Got what you wanted?"

Gregory held up his hands. "Sorry," he said. "I just came by to see how you were. If you don't want me here . . ."

"A little late for that, isn't it? I never wanted you here at all. And if I'd listened to what that little voice was telling me, my wife would be alive."

Gregory felt his anger building. "It's not my fault. The rigging collapsed. It was an accident."

"Accidents don't just happen."

"Of course they happen."

"There's always a cause."

"And that's me?"

"If the shoe fits . . ."

"Look, I don't want to fight. I know what you're going through—"

"You have no idea what I'm going through!"

Gregory backed up. "Fine," he said. "Fine. I'm here if you need me. Give me a call if you want. But I think it's better if I leave you alone right now."

"You're here if I need you? Where were you when I needed you to make sure your lights and sound system were safe enough not to kill people, huh? If you hadn't been too fucking cheap to get a professional to put it in, this never would've happened!"

"You're the one who wanted Odd to handle it!"

"And he failed! You and Odd are the ones who fucked up here. You killed my wife and Irma Slater and Houston Smith and Linette Daniels and I'm going to sue your ass for everything you've got, you cocksucking little milk-drinking faggot!"

Gregory pushed him.

They hadn't had a physical altercation since they were little, since junior high, when Paul had gotten blamed after Gregory keyed the gym teacher's car, but they got into it now, escalating instantly from shoving to punching. They were both horrendously out of shape, but anger and adrenaline made up for lack of fitness and expertise, and the fight was vicious. There was no one else around; neither of them was concerned with maintaining a manly facade, and they kicked and punched and pulled and grabbed in animalistic fury.

Paul yanked Gregory's hair, pulled him forward, then punched him in the stomach, knocking him down, and though he could barely breathe, Gregory rolled out of the way before he ended up with a hard kick in the midsection. He staggered to his feet, faced Paul, and though he didn't want to think it, the thought arrived unbidden: *I wish I had my gun.*

Paul came at him again, and Gregory kicked out, the toe of his shoe connecting with his friend's gonads, and Paul fell to the floor, clutching his crotch, curling in on himself, whining in a high, doglike squeal.

A rectangle of light appeared, approached, and then overtook the two of them, and Gregory turned to see

Wynona opening the door. "What is going on here?" she said, looking around.

Paul moaned, and Gregory stared at her dumbly.

The teenager walked in, walked past him, and crouched down next to Paul. She looked up at Gregory disgustedly. "Haven't you done enough?"

He backed toward the open door, letting his fists fall open.

"You killed his wife, now you want to kill him too?"

"I didn't kill anybody," Gregory said. His voice sounded slurred, dumb, confused.

"Just get out of here," Wynona told him, helping Paul to his feet.

He looked at the two of them, then turned and hurried out of the café.

You want to kill him too?

He *had* wanted to kill him, Gregory thought. If he had had his gun, he would have.

And as he got into the van and drove away, he realized that he didn't feel ashamed about that at all.

Seventeen

1

"Look!"

Tompall looked.

It was Jesus.

The picture was grainy and smudged, like a textbook photo of the shroud of Turin, the features of the face hinted at more by what was not clear than by what was. He picked up the sheet of paper, looked at the one beneath it.

Same thing.

Ditto for the one beneath that.

And the one beneath that and the one beneath that . . .

All of the copies made on the machine were imprinted with the countenance of Christ.

"This is a joke, right?" Tompall turned toward his assistant.

Johnny shook his head, his eyes wide.

"Well, what did you do?"

"Nothing!" Johnny's voice was high and nervous. "I just copied these articles for Mrs. Kness. She wanted twenty copies of each, one for each student in her class, and I put them through, had them collated . . . and this is what came out." He handed Tompall the originals, and Tompall sorted through the articles.

Nothing out of the ordinary here.

He opened the copier, checked the camera, checked the glass, even checked the ink and toner, though that could not possibly have a bearing on what had happened.

Finally, he made a copy himself.

Instead of a reproduced article on sea turtles, the photocopy showed the picture of Jesus.

He replaced the paper in both trays, made several copies, varied the reproduction size, but the result was always the same.

"Jesus," he breathed, and the exhalation was not one of identification or recognition.

"What should we do?" Johnny asked.

"Try doing these on the other machine. And get me something else to copy. We'll see if it's the articles or the machine."

It was both.

No matter who copied what, or which machine they used, the result was always the same.

Tompall was sweating, not only afraid but frustrated. He didn't know if this was a miracle or a haunting. He didn't really care. He just wished it had happened to someone else. He had orders to complete here. The town hall's new budget book by Friday. Ab Reese's pharmacy calendars by Monday. Not to mention all the piddly-ass little photocopies that they were given each day—wills and tax forms, letters and checks.

"You think Christ's trying to tell us something?" Johnny asked.

Tompall looked at him. "Just shut the fuck up."

He unplugged both machines, plugged them in again, used Windex to wipe the glass, then, as an experiment, took one of the first Jesus pictures and tried to make a copy of it.

This time, the result was a little bit different.

He and Johnny stared at the legal-sized paper. In this one, Jesus was smiling, and there was a little cartoon speech bubble, like the ones in comic books, coming out from his mouth.

"The Molokans killed me!" Jesus was saying.

Johnny read the words. "You think that's true?" he asked, his voice hushed.

Tompall shook his head slowly, wiped the sweat from his forehead with a paper towel. "Who knows anymore?" he said, staring at the image. "Who the hell knows?"

"You think we should tell someone?"

"Not yet," he said, and he took the picture with the cartoon bubble, placed it on the glass, and hit the Copy button on the machine.

2

"Adam?"

Babunya's voice sounded tired, and he looked up from his comic book to see her standing in his doorway. "Yeah?"

"What are you doing?"

"Reading."

"You are very quiet." She walked into his room, looking around at the mess. It was the first time she'd come in here since they'd moved into the house, and he wondered what the reason was for her visit now.

"How are you?"

He looked at his grandmother and realized that he'd been avoiding her. He'd always been close to her, and they'd talked a lot when they'd first moved here, but in the weeks and months since, he'd made an effort to stay away from her, although it was not something he had even recognized until now.

The banya.

It was the *banya* that had come between them. He hadn't liked lying about going there, and it had been easier just staying away from her. Even after he had stopped sneaking over to the bathhouse, he'd found himself avoiding his grandmother.

Why? he wondered.

He could not really say.

She had obviously noticed, and he assumed that she was now attempting to cross that breach, to break down that wall. He wanted to be able to meet her halfway, to be as close to her as he had been before, but he felt himself stiffen as she approached. Part of him wanted her out of his room, wanted to guard the secrecy he'd been cultivating.

Why? he wondered again.

Once more he did not know.

"I'm fine," he said rather formally, in answer to her question.

She walked over, smiling, intending to sit down next to him, but she stopped just before reaching the bed, focusing on something to the left of him, on the floor. Frowning, she reached down, picked up Sasha's panties from the space beneath the box springs where he'd shoved them.

She looked at him evenly, and he wanted to protest that he didn't know what they were, didn't know how they'd gotten here, but he found himself turning away under her strong gaze, and though he opened his mouth to speak, no words came out.

She slipped the panties in the pocket of her housecoat and sat down next to him.

"Is not your fault," Babunya said softly, putting an arm around his shoulder. "You good boy. I know that. You always good boy. You were born with happy face. The first time I saw you, in the hospital, I saw you had happy face. Sasha and Teo, they don't have happy face like you. I know this not your fault."

He was crying, though he didn't want to and could not remember the last time he had done so, and he hugged Babunya, filled with guilt and a deep, humiliating shame. At the same time, he felt liberated, as if he'd been keeping a secret for a long, long time that he had finally been allowed to tell. He thought of the *banya,* thought of the spot above the highway where they'd been arrested. He wiped his eyes. "What's happening?" he asked.

"Evil," she said, and the word, spoken so plainly and straightforwardly, made the hair on his arms bristle.

He licked his lips. "The *banya*?" he whispered.

She sighed. "Evil always come back. The Devil work in many ways. Even good people influenced by evil. That what happen to you. That is why you throw rocks at cars and . . ." She glanced down at her housecoat pocket, looked quickly away.

"I didn't mean to," he said. "I don't even know why I did it."

"I know." She squeezed his shoulder, looking at nothing, thinking to herself. "I know," she repeated absently.

"I thought you said we had guardian angels, that they would protect us."

She looked at him, nodded solemnly. "That true. We all have them. But they only protect from *earthly* thing, not protect from evil spirit."

That word again: *evil.*

"Our house is haunted, isn't it?"

"Perhaps."

"People were murdered here before, you know. My friend Scott said that the dad murdered his whole family. Maybe it's their ghosts that are . . ." He trailed off. *That are what?* He did not know how to complete the sentence. Everything that scared him, everything that had happened, was vague, unspecific, feelings and impressions more than concrete events.

Except for the stuff occurring around town. The murders. The deaths. The cactus baby. The animal attack on Teo's school.

Those things couldn't have been caused by something in their house, could they?

"Is not ghosts from house," Babunya said. "Not *just* ghosts," she amended. "There are many spirits in town. We pray at church and try to get rid of them, but too many here." Her voice lowered. "Devil send them."

Goose bumps pimpled his skin.

Babunya stared at the wall, at nothing, and when she spoke again it sounded almost as though she was talking to herself rather than to him. "Spirits here but they are . . . uninvited." Her voice sounded uncertain, as if that was something she did not entirely believe.

Adam felt cold. *Uninvited.* He'd heard that before, and he looked at her. He took a deep breath. "The Indians think the same thing. My friend Dan says that they call them uninvited guests. They have some Indian word for it."

"Uninvited guests." She repeated the words as if trying them out. "Uninvited guests." She nodded slowly. "Dan's people very wise."

"Maybe we should talk to them. Maybe they know what to do."

"We know too. Molokans know better."

"But—"

"Evil happen here long time ago and evil attracted here now."

"That's what he said! He said it was the mine—"

"Is not mine." She closed her eyes, breathed deeply. "Sometimes evil want to come back but cannot because everything protected. But sometimes it find a way. A crack to sneak through." She was silent for a moment, and when she spoke again, her voice was barely above a whisper. "This time I make that crack."

She looked at the wall again, but Adam knew she was seeing something else. He was frightened, had no idea what she was talking about, had a million questions, but he sensed that this was a time to keep quiet, and so he said nothing. She would explain, he knew, in her own time.

She sighed. "It because of who I *forget* to invite that other . . . spirits invite themselves."

Adam thought of Rumpelstiltskin.

"Jedushka Di Muvedushka?"

She nodded. "Jedushka Di Muvedushka. I don't realize it until now. A month ago, I went with church to see prophet. Molokan prophet. Very wise man. Holy man. He lives in cave in desert. We ask him what's wrong and he said town in danger. He told me it is my fault." She pointed to her head. "Told me here, not with words. I don't want to believe him, but I think it might be true. I think about Jedushka Di Muvedushka, but I still don't see how it is possible. Now God let me see. We move to house where evil things happen, have no protection, no Jedushka Di Muvedushka, and that allow evil to grow, get stronger. Once stronger, it spreads. Others come."

"Uninvited guests."

"Yes," she said, nodding.

Jedushka Di Muvedushka.

The idea of a little invisible man, a supernatural being living with them in their house, had frightened him at first, and though he had not exactly believed it, he had been glad they'd forgotten to invite the creature to come with them from California. He didn't like the thought of some . . . spirit watching them, monitoring them, keeping tabs on them in the privacy of their own house. If there was such a thing, he was glad they'd left it behind.

Now, though, he had changed his tune. The idea of an Owner of the House, an invisible being watching over them and watching out for them, no longer seemed so far-fetched. It was the same basic premise as a guardian angel. So maybe there was something to it. All legends were supposed to start with a grain of truth. And other cultures had stories of little men as well. Like the leprechauns in Ireland, the trolls and elves in other countries' fairy tales. Perhaps there was some basis in fact to this. Perhaps there *were* little people with magical powers and different countries called them different things.

And at this point, the thought of a little guy staying awake at night while they were asleep, battling evil, unseen enemies, was a comforting one.

But had everything in town, all of the deaths and hauntings and craziness, started because his family had forgotten to invite Jedushka Di Muvedushka to come with them from California and move into their new house? Had everything begun at this home? It was hard to believe . . . but it was not impossible. Scott had told him that the entire town was haunted, and perhaps it was, but everything had apparently remained dormant until they'd arrived, a fact that quite a few people had noticed.

He didn't want to blame Babunya, but he did. She obviously blamed herself as well, and part of him thought, *Good*.

But his parents had known about this custom as well, and *he* would have known about it had his mom and dad not tried so hard to keep them all away from Russian things, from their own culture. They were all at fault, they were all responsible, and maybe they were all being punished for it.

Maybe they deserved to die.

He had a sudden clear image of the *banya,* of bringing his family into it, like an executioner leading condemned prisoners into a gas chamber.

Was it his brain coming up with this? Or was he being influenced by something else? Was this what Babunya had been talking about?

He didn't want to think about it. His head hurt, and he pushed the thought away, forcing himself to see it for what it was.

Evil.

He looked at Babunya. "Did you tell Mom and Dad?"

"No," she said carefully.

"Why?"

"Because your father, I think . . ." She shook her head, looking concerned, and Adam felt scared. She was talking to him seriously, he sensed, like an adult instead of like a child, and while that was frightening enough, her hesitancy and confusion invested it with a dread that went even deeper. He thought of the *banya* again, and he knew that he had to confess.

"I went back to the *banya*," he blurted out. "I haven't been there in a while, but I went back a whole bunch of times after you told me not to, and I even took my friends there, and they're the same friends who were throwing rocks at cars with me." He was on the verge of crying again, and he stopped, looked at her, tried to gather his composure. "Maybe it . . . affected me," he said. "Us. Maybe we're all, like, contaminated or something."

He wished he spoke Russian or wished she spoke better English. This was something that it seemed important to communicate clearly, and he was not sure he could make his grandmother understand what he wanted her to understand.

She seemed to, though, and she nodded solemnly and touched his shoulder. "Yes," she said. "The *banya* is bad place. But you stop going there, no?"

"A while ago. I got scared. But my friend Scott went back and tried to take pictures and the pictures had ghosts on them."

"He stop too?"

"We all did. We all got scared."

"Good." She nodded. "That good. If you can stop, it is all right."

His head was still pounding. It was as if his brain was being squeezed, as if he was connected to some remote control and someone was cranking up the pain volume every time he tried to talk.

"I saw a Russian spoon up there," he said. "Where we were throwing rocks. On that little ledge. It was . . .

spooky. And there was, like, this little . . . cave. And it reminded me of the *banya*—"

"Spooky," Babunya repeated, still nodding, thinking.

"I want to tell Mom and Dad. I think we should tell them."

"No."

"Why not? Maybe they can—"

"No," she repeated. "Wait."

"Why? Wait for what? Things to get worse?"

"Remember what happen to other family in this house? Father kill his children . . ."

She looked at him, and he was suddenly filled with a knowledge he did not want to have. He knew what she was saying, and he could see the image in his mind, but he shook his head vehemently. "No. That couldn't happen."

Even good people influenced by evil.

Evil always come back.

She nodded slowly, as if agreeing with him, but he knew she didn't agree at all, and he wondered what she was thinking, what she knew. Maybe she was like a witch, he thought. Maybe she was psychic. Maybe she could see the future.

The idea should have made him more afraid of his grandmother, but for some reason it didn't. It made him feel safer, more secure.

Except when he thought about his father.

A look passed between them.

"Okay," he said. "I won't say anything."

Babunya smiled absently, patted his head. "You good boy. That why you have happy face."

She was obviously distracted, obviously thinking about something she did not plan to share with him, and for that he was grateful. She had shared too much already. He didn't like this adult talk, didn't like being trusted with knowledge he should not have to know, secrets he should not have to keep. He'd been eager to grow up, but he was eager no longer. He wanted to be able to be just a kid again, not to have to think about any problem other than his own, to let adults do all the worrying and thinking.

She stood, holding her back and letting out a small

"Oy." She looked down at him. "Stay here," she said. "Be nice to your father, but be careful. Make sure Teo be careful too. Try to obey everything he says."

Adam felt something close to panic. "Why? Where are you going? Aren't you going to be here?"

"Church. I will be back soon. Before dark."

"Babunya—" The urge to cry had returned.

"I will be back soon." She said some sort of prayer in Russian, smiled at him, and his headache seemed to fade away.

"Be good," she told him and kissed his forehead before she turned to leave.

He had been forbidden to contact Scott or Dan since the arrest, had seen them only in school, and even there paranoia had severely inhibited their conversations. It had been a tough two weeks. He could not leave the house on his own, could not go anywhere except school, could not stay after school for any reason, and he'd had a difficult time adjusting. He knew he'd been in the wrong, though, and he'd obeyed his parents' orders, spending his time reading, watching TV, doing his homework, writing letters to Roberto, even playing games with Teo.

But this was too big, too important. He had to break the prohibition. When he knew everyone else was occupied—Sasha gone, Teo outside playing, his parents busy, Babunya back at church—he sneaked surreptitiously out to the phone in his parents' bedroom and gave Dan a quick call.

Dan's mother answered. "Hello?"

"May I speak to Dan?"

He was whispering, he didn't want to get caught, and Dan's mother was immediately suspicious. "Who is this?"

He thought quick. "Robert. From Dan's English class. I have laryngitis and I'm calling to ask about homework."

"Oh," she said. "Just a minute."

He heard her call for Dan, and a minute later his friend came on the phone. "Robert?" He sounded suspicious too. There was no Robert in their English class.

"It's me. Adam. Is your mom still there?"

"No."

"I'll talk fast."

He explained about the meeting with his grandmother, gave a quick thumbnail sketch of Jedushka Di Muvedushka, told him his grandmother and the other Molokans thought that was the source of everything that was happening around town. "Even us," he said. "Remember that Russian spoon? That's why we were up there—"

"That's not why we were up there," Dan said.

"Well, maybe not. But you know what I'm saying. And get this. She says these spirits or whatever they are are *uninvited*. That's the word she used. 'Uninvited.' "

"Na-ta-way," Dan breathed.

"That's exactly what I told her, and she went off to her church right away. I guess they're going to try something. But I thought you should know, too." He thought once more about how long Dan's people had been here, how old they were. A shiver passed through him. "I thought you guys might know what to do. I thought you might have some kind of ritual or something that might work better."

"I'll talk to my father," Dan said. "He's not too thrilled with me right now, but I think he'll listen." There was a pause. "This is serious, isn't it?"

"I think so. My grandma seems to think so."

"We should've said something earlier. We shouldn't have waited so long."

Adam heard a noise in the hallway, and he quickly hung up, ducking into his parents' bathroom and flushing the toilet, then walking out, pretending to buckle his pants. His father walked into the bedroom, and there was something weird about him, something strange.

Adam was grateful that the toilet was still running. He tried to think of some reason why he'd come in here instead of going to the other bathroom, but his father did not seem to be interested or care. He walked past Adam and lay down on the bed, closing his eyes and laying a hand over his forehead as though he had a headache.

It was weird, weird and spooky, and he thought of what Babunya had said—

Remember what happen to other family in this house?

—and hurried out of his parents' bedroom back to his own.

He hadn't even had time to say good-bye to Dan, he thought.

Somehow that bothered him.

3

It had come to Agafia in Adam's bedroom, when she'd seen his sister's underwear wadded up beneath his bed. She had tried to remain calm for his sake, but inside she was in turmoil, filled with the sudden realization that the evil forces in this town were not just growing stronger and randomly killing people but were proceeding along other, quieter, more subtle lines as well. And when he told her he'd gone back to the *banya,* told her of the spoon on the ledge, she understood the extent of the influence. They were all at risk. Every one of them. Her family. Her friends. The Molokans. Everyone in town. Not just from without but from within.

Suddenly, it had all become clear, and she understood what the prophet had tried to tell her. It *was* the fact that they had not invited the Owner of the House that had led to this, that was the source of these murders and manifestations. That one breach had allowed spirits to gain a foothold here in town, had taken the lid off the pressure cooker. As Adam said, this was a bad house to begin with, home to evil of its own, and evil was like a magnet for other evil.

Evil always comes back.

Now spirits were overrunning McGuane, growing ever more powerful.

And their house was at the center of it.

She had blessed the home. Many times. Every time she walked into it, in fact. But that sort of mild defense did not make up for the lack of strong permanent protection, and she had allowed her reliance on habit to blind her to what was really going on. She had assumed that their house was safe because she was blessing it,

while the truth was that it was being invaded under
her watch.

It explained why none of the Cleansings had taken,
why none of the rituals had worked. Their focus had
been misdirected. They had concentrated their prayers
and energies on the church because that was where Jim
had been killed, but they should have been focused on
this house.

Perhaps they could have stopped it earlier.

No matter. They would stop it now. She phoned Vera,
told her to call the others immediately and gather them
together. She didn't say why, didn't say what the hurry
was, but she told Vera she would meet them at the
church, and she made it clear that it was important. She
did not want to speak in this house, did not want to
reveal too much in case something was watching, listening. She knew the church was clean, and she thought
it best to discuss things there. On the other end of the
line, Vera seemed strange, distant, but she agreed to call
the others and meet.

Agafia changed into a Russian dress, put on her white
sneakers, and went into the dining room for her Bible.
Gregory and Julia were both at home, and she could
have asked one of them to take her downtown in the
van, but she was wary of involving them. She had spoken
to Adam, and she would talk to Teo, but Sasha and
her parents were out. They were too old. There was a
possibility of corruption, and while it was not their fault,
she knew she could no longer trust them. Not until this
was over.

Agafia thought of the prophet's bony arm, wiping out
the small town on the sandy floor of the cave.

She could not allow herself to think about that. She
had to concentrate on what needed to be done now, and
she quickly called Vera back, but the line was busy, so
she dialed Semyon's number. No one answered.

She made several phone calls, calling everyone in the
church for whom she had a number, dialing Vera's number in between each, but she could not get hold of anyone, and she made the decision to walk. It was foolish,
perhaps, but it felt right, and, putting on her jacket,
clutching her Bible, she sneaked out of the house and

hurried up the drive, praying she would not hear Gregory's or Julia's voice behind her.

She headed for the church.

It was a long walk. She tired easily these days, and ordinarily she would have had to sit down and rest every so often, but the brisk air and pumping adrenaline gave her the sort of strength she had not had in years, and while she did not *speed* down to the church, she was able to make good time.

She remembered when she was younger and walked to the church all the time, when she and John and Gregory would get dressed up and all walk, and she found herself thinking that the years sped by far too fast, that life was too short.

It took only fifteen minutes for her to reach the street on which the church was located, and her step, which had been flagging, picked up as she hurried along the side of the road.

She did not see the building until she was nearly upon it—the bulk of the variety store blocked it from view—but as soon as she reached the vacant lot next to the church, she stopped dead in her tracks, her heart lurching painfully in her chest and causing her to gasp.

The church was covered with hair.

Not all of the other Molokans had arrived yet, but several of them had, and they were standing in the dirt parking lot, staring at the building. She hurried past the vacant lot, over to them.

Thick black hair had grown out from every inch of wood wall and stone step and shake roof, straight and shiny and several feet long. The church resembled nothing so much as some sort of fantastic beast from a children's fairy tale, but there was no sense of the benign magic so common to children's stories. This was wrong, this was evil, and it had been created not to amuse or inspire awe but to terrify.

Agafia had never seen such a thing before, and it was the absurd incongruity of the sight that made it so frightening. There was a cool, dry breeze blowing through the canyon, and the light wind caused the hair to waft left on unseen currents, waving slightly and giving the church beneath it the appearance of movement.

When had it happened? Last night? This morning? Had it occurred as these things usually did, under the cover of darkness, when no one was looking? Or had someone seen it? She imagined the transformation: the hair appearing, coming in, the church building suddenly growing darker, as though a shadow was passing over it, until the hair grew long enough to see and it became clear to anyone viewing the sight what it was.

Did this have any meaning? she wondered. And what was the significance of *hair*? She didn't know, but she walked onto the church property feeling cowed and intimidated, certain that this bizarre desecration had somehow been meant as a warning to *her*.

Vera turned in her direction as she walked over. "It is *you*," she said quietly. "You are the one who has brought this upon us."

"What?"

"It is your fault. This. Everything."

She understood now Vera's diffidence over the phone, and she shook her head. "No."

"Last night I dreamed of the prophet. He told me."

"What did he tell you?"

"He told me you had been influenced. He said you must be cast out." Vera looked at her evenly. "He said this is your fault. It is all your fault."

She wanted to explain that it *was* her fault, that she had forgotten to invite the Owner of the House and that it was from that that everything else had sprung, but she knew that at this point Vera would not listen to her. The other woman was fixated on her dream, she believed it utterly, and nothing anyone could say would dissuade her.

"Pray for me," Agafia challenged her.

"It is too late for that." Vera turned away. "Leave. This is no longer your church."

Pacifism or no pacifism, she heard hatred in Vera's voice, hatred and fear, and she could sense the threat of violence just below the surface.

Agafia turned away, feeling frustrated and frightened, not knowing what to do. Other people were stopping, drivers on the street braking to a halt so they could look at the transformed building. A crowd was gathering.

She looked again at the church, and this time she saw it in a different light. She'd been thinking of this as a religious occurrence, an act of defiance against God, but now she saw it as vandalism. That was why the hair made no sense, she realized. Like everyone else, she had been thinking in biblical terms, trying to equate what was happening to the words and prophecies in the Bible, but this had nothing to do with that.

This was not sacred, it was secular.

A hand touched her shoulder, and she whirled around. It was Semyon. He'd obviously been standing nearby, listening to her and Vera, and he was offering his support. "I do not believe it," he said. He smiled. "I know you, Agafia."

She smiled back, took his hand, gave it a small squeeze of gratitude, but the expressions on the faces of the others were hard and harsh, judgmental and unyielding.

She pulled him aside, walked with him out toward the street. "Listen," she said, quietly but earnestly. "We need Vasili. Someone needs to get him and bring him here. Our Cleansings are nothing, a squirt of water on a pile of dirt. There are . . . many entities. They are invading McGuane and there are more all the time. Nikolai knows nothing about this, and even Vera is in over her head. Maybe the prophet has some idea of what we can do to stop it."

"He wasn't much help last time."

"Prophets only know what God *wants* them to know, and only *when* God wants them to know it. Vasili has no control over what is revealed to him. And perhaps he has had some revelations since that will let us know what to do." She paused. "Besides, God may have nothing to do with this."

She saw the look on his face, and she stopped him before he could start. "We don't have time," she said. "But this has nothing to do with prayers or God or Jesus Christ. It has to do with Jedushka Di Muvedushka . . ."

He frowned. "That's just a . . . a tradition. A superstition."

"It is not!" she said fiercely. "My father saw him, and I'm sure you know plenty of other people who have,

too. And you and your family have always invited him
when you moved, haven't you?"

Semyon nodded a reluctant acknowledgment.

"So you believe. Don't tell me you don't."

He was interested now.

She took a deep breath. "I forgot to invite him when
we moved here. I cannot go into the details now, but as
I'm sure you know, that left our house unprotected. And
you know which house *that* is. You know what happened there."

He swallowed, nodded. "The Megan house."

"That is where it started. It grew from that." She took
his right hand in hers, looked into his eyes. "You see
what I mean? This may have nothing to do with church."

"The way it started might have nothing to do with the
church, but the spirits that have come in, the evil that
has come in since your house was unprotected . . ."

"That's why I hope the church can help stop it. I don't
have any other ideas. So get the prophet. Tell him.
Maybe he will know what to do."

"I will," Semyon promised.

"Vera will not listen to me, and that means Nikolai
will not listen to me, but you talk to them, you make
them know what is behind all this, what started it. And
make sure someone brings the prophet here."

"He may not come."

"At least talk to him, tell him what is happening, see
if he knows what to do."

The others were staring at them, and Agafia released
him, used her left hand to help hold up the Bible sagging
in her right. "Go," she said "Talk to them. Tell them."

He nodded, backed away. "I believe you," he said.

She smiled her thanks.

It was getting near dusk, and the air was growing even
colder. The others obviously had something planned,
and she hoped they'd at least called in someone else for
whatever ritual it was. She doubted it would work, but
there needed to be ten of them. Just in case.

They were staring at her, waiting for her to leave, and
so, clutching her Bible, Agafia turned and walked
through the long shadows of downtown back toward
home.

Only she didn't get that far. She was in front of the
hardware store, standing on the corner, looking both
ways, when to her right she saw a small, dark figure
crossing the road, a little man with a beard, and her
heart jumped.

Jedushka Di Muvedushka.

She had never seen him before, but she recognized
him instantly. There was about the small man an air of
the unearthly. Something about him bespoke an unnatural origin, and though he appeared calm and benign, she
was seized with fear at the sight of him.

When Father had seen the Owner of the House back
in Mexico, it had been accidental, pure luck, and it, too,
had been right around sundown. Father had never been
sure whether it was the special qualities of the light
which had given him that glimpse of the little man, the
fact that it was the time halfway between day and night,
or whether the Owner of the House had *allowed* him a
glimpse, but he had never doubted what he'd seen and
neither had anyone else in the family.

Agafia understood why. There was something so *there*
about the man, something so substantial about his presence that he seemed in a way more real than his
surroundings.

It was that observation which made her think he
wanted her to see him.

But whose Owner was he? she wondered. Where had
he come from? And why was he trying to communicate
with her?

He turned, smiled, beckoned.

She followed him to Russiantown.

She remained far behind, ready to run at any moment,
though she doubted she could actually escape him. He
did not appear to be after her, made no effort to chase
her, and though she was cold and tired and winded, she
followed him through empty alleys and empty streets,
along a route that seemed specifically designed to avoid
contact with anyone else, until they were halfway up the
canyon and in the ruins of Russiantown.

She could not recall the last time she'd been here, but
she remembered the layout perfectly, and she knew,

even before they reached their destination, where he was leading her and what he wanted her to see.

The small man passed through a yard of overgrown dead weeds higher than his head, then climbed up the rickety remnants of wooden steps to a doorway.

The doorway of their old home.

She stood before the ruins of the house, the memories of that last day and night flooding over her. She'd vowed never to return, had promised herself she would not come back to this spot, but here she was, and she faced the past boldly, unflinchingly, something which would not have been possible even a week ago but was absolutely necessary now.

She remembered what happened, remembered what they'd done.

It had been during the Copper Days celebration. Back then, the event had not drawn tourists and people from outside. It had been a local celebration, a miners' holiday. Only there weren't many miners anymore. The mine was closed. It had been closed since before the first Molokan had moved here, but that did not stop some of the more belligerent unemployed mineworkers from using them as scapegoats. They didn't blame Molokans for the fact that the pit had run dry, or the fact that the mining company found it cheaper to move on rather than attempt to extract copper from the remaining low-grade ore—they blamed Molokans for the fact that they were no longer working. The Molokan farm was doing well, and that helped to focus their anger, provided them with a contrast between the Russian community's growing success and their own falling fortunes.

Some of that hatred was directed at the Mormons as well, who were also surviving, if not thriving, during those tough economic times and who had stores of extra food in their homes and in the church. But it was the Molokans who bore the brunt of the resentment. They were foreigners. They talked funny, they dressed funny, and they didn't even believe in war. They wanted to live in this country, but they didn't want to fight for it, and that enraged many of the townspeople.

The seeds for what happened Saturday night had been sown Friday evening, during the first day of the celebration, when one of the bars had offered free drinks to all ex-miners. The First World War had just ended the year before, and the bar owner got up on his soapbox and started lecturing about what he'd seen in Europe and how important it was that every man be willing to fight when his country called him. The combination of alcohol, miners, and the subject of war had of course led to long, drunken diatribes against the Molokans and their anti-American way of life.

The horde of miners had slept it off Saturday morning, for the most part, and roused themselves for the fair in the afternoon, but by Saturday night they were at it again, paying for their own drinks this time, and angry about that as well.

This crowd was bigger. Not the whole town by any means, but a significant minority, and they added to their numbers as they barnstormed through the area, trying to drum up enough people to take some action, adopting a you're-either-with-us-or-against-us tack that intimidated a lot of fence-sitters into joining them.

Agafia remembered the first smell of smoke, remembered seeing the orange glow from the top of the plateau as the Molokan fields were set on fire. She remembered, after that, how the drunken miners and their supporters had come after their homes.

And she remembered what they'd done in retaliation.

It was something they had never spoken of since, something she never thought about and had almost convinced herself hadn't happened.

But it had.

Russiantown had been destroyed that night. There'd been no real plot or plan, there was nothing organized or thought out. Roving gangs of angry, intoxicated citizens, true believers and the sheep who succumbed to mobthink, drove, walked, stormed through Russiantown, wanting to lash out, wanting to cause harm. And doing so. There had been beatings and assaults as well as property damage. Three women had been raped, two of them in front of their husbands. Her own uncle had been hanged by the miners, tied up and dragged downtown by the mob at the height of the frenzy, strung up on the cottonwood tree in the park, and it was after his murder,

after seeing the suddenly lifeless body of a man who'd
been alive only seconds before, that the riot or whatever
it was ended, that the crowd, now cowed and silent, dis-
persed and went home, leaving rubble and broken lives
in their wake.

They had watched the hanging from out in the street,
her entire family, and though she had wanted to look
away, she had not.

Nor had her mother made her.

The faces of the men who performed the act, who
committed the murder, were seared into her memory.
She knew they would never be caught or tried or prose-
cuted—not in this town—but she committed their faces
to memory anyway.

Russiantown had burned to the ground, and the few
buildings that were not burned had been looted and torn
apart. Her family and John's and Semyon's and Vera's
and Alexander's had been the hardest hit, and someone,
she could not remember who, had told them that night,
as they were nursing their wounds and surveying the
damage and mourning the dead, as the fire wagons attempted to put out the fires so they would not spread
to the rest of McGuane, that there was a way to get
back at those who had perpetrated this wrong, that there
was a way to exact revenge.

If it had been an hour earlier or an hour later, perhaps
they would not have followed through, would not have
allowed themselves to be led in this direction. But pas-
sions were high, and word spread quickly among the
battered and displaced populace of Russiantown that
they had recourse, that there was something that could
be done to get back at the people who had destroyed
their homes and lives.

They'd gathered together with a man she did not know,
crouching in front of a fire next to a *banya*. The mood
had been somber and secretive, and they had called forth
a spirit from the forbidden texts of a prophet whose very
name had been expunged from Molokan records and
history. The prophet's words had been saved, passed
down haphazardly, here and there, by outsiders and mal-
contents, Molokans who weren't really part of the

church or the community, and though the existence of the words was known, it was not tacitly acknowledged.

Someone had found them, though, someone knew them, and after all these miles and all these years, the worst of them were spoken.

Jim had already been assisting Pavil Dalgov, their minister at the time, and it was Jim and the minister alone who had argued against revenge, who had told them in no uncertain terms that they were treading on the province of God. "Vengeance is mine, said the Lord," the minister kept repeating, and he ran down a litany of the ills that had befallen those who had gone outside the words of the Bible for comfort or satisfaction, who had trusted not in the Lord but in their own basest instincts. They would pay dearly for this sacrilege, he told them.

The warnings were ignored, however, the forbidden words were spoken, and it had come out of the fire, a blackened thing of charcoal and ash, a creature of death that bowed before them and waited for their orders, willing to do their bidding.

Names had been shouted: the names of those who had inflicted the damage, the names of those who had accompanied the murderers and egged them on. The creature disappeared into the shadows.

And those men had died.

And their wives had died.

And their children had died.

Horribly.

It had been a betrayal of their Molokan beliefs and their covenant with God, this . . . summoning, this intervention from the spirit world. They knew that almost immediately, knew that the minister was right, that they had done wrong. There'd been no satisfaction in the deaths of their tormentors, no sense of rightness or justice, only grief and despair and the guilt of the wicked, but afterward they'd told themselves that something good had come out of it because it had reinforced their faith, had brought them back spiritually to where they were supposed to be. They had sinned, they all knew it, and they had rededicated themselves to God and the Molokan life.

The demon had died after performing its assigned

duty. It had been created out of hate and magic for one thing and one thing only, and when that was done, it had dissolved into nothingness, its life extinguished with the death of its purpose.

Perhaps that had been the true start of it, Agafia thought now. Perhaps that was why she and the Molokans were being targeted. They were being punished for what they had done in the past. Judgment had finally found them. Her unprotected opening had allowed the natural workings of supernatural events to resume, had allowed impulses and forces that had been blocked and dammed for all these years finally to take their course.

Did that mean there was nothing they could do to stop it?

No. She did not believe that. God would not let such a thing happen. And God would not allow the innocent to suffer. The children, like Sasha and Adam and Teo, the people who had moved into town since those days, none of them had had anything to do with the events of that time, and God would not turn His back on them.

But were any of them really innocent?

She recalled the look in her future husband's eyes when he had helped to call forth the death spirit that night, and she remembered that there was something in the fierceness and determination of his expression that had appealed to her, that had drawn her to him. While she had not exactly been waffling in her commitment to him, it was that as much as anything else that had cemented her resolve to be his wife.

The sins of the father were visited upon the sons, she thought.

Evil always comes back.

No, she thought. God would not allow it. He would not stand by while the innocent were taken.

Jim had been innocent, though. He had fought against the summoning of the spirit. He had not taken part in any of it.

And he had been killed.

Evil did not play by God's rules.

And evil always came back.

In the doorway of what was left of her old house,

Jedushka Di Muvedushka turned, looked at her. His face was middle-aged, but his eyes were ancient.

He smiled, beckoned, but she refused to follow him any farther and would not walk into the house.

Whose Owner was he? she wondered again. Someone's who had been left behind when Russiantown had been abandoned? She remembered father inviting Jedushka Di Muvedushka to come with them when they moved, and she remembered, even on that terrible morning, the kids laughingly making room for him on the buggy, though they could not see anything there.

No, this one was not theirs.

Still smiling at her, the little man walked into the open entrance of her old house and promptly disappeared into the shadows.

She dreamed that night of the *pra roak*.

She was back in the cave, and she was alone with him. He looked up from his fire at her and grinned, and she turned away, wanting to leave, but the bones had blocked the path and she was barefoot.

He cackled, and she saw that he no longer had his unnaturally white teeth. His teeth were rotted, blackened stumps.

He reached out an arm and wiped out the town he had rebuilt in the sand.

"It's here," he said in English, and his voice was Gregory's voice. "It's time."

4

Gregory met Odd at the bar. Paul had severed ties with the handyman as well as himself, and the two of them had spent the past several days commiserating about it, feeling sorry for themselves, drinking away their troubles. It was clear to Gregory that the bartender didn't like him, that the man was one of those ignorant yokels who bought into that bullshit rumor that he and his family had brought bad luck or evil or whatever it was to McGuane, but as usual beliefs took a backseat to bucks, and since he and Odd were the bar's most loyal customers, the man put his personal feelings aside and served them.

He didn't participate in the conversations, though. And he kept a wary, careful distance.

He was listening, however. He kept his ears open, and he kept track of what was said and who said it, in case he needed the information in the future.

That ticked Gregory off.

It was one of *many* things that ticked him off.

There was nothing he could do about any of it now, but he, like the bartender, was keeping track, keeping score, and one of these days he was going to tally everything up and the bill was going to come due.

Gregory finished his beer, motioned for another.

The headaches had been really bad the past few days, much worse than usual, and he'd considered going to a doctor. Aspirin and Tylenol did no good, and it occurred to him that perhaps he had something serious, like a brain tumor.

Drinking took away the pain, though, and for the moment that was his medicine of choice.

The bartender brought him a beer, and Gregory nodded his thanks, smiling unctuously. The bartender ignored him and went back to the other end of the bar where he was pretending to dry shot glasses.

Gregory raised the mug to his lips, took a long, cool drink, then stared down at the dark wood countertop. He didn't know what was wrong with him. He and Julia had made up, or had pretended to make up, but for some reason he'd been avoiding her ever since. It was as if her capitulation had somehow tainted her in his eyes, and if he had found himself too often angry with her before, now he was simply disgusted. He had no respect for her whatsoever; in fact, it was hard to remember what had once convinced him to marry her.

He didn't want to go home tonight, and he realized that he was drunk when he found himself trying to concentrate nonexistent psychic powers on Odd in an effort to get his friend to invite him over to his place. He kept repeating the same phrase over and over again in his mind, concentrating so hard that he gave himself a headache: *Invite me to sleep at your house. Invite me to sleep at your house.*

Finally he gave it up and just came right out and asked.

"Julia kicked me out," he lied. "Do you know someplace I could stay the night, until things cool off?"

Odd squinted at him. "What're you talking about? A separation?"

"No, no. Just for tonight. Just this one time."

"Hell," Odd said, "Lurlene and I'd love to have you over."

That was what he'd been fishing for. "Thanks," Gregory told him. "You're a real pal."

The old man grinned. "At least you got *one* left."

Gregory nodded. He wasn't sure why he did not want to go home. And he didn't know why he wouldn't just go to a hotel if his goal was merely to stay away. But this was what felt right, and he was glad that Odd had invited him over.

Or else he would have had to kill him.

Where had that thought come from? Gregory didn't know, but it frightened him, and he pushed the mug away, declining to finish the last half of his beer. "I'm ready to go," he said. "Let's get out of here."

They were both too drunk to drive, and so they walked through town, ignoring the hostile stares of the passersby. Odd had said before that things had turned nasty, and he was right. There was a feeling of tension in town, tension combined with a wild unpredictability that reminded Gregory of the mood in Los Angeles just before the riots.

He thought of his father, wondered what his father would think of this.

Odd lived in a run-down one-story wood-frame home just behind the business district. He hadn't kept up maintenance on the house—ironic for a handyman—but the yard was carefully landscaped and, rare for this town, sported two tall citrus trees and a full lawn.

The old man pointed proudly at his grass. "Lurlene refused to live in a house without a lawn. Water bills cost me an arm and a leg, but it looks good, if I do say so my damnself."

Gregory nodded his agreement, and the two of them walked up the porch steps into the house. "Hon?" Odd called.

There was no answer.

"Probably in the kitchen." Odd led the way through the rather shabby living room, opening the swinging door that led to the kitchen.

Odd's face lit up. "Gregory?" he said, turning around proudly. "This here's my wife."

In the center of the kitchen was a cow.

A heifer.

Gregory stared in horror at the animal, which stood in the middle of the room placidly chewing its cud. There was a bale of hay on the floor next to the refrigerator, and dirty hoof marks marred the yellowed linoleum.

Odd kissed the cow on the mouth, and Gregory could see, through the gap between their ill-fitting lips, his tongue caressing hers.

Through the fog of alcohol, through the headache that still lay somewhere beneath that, a rational part of his brain was telling him that this was not right, that there was something wrong here, that whatever had led his friend to do this was dangerous and he should get the hell away from here as quickly as possible. But amazingly, incredibly, he was already rationalizing it, and whatever protests had been forming in his mind were quickly squelched.

Love was blind, Gregory told himself. And if he could marry an outsider like Andrea, well, Odd could marry a cow. Who was he to pass judgment on someone else's private life?

Again, there was a nagging hint of disagreement from somewhere deep within his brain, but that faded into nothingness.

Gregory walked over to the opposite side of the kitchen, slumped down in the breakfast nook, and smiled at his friend. "What's for dinner?" he asked.

5

Julia was frightened, Gregory had not come home last night, and his mother had been upset and agitated, ranting in Russian about evil spirits and Jedushka Di Muvedushka. Promise or no promise, this was the last straw. She was going to pull up stakes and throw their stuff in the van and drive back to California as quickly as her lead foot would take her. She had not slept at all, wondering whether Gregory was dead, murdered, lying in a ditch, or whether he had . . . what? Run away?

She didn't know, but she was scared. She'd called Paul in the middle of the night, but he said he hadn't seen Gregory in days. She'd called Odd, but no one had answered the phone at his house.

Maybe he was at Odd's, she told herself hopefully. Maybe they'd gotten to talking and lost track of time and he'd had a little too much to drink and he'd decided to spend the night there.

But why hadn't he called?

Because something had happened to him.

It was an idea she could not get away from.

His mother was even more worried than she was, if that was possible, and the two of them had talked about evil spirits and the Owner of the House, and the skepticism Julia had always feigned before had been completely stripped away.

Her mother-in-law's worry was of a different sort. Agafia seemed to believe with unshakable certainty that nothing injurious had happened to her son, that he had not been hurt or killed, but she was worried about . . . something else. She was wary with Julia, but though it did not disappear completely, that suspicion did break down a little as the night stretched on, and Julia learned that it was the house that made her mother-in-law so guarded, the fear that she, Julia, had somehow been corrupted or influenced that kept Agafia from trusting her fully.

The house.

It was terrifying to have her worst fears confirmed, but it was also strangely reassuring. Gregory's mother told her it was because Jedushka Di Muvedushka had not moved with them to this house that other spirits had been allowed in. Julia remembered the flippant and condescending reaction she'd had that first day when Agafia had been so worried about not inviting the Owner of the House, and she was ashamed of her attitude. If she'd had more respect, if she'd been a little less arrogant and a little more open-minded, perhaps she would have caught on to this earlier. They might not have been able to stop what was happening, but they might have been able to get away from it.

The house seemed even darker than usual to her, though it was morning and the brightest part of the day.

What was here? she wondered. What existed in this place with them? The ghosts of Bill Megan and his murdered family? A demon from hell? Some nebulous, shapeless, evil entity?

As ridiculous as those concepts would have sounded to her before, they all seemed perfectly plausible now, and Julia understood why Agafia was so wary. She thought of Sasha's behavioral reversal since they'd moved here, Adam's arrest, Teo's secrecy, her and Gregory's personal problems. They'd all been influenced in one way or another. She'd noticed it before, and she'd always attributed it to natural causes, but the pattern now seemed too clear to ascribe to such innocent origins.

She'd let the kids go to school earlier without telling them that their father was missing, without letting them know her fears, and she was glad now that she'd done so. It would make it easier to do what she knew she had to do.

She faced Gregory's mother across the kitchen table and told her that they were going to leave. "After I find Gregory, we're getting out of here," she said. "We're going back to California before anything else happens. Just pack enough for a week or so, and we'll get the rest later, when we sell the house."

"No," Agafia said in Russian. "I cannot leave. I am responsible for allowing this evil in, and I must remain to fight it. Only our church can put an end to this—"

"But your family comes first," Julia said, also speaking Russian. "Your first loyalty is to us. We need to get out

of this town before one of us is killed and ends up like
Jim Ivanovitch or my friend Deanna."

"I cannot leave. There is evil here."

"I know there is," Julia told her. "That's why we need
to get out. That's why I have to get the kids out
especially."

The old woman seemed to understand. "Take the children back. Keep them away from here."

"You too."

"No," Agafia said firmly.

Julia knew it was useless to argue, and so she gave in,
nodding her acquiescence. She did not know what the
old woman had planned, did not know what she intended to do, but she imagined Agafia standing in the
church, praying, attempting some sort of exorcism, and
she figured that if her mother-in-law was going to stay,
that would probably be the safest place for her. Besides,
Agafia seemed to know what she was talking about.
She'd been right about all of this from the beginning.
Perhaps she *did* know how to put a stop to it, though
to Julia the most logical tack would be for all of them
to leave. If it really was the fact that the Owner of the
House was not here to protect them and keep out other
supernatural entities, then shouldn't that breach be
closed with their departure?

"Go to Montebello," Agafia said. "Stay in my house,
Helen, across the street, has the key. I left it with her
and asked her to water my plants."

Julia had almost forgotten that her mother-in-law had
refused to sell her home, and now she was ready to weep
with gratitude for that bit of stubbornness. They would
not have to put themselves up at some hotel or stay with
friends or relatives. They had a place to go, a house
where they could live until they got resettled.

"Thank you," Julia said. She stood. "I'm going to try
and find Gregory. Then we're getting the kids and getting out."

"No," Agafia said.

Julia blinked. "What?"

"No!" The old woman slammed her hand down on
the table. "Get the children and go! But leave Gregory
here! I will take care of him!"

"I don't want Gregory to stay here. I want him safe, and with us."

"He is my responsibility. I will take care of him."

Julia looked at her mother-in-law. She had never been overprotective of her son, had never seemed to be one of those overly Oedipal mothers who resented wives and girlfriends and any other female intrusion into their boys' lives, but that was the way she was acting now, and Julia wondered if the same forces that she was so worried about affecting everyone else had gotten to her first.

She had no intention of leaving Gregory in this town if she could help it. If he wanted to stay, that was different, but Julia was determined to give him a choice and a chance and ask him to come with them back to California. He seemed to have been the most affected by living here, the most influenced, and if his mother was right, he should be okay if he got away from this town.

If he was still alive.

No, Julia agreed with Agafia there. She did not think Gregory was dead. Injured, perhaps, out of commission temporarily, but alive.

Could he be with another woman?

The possibility threw her. She had not thought of that before, and she was surprised at herself for not even considering such an obvious explanation for his absence. Their sex life certainly hadn't been lighting up the skies lately, and it was entirely possible that another woman could be at the root of his disinterest.

She pushed that thought away before pictures started forming in her mind. There was too much to think about right now, too many other things going on. She would get her family out of McGuane and back to California, and *then* she'd try to sort everything out.

"I'm still going to try to find him," Julia said, heading toward the stairs.

"He stay here!" Agafia called after her in agitated English.

Thank God Gregory had not taken the van yesterday. Julia found the keys on the top of their dresser in the bedroom, slipped on some tennis shoes, and went outside.

Where to begin?

She didn't know, but the café seemed as good a place as any. She started the van, executed a three-point turn, and headed up the dirt drive, turning toward downtown.

She was glad the kids were at school. It would give her time to pack, give her time to prepare without having to answer a thousand questions and explain everything she was doing. She would find Gregory, they'd get everything together, pick up the kids at school, and take off. The kids could ask questions on the trip.

The café appeared to be closed, and she had no problem finding a parking place in the front. The door was unlocked, though, and she pushed it open, walking inside.

It hit her all at once. She had not really had time to grieve, had not allowed herself the luxury of experiencing the feelings she needed to experience, but entering the closed café, seeing the fallen lights and the destroyed stage, the mess that had not been cleaned up, it was as if an emotional tidal wave slammed into her, crushing her. Her family's dissolution, Deanna's death, Gregory's growing distance. The cumulative weight of all that baggage came crashing down on her head, and the walls she'd set up to deal with it, the barriers she'd erected to keep the feelings at bay and allow her to think and act clearly until she had time to sort through the emotional wreckage, came tumbling down. She was very close to tears, very close to complete paralysis, when she heard Paul's voice from somewhere across the darkened room. "Deanna?"

She squinted, her eyes adjusting. "Paul?" she said gratefully.

He walked over, across the floor toward her. "He didn't come home last night, did he?"

Julia shook her head, wiping away the tears that were threatening to spill onto her cheek.

"He was at a bar most of the evening—and most of the day—with Odd, both of them just sitting there and getting plastered. And then he went home with Odd, spent the night at his place."

"He was at Odd's?"

Paul nodded.

"I called there and no one answered."

"Maybe they were passed out. Or maybe they just didn't want to pick up the phone."

The fear and uncertainty were replaced swiftly with anger. She felt her strength coming back. "He could have called. He could have let us know he was all right."

"He should have."

At least it wasn't another woman, she thought. At least he was alive.

But, damn it, how could he be so inconsiderate?

Paul was almost up to her, but he kept coming closer, showed no sign of stopping. She felt nervous all of a sudden, and then he reached her and put his arms around her shoulders, hugging her.

They had never touched before, and she felt uncomfortable with this close contact. This was no doubt a friendly hug, a chaste and harmless gesture of support, but she wasn't one of those touchy-feely people who went around hugging everybody in sight, who squandered personal contact on virtual strangers, and this sudden intimacy not only surprised her but made her decidedly ill at ease.

The hug continued a beat or two longer than it should have, and she tried to casually pull back, to move out of his grip in a way that seemed natural and inoffensive, but though he shifted position, let his left arm fall away, his right arm remained around her shoulder.

"Maybe he's still there," Julia said. "I should see."

Paul stroked her hair. "He doesn't treat you the way he should."

She wanted to back away, wanted to tell him to stop . . . but she didn't. She felt dizzy, almost lightheaded, and she didn't know why she was letting him do this, but she said nothing as his hand roamed from her hair to her shoulders, rubbing over her breasts.

What was going on here? She was not at all attracted to Paul, and he had never indicated that he was remotely interested in her. Perhaps, she rationalized, it was Deanna's death that was the impetus behind this inappropriate behavior.

What was behind her acquiescence? She knew that what he was doing was wrong, and she told herself she

wanted it to stop, but she made no real effort to end it
or to move away from him. It felt good to be touched
again, felt good to have a man's hands on her in this
way. And Paul was right. Gregory had been a jerk lately
and he *hadn't* treated her the way he should. She deserved better.

Paul proceeded slowly, and she let him unbutton her
pants, let him slide his hand down her panties. His fingers felt strong and sure, and she gasped as he cupped
her, as his middle finger slipped easily and gently inside her.

And then Gregory walked into the café.

Time stopped. She was suddenly aware of everything:
the ticking of the clock across the room, the sound of a
pickup passing by on the street outside, the far-off cry
of a hawk, her own pounding heart, and the silence as
she held her breath. Her senses were heightened, and
she felt with extraordinary sensitivity Paul's hand pulling
out from her underwear, saw too clearly the blank expression on Gregory's red face, heard her own huge exhalation as though it were the sound of a monsoon.

What happened next seemed surreal and not quite believable. There was no argument, no fight, no histrionics.
Paul simply turned and walked back across the café to
his office and Gregory held his arm out silently. She
buttoned up her pants and took his hand. She still felt
light-headed, and she wanted to apologize, wanted to
explain, but her thoughts were foggy and couldn't seem
to make the trip out of her brain and down to her
mouth.

Gregory held out his hand for the keys, she gave them
to him, and, still not speaking, they walked out of the
café to the van.

He didn't hit her until they got home.

The house was empty. Gregory's mother was gone,
the kids still in school, and the two of them walked silently inside. They had not spoken once during the entire trip home.

She looked around the empty house. They never kept
track of anything anymore, she thought. They used to
know where everyone in the family was at all times, but

like the rest of the supposedly stable building blocks that
had been the foundation of their relationship, that had
broken down here, too, and now they'd reverted to a
more primitive monitoring system, noticing only whether
someone was present or absent, not knowing or caring
about anything in between. Even after Adam's arrest,
they had not kept the close tabs on him that they'd
promised him and themselves.

They walked into the living room, Gregory carefully
closing the door behind them.

He slapped her.

It was a hard slap, straight across the face, and Julia
was almost knocked off her feet by the force of it. Blood
started pouring out of her nose, and she held a hand up
to it to stem the flow, tilting her head back.

Gregory punched her in the stomach.

She went down.

She had never really been in a fight before—even as a
child, she had avoided physical altercations—and though
she'd seen plenty of them in movies and on television,
she did not really know how to defend herself and did
not seem to be able to think fast enough to keep up
with the action. Gregory kicked her in the breast, and
by the time she thought to roll away, out of his reach,
he was grabbing her arm, yanking her back up, kneeing
her in the crotch.

The pain was unbearable. She felt like vomiting, could
not catch her breath. The sharp flashes of agony that
accompanied each of his blows spiked deep into her
body. It felt as though bones were breaking, organs were
rupturing, and as he continued to pummel her, she wondered if he was going to kill her, if she was going to die.

And then he stopped.

He'd said nothing the entire time, and he was still
silent now as he let go of her arms and allowed her to
fall back onto the floor. Her first instinct, a purely animal
reaction, was to curl up and protect herself, but he had
stopped attacking, at least for now, and she tried to
stand, couldn't. He stood above her, arms folded, staring
blankly, and though the pain was tremendous and each
slight movement brought fresh tears to her eyes, she
managed to crawl to the stairs and start the slow, ardu-

ous trip up, one hand on the posts of the banister, the other supporting her weight on the steps.

He followed her, stood directly behind her. She kept waiting for another kick, kept waiting for him to throw her back down the stairs, but he did nothing, just stared.

After what seemed like an hour, she reached the top and managed to crawl into the bedroom. She was barely able to close and lock the door. Crying from the pain and the effort and the emotional toll, she pulled herself onto the bed and lay there, grateful for the soft blankets and mattress.

He was smart, she thought. Aside from that first slap, he hadn't hit her in the face, hadn't hit her where it would show. It was what she'd heard about chronic wife beaters, the way they hid their violence from friends and family, and it was this bit of circumspection that most frightened her. It meant that this might go on for a while. It meant that he intended to do this again without letting anyone know.

It meant that he intended to stay.

He intended to stay.

That lay at the heart of her fear. For it was as if this entire situation had been specifically arranged in order to keep her here: the scene with Paul, Gregory's discovery of them, the beating. She remembered the fogginess in her mind at the café, the blank expression on his face as he attacked her, and she wondered if that was not exactly what had happened. It was too convenient, she thought. Gregory had been played like a puppet, used by whatever lived in this house to make sure that she and the kids did not leave town.

There was a loud smack against the door, and Julia jumped, her ribs hurting. "You stay in there!" he ordered. "You come out and you're going to get the beating of your life, you fucking slut! And I hear you say one word of this to Mother or the kids, and you won't be the only one punished!"

Julia held her breath, did not reply, terrified that he would break down the door and come after her again, but he did not. Soon she heard him walk away, heard his footsteps head down the hall.

There was an unfamiliar series of loud noises after

that—clatterings and slammings—then she heard him upstairs, in the attic, rummaging around.

She listened to the noises until she fell asleep.

Sometime later, the kids came home from school. He was back downstairs again, and though the sounds were muffled, she could just make out their voices. She heard him lie, heard him tell the kids that she was sick and needed her rest and couldn't be disturbed, but one of them, Teo probably, tried the knob anyway a little while later, and she was grateful for that stubborn spirit of disbelief. She said nothing, however, gave no indication that she was awake, believing Gregory fully, knowing that he would make good on his threats. She didn't want anything to happen to the kids.

You won't be the only one punished!

His mother came home soon after, and he fed her the same line, but Julia could tell that Agafia didn't believe it. Their conversation was polite, but there was a stiltedness to it, an undercurrent of formality, an obvious discomfort on both their parts. Gregory's mother seemed afraid of him, and Julia thought that the old woman was her last best hope. Agafia could obviously sense that something was wrong, that there was something amiss here, and she said nothing to her son about Julia's plan to take the kids and get out of town.

Agafia would figure something out, she knew. The old woman would find some way to help her, to get them all out of this.

She fell asleep thinking of plans for escape.

In the morning there was a knock at the bedroom door, and then *he* walked in. "I need clothes," he said shortly.

She'd locked the door. She knew she had. But Gregory had somehow opened it anyway, striding in, ignoring her and taking a pair of jeans from the closet and an old Yes T-shirt from the dresser. He threw off his dirty clothes, tossing them in the direction of the hamper, and put on the clean ones.

He looked at her disgustedly. "Get your lazy ass out of bed," he said. "Your children need breakfast. Do something useful for once in your miserable life."

It was an order, not an observation, and he stared at her as if he meant to be obeyed. Julia rose painfully. She had not changed out of yesterday's clothes, and now she left her jeans on—it hurt too much to try to take them off—but she removed the blood-spattered blouse and replaced it with a loose-fitting red shirt.

"Wash your face off," he said. "Then get downstairs."

He left the room, and she shuffled slowly across the carpeted floor into the bathroom. Her face was indeed a mess, smeared with dried blood, but it looked worse than it was and after two minutes with the washcloth she looked almost normal.

This was her chance. If Agafia was downstairs and Gregory left them alone for even a minute, they could talk, figure something out, formulate some sort of plan.

The stairs were difficult, and Julia held tightly to the banister, walking down one step at a time, stopping on each, like someone handicapped. Once on the first floor, she hobbled to the door of the kitchen that opened onto the hallway, and her heart sank as she saw the kids seated in the breakfast nook, Gregory pouring himself a cup of coffee at the counter next to the sink—and no sign of her mother-in-law.

The Gregory from upstairs was gone, and in his place was a falsely cheerful Stepford husband. "Mother already left for church," he said, as if reading her thoughts. He smiled brightly at her. "Feeling better, dear?"

Adam and Teo both looked worried, and she wondered how much they knew, how much they suspected.

Julia looked from their drawn faces to Gregory's beaming visage, and she forced herself to nod. "Yeah," she said. "I'm feeling better."

Eighteen

1

Frank Masterson gunned his Jeep and sped down the winding dirt trail that led to transformer 242. The sun was setting, and he was anxious to get this problem settled before nightfall. For one thing, he hated to work in the dark. And he and Shelly had tickets for tonight's Garth Brooks concert. The concert didn't start until eight, and there was an opening act, so Garth probably wouldn't go on until nine, but it was still a two-hour drive back to Tucson, and if he had a hope in hell of making it on time, he had to make it to the transformer, fix whatever was wrong, and start back within twenty minutes.

Shelly had predicted this would happen, and he hated it that her prediction was confirmed. He'd never hear the end of it. She'd bitch and moan all night, and the concert would be ruined. Then they'd fight over *that* and the whole thing would spill over into the weekend.

If he was lucky, it would be nothing. Those computers down at the office weren't worth shit in his book, and nine times out of ten the problem turned out to be not with the transformer or relays but with some glitch in a computer program. The company had spent millions of dollars over the last two years, upgrading their system, but it still wasn't half as efficient as the old one. Give him a good old-fashioned low-tech, labor-intensive *human* monitoring system any day of the week.

He picked up the phone from its cradle beside him, checked in again. "Frank here. I'm almost to 242. Any change in the readings?"

The voice on the other end was barely audible through the static. "Nope. 242's still offline and needs a reset, copy."

"I'll get back to you in ten." He replaced the phone in its niche. If it wasn't a computer error and the transformer simply needed to be reset, that wouldn't take long. He'd be in and out in five minutes. If it was anything else, though, he was screwed. He would have to call the office, have them patch him in to home, and lay out the situation for Shelly.

God, he hoped he didn't have to do that.

The trail wound out of the hills and led over a flat section of desert, ending up ahead at what looked like an iron scrap yard fenced in with chain-link and barbed wire. Lines and cables emerged from this mess in two directions, climbing up to lie in the arms of the monstrous metal power towers that had always reminded him of Japanese robots and that marched to the west and to the north across the open land.

He stopped the Jeep, hopped out and unlocked the padlocked gate. The sun was a brilliant orange half-globe on the edge of the horizon. To the east, he could see the coming night.

He had to hurry. Frank swung open the gate and jumped back into the Jeep, gunning it and braking to a sudden halt just before the blocky transformer building. From the rear of the vehicle, he grabbed his tools, diagnostic equipment, and a flashlight, just in case. He popped open the door of the building, flipping on the lights and walking inside, and headed immediately to the control panel, installed in a series of metal cabinets and insulated wall units at the opposite end of the room. Checking all of the appropriate gauges, he frowned. There was nothing wrong here. Everything was running smoothly. Everything was as it was supposed to be. He turned around—

A shadow flitted past the door.

Frank practically jumped out of his boots.

The movement had startled him, but that was not what *scared* him. Or it was only the start of it. For there was something strange and unnatural about the shape he'd seen, some sense he'd gotten from that fleeting glimpse that whatever was inside the gates here with him was . . . not right.

Evil.

That was the word that was echoing in his mind, and while he wasn't a churchgoer like Shelly, while he thought he'd left all that fire and brimstonery back in his mama's house, he offered up a quick prayer. He was smart enough to know that there were things he didn't know, and right now, out here in the middle of nowhere, that sense of ignorance seemed particularly strong. He was trying to hold on to some half-baked notion that this was an animal or a homeless man, but his emotions, his brain, and his gut instinct told him otherwise, and he wished to Christ they'd sent Tyler out on this call instead of him.

There was a pounding on the roof.

He glanced again at the instrument panel, saw that nothing was wrong, and thought that whatever this creature was, it had caused the system anomalies they'd recorded back at the office and had purposely tried to make them think there was something amiss.

But why?

Maybe it wanted to lure someone out here.

For what?

He didn't even want to think about that.

From his tool kit, he withdrew his heaviest socket wrench. He didn't have a hammer with him—it was back in the Jeep—but this would do in a pinch, would enable him to fight off whatever came at him until he *could* get to the Jeep.

Outside, the light was failing fast. Already, the sun had dropped below the horizon, leaving only an orange glow where its specific shape had been. The lights in the transformer room made the dying light outside seem even darker.

Dying light?

Frank hurried toward the open door. He flipped off the inside lights, closed the door behind him, and in the brief second before it hit him and knocked him down, he saw a dark shadowy figure swoop down from the roof of the transformer building. He landed on his back, star-

ing up for a moment at the steel girders and the inter-
secting power cables and the purple sky above.

Then something dark passed between him and the sky.

The face that pulled close to his was wrinkled and
horribly old, wizened and evil, and he screamed as the
hideous creature bent down to kiss him and rubbed its
slimy skin against his cheek.

2

The blackout occurred at 6:45.

Julia heard over the radio that it had affected five
western states and that electric company representatives
believed it to be the result of a downed transformer in
either eastern Arizona or western New Mexico. Similar
blackouts had occurred because of heavy monsoon activity in the past, but there was no lightning this time, no
storms in any of the Four Corners states, and experts
were at a loss to explain what had brought about this
failure.

Big cities, they predicted, would be quickly back on
line, would have power restored within the next three
or four hours, but it might take three days before the
entire power grid was again up and running.

Where did that leave McGuane?

She wasn't sure.

Julia sat in the kitchen, waiting for Agafia to return.
Her mother-in-law had been gone all day, and in Julia's
fantasy she was gathering the other Molokans together,
hatching a plan to get her and the kids out of here, but
the truth was that she was probably trying to perform
one of her exorcisms or rituals, attempting to get at the
root of the problem rather than focusing on their specific
situation. Like most true believers, Agafia would put her
cause ahead of her family—and Julia resented her for
that.

The atmosphere in the house was tense. Aside from
those few angry words in the bedroom and his false
cheer at breakfast, Gregory had not spoken to her
since . . . since the beating. He was not only hostile
and angry, which she would understand, but there was

a distracted distance in his attitude that frightened her. He had shadowed her all day, not letting her out of his sight, and it was only after the kids returned from school that he finally went upstairs and locked himself in the attic. Her hands were still shaking nervously, but at least he was out of her hair for the moment, and she was grateful he'd decided to leave her alone.

The kids were on edge, too. The hyperfriendly Gregory of the morning was gone, and since Adam and Teo had come home, their father had been avoiding them, not speaking to them either, and she found that troubling. She wanted to grab the kids and take off, let them know what was really happening, but Gregory was holding the van keys and they certainly wouldn't get far by walking.

Adam and Teo had been hiding in Teo's room ever since they'd come home—it was downstairs, farther away from *him*—and they emerged into the living room as soon as the lights went out. Julia broke out the candles, setting three on the coffee table and four others around the perimeter of the room, letting Adam and Teo light some of them, lighting the rest herself.

Sasha had still not returned home, and that worried her. Not as much as it would have ordinarily, though. She was concerned for her daughter, but part of her couldn't help thinking that she would be safer away from this house, away from her father. Julia found herself hoping that Sasha would stay with a friend until daylight.

There was the sound of a crash from upstairs, and Gregory's shouted curse, and Adam and Teo both looked at her. She tried to offer them a reassuring smile, but she was still in quite a bit of pain and it probably came out closer to a grimace.

None of them said anything.

Julia looked out the window once again, hoping to see a Molokan cavalry coming to the rescue, but there was only blackness, only night, and the three of them sat together in the living room, waiting, listening to the battery-powered radio, trying to ignore the sounds of Gregory up in the attic.

3

The lights went out at the perfect time.

Sasha had taken off her clothes and crawled into the bed, and Wilbert was just starting to undress.

The truth was that she didn't really want to see him naked. The beer gut distending his T-shirt was bad enough when he was fully clothed, but staring at that hairy blubber hanging over an erection would be a serious turnoff, and she was glad when the lights winked out.

She was not so glad when he hit her.

She did not know why it happened, did not know if it was an accident, if he simply hadn't been able to see her in the dark and her face had been in the way of his hand's intended destination, or if the blow was intentional, but it made her angry, and she yelled at him, making sure he got her message loud and clear. She was doing this ugly porker a big favor by fucking him, and if he was going to try and pull this shit, she'd kick him in the goddamn balls, grab her clothes, and get the hell out of his rat-infested trailer.

He did not respond to her tirade, and against her will she felt the first faint stirrings of fear.

"Aren't you even going to apologize?" she asked, keeping her voice angry.

No answer.

She could feel his weight on the bed next to her, so she knew he had not left, but still he said nothing.

Now she was definitely afraid. She did not like the fact that he was not speaking, that the room was silent. "Wilbert?" she said hesitantly.

Silence. A slight shifting of weight.

"Wilbert?"

"Boo!" he said.

Relief flooded through her. "Wilbert!"

He was laughing, rolling around on the bed.

And there was someone else in the room laughing as well.

She heard several people laughing.

Her mouth suddenly went dry.

There were others here.

She started to sit up. He slapped her again, and now her mouth was no longer dry. There was blood in it.

A strong hand pushed her down, and then he was on top of her. The other laugher had not yet stopped, and even as Wilbert spread her legs apart, she was listening carefully, trying to determine how many different voices she could pick out.

Three.

Five.

Six.

She could not differentiate how many others.

There was a scream from the next room.

Cherie.

It was too dark to see, but Sasha closed her eyes anyway. This was a nightmare, like something out of a movie. She should have learned her lesson last time, should have stayed as far away from these rednecks as possible, but . . . but something had made her do it.

And as Wilbert's bulk settled on top of her and the laughter grew, she began to cry.

4

Jesus H. Christ.

Sheriff Roland Ford paced in the dirt in front of his office, rifle in hand, waiting for those dipshit policemen to show up. The two departments were pooling their resources tonight, and though he did not like the idea, he recognized the necessity for it. Neither could handle this situation alone—there was so much going on that they needed to coordinate who was going to do what. It was like New York out there rather than McGuane—a night filled with looting and random violence. He found it hard to believe that one extended blackout could cause so many problems.

From far off up the canyon he heard the sound of sirens. Fire, it sounded like. Or ambulance.

He shook his head. What the fuck was going on here? It was as if lights and electricity were the only things maintaining people's sanity, the only things upholding civilization, and without those basic technological comforts, they panicked, reverted to savagery. It made no sense on any sort of rational level, and he had to admit that he did not understand it. As someone who often went camping and hunting, the night held no terrors for him, and he could not figure out why seemingly well-adjusted adults would overreact to such an unbelievable extent.

Of course, not all of them were well adjusted.

Two separate local militia groups had appointed themselves the official protector of McGuane, and they were fighting it out in the park over jurisdiction. A bunch of overweight, undereducated losers who wouldn't even be able to make it through the sheriff's academy's female course, they were now proclaiming themselves the only real law in town.

Word was that they'd tried to lynch a man, a Mormon elder who had dared to question their right to even participate in law enforcement, and Tom Sobule, the town's newest police recruit, had had to fire his sidearm into the air in order to rescue the man and head off a confrontation. They hadn't been brave enough to actually go up against a real officer, to abandon all pretense of the rule of law and degenerate completely into anarchy and vigilantism—but the night was still young.

Since then, the two militia groups had gotten into it with each other. If he was lucky, they'd kill each other off, and his men could just go in and arrest the last man standing.

Or take him out if he wanted to fight.

They'd had blackouts before, and he failed to understand what made this one different. The others had been local, confined to McGuane or, at most, Rio Verde County—they had not involved whole states—but he found it hard to believe that the size of the affected area had any bearing on the behavior of people in town. Did they learn that the blackout was affecting Arizona, New Mexico, Colorado, Utah, and Nevada and automatically assume that it was the end of the world or the collapse of the country? The militia nuts, perhaps. But he could not see ordinary, everyday citizens believing such lunacy.

Yet it was those ordinary, everyday citizens who were out there looting and fighting and doing who knew what.

Roland sighed. The truth was, it wasn't just the black-out. Something else had caused this unrest, something had led them to this point. The blackout was just the catalyst, the excuse. The real reasons went far deeper, and while he prided himself on his fairness and open-mindedness, while he did not like to pick on one specific group of people or indulge in any kind of scapegoating, he could not help but think that the Molokans were somehow at the root of it all. Things had been getting increasingly strange around here for quite some time, but it was the hairy church yesterday that had really kicked the situation into high gear. Though the Russians might be victims just as much as everyone else, he could not seem to maintain the objectivity he knew his job required, and he found himself thinking that they were somehow responsible, that, intentionally or unintention-ally, they had brought about this craziness.

And it was crazy.

A woman had called in to his office, claiming that the sheets that had been drying on her clothesline were fly-ing around the outside of her house, trying to find a way in. A girl had called saying that her younger brother had tried to stab her and she'd had to lock the boy in a closet. Two kids had run down to the police station afraid that a giant lizard was chasing them.

There were reports of rat armies and cat attacks, and throughout the canyons came the almost constant echoes of gunfire.

Roland hoped to God it was animals that were being shot.

It was chaos out there. There was so much going on that it was impossible to know what was happening. Even with all of the shifts called in, the sheriff's office was severely undermanned, and that was why, against the strong feelings of his gut, the instinct he usually trusted above all others, he'd agreed to throw in with the cops.

Someone somewhere screamed in the darkness, and a moment later the police car finally pulled up. Two offi-cers got out, clutching flashlights, and Roland ushered them quickly inside the building. "About time," was all he said.

The emergency generator was on, but that meant that only the backup lights were lit, and the office was still dark and gloomy.

All of the phones were ringing, but there were only two receptionists, and they were answering the calls as fast as they could.

He led the policemen into his office, closing the door behind them.

"No, Mrs. Kennedy," Alice was saying as the door closed. "There's been no reports of any spacecraft landing anywhere in Arizona. . . . No, I don't know anything about little alien men."

Semyon Konyov sat at the picnic table in the yard next to the church while he waited for the others. Peter and Nikolai had driven out into the desert to get the prophet, and the others had gone in search of Russian Bibles, since theirs were still inside the church and could not be retrieved.

Agafia was waiting at his house. The rest of them had not wanted to hear from her, still blamed her for this, still thought she was tainted and corrupt, her information lies, but he had lied himself and pulled a Vera, saying that he'd seen the answer in a dream. He told them everything Agafia had said to him, pretending the words were his own.

And Peter and Nikolai had gone to get the prophet.

Semyon looked toward the street. Where were the others? His candle was burning low, and his flashlight batteries were almost dead; he'd turned the light off some time ago in order to conserve them.

It occurred to him that they had been killed, that something had gotten them, but he pushed that thought out of his mind. He turned around, looked back toward the church, saw the dark hair waving slightly in the almost nonexistent breeze. Quickly, he looked away.

The night had been noisy, the town alive with fights and screaming, gunshots and sirens, but most of it seemed to have been coming from elsewhere in the canyons.

Until now.

There was the sound of an engine drawing closer,

bringing with it angry voices, and he was embarrassed to discover that he was afraid. He closed his eyes and offered up a quick prayer, asking the Lord for strength.

He opened his eyes and saw headlights. A pickup was pulling up, coming to a stop in the church's small parking lot. The truck's bed was filled with cowboy-hatted, overalled men carrying shotguns.

He had a quick flashback to a similar scene, in another time, a time he had not thought of for decades.

Flashlights played across the hairy front of the church. Several of the men leaped out of the truck onto the ground, and one of them screamed at him. "This is the last straw, man. The last fuckin' straw. You milk drinkers think you can just come to our town and do whatever the hell you want? Well, we're not going to put up with that shit no more!"

Semyon stood, scared, flustered. He walked toward the men. "No—" he began.

A shot rang out.

He stopped in his tracks, and one of the men laughed.

Had they shot at him? He didn't know and he was afraid to find out. His first instinct was to run, try to find help, but he knew there would be no help this night, and though he was trembling with fear, he remained in place. "Go!" he said. "Go home now!"

"Go home now!" Someone made fun of his accent, and the others started laughing.

They started shooting up the church, aiming their guns at the front of the building, taking turns, some focusing flashlights while their companions shot. The bullets sank into the hair at first, but after several minutes and several rounds, chunks of hair-covered wall began to be blasted away, pieces falling, flying off. Semyon turned on his own flashlight, and he saw something completely unexpected, something he never would have believed.

The building was bleeding.

What was under that hair now? he wondered. He could not imagine. It was obviously not a building. The voices of the shooters became at once angrier and more frightened as they, too, saw the dark liquid spreading out across the dirt.

Semyon gathered up his courage once again. "This our church!" he said. "Leave us!"

"Shut up, old man!"

He felt the bullet pierce his chest, felt it rip through his body, shattering bone and organ, stopping somewhere deep inside him. He staggered to the right, clutching the burning, bleeding section of his torso where the bullet had ripped into him. He fell against the wall of the church and was immediately engulfed in a forest of hair that clutched at him and pulled him into itself.

It felt soothing, was the last thing he thought. *It felt good.*

The lights led Wynona down into the mine, her feet slipping on the gravel of the extant road that wound down to the bottom of the pit. The lights were beautiful, appearing and then disappearing, forming patterns, and she thought that she had never seen anything like them.

They'd come to her bedroom window, tapping musically on the glass, and they'd drawn her outside, leading her down Ore Road all the way to the realty office before flying into the air above the pit and dispersing with a whirling flourish that no fireworks could ever hope to match.

The lights had floated down, settled and winked up at her from their various locations throughout the massive pit, beckoning to her. She'd found a hole in the chain-link fence, climbed through, and started down the old truck trail to meet them.

The gravel was slippery, and several times she nearly fell, but she always managed to keep her footing.

She finally did fall twenty minutes later, when she was halfway down, her right foot flying out, throwing her off balance, and she landed on her back on the road, the hard ground knocking the wind out of her.

She tried to get up, but she could not, her left arm wouldn't work right, and she prayed that it was only sprained and not broken.

Throughout the pit, the lights flew up again, coming together, swirling, dancing, then flitting over to where she lay. If she could not come to them, they would come to her, and for a brief second Wynona was delighted, filled with an exuberant sense of joy.

But something changed before they even reached her, and as suddenly as it had come, her exultation disappeared, and she was left with a strange sense of dread that caused her to once again try to sit up and get back on her feet.

She rolled onto her right side and was up on her elbow, when the gravel beneath her shifted again, and she fell back down.

The lights danced above her head and landed on her body. Up close they no longer looked so beautiful.

They looked like they felt.

Terrible.

And the night continued on.

Nineteen

1

The voice talked to him.

It was a real voice, not an imaginary voice, not something he heard in his head. It was out there and it spoke to him, talking calmly and rationally about things that were not calm, not rational at all.

Gregory sat up on the bed, squinting at the brightness of dawn. He had not shut the drapes last night, and morning light streamed through the window—or came as close to streaming as was possible in this house.

Where was his mother? Had she ever come home last night? And where were Julia and the kids? Were they still in the house asleep, or had the treacherous little shits sneaked out on him? He felt for the van keys, was gratified to find that they were still in his pocket.

The voice continued to talk. He'd been hearing it all night, he realized. It had been speaking to him even as he slept, and he had incorporated its monologue into his dreams. He was awake now, though, and while he could not see the source of the voice, he knew it was in the room with him, and for the first time he listened specifically to what it had to say, to what it was trying to tell him.

"Remember when you caught Julia and Paul?" the voice whispered. "His hands were down her pants. How many fingers do you think were up her snatch? One? Two? Three? How many can she take up there? You think she was wet? You think he went sluicing through her juices?"

Gregory's jaw muscles clenched. He didn't want to hear this, didn't want to think about it.

But he could not stop listening.

"It's not the first time she did it," the voice said insinuatingly, and there seemed to him something familiar about it. "She's fucked half the town. She blew Chilton Bodean before he bit the big one, sucked him dry, swallowed it down and begged for more. Your old pal the bartender? She licked his balls for over an hour while he worked behind the counter, crouching down and following him on her knees, servicing him as he served the customers."

He recognized the voice now.

It was his father's.

It switched to Russian. "Your mother was the same way, that whore. She'd spread her legs for Jim Ivanovitch, let him have her in whatever way he wanted, then come back and deny me my husbandly right. Bitch."

He heard hatred in that voice, the threat of violence.

"I waited, though. I bided my time."

"Did you kill Jim?" Gregory asked.

The voice was smooth. "Of course I did." It was back to English. "Think I could let him bang my woman? Think I could let him fuck your mother? That little hypocrite. 'Thou shalt not commit adultery.' It's one of the ten, and that lying little prick was giving your mother a sperm bath when he was supposed to be praying and reading the Good Book. Could I stand by while he fed my wife his tubesteak?"

It occurred to Gregory that his father's English had never been this fluent, his command of slang and colloquialism never this well developed, but though he had the thought, it did not affect his belief in its authenticity, did not dissuade him from accepting his father as the true and ultimate source of the voice.

"I did what I had to do," his father said. "As a man."

Gregory nodded. His father was right. What he said made sense. Gregory stood, smoothing the wrinkles of the clothes in which he'd slept.

"Are you going to let Julia get away with this? Are you going to let her spread her legs for every swinging dick that comes along?"

"No," Gregory whispered.

"Get the gun," his father said softly. "You know you want to. Get the gun and stuff it up her pussy where all those other men have stuffed their cocks, and blow their leftover sperm out with a bullet. That'll teach her. That'll teach all of them."

Gregory nodded.

"That's what you bought the gun for, anyway. Use it. Do it tonight. Surprise her when she's asleep, when she's thinking about the taste of his hot sperm, when she's dreaming about riding his cock. Do it then. Do it then."

The voice continued to talk, but Gregory no longer heard it. It was like a radio that was on in the background, white noise, he could tune it in or out at will, and right now he had heard enough. He didn't want to hear any more.

But he knew his father was right, and he was filled with a righteous anger, a molten core of fury that he knew he would have no trouble sustaining until tonight.

Part of him wondered why he had to wait, why he couldn't just do it now, but that was like the thought concerning his father's English. It was irrelevant, and he pushed it aside, ignored it.

He walked out of the bedroom, went immediately up to the attic, and pulled the ladder up, closing the door behind him as he headed to his gun shelf.

2

Teo was scared.

There was something wrong with her dad.

And something bad had happened to Sasha.

Her mom and Adam were scared, too, and that made it even more frightening. No one had talked to her about any of it—her mom had simply told her to stay in her room and not come out—but she had the feeling that it was the *banya*'s fault. She could not help thinking that if she had not stopped going there, not stopped seeing it, that none of this would be happening. She was being punished by the *banya* for her ingratitude, for the way she had treated it.

And it was taking out its anger on her family.

Teo felt like crying, but she forced herself not to, forced herself to be brave. She wanted to go back out to the *banya* and confront it, but her mom had ordered her not to leave her room—and she was afraid to do so anyway.

Her dad had been acting weird for the past few days, and she and Adam had talked about it, but neither of them had known how to bring it up with their mom. Besides, she wasn't in the best shape herself. Whatever flue or illness she'd had, it had left her weak, and neither of them wanted to make things any more difficult.

But Dad was being weird.

Scary.

He *was* scary, and she wasn't quite sure why. He wasn't acting mean or angry or anything. He was either really, really cheerful or just sort of quiet and distant. But . . .

But neither of those was her father.

That was it exactly. He wasn't himself. He didn't seem like her dad. He seemed like a fake father, like someone who looked exactly the same and was trying really hard to be him but just couldn't quite pull it off.

And that, she supposed, was what made her think of the *banya*.

That and the sense of danger.

For there seemed something dangerous about her dad right now. Beneath the cheerfulness, beneath the bland niceness, was something else, something deeper, something that reminded her of the swirling blackness of the *banya* shadows. She knew that Adam sensed it too. Their mom probably did as well, but she was staying away from all of them, keeping to herself.

She wished Babunya was here. Babunya would know what to do, and even Adam admitted that he'd feel safer if their grandmother was around. But Babunya hadn't come home yesterday, still wasn't back this morning, and no one seemed to know where she was.

Sasha was back. She'd come home late last night, looking like she'd been beaten up, and Mom had been hysterical, rushing her into the bathroom to get cleaned up and bandaged. Her dad had acted like he didn't even

care, and Teo supposed that was the first time she'd
thought that maybe the *banya* was behind this.

That was the first time she'd sensed the danger.

She wished they were back in California. Things like
this had never happened there. As she stared out the
window of her room at the yellow-leafed cottonwood, at
the cloudless blue sky and the tan rock of the canyon
cliffs, she did what she had been trying so hard not to
do. She cried.

3

Agafia had fallen asleep on Semyon's couch, waiting
for him to return. But by morning she'd known that
something was wrong, that something had happened to
him. He was supposed to have come back immediately
after telling the others to bring the prophet to her house,
that that was the location of the breach, the source of
the *neh chizni doohc*. She and Semyon were then supposed to go together and try to rescue Julia and the
kids. She knew there might be a problem with Gregory,
that he might not want to let them leave, but with Julia,
the kids, Semyon, herself, and the power of prayer and
God's grace, she had no doubt that they could get away.

Semyon had not returned, however, and she'd eventually fallen asleep, waking up this morning to find that
she was still alone in the house.

And she'd hurried immediately back home.

Or hurried back as fast as her old legs could take her.
All of the running around the past two days had taken
quite a toll, and she ached all over: her leg muscles were
sore, even her lungs hurt when she breathed. She considered herself to be in pretty good shape for her age, but
that age was 74, and as much as she would like to deny
it, she was not a young woman anymore.

God gave her strength, however, and Agafia hobbled
doggedly along roads that had not changed or improved
much since her own teenage years, grateful that the way
was mostly downhill. Semyon's house was not too far
from theirs, and in less than fifteen minutes she was
walking up the porch steps.

Luckily, they were all home.

Luckily, they were all right.

She didn't know what she'd been thinking. She should have made sure Julia and the kids were out of here and safe first, before she'd even gone to Semyon's, and she was filled with guilt at the thought of her irresponsibility. It was pure luck that it hadn't turned into a disaster, that she hadn't come back to find them butchered.

What could have made her act so stupidly? She looked around the living room, dark even in the day, and she wondered if she had been influenced by whatever power had taken up residence here, if she had done what *it* wanted her to do rather than what she knew to be right.

Of course, now that she was thinking clearly, logically, did that mean that its influence was gone?

Or did that mean that it now *wanted* her to help Julia and the kids get away?

Neither, she assumed. It probably meant that Gregory was enough in control here to enforce its will and it didn't need to expend any extra energy trying to influence the other people in this house.

She'd noticed the difference in atmosphere the moment she'd come back, the second she'd walked through that door. Tension hung thick and heavy in the air, and the feeling here was far different than the one at Semyon's. As always, she'd said a prayer before even walking inside, and she was grateful now for even that small bit of protection.

There was *hrehc* here.

Evil.

She and Julia huddled around the kitchen table, trying to decide what to do. The phone was dead. It had not exactly been a surprise, but it still brought home to them the seriousness of their predicament, the lengths to which the spirits here would go in order to cripple them, to thwart their efforts to escape. They were both wary, conscious of the fact that they might be under surveillance, that it was more than possible they were being spied upon.

Gregory had the van keys, and Julia had proposed going up there, confronting him and trying to take the keys from him, but it was too dangerous, Agafia told her. Even if both of them went up to the attic, they would not be facing just Gregory, they would be facing Gregory and whatever *else* lived in this house. Agafia doubted that even with weapons and a Bible and prayers of protection, the two of them could stand up to that sort of power alone.

Semyon had driven his car last night, but he had another old Chevy in his carport, and Agafia wondered aloud if there weren't keys for the vehicle somewhere in his house. There was no guarantee that it would work even if they did find the keys, but taking Semyon's Chevy was a possibility. She had not driven since coming to McGuane—Gregory had not let her do anything but ride in the van—but if worse came to worst, she could try to drive the car.

"Or I could drive it," Julia said.

"Even better," Agafia told her in Russian.

They talked quietly. Sasha was still asleep in her bedroom, and when the two of them went in to look in on her, they could see that she was not ready to go anywhere. Even if they could sneak out of the house, even if Semyon's old car worked, even if they could find the keys for it, even if they could get it back here, they would have to carry Sasha out, and they both doubted that Gregory would allow them to do that.

Agafia did not like the fact that Sasha was upstairs, in her own bedroom. The girl had gone there herself, apparently, had insisted upon it after Julia had taken care of her cuts and put some salve on her bruises, but it was still too close to Gregory and the attic, and it made her nervous. If they were lucky, Gregory would remain upstairs until they had a chance to get out of here or to figure out how to call for help.

If they were unlucky . . .

She didn't even want to think about that.

As Julia bathed her daughter's forehead with a cold washcloth, Agafia had an idea. She took Adam with her out to the carport, where the two of them picked up a ladder and brought it back into the house. The attic door opened only one way—down—and they positioned the top of the ladder against the trapdoor, wedging the bottom between the wall and the floor in order to block

the door and keep Gregory from opening it. Adam knew
what they were doing, but he said nothing about it, and
Agafia wondered what was going through his mind as
they trapped his father inside the attic. It could not be
healthy, it could not be good, for a young boy to have
to do something like this.

All three of them walked downstairs to where Teo sat
alone in the living room, reading a book and listening
to the radio. Adam went to join her, and Agafia looked
at her daughter-in-law. She suddenly had another idea.

"You take Adam and Teodosia," she said in Russian.
"Take them to . . . I don't know. Take them away from
here. I will meet you with Sasha as soon as she is strong
enough to walk."

Julia shook her head. "She's my daughter. I can't
leave her. Besides, what do you think would happen
after Gregory discovered we pulled something like that?
You think he'd just wait around for several days until
Sasha's condition improved, and then let you two go
walking out of here? No. He would cripple you if he
had to. He'd do what he needed to make sure you two
couldn't go."

Julia thought for a moment. "*You* take Adam and
Teo," she said. "I'll stay here with Sasha. Go to your
friend Semyon's house. Draw me a map."

Agafia shook her head. "I need to be here. Only I
can fight against this."

"Then I guess we all stay. I can't send those two out
alone. Who knows what's out there? At least we *know*
what we have to deal with in this house." She glanced
up at the ceiling, but Agafia knew she was thinking of
the attic.

And Gregory.

They were both silent for a moment, looking at each
other.

Agafia smiled, tried to be reassuring. "Don't worry. I
can handle him," she promised.

But she wasn't sure of that.

She wasn't sure at all.

Julia removed all of the knives from the kitchen, saving one for herself. Agafia helped her look through the

other cupboards and closets, trying to weed out things that could be used as weapons, attempting to make the house attack-proof. Everything they found, Julia took outside, tossed into the weeds at the side of the drive.

"That should help," she said.

None of them went outdoors after that.

The day was strange. It was only a blackout, but it felt as though they'd been hit by a hurricane or a tornado and were between storms, waiting for the next one to hit. It was like being under siege.

The radio had been on the entire time, and the batteries finally gave out around dusk. There were a few other batteries, but Julia wanted to save them for her flashlight, and Agafia agreed that was a good idea. It was quiet without the radio, though. Too quiet. Even Gregory in the attic was silent, and Julia broke out a deck of cards and played War with Adam and Teo in the kitchen, getting up periodically to check on Sasha.

None of this would have happened, Agafia thought, if she had made sure to get them out before leaving yesterday, if she'd just taken them with her to Semyon's. But that game could be played forever. None of it would have happened if they had returned to California a month ago, if one of them had remembered to invite Jedushka Di Muvedushka to come with them, if they'd never moved back to McGuane, if Gregory had never won the lottery . . .

She fell asleep after a makeshift dinner, on the couch again, and when she woke up, only Julia was in the room. The single candle that was still burning was low, and the room was bathed in shadows that did not all appear to be natural.

"Where are Adam and Teodosia?" she whispered.

Julia looked over at her. "In their rooms. Sleeping."

"Why aren't they sleeping in here?" She was instantly filled with dread—and anger at what she saw as her daughter-in-law's stupidity.

"Because the bedrooms have locks."

"You let Adam go upstairs—?"

"I've been up there myself half the time. With Sasha."

"You should have put him in my room."

Julia blinked, stared at her blankly. She obviously

hadn't thought of that, and Agafia again wondered how much influence this place was exerting on them, how much their thought processes were being affected just by remaining in this house.

There was a movement of shadow in the far corner that did not correspond to the flickers of the candle. Agafia picked up the flashlight, quickly shone it in that corner, and was gratified to see nothing there.

She turned the flashlight off. Her head hurt, and she was dimly aware that she'd had a dream, some sort of nightmare about the *banya*.

The *banya*.

Something clicked in her mind, a connection that had not been made before, and while it was not something she could explain, not something that was specifically spelled out, she suddenly realized that the *banya* was just as central to what was happening as the house was, and she thought that maybe *it* was the doorway through which—what did Adam say the Indians called them? uninvited guests?—were coming, and that perhaps the tide could be stemmed there.

Why hadn't she figured that out earlier? How could she have been so blind?

She pushed herself up and off the couch, grabbed her Bible from the table.

"What are you doing?" Julia asked her.

They'd been speaking only Russian for most of the day, not wanting the children to understand what they were talking about, and they were still speaking it now even though they were alone.

Agafia picked up one of the unlit candles, placed its wick next to the burning flame of the candle on the table. "I am going to the *banya*."

The statement sounded frightening even to herself. It was too dramatic, too self-important, but she *felt* dramatic, this *seemed* important, and there was an urgency about it, a powerful impetus to do this right now, this second, a sense that there was no time to waste and that if she did not hurry, whatever window of opportunity was open to her would be closed.

Something had been trying to communicate with her for quite a while—

God?

—and she did not know why she had not paid more attention to her dreams, why she had . . . not exactly ignored them, but not acted upon them, not pursued the truths they were trying to reveal.

She hurried over to the closet in the entryway, placed her candle and Bible on the table next to the door, and took out her jacket, putting it on. Julia was following her, unsure of what to say, unsure of what to do, and Agafia turned to her. "Keep your knife close," she said. "I will be back as soon as I can."

Julia seemed about to say something, but instead she just nodded.

"Get Adam downstairs. Put him in my room. When I get back, we'll try to bring Sasha down." She picked up her Bible and candle, said a quick prayer of protection, blessed Julia, the kids, the house, then hurried outside without waiting for a response. The sense of urgency was now almost overwhelming, and the feeling within her was something like panic. She could not run, because she did not want to put out the candle, but she walked as quickly as she could toward the back of the property, past the cottonwood, toward the *banya*. The thought occurred to her that she should have brought the flashlight instead of the candle, but she figured that Julia and the kids needed it more than she did.

Should she have brought any of them with her?

No. Julia was right. At least they knew what was in the house. Out here . . .

Who knew what she would find?

The ground was getting rough, the candlelight was not particularly effective, and she was forced to slow down so that she wouldn't trip. From somewhere far away, she thought she heard the sound of wind.

Uninvited guests.

She had focused before on the word "uninvited," but it was "guests" that grabbed her attention now. For that was what they were. Not indigenous spirits or beings that lived here, but *neh chizni doohc* that had arrived from elsewhere. Visitors.

Why had they come, though? What did they want?

Agafia traveled quickly, working on instinct or being

led by God, she was not sure which. She could not really see the path, but she was following it, and just as she emerged from the boulders, the moon appeared above the high cliffs to the east, bathing the scene in front of her with light.

And she saw Jedushka Di Muvedushka.

Laughing, the small figure sped out of the *banya*, took off up the hillside, clambering over rocks, cavorting playfully in the moonlight. Did he see her? She didn't think so, and that made his exuberant little dance all the more eerie.

There was a rustle off to her left, and Agafia whirled so fast in that direction that her candle went out. Her heart was pounding and she was prepared to see shadows with teeth or snake-skinned demons, but instead she saw a line of people, several of them carrying flashlights.

Molokans.

One of them moved forward, toward her. It was Vera, and Agafia had never been so happy to see anyone in her life. She could tell by the expression on the other woman's face that Vera no longer believed her to be corrupted, and her relief was so great that she wanted to cry. Semyon had obviously gotten through to them. She scanned the row of faces looking for him, but he was not among the Molokans gathered before her.

Why were they at the *banya* instead of the house? She'd told Semyon to make sure they went to the house.

She looked at Vera and understood. The old woman had had another dream. And it had pointed her here.

"I am sorry," Vera said, moving closer, throwing her arms around her, and hugging her close. Agafia remained holding onto her Bible, but she tossed the unlit candle aside and hugged her old friend back with one arm.

There was a lot to be said but no time to say it, and Vera's apology covered all of it for now.

"Did you see him?" Agafia asked, nodding toward the hillside.

Vera nodded grimly.

"Whose house is he from?"

"No one knows."

"You have been watching him?"

Vera nodded, looked at the others. "We did not know what to do."

It was a tacit acknowledgment that *she* was now the leader, that she was the one who would decide how they would act, and Agafia had never felt prouder in her life. She scanned the faces, looking for Nikolai, but the minister was nowhere to be found.

"Where is Nikolai?" she asked. "Where is Semyon?"

"Nikolai went with Peter to bring back the prophet, as you said." Vera met her eyes. "Semyon has disappeared."

There was no time to waste, no time to dwell on what they should have done or could have done, and Agafia nodded. She pointed toward the *banya*. "I'm going to look."

Even as she said it, a shiver ran down her spine, but the others trained their flashlights on the bathhouse and followed along with her, and she was grateful for both their presence and their courage. Although she had no light of her own, the moonlight was bright enough to see by, and she did not stop until she was directly in front of the *banya*'s open door. Vera shone her flashlight into the darkness.

The inside of the *banya* was filled with bodies.

Bodies of Jedushka Di Muvedushka.

Agafia took an involuntary step back, nearly stepping on Onya's toes. The bodies were barely there, shimmering like spirits, the flashlight beams granting them even less substance than the refracted moonlight, but she could see them piled one on top of the other, like logs, and in a sudden flash of insight, she understood what had happened.

Jedushka Di Muvedushka had followed them from California.

And he was killing off all of the other Owners in McGuane.

It explained the increase in supernatural activity, the reason why these supernatural forces had been allowed to spread outward from their home. There had been no protection. Anywhere.

Agafia stared at the stacked ephemeral bodies, stunned. A flashlight beam played across the back wall of the bathhouse, and she saw that the figure on the wall had changed. Its head had grown, its body had shrunk, and it no longer looked like a typical Molokan man. It looked like what it was.

Jedushka Di Muvedushka.

Slowly, tentatively, she walked inside. The power here was incredible. She could feel it. It was stronger than it should have been, it had obviously been fed. She recalled Father telling her when she'd asked that the Owner of the House ate mice and rats and possums, kept vermin away from the house and fed himself at the same time.

She could not recall seeing any rodents or pests on their property since they'd arrived in McGuane.

She could not even remember the last time she'd seen a bird on their land.

Vera had already started chanting. A prayer of forgiveness, a prayer of healing. It did not seem entirely appropriate, but like the others, she fell in behind Vera, repeating the words, holding tight to her Bible, and there actually did seem to be a slight lessening in the oppressiveness of the air. When they finished and she opened up her eyes, she could no longer see the small stacked bodies.

Why had she not been killed?

Why had no one in her family been killed?

That was what puzzled her. Jim was gone. People she didn't even know, who had no connection to the family, had been murdered. But so far she and all her family were still alive.

Perhaps Jedushka Di Muvedushka could not actually harm them. Perhaps he merely wanted to shut down the defenses to show them what they were missing, how he could have protected them had they not abandoned him. More likely, he was out for revenge and wanted to destroy them, but wanted to do so in as subtle a way as possible, to drag it out, to prolong their suffering. Nearly the entire town had been turned against them now; it made her think of how things had been in Russia before the Molokans had left. The persecution. The public beatings.

She thought of Russiantown.

Was that the point of all of this? Spite and revenge? She had learned from Father—and had always believed—that the devil, like God, had a grand scheme, a master plan, and that he would use whatever means were at his disposal to convert the good and recruit the wicked and sow the seeds of death and destruction wherever and whenever possible. But was that really the case? It seemed to her that this had all been brought to bear not as part of some cosmic design but to satisfy the petty desires of a minor spirit.

Was evil really that small?

Perhaps it was. That thought gave her hope.

The Molokans all crowded into the tiny building. There were seven of them, and they could barely fit, but they stood close to each other, holding hands, and without speaking, without planning, began to perform the Cleansing. After all of their previous efforts, they knew the words by heart, and as they chanted, Agafia wondered what would happen if the Owner of the House returned. Would he be repelled by the force of their prayers?

Flashlights had been switched off, and before they were even halfway through, the darkness around them was moving, sliding sinuously between their legs, wrapping itself around their heads. They remained focused, kept praying, and the movement within the bathhouse became more agitated.

After this, they would walk back to the house, get her daughter-in-law and her grandchildren. The Molokans had obviously come in cars, and even Gregory could not hope to combat so many allies. She and the children would escape and go to one of the others' houses and decide on a further plan from there.

Agafia felt good, invested with power by the Holy Spirit, and though she knew it was inappropriate in this place and under these circumstances, she wanted to jump, wanted to give herself over to the Lord and let the Spirit overtake her.

It was then that the sandstorm hit.

Twenty

1

The wind began blowing, sand scraping loudly against the windows and the sides of the house. Visibility was worse than in fog, and through the small attic window Gregory could see only blackness: no moon, no stars, no lights.

He thought to himself, *It's time.*

He stood up slowly. He'd been sitting here for hours, in the same position, revolver loaded, waiting, and the muscles in his legs were sore. His father had stopped talking to him some time ago, but he'd stopped listening long before that. He didn't really need his father to tell him what needed to be done.

He knew.

Oh, he definitely knew.

Gregory opened the trapdoor, carefully lowered the ladder, and climbed out of the attic as quietly as possible. The hallway was dark, but he didn't need light to see. Something had happened to him after all those hours in the attic. His eyes had not merely adjusted to the dark, his vision had been enhanced. It was like a cat's, and though the world was in black and white, it was clear, clearer than it had ever been before. He saw the empty corridor before him, saw the metal ladder that someone had brought in from outside and that for some reason had been laid along the side wall.

He started walking.

He understood how Bill Megan had felt, why he had had to do what he did. It was the only possible response, the only way to make sure that mistakes were paid for and that they would not happen again. It was just, it was justice, and there was something both invigorating and fulfilling about knowing that he was about to put things right.

The gun felt good in his grip, like a part of him. He walked slowly, silently, careful not to put too much of his weight on the creaky boards. Outside, the wind increased in volume, the susurrous sand growing in intensity. It sounded to him like music.

Sasha's door was the first one he came to, and he pushed it open, gun extended. He walked into his daughter's room. She'd pulled her blanket up, bunching it around her midsection, and the bottom of her body was exposed to the open air. She was lying on her side, and her legs were scissored so that he could see her crotch. Her panties were pulled tight, and he saw the slight bulge of her pubic mound, the crease of her vulva. There was what looked like dried blood on the material, but he ignored that, saw only the outline beneath the stained underpants.

She stirred in her sleep, her legs spreading wider, and he understood what was going on here.

The slut wanted him to fuck her.

The anger began building within him, the rage he'd been conserving all day blossoming into a white-hot, righteous wrath. Here she was, beaten and bruised, and all she could think about was getting that little hole filled up again as quickly as possible. She was just like her mother, hungry for dick, any dick, wanting only to be filled up with man meat, and he was sickened thinking that she wanted to have intercourse with him, her own father.

The beating she'd received from whatever guy had banged her had obviously not been enough to teach her a lesson, and now it was up to him to point out the error of her ways, to make sure she never did anything like this again.

He walked over. She was only pretending to be asleep, and he kicked the bed hard, forcing her to give up the ruse. She sat up, acting as though she was startled, her eyes opening wide with what could have been terror but was obviously lust.

She saw the gun in his hand, looked into his eyes, knew what he intended to do.

"No!" Sasha screamed.

He shot her in the crotch, giggled as a wash of blood spread over her nightgown. "You're not going to be able to put anything else in there, bitch."

She was thrashing around, making a funny gurgling sound, and he could not help laughing. The blood was everywhere, and an intoxicating charge surged through him as he looked at what he'd done. He thought of the Molokans' wimpy little prohibitions against violence, their stupid outmoded adherence to the letter of the Bible, and he knew he was more alive in this moment than they would ever be.

Why hadn't he done this before?

Sasha was still jerking spasmodically, arms outstretched, back arched, and he lifted the revolver, pointed it at her midsection and fired again.

More spasms, more blood. Then she finally stopped moving, and he smiled to himself as he opened the door, walked out into the hall.

"Next," he said.

2

Adam heard everything through the walls between their rooms, and even as the agonizing emptiness of loss ripped through his guts, even as that was replaced by terror and fear, he was thinking, moving, and he looked quickly around his bedroom for, first, someplace to hide, and, second, a weapon.

There was no place to hide, and if he jumped out the window from this high up he'd probably break his leg and be caught, so he concentrated on finding something to fight with, but for a brief, panicked second it looked as though he was going to be screwed. There was nothing here he could use.

Then he remembered, and he grabbed the flashlight from underneath his bed. It was a big one, an old one made out of metal, and he and Roberto had often made contingency plans to use it as a weapon should anyone

attempt to break into their tent while they were camping
in the backyard. It was no match for a gun, but he had
no choice. It would have to do.

He ran over to the door, stood next to it, flashlight
held high. He hadn't even known that his dad had a gun,
and the revelation shocked him to the core. Even after
all that had happened, even after they'd tried to trap his
dad in the attic, he hadn't really believed that his father
would snap like this, would go this far. He might get
angry, yeah. Might threaten them and throw things
around. But murder them? Kill his own children? That
he never would have believed.

But he'd heard it.

He knew it was true.

And he knew he was next.

His hands were sweaty, his heart pounding. It was
hard to breathe, but though the wind outside seemed
deafening, he did not allow himself to suck in the air he
needed. He was afraid it would be too loud, his dad
would hear. He rationed his air, forcing himself to keep
his mouth closed, to breathe through his nose and take
short, shallow breaths.

In the hall, his father's footsteps drew closer.

The flashlight slipped out of his hands.

It fell to the floor, banging loudly against the hardwood, the clattering noise of its landing distinct even
above the sound of the sandstorm. He crouched down,
scrambled to pick it up.

He heard his father's careful footstep on the hall floor.
"Son?"

He was so scared that he wanted to cry, felt like he was
going to wet his pants, but he remained in place against
the wall, next to the door, the hard plastic nub of the light
switch digging into his back. He would only get one
chance, he knew, one shot—if that—and he'd better
make it good. Most likely, he would be killed instantly.
His father would probably be expecting something: he'd
heard the flashlight fall, and he would no doubt come in
like a cop, swinging his gun around in a semicircle, ready
to shoot at the slightest sign of movement.

Adam held his breath.

His father walked through the door.

He swung hard, hitting his dad in the head. He swung with all his might, with a ferocity he had never been able to manage playing baseball during PE, and the blow connected, the shock wave passing through the metal into his hand and almost causing him to drop the flashlight.

His father fell to the floor.

"Thank God," his mother cried. "Thank God!"

He picked up the flashlight, turned it on, shone it toward her. She stood in the hallway, knife raised, both arms shaking, her knees practically buckling. She'd obviously heard the shots from downstairs and had come up here to save him, and though she hadn't had to attack his father, the fact that she was willing to do so filled Adam with gratitude, relief, and a childish sort of happiness. It was a brave, selfless love that had brought her up here, into the mouth of danger, and at that moment he felt closer to her than he ever had before.

His father was on the ground, bleeding, lying perfectly still, and Adam rushed over his unmoving body to give his mother a quick, hard hug. She squeezed back, but she was already moving away, bending down, checking to see if his dad was . . . what? Unconscious?

Dead?

He'd automatically assumed that he'd just knocked his father out. But what if he was dead? What if he'd killed him?

The gun had fallen out of his father's hand, and his mother picked it up gingerly. In movies, people always knocked out the bad guy, then forgot to pick up the gun, leading to another inevitable showdown, but his mom was no dummy, and there was no way that was going to happen here.

She stood up, and he still didn't know if his dad was alive or dead, but Adam assumed he was alive because his mother said, "We'd better get out of here."

The flashlight in his hand was bloody, but it was still working, and he wiped the bloody end on his jeans and waited while his mom quickly ran to Sasha's room, went inside, then hurried back, her face white, blanched. She bent down again, dug through his dad's pockets, looking for something, and finally withdrew a key ring. She stood, grabbed his hand. "Let's go!"

They practically flew down the stairs, and he tried to concentrate on the task immediately at hand—escape—but his mind kept going back to Sasha.

There were tears streaming out of his eyes, down his cheeks, but he was not really crying, and he was able to speak clearly. "Where's Teo? Where's Babunya?"

"Teo's in her room."

Teo *was* in her room, crying, but she'd been smart enough to lock the door, and she did not immediately open it. Even when they pounded and yelled for her to open up, she did not do so right away. It was only after Adam said, "He's just knocked out! We have to get out of here before he wakes up!" that she finally unlocked her door and came out.

Adam grabbed his sister by the arm and the three of them rushed out of the house into the sandstorm. Dirt and grit sprayed into his face, needling his skin, little jabs of pain like pinpricks, causing him to turn away, squinting. The wind was tremendous, cold and powerful, strong enough to practically blow him off his feet, and he held tight to Teo's hand.

The van was parked in the drive, in front of the carport, but as he started toward it, his mom pulled him away, in the opposite direction.

Where were they going?

"The *banya*!" his mother yelled over the wind, as if reading his mind. "Babunya's there!"

He pulled ahead of her, in the lead, running down the path toward the bathhouse, dragging Teo with him, his feet moving from memory. The last thing he wanted to do right now was go out to the *banya*, but Babunya was probably out there praying or something, and they couldn't just leave her. He thought fast. If they got her, brought her back, they could probably be in the van and gone before his father came to.

They *were* like stupid movie people, he realized. They should not only have taken his father's gun, they should have tied him up before they left so he wouldn't be able to come after them when he did regain consciousness.

But Adam didn't know where ropes were or even if they had any, and he thought that maybe they had done the right thing after all. It might have wasted too much time had they stopped to figure out how to restrain him.

Time, he suspected, was the one thing they didn't have.

They reached the boulders, ran past them. He could not see the *banya,* but he knew it was ahead and he led them straight to it, stopping in front of the open doorway, and shining his flashlight inside.

Babunya was in there.

She was standing in the center of the bathhouse with a whole bunch of old Molokans who looked like they were dressed for church. It was creepy to see them all inside the bathhouse, dressed in white, in the dark, while outside the wind and sand blew wildly, but . . . but somehow the *banya* didn't seem quite as spooky as it had before. It was as if whatever had been in here, whatever had possessed this place, had fled, leaving behind only the eeriness of an ordinary abandoned building. Behind them, he noticed, the shadow on the wall had disappeared.

He felt a small shove on his right side, and then Teo was pushing past him, running inside, throwing her arms around her grandmother.

"He killed Sasha!" Teo cried. "And he tried to kill Adam!"

His mother's hand was on his shoulder, and then all of them were moving into the *banya.*

"It's Dad," he explained. "I hit him in the head with this flashlight"—he held it up—"but I think it only knocked him out." He cast a quick look out the door. "He's after all of us. He's crazy."

Babunya nodded. "I know."

They started talking in Russian, the Molokans, and he had no idea what they were saying, but the tone was easy enough to read: they were scared. He heard high, fast syllables filled with far too many consonants. He looked over at his mom and she was listening intently, but he had the feeling that even she was having a difficult time keeping up.

Teo glanced around, frowning. "What happened?" she asked. "Is the *banya* dead?"

She'd been here too, Adam realized, and the thought of that made his blood run cold.

Babunya smiled at her, hugged her. "Yes," she said

in English. "We kill it." She walked over to his mom
and said something to her in Russian.

His mother nodded.

"Come on," Babunya said. "Work here done. We
have to go." She moved forward, gently took the gun
from his mother's hand. "Others are waiting."

Like his mom, Babunya held the weapon as though it
was a hand grenade about to go off. He realized that
the gun was what his father had used to kill Sasha. It
was what had murdered his sister.

Murdered his sister.

It still didn't seem real to him. In some ways it seemed
too real—the horrific specifics of it were imprinted on
his mind and would be there forever—but at the same
time, the knowledge was too large to grasp any way but
intellectually. He *knew* Sasha was dead, but he hadn't
really *felt* it yet, not the full force of it, and he was afraid
of what would happen when he did.

"Oh, shit!" his mother said. "Oh, shit!" She started
beating her rear end, hitting her pockets in the front.
She looked at the ground around her, turning in a circle,
then glanced up at Babunya. "The keys! I lost the keys!"

Adam's heart lurched in his chest. "The van keys?"

"Oh, shit!"

"There are cars," Babunya said, nodding toward the
other Molokans. "We go with them."

His mom sounded as though she was about to cry.
"But—"

Babunya put a hand on her shoulder. "We go with
them."

3

When Gregory came to, his face was stuck to the floor.
His head had stopped bleeding, but the congealed pool
of blood had cemented his hair and cheek and left temple to the hardwood of the upstairs hallway, and it felt
like his face was being ripped away as he pulled himself
free and stood up.

He did not scream, though. He did not cry out from
the pain.

He welcomed it.

He thought of his family, smiled to himself. They were stupid. They should have killed him when they had the chance. Now they would have to pay for that mistake. And from somewhere down the hall he heard the voice of his father, agreeing with him. "Kill them all," his father said. "They don't deserve to live."

No, they didn't, Gregory agreed. He put a hand up to the side of his face, it came back wet and red. His wound had been newly reopened, and it hurt like a motherfucker. Adam would pay for that. He'd been planning to dispatch the boy like he had his sister—quickly—but his plans had changed. Now the little shit was going to die a slow, horrible, painful death.

He hobbled down the hallway, using his hand to guide himself along the wall because of his closed eye and the subsequent loss of depth perception.

He used the handrail on his way down the stairs.

"Kill them all," his father whispered again.

He did not even bother to answer. His father had become irrelevant, and Gregory was acting now on his own reasons, for his own purposes.

The house was silent and the sound of the wind and sand outside was maddening. His head was aching, a sharp pain that seemed to run down the entire left side of his body, but the pain was good and he was grateful for it. It spurred him on, enabled him to remain focused on what he had to do.

Hunt down his family and kill them.

Bill Megan had been lucky. He'd been able to take out his family easily, with no difficulties or complications. Gregory wondered if he'd had a silencer on his gun. Maybe that had been the problem, not having a silencer, and he cursed his Molokan upbringing for not allowing him to be more familiar with firearms.

His mother would pay for that.

He staggered through the living room, reached the front door, pulled it open. The wind and sand stung his face, blowing into his wound and amplifying the agony tenfold. He looked down, steeling himself against the onslaught—

And something caught his eyes.

A key ring.

He bent down. Smiled. The stupid bitch had tried to steal his keys, but she'd dropped them on the porch, right on the welcome mat, like a present for him. He laughed, the laughter spiraling upward, out of control, until he finally forced himself to cut it off.

He walked through the stinging sand out to the van, got in.

He could see out of only one eye, but there was not much to be seen in the sandstorm anyway, and he drove by instinct, drove from memory, heading up the drive, down the road, through the dirty black night toward the center of town.

He drove directly to the gun store, and as he'd hoped, its doors were wide open. The place had obviously been looted, but there were still plenty of weapons available, and he chose a revolver exactly like the one he'd had. He was familiar with it, knew how it worked, and he wouldn't have to waste any time adjusting to a new weapon. He walked behind the counter, grabbed a box of ammunition from the cupboard beneath the display case, loaded the gun, and put the rest of the ammo in his pockets.

Outside, through the blowing dust, he saw what looked like Paul's car parked in front of the café, and he smiled. He should've known that little pussy would be living in there now. He was probably crying himself to sleep. Or trying to hump the chalk outline the pigs had drawn around Deanna's dead body.

Or both.

He was glad Deanna was dead. He'd never liked that bitch, and it served her right that she'd met her end in her husband's café. He wondered what her last thoughts had been. He hoped they were desperate and despairing.

He walked against the wind, keeping his head down, until he reached the café. The door was closed and locked, but he raised his revolver and held it against the door handle, pulling the trigger.

There was a loud report that was swallowed instantly by the wind, and the door swung open, its lock and handle shattered.

His night vision was still intact, and, out of the sand,

he could see clearly, though there were no lights on in the café and no illumination filtered in from outside. He didn't see any sign of Paul, but the café owner was a lazy fuck, and Gregory knew there was no way in hell that Paul would walk home and leave his car. Especially not in this kind of weather.

Revolver extended, he walked along the side of the counter to the short hallway that led to Paul's office. He kicked open the office door.

Paul looked up groggily, squinting into the darkness. "Who's there?"

"Hello, Paul."

"Gregory?"

"Who else?" He remembered what it had been like to see his friend's hand shoved all the way down his wife's open pants, fingers working on her, and he was filled afresh with rage and hate. "Didn't expect to see me here again, did you?"

"N-no." Paul could obviously tell that something was not right, and Gregory smiled at the wary expression on his face, enjoying the slight hesitation in his voice.

He thought of the last time they'd fought, the words that had been said. He advanced slowly. " 'Milk drinker'?" he said softly. " 'Faggot'?"

His head hurt like a motherfucker, but the pain cleared his brain, sharpened his thoughts, and he was able to remember in vivid detail the particulars of the fight, the unfair way he had been kept from complete and total victory. Paul was going to get what was coming to him this time. There was no Wynona to save his ass now, no teenage bim who was going to arrive at the last minute and rescue him.

Paul could still not see him, but the café owner stood, facing the direction of his voice. He walked out from behind the desk, and it was obvious that not only had he been sleeping—he was drunk.

Good.

"You called me a homo," he told Paul.

"Did I?"

"*You're* the homo."

Paul grinned into the darkness. "Then why'd your wife want to fuck me?"

Gregory shot him in the knee.

Paul went down screaming, a bloody spray of bone and cartilage flying out every which way, splattering against the wall and the desk, soaking the carpet. Gregory was surprised the shot had been so true. He could see perfectly in the pitch-black room, but it was out of only one eye and his depth perception was completely gone.

God must be looking out for him.

No, he thought soberly, not God.

Paul was screaming nonstop, a piercing, agonizing cry that sounded more animal than human. It was an irritating sound, an excruciatingly grating sound, and he stared at the writhing figure on the floor, willing it to stop.

He realized dimly that he and Paul had once been friends, but that seemed so long ago and so far back that it was almost as though it had been in another life, in another world, in an alternate universe.

The screaming did not abate—got worse, if anything—and Gregory took a step forward, reached down, placed the barrel of the gun next to Paul's Adam's apple and blew a hole in his throat.

Blood was gushing, spurting everywhere now, and he knew instantly that he'd made a mistake. Paul was thrashing around and was no longer screaming—he no longer had a voice box, no longer had a throat—but he was dying, and Gregory had wanted him to suffer longer, had planned to draw out his death and torture him before finally allowing him to give up the ghost.

He stared down at his dying ex-friend. In a suddenly lucid moment, it occurred to Gregory that something was wrong. He was not the person he used to be, not the person he should be. He knew it, and he wanted it to be different, but his thought processes seemed to be overridden by an outside imperative, a will greater than his own, and the insight vanished as quickly as it had arrived.

Paul died.

And that made him feel good.

He walked back through the café and out onto the street, bracing himself against the coldness of the air and the strength of the sand. He thought for a moment, then started down the cracked sidewalk toward the bar, the bar where his father had been humiliated and where for the past few months that smug prick of a bartender had made it clear that he was doing him a big favor just by allowing him to drink here.

MOLOKAN MURDERERS

Whoever had spray-painted that graffiti gem had been more right than he'd known.

And the bartender was about to find that out for himself.

Gregory clutched the revolver tightly, holding it out in front of him. He didn't know what time it was, but it couldn't have been that late because through the sand and darkness he could see the glowing neon of a battery-powered beer sign, colors that he knew to be red and blue but that appeared to him as shades of gray.

The Miner's Tavern was still open.

He walked inside. Candles were lit on the tables and on the bar, providing the only illumination save for the beer sign. The place was empty except for the bartender, and perhaps that was just as well. He thought of his father, humiliated here, degraded, cowed into being less than a man, and without stopping to confront the bartender or explain what he was doing, Gregory started shooting.

He stopped only when the hammer clicked on an empty magazine, but the bartender was already long dead.

He popped out the empty round, popped in another, then walked out of the bar.

Playtime was over.

It was time to get back to business.

It was time to kill his family.

4

The Molokans' cars had been parked on the road that ran by the burned house on the other side of the *banya*. It was closer and quicker this way, and they didn't have to go anywhere near their own home and risk seeing his father again. Adam was thankful for that.

He rode in a big car with his mom, Teo, and two Molokan men he didn't know, moving slowly through the sandstorm. Babunya was traveling in one of the other two cars, and all three vehicles pulled up in front of the church together.

The wind was still blowing crazily, but the downtown buildings kept the worst of the dust out, and at least they could see here. The cars pulled into the small parking lot, and they all got out at once.

At the front of the church were the rest of the Molokans, twenty or thirty of them, old men and old women in white Russian clothes.

But it was the people with them who were the surprise. Indians.

Standing next to the Molokans were several men from the reservation, dressed in what looked like the traditional clothing of their tribe. Dan and his father, the chief, were in the front, and Dan smiled at him, waved. Adam felt hope flare within him. Despite the reassurance he'd gotten from Babunya and her friends, despite the fact that they seemed to know what was happening and what to do about it, the Molokans seemed to him too old to be effective in any kind of fight. He did not think they would be able to stand up against the sort of power and force that could summon ghosts and kill people and haunt houses and possess his father.

But the stoic men of the Indian tribe seemed healthy and fit and reliably steady. He believed in them, he trusted them, and he knew from the clear, hard expressions on their faces that they could handle whatever trouble was thrown their way. They were clutching long spears painted with bands of alternating red and black and blue, fringed at the top with loops of leather cord and white feathers, and the fact that they carried weapons rather than Bibles made him feel a little more confident as well.

Although . . .

He squinted, looking closer.

They were not spears after all, he saw. They might not even be weapons. They were . . . painted sticks.

Dan said something to his father, started toward Adam. Adam looked up at his mom, wondering if it was all right for him to talk to his friend again, but he could tell by the expression on her face that their little rock-throwing incident and subsequent arrest was the last thing on her mind, and he hurried across the dirt to meet his pal.

Dan was the only Indian dressed in regular street clothes, and he and his family were the only Molokans similarly attired. Dan grinned at him as he approached. "Came through for you, didn't I?"

Adam nodded. "Thanks, dude." There was so much he wanted to say, so much he needed to explain, that he didn't know where to start. The next words out of his mouth were totally off the subject.

"You seen Scott?"

Dan shook his head. "I haven't been allowed to see either of you."

"Until now."

The other boy smiled wryly. "I guess they finally figured out that it wasn't really our fault."

"It wasn't?"

Dan laughed. "Well, we'll let 'em think it wasn't."

"So what's the plan? Do you guys . . . know what's going on here?"

"Yes."

"My dad went crazy and killed my sister Sasha. He tried to kill us, but I knocked him out with this flashlight, and then we ran over to the *banya,* where my grandma and those other Molokans did some sort of exorcism to force out the demons or ghosts or whatever was living in there." The words tumbled out of him in a rush, and he was grateful to see Dan nodding at everything he said, not surprised, just accepting it.

"I told you," Dan said, "weird things have always happened here. Like Scott said, it's a haunted place."

"But this is different."

"Yeah."

"Uninvited guests."

His friend nodded. *"Na-ta-whay."*

"What do you guys think we need to do?"

Dan looked at him evenly. "Find it. Kill it."

"It?"

"There's a leader, a ringleader. Kill it and the others will scatter."

Dan seemed so much more knowledgeable than he himself was, so much more mature than he felt. He wondered if that was an Indian thing or if that was just how Dan was.

The adults were talking now, and Adam listened in.

"They try get Vasili," an old fat woman said in English even more halting than Babunya's. "They no come back."

"Maybe it's only the sandstorm," he heard his mother say. "Maybe they just got lost or didn't want to chance the roads at night in this wind."

The woman said something in Russian.

His mother turned toward Dan's dad. "What do you think it is?"

The chief said basically the same thing his son had, about there being a host of evil spirits, about killing the leader, and he used some long, unpronounceable word to describe the creature.

His mother recited the name back to him perfectly, and for the first time, the chief allowed himself a small smile. "Very good."

"We call him Jedushka Di Muvedushka," Babunya said.

"So you know what this is, too?"

"Of course."

"It is a mischievous spirit. It likes to play."

"Play?" his mother repeated.

Dan's father nodded grimly. "We are nothing to it. We are toys, meant to be used and discarded. It orders around the other spirits, makes them do its bidding, murders us, hunts us down. All for its entertainment." He leaned forward. "That's why it must be killed," he said fiercely. "I know Molokans are pacifists—"

"Cannot kill what not alive," Babunya said.

"*We* can kill it."

Adam looked from one to the other, following the conversation. Creatures who used people as toys, for entertainment? It sounded like Greek mythology, like all of the gods and creatures they'd learned about in English class who had alleviated their boredom by playing chess with human lives.

Once again, he thought that maybe the legends of all cultures had some common root, and the idea made him shiver.

Because that root was right here in McGuane, the grain of truth at the core of it all located at the overlapping intersection of Russian and Indian myths.

He was struck by the fact that more than half of the Molokans were women but that there were no women among the Indians. It was a strange observation to be making at this time, and though it wasn't a contest, he thought that his people were more progressive, more modern than Dan's tribe, and for the first time he felt genuinely proud to be Russian, to be Molokan.

His mother looked from Babunya to the chief to the other Indians to the other Molokans. "So what do we do now?"

The chief looked at her, looked past her at the others. "We have to go back to your house." His voice lowered. "And kill it."

5

There were shapes in the sand, outlines. Small, light figures that cavorted behind a curtain of tan; larger, darker, unrecognizable creatures that slouched through the windblown dirt, barely seen. It was as if the duststorm was a cover, a cover for . . . for what?

An army of monsters that was invading McGuane.

Scott turned away from the window. That was the thought that came to him, and while he knew it sounded crazy, he believed it. As he'd told Adam, McGuane was a haunted place, and it seemed to be getting worse by the minute.

His parents were fighting again, screaming at each other in the bedroom. Earlier, he'd taken advantage of the situation and tried to call Adam from the phone in his dad's den, but the line had been busy. He'd tried again just now, but a recorded voice said that line had been disconnected.

He didn't like that.

And he liked the shapes in the sandstorm even less.

For some reason they reminded him of the bathhouse, of the pictures he'd taken.

Like most of the people in town, his parents were blaming the Molokans for bringing this curse upon McGuane, and he was glad they hadn't seen the shapes in the sand. They stupidly thought it was Adam's influence that had made him throw rocks at cars on the highway and had led to his arrest—that was one of the things he'd wanted to talk to Adam about—and their anger had grown from there. Part of his parents' current fight had been about his dad going off to "smoke some Russians." Luckily his mom had refused to let him go, yelling at him, telling him he could pretend all he wanted outside these walls with his friends, but in here, where it counted, in the bedroom, she knew he was not a man.

The argument had branched out from that starting point to cover the usual issues and grievances, and for once he was glad his parents were fighting. It kept them occupied.

Ordinarily, he hit the road when his parents got into it like this, going over to someone else's house, hanging out at French's. But tonight he stayed home. Their screaming was the worst he'd ever heard, but he knew it was preferable to what was happening outside, and as he looked through the window at the obscured world out there, he thought that no matter how tense things got in here, right now there was no place else in town he'd rather be.

The cells were full. The sheriff tried once again to radio the Rio Verde sheriff's station to ask if they had any open cells where prisoners could be transferred, but, as before, he was unable to get through.

He tried Willcox, tried Safford, tried Benson.

No answer.

Roland slammed down the mike on the radio set, frustrated. Tish, holding down the front desk by herself, looked over at him, worried, and he forced himself to smile reassuringly at her.

"Still no answer?"

He shook his head. "I'll try again in a few minutes." He started to walk back to his office but noticed something strange when he passed the hallway leading to the holding area.

Silence.

He frowned, listening. The prisoners were awfully quiet all of a sudden, and that didn't sit well with him. Not with things going the way they were. He made a detour down the hall, knocked on the metal door that led to the holding area. "Tom!" he called.

He expected the door to be opened immediately, but when there was no response, he called his deputy's name again and quickly pulled out his own keys, a feeling of dread growing within him. "Tom!"

He pulled open the door.

Tom was lying unmoving in the middle of the corridor that ran between the two rows of cells. In the cells themselves, the prisoners were dead. All of them. Pressed against the bars, faces blue-black from lack of oxygen, eyes bulging from their sockets in contrasting white.

A cold fear gripped Roland's heart and he turned around, wanting to get out of here as quickly as possible, not even bothering to check on Tom's condition to make sure he was dead.

The metal door slammed shut in his face.

Faron Kent pulled to a stop in front of the temple. He'd been born and raised Mormon, had left the church only when he'd married Claire, but he still considered Mormons his people, and when he saw all of the cars and trucks parked in front of the temple, he knew where he had to go.

He'd just come into town, and he'd almost pulled off to the side of the road to wait out the sandstorm once he'd come through the tunnel and experienced its ferocity. There'd been only a slight wind in the adjoining canyons through which he'd driven, nothing at all on the flat desert plain before. Which mean that this freakishly localized weather could not possibly last the night. It was probably safer to pull onto the shoulder and catch a couple winks than attempt to maneuver these narrow roads with zero visibility.

But . . .

But he saw shadows in the sandstorm. Figures. Creatures. And he *heard* things. And he thought it safer to try and navigate the roads than pull off and wait for . . . what?

As he drove down the sloping highway into town, as the sand and its hidden inhabitants swirled about his car, old buried beliefs from his upbringing suddenly kicked in, and he found himself wondering if this was the end, if these were the last days.

It did not seem that far-fetched, and when he saw all the vehicles parked in front of the dark Mormon temple, he immediately and impulsively pulled in.

Even as he braked, however, the wind was lessening, the sandstorm dying down. There were still no lights on in McGuane, other than what looked like headlights further up the road, but a faint glow of moonlight from above the storm could now be seen filtering onto the scattered buildings.

And the mine.

For that was the only place where he saw movement, the open pit across the highway, and the movement that he saw, that instantly grabbed his attention, scared the living shit out of him.

There were creatures crawling out from the mine, emerging from the pit onto the ground above, creatures of dirt and gravel, monsters made from copper tailings and animated with some hellish spark of life.

The last days.

His first instinct was to run inside the temple for sanctuary, but his experiences during the intervening years proved far stronger than the influence of his upbringing, and he reached for the rack behind him and pulled his shotgun down.

He got out of the pickup, locked and loaded, and strode bravely across the highway. He pointed his shotgun, aimed it at the first sand creature and pulled the trigger.

With a short, high wail, the creature dissolved into dust.

Ashes to ashes, dust to dust.

He targeted the next monster pulling itself up, its min-

eral fingers still clutching the edge of the pit, and when
its head exploded in a shower of dirt, it fell back into
the mine.

Behind him, a few of the braver men were walking
out onto the steps from inside the temple to see what
was going on. The wind had died down enough now that
the sound of the shotgun blasts had carried.

"Grab some weapons!" he yelled as loud as he could.
"I need some help here!"

There was a second's hesitation, then two men
sprinted down the steps and out to their pickups. A moment later, three others ran out of the temple to help.

He smiled, feeling good, feeling strong, and blew the
next monster into a cloud of dust that dissipated in the
wind.

6

They were starting toward the cars when Agafia saw
Gregory staggering up to the church through the blowing sand.

Even with the flashlights pointed at him, he remained
only a silhouette, but she would have recognized her
son's shape anywhere, and she drew in her breath
sharply. He was lurching to the left, and it was obvious
that there was something seriously wrong. Her first instinct was maternal, and she wanted to run to him and
hug him and pray over him and make him feel better.
But pragmatism took over instantly, and she ordered the
others back into the shot-up and now hairless church,
warning them to stay down. Julia shoved the kids
through the door, and Adam's little friend went with
them. The older Molokans obeyed as well, but some
merely doused their flashlights and moved off to the
right or to the left, waiting to see what was going to
happen. The Indians, following some plan of their own,
broke up and began moving into the dust storm, into
the night, attempting, she assumed, to sneak up behind
Gregory.

He came closer.

She kept her flashlight trained on his indistinct form.

The sight of him with a gun in his hand was not only shocking but repulsive, and her first thought was that she was glad his father was not alive to see this.

She still had in her own hand the gun she'd taken from Julia—

the gun he'd used to kill Sasha

—and though she had no intention of using it, did not even know *how* to use it, she grasped it as she'd seen in movies and on television and pointed it at Gregory, illogically hoping that it would scare him away.

He shot at her.

Agafia jumped back, almost fell, and did drop the flashlight, though she managed to hold on to the revolver. She chanced a quick look behind her, but did not see anybody dead or injured, and she prayed that he had not hit anyone.

Gregory ran forward as fast as he could.

It was totally unexpected behavior, and in this place and under these circumstances, it appeared to be the move of a madman.

Screaming crazily, shooting at the church, causing everyone to scatter, he ran toward her, past her, up the steps—

And pointed his gun at Julia.

Agafia knew she had to act fast. He was not playing around, not trying to gain leverage or make demands. He wanted only to kill his wife, and Agafia stepped up, shoving her gun hard against the side of his head, the side with all the blood. He winced but did not drop his weapon, did not waiver from his intent.

"Forgive me," Agafia said softly in Russian, not knowing if it was Gregory to whom she was speaking or God.

She pulled the trigger.

Gregory dropped.

Julia screamed. It was a cry of sheer pain unlike any she had ever heard, and Agafia felt a twin of that pain within herself, a cry that wanted to escape and be let out but that she kept bottled up inside for fear if allowed free rein it would never end.

They were staring at her with horror, all of the other Russians. Aside from Gregory, she was the only Molokan she had ever known who had willingly and intentionally taken a human life, and that sin weighed on her like a mountain on a peasant's back. Awareness that the life she had taken was also the life she had created, her son's, made her crime that much more heinous, made Agafia feel empty inside. She almost expected God to strike her dead right here and now, but as the others started moving forward, as the Indians emerged from the storm, she understood that that was not going to happen. She would not be taken, she would not be granted an easy way out. She would have to live with what she'd done, with what she was.

Evil.

She thought of Russiantown.

But she could have done nothing else. It was either her son or her daughter-in-law, and she had chosen. If she'd done nothing, Gregory would have killed *her* next, and the kids, and then however many others he could have before someone stopped him, so she'd made the decision to do it herself. It was something she would not have been able to carry out had she had time to think about it, but running on instinct, she'd made the split-second decision to kill him.

It would be God who judged her finally, and she was prepared to accept His verdict no matter what it was.

Julia was next to her, next to him, on the ground, touching Gregory's face, but she was already pulling herself together, obviously attempting to be strong for the children, and Agafia admired that. Julia was tough. She was a survivor and, no matter what, could always be counted on to do what had to be done. Agafia was proud of the choice her son had made.

Her son.

She had no son any more.

She had murdered him.

Again, the scream was within her, threatening to escape, but she pressed it back, would not let it out. She looked down at Gregory's bloody body, then turned away, looked over at the others watching her, staring at her.

She took Julia's arm, pulled her up. "It not over," she said in English. "Indians are right. We go back to house. Finish it."

Twenty-one

1

They parked on the road.

Julia made Adam and Teo stay in the van, with the doors locked. They were both stunned, shell-shocked, and neither objected nor even responded. Dan was in there with them, and one of the old Molokan men volunteered to remain outside and guard the kids.

The rest of them walked up the drive to the house.

There were at least forty of them—Molokans and Indians—and the sheer number of people made her feel safer, more secure. There *was* safety in numbers, and even up against something as vast and incomprehensible as the supernatural, she felt reassured being part of a crowd.

The wind had disappeared as suddenly as it had arrived, but the blackout continued, and after all the howling, this new silence seemed creepy and somehow ominous. Most of them had flashlights, and the way before them was well lit. Ahead, at the end of the drive, its black bulk still too far away to be illuminated by their lights, was their destination.

The house.

Where Sasha lay murdered in her bed. Julia focused on Jedushka Di Muvedushka, trying to figure out where the Owner of the House might be hiding. Like an alcoholic, she was taking everything one step at a time. She concentrated only on the present, only on the here and now, only on what lay immediately before her—

not on the fact that her husband, her lifemate, her love,

*had been shot and killed by his mother on the steps of the
Molokan church while their son and daughter watched*

—and she purposely kept herself from thinking about
the larger issues and implications, about what she was
going to do after this was all over, about what was to
become of the rest of her life.

They reached the porch.

"I'll go in first," the chief said, moving in front.

Agafia pushed past him, motioning for Julia to follow.
"No," she told him. "Our house. We go first."

Julia did not want to be first. She wanted to remain
right where she was, safely in the middle of the crowd,
borne along by the momentum of those around her, carried on the tide of consensus. She didn't want to have
to make decisions, didn't want to think about—

*his brains blown out of his head by his mother seconds
before he was going to shoot* her, *and the expression on
his face in the second before it disintegrated into a wash
of red, that knowing, horrified look that she would remember to her dying day, that was imprinted forever on
her mind, that would always cause her to wonder if at
the last minute he realized what he had done*

—what to do, but she accompanied her mother-in-law
up the porch steps, the others falling in behind them.

They walked into the house, and as scary as it should
have been, the atmosphere was dissipated by the number
of people tramping through her living room. They were
like an army, and Agafia was the general, directing half
of the Indians and Molokans to explore the first floor
and the back porch with Vera and the chief while the
rest of them went upstairs.

Julia realized that she did not know the chief's name,
that none of them had even bothered to ask. Of course,
she didn't know the names of most of the Molokans
either, and somehow the fact that she was here with
strangers lent to the proceedings a dispassionate, objective air that further served to dispel the aura of horror
that overhung the house.

The downstairs people started searching the kitchen
and the first floor bedrooms while the rest of them went
upstairs with Agafia.

They planned to go through this floor, then, if they

didn't find anything, check out the attic. The thought of going up into the attic scared her—

it was where Gregory had hidden, where he'd stored his gun

—and she decided that she would remain here and let some of the hardier people, the Indian men, check for her. She could not go up there. Not now. Not yet.

There was a press of bodies behind her, and she moved forward, flashlight extended. They started with the hallway, checking the linen closet.

Nothing.

Their bedroom, bedroom closets, master bath.

Nothing.

Adam's bedroom. Nothing.

Sasha's bedroom.

Julia sucked in her breath as the flashlights shone into the darkness and illuminated the bed.

It was him. The Owner of the House.

Jedushka Di Muvedushka.

He was crouching over the body of Sasha, and it was obvious that he'd been playing with her. There were patterns drawn in blood, obscene renderings on the wall above the headboard, and her limbs had been repositioned in a disgusting way that he obviously found comical.

She recognized him instantly. She had seen him before, in Russiantown. He was the figure she had encountered in the ruined buildings of the old Molokan neighborhood. She remembered perfectly the scrunched-together face, the abhorrent configuration of features, the aura of tremendous age. He was wearing traditional Russian clothing, but his white shirt was covered with red, and his stubby hands were drenched with blood.

Fear, horror, revulsion, sadness, despair, anger—all vied for supremacy within her, but it was anger that came out on top, and she was the first one to step through the door into the unnaturally cold room. He could not do that with *her* daughter's body. Supernatural being or not, he could not desecrate her corpse and get away with it.

She acted without thinking, throwing her flashlight as hard as she could at the little man and feeling a small twinge of satisfaction as it bounced off his head and made him wince. "Leave her alone!" Julia screamed.

She felt Agafia's reassuring hand on her arm.

"Get out of my house and leave my daughter alone! All of you!"

He looked at her, and in a sudden flash of insight she realized the truth.

There were no others. No ghosts, no demons, no other creatures, no other beings.

Only him.

Agafia was wrong. It was not that supernatural forces were attacking the town because he wasn't there to protect them. It was simply that he was pissed off that they hadn't invited him along when they'd moved.

And he was out for revenge.

The powers at his disposal, the ones he was supposed to turn outward against their enemies, he had turned inward against them. Not only was he not protecting them, he was attacking them, and in his face was the purest example of rage and hatred that she ever hoped to see. It was terrifying, the sheer power and intensity of those emotions, and her next invective died in her throat as she involuntarily backed up.

There were shouts coming from the stairs, everyone was running up, but there wasn't enough room for everybody in the hallway, and she heard the people at the tail end calling out in confusion.

There were all these men and women against this one dwarfish creature, but the deck still seemed stacked, the odds in Jedushka Di Muvedushka's favor, and it was clear that everyone knew it. The cold air was thick with power, an almost electrical charge that Julia could feel on her skin, in the shallow breaths she inhaled. Despite the rush of bodies, she and Agafia were still the only ones in the bedroom. A half-dozen flashlight beams were trained on the blood-spattered little man, but the men and women holding the lights remained out in the hall, afraid to come in.

The left-behind owner smiled at her, revealing small, sharp baby teeth, but there was no mirth or humor in the gesture. "There is only me," he said, confirming her thoughts.

"The *banya*?" Julia said. "The hauntings? The murders?"

Jedushka Di Muvedushka grinned. "All me." He chuckled. "My sandstorm, too."

"It is not him," Agafia said quietly in Russian.

"What?"

"It is not the right one."

The little man chuckled, spoke Russian as well. "Then I guess I'm the wrong one."

Julia understood. It was not their Jedushka Di Muvedushka. It was another one. A bad one.

An evil one.

She should have known that, should have been able to guess, but it made no practical difference, had no bearing on anything at this point.

"The *banya*," Agafia said. "It used to be the Shubins'. They must not have invited him to come. They must have left him behind."

And he'd been sitting here all these years, growing angrier, more bitter.

Stronger.

"Yes," he said, grinning.

Around them, the house shook. Some of the Molokan women in the hallway screamed. Flashlight beams darted around. Color was bleeding from the walls, leaving them black and white. Hovering outside the window was a miniature funnel cloud, a dust devil.

A dust devil with a face.

Gregory's face.

The Owner of the House laughed, the same ancient laugh she remembered from Russiantown, and Julia was chilled to the bone. The creature's voice, when he spoke, was equally ancient. "I'm glad you all came. I'm glad you're here."

And a naked, dirty old man with a beard that hung down to his knees walked through the door.

2

"You have found him."

Agafia heard him before she saw him, heard his voice

in her mind, and she turned to see a commotion in the hallway, a jostling of bodies made apparent by the suddenly skewed flashlight beams.

And then the prophet walked into the room.

The feeling that coursed through her, that washed over her, was not gratitude, not relief, not joy, not hope, but some amalgam of the four that was stronger and more intense than all of them put together.

Peter and Nikolai had found him. And they'd brought him here. She felt like crying but knew she could not allow herself that luxury.

Agafia looked at the *pra roak* and wanted to apologize for not doing something sooner, for not realizing what was happening and putting a stop to it before it reached this point, but there was no time for that either, and she did not really know what to say.

"It is not *your fault,"* that voice in her mind said, and she saw on that wrinkled old face a look of contrition.

She blinked. *He* was apologizing to *her*?

"It is not your fault."

That was true, she realized. Perhaps if they had invited their Jedushka Di Muvedushka to move with them from California he could have fought off this onslaught from his brethren, but it was equally likely that he would have ended up dead like the others, piled in the *banya*. It was the Shubins who had brought this about by ignoring tradition, by not following the Russian custom and inviting the Owner of the House to come with them, and it was their Owner that lay at the root of this disaster.

Although perhaps it was not even *their* fault that things had turned out this way. This was a haunted place, according to Adam's Indian friends, and maybe it was just the coincidental combination of a free and angry Owner and the indigenous spirits of this wild land that had led them to this pass, a unique mingling of the unseen forces of separate cultures, an accidental cross-pollination of different strains of *neh chizni doohc* that ordinarily would never have come into contact with each other but that had here created a monster.

The shaking of the house grew more intense, and Vasili closed his eyes and clasped his hands as around him the darkness began to swirl, gathering into shapes that she almost—but not quite—recognized and that spoke to her on some deep level she did not even know she possessed.

She held tightly to Julia's arm, tried with all her might not to look at Sasha's profaned form.

From the far edges of the room came a sound like the screeches of a tortured rat.

The *pra roak* began speaking in his upper-class Russian, a prayer Agafia could barely understand and that she had never heard before. She did not know if it was a prayer he had made up himself or a legitimate Molokan invocation that she was simply not familiar with, but either way it infuriated the little man, who began screaming crazily in a language that was clearly not human.

The swirls of darkness grew more solid, the black-and-white walls fading into monochromatic gray. The prophet's beard burst into flame, orange fire starting at the bottom of the long, tangled mess of hair and flashing upward toward his face.

Yet still he kept talking, praying, his voice remaining calm even while the Owner's inhuman screams grew ever more frenzied and intense.

The little man stomped his foot on the ground, pointed at Vasili, and the prophet's genitals disappeared, smooth skin appearing between his legs and tightening the wrinkles on his thighs and stomach. The window of the room shattered, flying inward, and the dust devil snaked through the opening and slammed into the *pra roak,* its Gregory face contorted with rage.

Except . . .

Except the prophet was not knocked down by the wind. Instead, it only put out the fire that had engulfed all of his beard save a last bit of stubble on his cheeks.

And the tide shifted.

She was not sure exactly how it happened, but suddenly the dust devil was faceless and fading, the Owner's screams were like background noise and the *pra roak*'s simply stated prayer was loud enough to be heard by all.

The Owner's eyes widened in terror.

Now each line Vasili spoke was like a whip across Jedushka Di Muvedushka's body. The small man recoiled, falling off the bed, rolling on the rug, jerking in spasms that coincided precisely with the end of each spoken phrase.

And he changed.

The clothes went first, melting off him, turning to liquid and running off his form, vaporizing into a foul-smelling gas before ever hitting the floor. The skin went next, then the hair and facial features. Layer by layer, the human veneer was stripped away, the pretenses of mortal existence cast aside. What was emerging was a monster. A squat, greenish-black creature with a strange, inky halo that gave off a smell like rotten garlic, a hideous, hellish being that looked like nothing Agafia had ever seen or imagined and that bespoke both plant and animal origins.

The chief and his men had pushed through the crowd and were now entering the room, and their eyes widened at the sight. They began speaking excitedly to each other in their own language. This was obviously something they recognized.

Evil had many forms and disguises, she thought.

But underneath, it was all the same.

The *pra roak* had moved on to another prayer, a prayer of binding that was part of the Cleansings she and the other church members had attempted to perform. She began chanting along with him, and from the doorway she heard Vera's voice chiming in. Others took up the chant. Peter, Nikolai, Onya. The chorus of voices grew, and Agafia was gratified to hear the creature's grunts and cries and hisses of pain.

The house had stopped shaking, and no longer were there shapes in the darkness, figures formed from shadow. The dust devil was gone. It was all Jedushka Di Muvedushka could do to protect himself from this onslaught of prayer, and he was wailing, gnashing his teeth.

At the end of the prayer, Vasili stopped speaking. The rest of them stopped with him. The freakish creature on the floor was immobile, frozen into a position of supplication. Only his eyes and mouth could move, the eyes darting angrily back and forth as if to escape this position into which he had been fixed, his mouth issuing cries of pain and fury.

The Indians moved forward.

"Kill it," the chief said coldly.

They began beating him with their sticks.

The colors on the sticks changed, and with each hit, with each contact, the sticks seemed to desolidify for a brief fraction of a second, to wiggle and wobble in the men's hands like snakes, like something alive, before stiffening once again.

Jedushka Di Muvedushka devolved under this assault, its form growing less specific, more generic, turning from what was recognizably a monster into a doughy, shapeless mass of quivering flesh that resembled a lump of polluted gelatin. Somewhere along the line, it lost its voice, and the electric change of power that had permeated not just this room but the entire house faded away into nothing.

The stench grew worse, and it was all Agafia could do not to throw up.

Was this what they were all like underneath? she wondered. All of the Jedushka Di Muvedushka? Or was their substance determined by their morality—were the evil ones made of this and the good ones of something nicer?

She didn't know, but she suspected the latter. Somehow she found it hard to believe that the pleasant little man Father had seen, who had braided their horse's hair and helped them through hard times, had anything in common with this hateful evil creature.

But who was to say?

She looked at the grotesque blob next to the bed and shivered.

The sticks were no longer changing color, and a few moments later the Owner of the House was gone. There was nothing left on the floor but a black puddle of brackish liquid.

Vasili mumbled something, dropped to his hands and knees and, like a dog, began lapping it up.

Agafia grimaced. She looked for the first time at Sasha's bloody body atop the bed, then quickly back at the blank and stricken face of her daughter-in-law. Glancing

at the silhouetted forms behind the flashlights, she made
out Vera's bulk, and though the two of them could not
see each other's faces a wordless understanding passed
between them.

The prophet was snorting like an animal, finishing up
the puddle.

Following Vera's lead, Agafia lowered her head and
prayed, giving thanks to God.

3

Her mother-in-law remained upstairs, as did several
of the other Molokans and the naked old man who was
licking up what was left of Jedushka Di Muvedushka.
The rest of the Russians, the Indians, and herself walked
downstairs and outside, exhausted.

The moon was up now, the stars were visible, and
while most of the flashlights remained on, they weren't
really needed. The wind had disappeared, and looking
up the drive, she could clearly see the cars on the road
and the van in which her children waited.

She walked alongside the chief, Adam's friend's father. The Indian man was talking to her, but she wasn't
paying attention and couldn't understand what he said,
and she nodded dumbly, pretending to be listening.

Julia felt numb. She'd been thinking of the present,
keeping the future at bay, worrying only about whether
they would get out of this alive, but now Jedushka Di
Muvedushka was history, the crisis was past and the future was here. She could avoid it no longer.

Sasha was dead.

Gregory was dead.

Her firstborn and her husband were gone, and it was
brought home to her in strange ways:

The knowledge that Sasha would not need the college
fund they'd started for her years before they'd won the
lottery.

And the realization that from now on she would be
making all the decisions alone. There was no one to
whom she could turn for support or advice, and if Adam

or Teo disagreed with her, they could no longer appeal
to their dad.

Their dad was dead.

And he had killed their sister.

Gregory *had* shot Sasha, but she did not blame him.
It might be nothing more than rationalization, rationalization borne of love, but in her mind he had been
guided and corrupted by a power far stronger than himself, under the influence of such an evil force that an
army of people from two different cultures had to band
together to defeat it. Her death was not his fault. Sasha
had not really been murdered by her father—he had
been someone else at that point—and Julia could not
find it in her heart to blame him.

She *did* blame Agafia for murdering her son, though
she knew that was unfair. Agafia had done it to save her
life. And her life *had* been saved, as had probably many
others. The old woman had gone against her religion,
her upbringing, her beliefs, had sacrificed not only her
son but the best part of herself for the rest of her family.
Julia knew it had been an impossible situation and an
instant decision had to be made, but she could not help
second-guessing and wondering if Agafia couldn't have
shot his leg or hit him over the head or somehow just
injured him rather than killing him.

She could not see herself absolving her mother-in-law
for what she'd done, could not find it in her heart to
forgive her. At least not at this point. But she knew, for
her own sake as well as the kids', she would have to
somehow work through it.

She ran the last few steps to the van—

The van that Gregory had bought

—and before she even reached it, the door was opening, and the kids were tumbling out, rushing up to her.

She hugged her children—

the two children who were left

—and she thought about Gregory and thought about
Sasha and thought about the life they'd had and the life
that they were no longer going to have, and she held
them tightly and she began to sob.

Epilogue

They went back to the old house in Downey, he and Babunya.

She drove her old car, her Pontiac, and she drove it in an old-lady way: seat far forward, posture ramrod-straight, steering wheel gripped tightly at the top, chin practically touching the wheel. Before, Adam would have been embarrassed to be seen with her like this, would have ducked far down in his seat and hoped that no one he knew would see him.

But nothing embarrassed him anymore.

They were staying at Babunya's house in Montebello until they found a place of their own, and though it was nice being back in California, it felt strange to be living in someone else's house—even Babunya's—and he was anxious for them to move into their own home.

Teo and his mom were at Aunt Tanya's house this morning, looking over real estate brochures, and his mom had wanted him to come with them, but Babunya told her that she was going to go shopping and that she needed him to help carry the groceries out to the car.

Instead, they'd come here.

He didn't like to think about what had happened. He avoided talking about McGuane or anything that had happened there, and he tried not to let even a stray thought about those months cross his mind. He'd promised Scott and Dan that he would call them, but he hadn't, and he was glad that they did not have Babunya's phone number or address. He did not want to talk to either of them.

He just wanted that part of his life to be over. He just

wanted to put it behind him and forget it had ever occurred.

Babunya pulled up in front of the house.

He looked at the front lawn, the garage, the corner window of what had been his room, and he suddenly felt like crying. He had not cried since the funerals, not even in the privacy of his own bed alone at night, but he felt like crying now, and it was all he could do to keep the tears from coming. He glanced away from the house, down the street, wondering if Roberto might be around, but it was a school day, and the street was deserted.

A stray tear escaped from his right eye, and he quickly, angrily, wiped it away.

The house was for sale. The people who had bought it from them had obviously done so only for investment, and there was a realty sign on the lawn, emptiness visible through the curtainless windows.

His mom must know that the place was for sale, but apparently she didn't want to go back there. He understood how she felt. There were too many memories. It would be nice to live near Roberto again, to go back to his old school and his old friends, but he didn't really want to take up residence in this house again, either. It would be too harsh a reminder, and it would be better for all of them if they found some place new, got a clean start.

"Come," Babunya said, unstrapping her shoulder harness and opening the car door. "We go inside."

He nodded silently, unbuckled his own seat belt, opened his door, followed her. They'd talked about this ahead of time, and he knew what they were going to do, but he still wasn't sure how he felt about it.

The locks of the house had obviously not been changed, and Babunya took her old keys from her purse and unlocked the front door. She said a quick prayer, walked inside.

Adam held his breath as he walked through the familiar doorway, into the furnitureless house. He glanced around. It had looked exactly the same on the morning they left, but time and distance had altered his perspective, and it felt weird to be back. It was his home but at the same time not, and he felt lost, adrift.

They walked slowly through the rooms, Babunya repeating the same Russian prayer as they moved from the living room to the family room to the dining room to the kitchen. Memories and emotions were pressing in on him from all sides, threatening to crush him, and it got harder and harder to breathe as they made their way through the once-familiar house. He wanted nothing more than to bolt, to run, to get the hell out of here, but he remained next to Babunya, concentrated on keeping his emotions at bay.

They came to the last room. His parents' bedroom.

Once again the tears threatened to well up, and he would have probably started crying had his attention not been distracted at that moment, had he not seen movement in the far corner of the room, a faint shimmering.

Babunya had just finished her prayer, and he looked over there, where the dresser used to be, and he thought he saw him, Jedushka Di Muvedushka, the Owner of the House. He didn't look like that Rumpelstiltskin picture, didn't look like the shadow on the wall of the *banya,* didn't look like a leprechaun. Indeed, he was not strange or unusual in appearance at all. He looked like a miniature man, a little Russian, and he was dressed in white Molokan church clothes, and had a long gray beard and the kindest eyes Adam had ever seen.

Adam glimpsed him only for a brief second, if at all, and then he was gone.

There was nothing there.

After everything that he'd been through, after everything that had happened, he would have thought that he'd be scared, that contact with anything even remotely supernatural would terrify him, but there was nothing terrifying about the small man, and in the brief second that he thought he saw him, he'd felt strangely at peace and at ease—something he had not felt for a long time.

Babunya looked at him, smiled.

She'd seen him too.

Looking toward the corner, she said some words in Russian, then nodded to him. He repeated them in English, just as she'd coached him: "Owner of the House, please come with us and protect us."

The little man appeared again, flickering into an existence that was still only barely visible. He nodded politely, started walking toward them . . . then faded into nothingness.

Adam looked over at his grandmother. "Is that it?"

"He with us," she said. She put an arm around his shoulder. "He protect you in new home. Do not worry."

Adam said nothing, and the two of them walked silently back through the house, outside.

He with us.

He would have laughed at that before, would have thought it was stupid, but now it cheered him up, made him feel better.

He protect you.

They walked out to the car, got inside.

On their way back, they stopped at a grocery store, bought some food for tonight's dinner, and she bought him a *Spiderman* comic book that he read to himself on the silent trip home to Montebello, where Teo and his mother were waiting.